CW01558991

LOVE TO HATE YOU

WHITLEY COX

WHITLEY COX

Copyright © 2022 by Whitley Cox

All rights reserved.

No portion of this book may be reproduced in any form without written permission from the publisher or author, except as permitted by U.S. copyright law.

PRINT ISN: 978-1-989081-55-6

Cover Artist: EmCat Designs

Editing: Chris Kridler

Beta-read: Postive Proof

For the husband.
Dude, I like really, really, really love you.
You're smart, you're kind, you're funny, you're weird, and you're hot.
I hit the jackpot.
You also have a GREAT ass. So bonus points for that.
Anyway, I love you so fucking much, so I'm dedicating another book to you.
xoxo

CONTENTS

CHAPTER ONE

Eli

TELLING A NEUROSURGEON HE could take his price tag and shove it up his scrawny ass was NOT the best way to guarantee he didn't "slip" and slice your medulla oblongata with his scalpel. So I kept my mouth shut as I waved goodbye and thanked him for absolutely fucking nothing. Just like I did every time I came to his office.

I wanted to flip off his receptionist, too. Tell them all to go fuck themselves.

A guy shouldn't go broke in order to fucking survive. I shouldn't go up to my fucking eyebrows in debt in order to keep my vision.

What the actual fuck?

It's not their fault. It's the system's fault. It's a broken system.

Yeah, and my health insurance was nonexistent, so the neurosurgeon had to charge me my monthly rent plus a limb for a visit and a checkup. And those scans to see how big the tumor was ... I could get a first-class ticket to Bora Bora for that. Well, maybe not *first*-class, but definitely a window seat in business class.

And don't even get me started on that surgery price tag. Who besides fucking Elon Musk could afford to pay that without taking out a second mortgage or raiding their kids' college fund?

And since I had no kids or their college funds to raid, or a fucking mortgage, I was really up a fucking creek, paddleless, with a giant hole in my hull, a bailing bucket the size of a spoon, and rapids up ahead.

Clenching my teeth hard enough I was probably going to have to spend even more money at the chiro to fix my jaw—or at the very least the dentist to give me a crown—I shoved open the door to the clinic and winced when the sun tried to burn my retinas.

I'd say "life wasn't fair," but I'd learned that a long fucking time ago.

Life was shit most of the time.

The world was shit.

And people were shit.

If you were super fucking lucky, once in a while you'd meet a decent human or something good might happen to you. But for me, those moments were rare.

Making my way down the sidewalk of the business complex, I peered into all the other businesses. I needed something to distract me. Something to take my mind off how just damn hopeless I felt.

I could wake up blind tomorrow thanks to the tumor in my brain, and I wouldn't be able to get the surgery because I simply couldn't afford it.

I lobbed a heavy sigh and shoved my hands into the front pockets of my jeans as I stopped in front of a pet store to admire the fish swimming around in the tanks, waiting for someone to come buy them and take them to their new forever home.

A couple of elderly women sat in salon chairs getting their white hair coiffed inside the hairdresser next door, and people—mostly families—sat at booths inside Linda's Diner on the corner having lunch.

My stomach grumbled at the thought of lunch.

I threw on my sunglasses but kept looking through the window of the diner. The smell of fried food filled the air, and my mouth started to water. I'd only lived in Linley Park, Maine, for a little over a year, but I knew well that Linda's made really good homemade, thick-cut wedge fries. And with their homemade gravy, they were to die for.

The place was packed like it always was. Which was why I'd had to park so far away from the surgeon's clinic because I couldn't find any parking right out front.

Not in a million years did I think I'd wind up in a rinky-dink little coastal town like Linley Park, but here I was. And it was all because the specialist who was monitoring Keith, the tumor in my brain, lived here, having left the hustle and bustle of Manhattan in an attempt to ease himself into retirement.

And since no fucking way did I want to live in Connecticut and risk running into my father or his horrific wife, I decided to just move to where the good doctor lived in the event I one day woke up blind, he could just cut into my brain on his lunch hour.

So now, after nearly a decade of being a nomad, I lived here. In this town. That had only four gas stations.

It just made sense. I hadn't had a place to call home when I got my diagnosis, so it was just easier to set down some temporary roots until I either located the money for the surgery or went blind.

I guess the town wasn't so bad. I found a job easy enough—not that I *enjoyed* roofing, but I was decent at it and the pay was good. My apartment was cheap and clean, and I could walk to the beach or go off and find some trails to hike. I just hated that everything besides one or two bars shut down by 8 p.m. There were places in Asia and Europe that didn't even open until nine or ten o'clock at night. Bars and restaurants opened their doors for the late-night crowd and kept the beer and food flowing until the sky started to get light again with the threat of a rising sun.

But not here.

Not little ol' Linley Park.

Some people called it quaint. I just called it inconvenient.

Looking past my own reflection in the window, I watched all the hungry patrons, wishing I was them and sitting down to a big, juicy—

What the fuck?

I took a step back. Was that tumor pressing on my optic nerve starting to make me hallucinate, too?

I blinked and scrubbed at my eyes, then opened them and zeroed in on the couple sitting on the inside booth.

She looked fucking angry.

But then again, she always looked angry.

Even though I hadn't seen her in over eight years, I would recognize that scowl anywhere. The rest of her had changed though. The rest of her had changed a lot.

The guy she was with was rolling his eyes and shaking his head, gesturing with his hands while his elbows rested on the table. He was pleading with her, but the more he did it, the angrier she got.

With a slam of her palm to the table, she got up, grabbed her purse, and stalked out.

I hid behind a concrete pillar and watched as she haughtily threw open the diner door, and in dark wash skinny jeans and a black leather jacket with a white T-shirt underneath, she climbed up into a big white Jeep parked right out in front of the diner.

Since it was a warm May day on the coast of Maine, the sides and roof of her Jeep were already off, and when she turned over the ignition and backed out, then peeled off into the street, her dark brown hair with the thick, bright red streaks in it trailed behind her.

Before I knew what I was doing, I scrambled to my truck, climbed in behind the wheel, and was pulling out into traffic, racing to catch up with her.

I managed to make it to the same light she was stopped at but three vehicles behind.

Even with my windows up, I could hear her music. Some indie alternative rock band I hadn't heard of.

The light turned green, and she accelerated. I kept the distance between us, because if she saw me, that scowl would only deepen, and she'd probably try to run me off the road.

For fifteen minutes I followed her.

Did she live here?

When the fuck had she moved to Maine from Connecticut?

I didn't talk to my dad, so I had no idea what was going on with that side of the family and preferred to stay the fuck out of the loop as it was.

After four more sets of lights, she pulled into the parking lot of another retail complex, but rather than parking out front, she swung into the back where staff parked.

I decided to keep my stalker tendencies to a minimum and pulled up to the curb, then unbuckled my belt and sat like an imbecile, watching as she climbed out of her Jeep and walked straight into the back door of a veterinarian clinic.

Obviously, she worked there, if she was using the staff entrance.

So she lived here in Maine, then.

Since when?

Granted, I'd only been here a little over a year, but had we been sharing the same airspace, walking the same trails and going to the same beach for a whole damn year?

Already disgusted with myself and how far I'd gone out of my way to follow her, I climbed back into the driver's seat, pulled out into traffic and then into the parking lot in front of the vet clinic.

East Coast Animals Veterinary Hospital. There was a cute picture of a dog, cat and horse beside the hospital name. And below all of that were three names: Dr. Unger, Dr. Chu and Dr. Hartford.

Holy fucking shit.

She was a vet.

Like an actual doctor of veterinary medicine.

I knew she'd gone to college. That there had been a no-brainer since she had always been smart—not necessarily as smart as me—but she was still smart.

I started searching her name on social media.

Never in the eight years since the last time I'd seen her had I ever had even an inclination to see what she was up to.

I could not have given an ounce of a fuck.

But now, seeing her, I gave at least an ounce.

Probably more.

There were loads of pictures on her social media—mostly of her with animals wearing scrubs that had *Dr. Hartford* stitched below the name of the vet hospital. Then there were a bunch of her with that guy from the diner, and then a few really old ones with ...

I exited out of the window on my browser before my stomach got too tight.

I couldn't look at those pictures right now. Not if I wanted to stay out of the pit of depression that inevitably accompanied looking at pictures of Eden—my twin sister.

Five doors down, and on the corner of the shopping complex, there was a café. I backed out of the parking stall I was in in front of the vet hospital and found a stall directly in front of the café. Against all the voices in my head telling me to go home, I grabbed my laptop from the back seat of my truck, as well as my tablet, and headed into the café. I was still hungry, so I ordered a Southwest steak panini and a medium coffee.

I set up my laptop, brought up the project I'd been secretly working on for the past five years, and dove into my sandwich, making sure to keep at least one eye on the front door of the vet hospital in the event she came out.

What would I do then?

I had no clue.

All I knew at the moment was that I hadn't seen this woman who had been an integral part of my childhood in eight years, and although ultimately we hated each other, the drive to find out exactly what she was up to now fueled me in a way that I couldn't quite comprehend.

Alexandra Hartford had been my twin sister's best friend since kindergarten. She had slept over at my house probably thirty times in thirteen years and sat across from me at the dinner table twice as much. She was in every single one of my classes from kindergarten right through to our senior year, and for thirteen years, she was my mortal enemy. The bane of my existence. The eternal thorn in my side.

We hated each other.

Tormented each other.

I could not come up with one good thing to say about her, even when it was an assignment in an anti-bullying campaign put on by the school. You had to write one positive adjective that described each classmate, then that list would be given to each student to help bolster their confidence and remind them that they had a lot of positive qualities.

In the end, I'd put *Alexandra Hartford can write her name.*

Of course, I'd gotten in trouble because that had not been the assignment. We were told to put a single adjective.

She'd put *fragrant* down for me, which I knew had been a backhanded way to tell me that I stunk. So in the end I wrote down *shiny* as a way to tell her that her skin was oily and I could use her face to regrease the chain on my bike.

We'd never gotten along. Not for even a second.

So it made the fact that she was my twin sister's absolute best friend in the entire world a constant bone of contention in our family. Add in the fact that our fathers owned an accounting firm together—and were best friends—and our mothers were best friends, and there had been absolutely no escaping Alexandra, no matter how hard I tried.

And boy, did I try.

Most people thought that we'd eventually grow out of our feud, but as we got older, things didn't get better.

She was sarcastic and snide. Opinionated and not afraid to argue until she was blue in the damn face. And yet she wasn't extroverted or loud.

She preferred to wield her evil silently.

She was like a fart after turkey chili—quiet, deadly, and something you really didn't want to be stuck in a room full of people with.

She'd also been a tomboy who preferred to play sports with the boys and would shoulder-check you just as hard as any guy during touch football or soccer. She was a brute.

And I hated her.

And she hated me.

Unfortunately, though, that brute had gotten hot.

That didn't mean she wasn't still ugly on the inside, though. Whatever had gone down in that diner, she undoubtedly deserved. The guy was probably getting out of dodge after she showed her true colors and went all psycho bitch on him.

Maybe I should find that guy and go have a beer with him, get the dirt on Alexandra that way.

I finished my sandwich, sipped my coffee, and brought up the working document on my laptop.

I had no idea what my plan was, but I knew that despite how much I hated the woman who was probably giving a Doberman an enema right now and enjoying the look of panic on the poor dog's face, I needed to know more about her. I wasn't ready to just walk away and not give a fuck.

Why?

I couldn't say.

But I was going to sit there, work on my laptop and watch the door until her Jeep drove away again.

Then I'd probably follow her some more.

I growled at how I was behaving.

This was stalker behavior. One hundred percent.

But I didn't give a fuck.

Alexandra Hartford had, for all intents and purposes, ruined my fucking life. She'd ruined my family and was the reason Eden was ...

I squeezed my eyes closed.

Not right now.

I'd think about that more when I wasn't in public. When I was home with my punching bag and could kick the shit out of something that wouldn't break and cost me a fortune to replace.

It didn't matter that she was now, technically, my stepsister.

First and foremost, Alexandra Hartford was my enemy, and it just didn't sit well with me that her life was thriving after the way she'd ruined so many others.

No, Alexandra Hartford needed to pay. Now I just needed to figure out how to make that happen.

CHAPTER TWO

Eli

AT TEN AFTER FIVE, Alexandra's Jeep pulled out of the parking lot behind the animal hospital, so I raced to my truck and followed her. We didn't drive long before she was pulling into yet another complex, climbing out, this time with a small duffle bag and a yoga mat.

Trying to get a little *Zen*, Alexandra? Balance your chakras and find some peace after all the hell you've caused?

I laughed at that thought as I brought up the website for the yoga studio.

And of course, she was a goddamn teacher there.

She was scheduled to teach today's five-thirty flow yoga.

Drawing in a deep inhale, I parked my truck a few spaces over from her Jeep, a spot that, hilariously, lent me a decent view into the studio lobby.

She wasn't in there.

She was probably changing in the back somewhere.

I waited, and sure enough, she emerged five minutes later, and my dick betrayed my hatred for her and twitched like a fucker in my jeans.

She wore tight olive-green yoga capris, a black sports bra, and nothing else. Her hair with the red streaks was tied up into a high ponytail on the back of her head, and thick pieces fell down and framed her face. But it was when she turned around and showed me her back that my dick really woke up.

She had a massive tattoo on her back.

A huge tree with cherry blossoms wound up from beneath her pants, all along her left hip, ribs, and shoulder blade. A few branches extended out over her arm. It was made up of gray and pink and no other colors. It was beautiful.

She was smiling and laughing with the woman behind the reception desk and then warmly greeted people who came in carrying their own yoga mats and shoulder bags.

By the way her blue eyes glittered and her smile so easily coasted across her face, one might be led to believe that Alexandra wasn't the reincarnation of the devil himself, but an actual human with emotions and a soul.

But I knew better.

She had just perfected the art of faking it and was duping these poor schmucks into thinking she was human.

All the people in the lobby disappeared through a door, leaving just the receptionist.

I waited fifteen minutes until I knew the yoga class would be in session, then I got out of my truck and headed inside.

"Hello," the cute blonde with brown eyes said, flashing me a flirty smile.

"Hi." I tossed on a bit more swagger to my walk as I gave her my own flirty smile and leaned my elbow on the counter. "How are you?"

She batted long, false lashes. "Great. You here for a class?"

"I thought the five-thirty class already started?"

She nodded. "It has, and we don't accept late arrivals after five minutes. But there is a six-thirty class. Alex isn't teaching, though. It's Raven."

"I'm actually new to yoga, but my doctor recommended it to help me destress, you know?"

The blonde nodded vigorously. "Totally. After I've had a rough day with school, I definitely need my sixty-minute freedom flow to help center me again."

"You're in school?" She didn't strike me as jailbait, but then again, Gen Z's were wearing way more makeup and dressing like adults than I remember my own generation doing.

"Second year of college. I'm studying to become a dental hygienist."

Not jailbait but damn close. "That's a great career. You'll never not be able to find work."

She beamed. "That's the hope. My boyfriend is premed, so the plan is to just get work wherever he ends up for school and residencies and stuff."

If they lasted that long. I hadn't met one couple that had ever gone the distance. Not one. Which was why I didn't even bother with relationships anymore. Fuck buddies or one-night stands made of Teflon. No clingers. I needed to be able to slide those ladies right off when the night was over.

"I'm looking for something introductory, you know? Just to try it out. What do you suggest?"

She grabbed a brochure from a stack next to my elbow. "No matter what you choose for your first class, it's free. We call it our karma class. But if you're new to yoga and looking for a gentle introduction, nothing too complicated and more relaxing than anything else, then I suggest our candlelight freedom flow. Alex is teaching it tomorrow at five-thirty." She leaned in and brought her voice down to a whisper. "And in my opinion, she's the best teacher here."

Her eyes darted back and forth as if making sure no other instructors were going to pop out like prairie dogs and accuse her of favoritism.

Sitting back, she shrugged. "I mean, they're all great."

I grinned. "Your secret is safe with me. But tell me, what makes Alex so great?"

The girl's eyes gleamed. "Well, not only is she like one of the nicest people I've ever met, but she's just a really great instructor. She comes around and helps each person adjust and tweak to reach their full potential. She's encouraging but doesn't make you feel bad if you can't quite reach a certain posture. She gives great alternatives. The way she moves you into each new position is fluid and flawless. She reminds you of your breath constantly, which is so important, because normally I hold my breath when I'm holding a position, and that's definitely not what you're supposed to do. And she's also like crazy bendy. She can put her leg over her head and makes binding look easy."

My mouth hung open for a second.

I didn't blink.

Sorry, did she just say that Alexandra could put her leg over her head?

And what was this about *binding*? I didn't even know was binding was, but I was sure as fuck going to Google it when I got home.

"There's a window on the door if you want to take a peek into the classroom," she offered. "They do it in the dark with LED candles all around. Nobody will be able to see you. It's a one-way mirror."

Nodding, I walked over to where she pointed and peered through the cutout of glass. Sure enough, the room was dark, only lit up by the green emergency exit signs and the dozen or so LED candles placed throughout the room on the floor.

Everyone was facing the opposite wall in what looked like something I could vaguely remember being called warrior pose or some shit. Not that I'd ever taken a yoga class in my life, but if you live long enough, you pick up on stuff.

I certainly knew what downward dog was. Doggy style was one of my favorite positions.

I scanned the room for the olive-green pants, black tank top and back tattoo. I was not disappointed when I found Alexandra leading the class, her ass cheeks popping in those pants like two ripe peach halves.

My eggplant was certainly getting thicker.

"You need to sign up for the classes since they're almost always full," the girl at the front desk said, breaking me out of my trance and getting me to blink, since my eyeballs had been glued to Alexandra's ass. "Particularly Alex's classes."

I returned to the front. "I'd like to sign up for tomorrow's five-thirty class, please."

She grinned wide and slid a clipboard with a couple of sheets of paper clipped to it and a pen across the counter to me. "Perfect. If you can just fill out this waiver, then you'll be all set to join tomorrow."

I gave her another megawatt smile. "Thanks ..."

"Savannah," she said.

"I'm Eli."

"Nice to meet you, Eli. I'm sure you'll love it here. We're a very chill group. No judgment. Your practice is yours and nobody else's. And be sure to let your instructor know if you have any injuries or anything."

Yeah, I wouldn't be doing that. But I nodded anyway, took the clipboard over to a bench, and filled it out.

"Do you have a yoga mat, Eli?" Savannah asked as I went through the personal health and injury history list.

"I do not."

"Well, we've got some for rent for five dollars, or all our B Mats are on sale for seventy-five, regularly eighty-five."

"I think I'll rent one for the first class, see how I like it, then take it from there." I finished filling out the form, got up, and handed it back to her. "I'll see you tomorrow, then."

Her teeth scraped along her bottom lip. "You will."

Wrapping my knuckles on the counter twice, I winked at Savannah—who was at least ten years younger than me and at the moment making me feel even older—then headed back to my truck.

Savannah said the six-thirty class was being taught by someone else, so chances were, Alex would be leaving once the class she taught was over.

Did I stick around and wait to see where she went after that?

Or did I stop being a weird psycho-stalker and head the fuck home?

I stuck around.

This time, I brought out my tablet and the illustration software program I had. I was deep in my "doodles" when the front door to the yoga studio opened and people began to pour out.

I put my tablet in the passenger seat and slid down in my own seat behind the steering wheel.

Alexandra was the second to last person to leave, and she climbed right into her Jeep and took off.

Like a fucking crazy person, I took off, too, making sure I stayed a solid three cars behind her.

She drove to the outskirts of town into the industrial area and parallel-parked her Jeep in front of a big picture window of an old red-brick two-story building. It looked like it'd once been a factory of some kind with its big smokestacks on top, but such was not the case any longer.

I parked across the street, but from where I was, I could see right into where Alexandra got out and headed. A sign overhead said H&J Muay Thai.

No fucking way.

Did she box?

It was only six-fifty, but the building's east side was in shadow so I could see in. There were a couple of sparring rings, weights for lifting, punching bags, speed bags, and various other equipment used for mixed martial arts training.

She nodded and smiled at the guy behind the front desk, took a sip of her water bottle, and set her bag down on the outside of a ring. From there, she reached into her duffle bag and pulled out another sports bra, then tugged it over her other sports bra that she was still wearing. Then she went about bandaging up her hands. There were two other fighters in the ring, and a few guys stood around watching them fight. Every spectator acknowledged Alexandra with a big smile, and a couple of the beefier guys even came in for a hug.

She laughed and smiled through all of it, swatting a few of the bare-chested ones on the arm or chest.

Heat flooded my veins when I saw her getting chummy with some of the guys, kind of like she was one of the guys. But it was also unmistakable the way a couple of them looked at her. Stared at her tits and her ass. I could tell, even from across the street, that they wanted her.

She grabbed a pair of blue boxing gloves out of her bag, and with the help of one of the guys, she strapped them onto her hands.

The hair on my arms stood up, and the heat in my veins intensified until my blood sizzled. A prickling sensation developed on the back of my neck, and that was when I realized I was clenching my jaw extra tight. One of the guys winked at her, and I nearly chipped a fucking tooth.

When the fight in the ring ended, the sparring partners climbed out under the ropes, and Alexandra and one of the guys she'd been laughing with entered.

They bounced on their feet a few times, laughing and smiling with each other, then they tapped gloves and started to spar.

She was good.

Like really fucking good.

Like scary good.

The focused look on her face drew me in. I couldn't look away.

Every swift lift of her leg, every smooth shift of her hips and swing of her arms, it was like watching someone dance a dance they'd known since birth.

The scrunch of her brows and the determination in her eyes reminded me of that time in gym class in the eighth grade when we raced around the track and were neck and neck until the bitter end.

I beat her by half a second.

And I wouldn't let her forget it.

Her leg came up, and she kneed her opponent in the chest. He didn't have time to block but did so after the fact. That opened up his face, and she went at him like a fiend.

Holy shit.

She had him against the ropes and was just wailing on him with her fists. He wasn't able to block her fast enough, and when he tried, she lifted her knee again and got him in the hip or gut.

Her opponent managed to get off the ropes and back out into the middle of the ring, but Alexandra wasn't letting him get away.

He tried to come at her, but she blocked ninety percent of his punches, and I wasn't sure he made contact with her stomach once. She blocked everything. Was too fast for him. He wasn't doing so hot.

But Alexandra was on fucking fire.

The rest happened so fast that had I been blinking, I probably would have missed it. She went in with a left hook. The guy blocked but not well enough. He was also distracted with that block, which allowed her a chance to come at him with a right cross, get him right across the face, and send him spinning around and falling to the ground.

Holy fucking shit!

I clutched my face in disbelief.

She laid him flat.

Jesus Christ.

Pride surged through me at just how amazing she was.

Grinning, she removed her mouthguard—I hadn't seen her put it in but whatever—and turned to say something to the men clapping for her on the outside of the ring. Then she leaned forward and offered her hand to the guy whose ass she'd just kicked and helped him up.

His scowl just sparked more applause and cheering from the audience.

If I hadn't been watching her for most of the day, I'd wonder where the hell that raw anger was derived from, but if what went down in the diner was in fact a breakup, I had a pretty good idea.

I stuck around a bit longer, wanting to see if Alexandra got back into the ring, but she didn't. Two more guys climbed under the ropes and started swinging fists, but Alexandra didn't.

She didn't even hit the weights.

But what she did do was grab a mop and bucket and start cleaning the place.

And she was still cleaning when the rest of the guys there left, waving at her as they walked out the open door, and even after the guy who'd been behind the counter turned off a few lights and locked the door behind him.

Alexandra was their cleaner?

What the fuck?

Didn't vets make decent coin?

This wasn't adding up.

I fiddled on my tablet a bit more, drawing and coloring in the images I'd drawn earlier that day and waiting for her to leave. It was almost eleven by the time she turned off all the lights, locked up, and headed to her Jeep.

I thought about following her home but decided that I'd already stepped way too fucking far into stalker territory already and I wasn't ready to cross any more lines.

I'd see her tomorrow at yoga.

And hopefully by then, I'd know why the fuck I was doing what I was doing and following around my childhood enemy.

CHAPTER THREE

Alex

KICKING THE SHIT OUT of Wayne wasn't enough.

Finding my Zen at yoga hadn't been enough either.

I wanted to maim.

I wanted to destroy.

Where the fuck did Cade get off dumping me a week before we were all set to move in together?

I slammed the door to my apartment and tossed my duffle bag and keys on the kitchen counter, hitting a cardboard box labeled "kitchen shit" in the process.

And why did my keys hit a cardboard box labeled "kitchen shit"? Because I gave up my apartment and was all packed up with the intention of moving into my boyfriend's place in a week.

Correction—*ex-boyfriend*. Because that motherfucker just dumped my ass.

I wanted to let out a banshee scream, but I had neighbors, and they already didn't like the fact that I hit the punching bag at seven in the morning every day.

But fuck them! I wasn't going to be here for much longer—since the landlord had zero problems re-renting the place—so even though it was after eleven at night, I screamed at the top of my lungs. "That motherfucker!"

I waited for the stomp from Mrs. Potter upstairs.

Thump thump thump!

The woman was such a bitch. She had no problem vacuuming at five-thirty in the morning on a Sunday, but God forbid I want to work out for half an hour before I headed to work.

I wouldn't miss her one bit.

I would, however, miss my apartment.

It was perfect.

Big windows in the living room that let in all the morning sun, high ceilings, new kitchen cabinets and countertops, an induction stove.

This place was amazing, and I'd given it up so that Cade and I could take the next step in our relationship. He'd insisted we move into his place since it was a two-bedroom. And at the time, it made sense. So, against the voice in my head telling me it was a bad idea, I gave my notice to my landlord and started planning to move in with a man I'd been dating for over two years.

Big. Fucking. Mistake.

Ripping my sports bras off my body—since I needed to wear two when I boxed—I chucked them to the floor in the living room, then peeled out of my leggings as well, adding them to the pile.

A hot shower would do me some good.

Of course, I had to go digging for a fresh towel in one of my boxes labeled "bathroom shit," but eventually I found one.

As the warm water sluiced over my skin, I leaned forward and rested my head on the shower wall. What was I going to do?

I was effectively homeless in T-minus seven days, and to make matters abundantly worse, I was now dateless for a wedding in San Diego that I had to attend in exactly three weeks.

And I absolutely could not show up to this wedding without a date.

Allegra Ruiz was the *it* girl at our veterinarian school.

And yeah, we had an *it* girl in vet school. Stupid as fuck, I know.

But regardless, she was it.

Her parents had money, raced horses or something, and she grew up burning hundred-dollar bills in their wood stove to keep warm. Or so I assumed.

We were frenemies. And since we followed each other on social media, she knew that I had a boyfriend and worked at a vet hospital in Linley Park, Maine, and that I wasn't nearly as successful as she and her fiancé were with their enormous animal hospital to the stars in L.A.

Apparently, Allegra and Ford (her husband-to-be) treated pets owned by the likes of Ellen, Lady Gaga and Hilary Duff.

When the save-the-date and then the invitation came through—last year—I'd been happily dating Cade and RSVP'd yes, thinking that my hunky contractor, business owner boyfriend would be the perfect arm candy for the wedding. I also figured I'd have paid off my student loans by this time and that Cade and I would be living in a big house and be planning our own wedding.

Yeah, that wasn't happening.

None of it.

Cade's dad had medical bills he needed help with, which ransacked a lot of Cade's savings. My student loan debt was still alive and well, and after two and a half years, we were only just now planning to move in together.

Well, not anymore.

But still, I couldn't *not* go to this wedding.

As much as I'd rather cancel, that voice in the back of my head that sounded an awful lot like Allegra was harassing me.

You made a commitment. You agreed. You RSVP'd "YES".
We will all talk about you behind your back and troll you on
social media if you don't come.

Then a voice that sounded like Eden would tell the Allegra voice to shut the fuck up. But Eden's voice would still ultimately tell me to go, only with more encouraging words. *You haven't had a vacation in ages. You deserve this trip. You deserve to show those bitches all that you've become and accomplished. You are not the shy, wallflower they remember. You are a beautiful fucking rose with big-ass thorns and you smell delicious.*

Eden had said that to me on more than one occasion when I'd get down on myself about something or my shyness as a kid kept me from doing something. "You are a beautiful fucking rose with big-ass thorns and you smell delicious, now let's go get some Ben & Jerry's and watch Saved by the Bell reruns."

I smiled at one of the many incredible memories I had of my best friend.

My only *real* friend. Ever.

I'd been so lost and lonely after Eden died that when I met Allegra and her clique our first year at PenVet, I clung to the fringe of their group, and the small connection they allowed me, like a limpet to rock on a stormy shore.

Any idiot could see that they didn't really think of me as a real friend—or even an equal. I was a target for their teasing and insults. But I didn't care enough to go find a social group that wasn't toxic. My heart was too broken to care. They couldn't break it any more than it already was. I wasn't alone, but their jabs didn't really penetrate either. It was safer all around.

You're not that person anymore. Eden's voice rang through my head again. *You're so much stronger. And you shouldn't have to prove anything to them. But I do think you should go and flaunt your fabulous ass, tits, and the rest of that rockin' body in front of all of them. You deserve to have fun. And don't forget that the wedding is an open bar. Take advantage of that shit, girl.*

Even as just a manifestation of my mind, Eden made me laugh.

But even manifestation Eden was right. I needed to go to this wedding with my head held high.

But I also couldn't go alone. I was strong, but I wasn't *that* strong. I needed a date, otherwise, I'd never hear the end of it. They'd make my life hell; humiliate me for being dumped by Cade.

Fuck Cade.

After washing my hair and my body, I turned off the tap, grabbed the towel from the towel bar and tucked it around my body.

I'd moved to Maine thinking that it wasn't *so* far away from my dad in Connecticut that I couldn't go visit him for a weekend but it was far enough away from my past and my mom that I wouldn't run the risk of running into anybody I knew or my mother when I went grocery shopping.

But so far, I wasn't loving where I lived.

Yes, it was beautiful, with the forest, mountains and trees behind me and the ocean in front, but no matter how hard I tried, I just couldn't get *settled*.

A feeling of restlessness continued to bounce around inside me like a pinball. I was never able to just sit and relax. I had a couch I barely sat on, a kitchen table I *never* sat at, and a Netflix account collecting dust.

I was just too busy to relax. Between work, teaching yoga and going to spar with the guys at the Muay Thai gym, I had no time to lounge in front of the television and binge the latest shows. Hector at H&J Muay Thai was nice enough to let me spar there for free as long as I cleaned up the place, gave it a thorough mop and wiped it down three times a week.

I was grateful for the financial reprieve since I really didn't want to stop going there but also couldn't afford the hefty monthly fee.

Well, that wasn't true. I *could* afford it, but I was saving like a miser so I could one day buy my own place. It was another reason why Cade and I were moving in together, so we could save in order to one day soon buy. I also still had that pesky student loan debt that I was whittling away at.

My hair dripped, so I finished drying my body, then wrapped the towel around my hair, wandering out into my apartment naked.

I already knew my fridge was pretty much empty. So was my freezer. I was trying to *not* pack up a bunch of food and then struggle to find space for it at Cade's place. So I'd deliberately kept my grocery shops to a minimum.

Now I would starve because of it.

Well, not *starve*. But I'd probably have to make mac 'n' cheese with no butter and half the suggested amount of milk because of how little I had to work with.

I went on the hunt for a saucepot, filled it up and put it on the stove to boil.

The water was bubbling in ninety seconds, and ironically, after everything I'd been through today—getting dumped and having to put down two different dogs because their poor sweet bodies were riddled with cancer—the fact that I was going to have to say goodbye to my induction stove was what finally brought me to tears.

Standing there naked in my kitchen, with my hair wrapped up in a big gray towel, with my tits hanging over a boiling pot of water, I sobbed like a baby.

No matter how hard I tried to get ahead, I just constantly felt like I was drowning. Drowning with weights stacked on my shoulders.

I couldn't catch a break if it was thrown directly at my face and the size of a damn beach ball with zero wind resistance.

My salty tears slid into the boiling water as I poured the tiny no-name macaroni noodles out of the cardboard box.

Then I had to go on the hunt for a spoon to stir it all with.

I found an enormous stir spoon but nothing else.

It would have to do.

My mind drifted back to Allegra and this stupid wedding.

I thought I'd left the cliques of high school behind when I went to college, particularly a college out of state. But I realized there was no escaping it. The bitches were just different.

The funny thing was that during elementary, junior and high school, I hadn't really had to deal with too many catty girls. I was and still am a tomboy, so most of my friends were guys, except for Eden of course.

Granted, when those guy friends got girlfriends, their girlfriends hated me, but I just stepped back and let the girlfriends ruin the relationship on their own with their unnecessary jealousy, which inevitably they did.

There was only one guy I couldn't be friends with.

The one who made my life a living hell for thirteen straight years, Eli Evans, Eden's twin brother.

From the day we all met in kindergarten until the day we graduated, he was a thorn in my side. The bane of my existence. The dark curly pube on the public toilet seat of my life. Okay, that last one was gross and graphic, but that doesn't make it any less accurate. Not that my life is a public toilet seat ... Ugh!

The fact that I was over at his house having playdates with his sister and then just hanging out as we all got older made it all the worse.

I put myself in his path of torment.

I didn't have a date for prom because Eli circulated it among our entire graduating class that I liked to turn my entire bathroom into a Dutch oven and sit and smell my own farts. He spread the rumor that that was why I smelled so "funky." When in fact I didn't smell "funky" at all. But it was enough for guys and girls to follow me around the halls and sniff me and then make cringey faces.

And then there was the time we had to race each other around the track and field track and I was just about to beat him when he said to me a second before we crossed the finish line, "There's blood all over your ass. Did you leak through your tampon?"

How he knew I had my period, I didn't know. But either way, it tripped me up enough and got in my head that I stumbled and he won. And then that bastard lorded his victory over me for ages.

My tears had dried up, and my noodles were cooked.

I drained them in the sink using the lid from the pot, then added a splash of milk and the cheese powder from the package.

Dinner of champions right here. This was exactly what I needed to be putting in my body after a yoga class and an intense round of boxing with Wayne.

Well, okay, intense wasn't the word I would use to describe what it was like sparring with Wayne. He was new to the Muay Thai world and still had it in his head that he needed to take it easy on me.

That just fueled me to *not* take it easy on him and kick the shit out of him. All the guys standing around the ring ribbed Wayne good since we all knew he was having a hard time swinging punches at a girl, as the good Southern boy's "mama raised him right." He'd learn sooner or later that I was just as capable as the rest of them and not somebody he needed to take it easy on.

Stirring the mac 'n' cheese, my mind drifted back to my day.

Yes, I was upset that Cade dumped me, but I wasn't going to waste any more tears on that fucker. Especially not after he gave me his reasons why.

I'd say he was a pussy, but pussies are strong as fuck and push humans out of them. So instead, I'd call him a limp dick. Because that was precisely what he was. A limp fucking dick.

I needed to tackle my problems one at a time.

First, I needed to find a new place to live.

Next, I needed to find a date.

Cade and I had each taken ten days off with the plan to rent a car and drive across the country to San Diego, hitting all the major US attractions along the way, then we would fly home.

I still had those days off and the rental car booked. Despite my frugal nature and determination to put every spare penny I had toward paying off my student loans, I had socked away some money specifically for this trip.

I hadn't taken any kind of vacation in eight years, not since another boyfriend and I went to Thailand for a month, which was where I fell in love with Muay Thai.

Not bothering to find another bowl or a smaller spoon, I leaned against the counter and shoveled giant globs of bright orange mac 'n' cheese into my mouth, blowing on it, but not long enough, and then juggling it with my tongue because it was still too fucking hot.

I'd never been a patient person.

Well, not with myself or other people.

With animals, I had all the time in the world and would gladly sit with a dog or a cat for two hours petting them until they felt comfortable enough to let me examine them or clean their teeth. We were an animal hospital that did not put pets under to clean their teeth, but rather we gave them a mild sedative, spoke kindly and softly to them, and cleaned their teeth while they were awake. Large procedures like extractions and stuff, of course, we put them under, but not for simple cleanings.

That was another thing. Cade and I were going to get a dog.

I didn't have the lifestyle that would be fair to a dog if I lived alone, but with Cade and I together, we could give a pet the love and attention it needed.

Fucking Cade.

Maybe I could put out an ad in the local *Penny Saver* asking for a wedding date, all expenses paid. The guy just needed to be really hot, pretend he was obsessed with me, and agree to hit all the major tourist attractions with me on our road trip so that we could take selfies and load them to social media so our relationship looked real.

Easy peasy.

I sucked in a sharp breath when a hot cheesy noodle landed on my left breast. "Fuck."

Picking it off, I popped the noodle into my mouth, then wiped the cheese sauce off with my finger.

This was what I had been reduced to.

Standing naked in my kitchen, eating mac 'n' cheese out of the pot with a shovel, and picking burning-hot noodles off my breasts.

A tear slid down my cheek as emotion clawed its vicious nails at the back of my throat and immobilized my jaw. I struggled to swallow down the wad of chewed pasta.

Not even bothering to finish what was left in the pot, I tossed it into the sink along with the spoon and headed to my bedroom to go and find something to wear.

I tugged on a pair of loose, flannel pajama pants but then immediately yanked them off when I realized they were Cade's.

Motherfucker.

No way was I wearing these.

And no way was he getting them back. I'd burn it all before I showed up at his apartment with a box of his crap like some teary-eyed wimp. Burn it all to a fucking crisp.

It took me a while to find my own pajama pants. These ones had little cartoon dogs and cats on them, but they were clean and they were mine. With a black sports bra on, I grabbed my laptop and sat up against my headboard in bed.

First, find a new place to live. Even if it was shitty. I just needed a place to store my stuff and lay my head at night.

Second, find a date for Allegra's wedding.

I was just punching in *Craigslist Linley Park* on Google when a notification made my laptop go *ping*.

It was, of course, from the blushing bride herself, Dr. Allegra Ruiz.

I'd gotten at least one of these notifications a day for the past two weeks. It was always something new that she needed her guests to know about the wedding.

Yesterday, she emailed everyone to let us know that after careful consideration, children were *not* permitted at the reception, but they could attend the ceremony. I felt bad for the guests who were parents and now had to scramble to find last-minute childcare.

I understood not wanting to have kids at a wedding, but when you send the invitations out nine months before the wedding, state that preference right off the bat so your guests can make the necessary arrangements well in advance.

Ugh! She was just so inconsiderate.

I clicked on the notification for today.

Hola, everyone, we're only three weeks away from the big day. How excited are you?

We just want to let everyone know that with the wedding happening so soon and all the expenses that Ford and I have incurred, any no-show guests who RSVP'd "YES" will be billed for their missed meal(s) and unclaimed party favor(s).

Can't wait to see you all and dance all night long.

And also, please remember, no mustard yellow, burnt orange or seafoam green clothing, please. Thank you. Kisses.

Adios,

Mr. and soon-to-be Mrs. Ford Ruiz-Grady

I stuck my finger in my mouth.

Gag!

Allegra was literally the worst.

I exited out of Allegra's note and brought up Craigslist and apartment listings.

It was slim pickings.

I shot off half a dozen inquiries, emphasizing the fact that I was a veterinarian, neat-freak, and pet-free.

It was past midnight by the time I closed my laptop, only to sit there on my bed, staring at the piles of boxes.

My life in boxes.

My bloodlust from earlier had gone down the drain with the bathwater, leaving nothing but hopelessness in its place.

I didn't even have a best friend I could call and commiserate with.

Nobody who I could text and then thirty minutes later they would show up on my doorstep with wine and our boyfriends Ben & Jerry.

I didn't have a person, because my person—my best friend in the entire universe—was dead, and it was all my fault.

CHAPTER FOUR

Eli

IT WAS NOW DAY two of me hanging out in the café in the same complex as Alexandra's vet hospital.

The same barista from yesterday smiled when she saw me and asked me if I'd like the same thing as yesterday.

Surprised and delighted with such attentive customer service, I said yes before I could say no and that I'd just eaten breakfast.

I was toiling away on my super-secret project, in a real typing groove with the words just flowing, when a flash of dark blue scrubs walking past the window next to my table caught my eye.

Dark hair with thick streaks of fire-engine red got caught up in a gust of wind, and she hastily tried to tame her locks as her co-worker, another woman in dark blue scrubs, opened the door.

I sank down in my seat, grabbed my ball cap from my laptop bag, and pulled it far down over my face.

She was all smiles, greeting the barista like they were old friends, laughing with a few other café staff, as well as the other vet in scrubs.

To the average person who didn't know the real Alexandra Hartford, one might think she was a friendly person with a soul.

But I knew differently.

I actually found it kind of comical that she was a vet, since weren't animals supposed to have a sixth sense about people and go berserk around those with no soul?

Maybe she just shot them with a heavy tranquilizer before they had a chance to really figure out that she was a demon inside the shell of a hot chick with a great ass.

After they placed their order, Alexandra and her colleague stepped to the side to wait for their order. But to the side was actually directly in front of me and well within earshot. It also put Alexandra's rocking ass—even in scrubs—at eye level.

Even though I hated her, even though I knew it was wrong, the primal beast inside of me with way too much testosterone and not nearly enough brain cells zeroed in on those cheeks and ogled.

They looked fucking dynamite in yoga tights, but she still managed to pull off loose scrubs like a boss, too.

Blinking and dropping my gaze from her ass, I tuned out the rest of the world and tuned in to their conversation.

"So why did he end it?" the woman with blonde hair in a ponytail asked. I would put her around forty-five years old.

Alexandra cleared her throat. "A *multitude* of reasons." She used finger quotes when she said multitude.

"Which are?" the blonde asked with a sarcastic tone.

"He said he didn't like the fact that I made more money than him."

The blonde scoffed. "He's a contractor."

"Yeah, but ... his business is in its fledgling state, and there's a lot of competition out there. Plus, he's had like four guys quit in the last two weeks ..."

"Management style?" the blonde asked. "Meaning he has none and people hate him."

Alexandra merely shrugged. "He said he didn't like that the majority of the people I hang out with are men—aka the guys at H&J."

"Dear lord," the other woman murmured.

"And he said that it emasculated him how strong and able to kick his ass I am. He doesn't like the fact that I could beat him up."

"What the fuck?" the blonde said and thankfully loud enough because I said the same damn thing.

I held my breath, hoping they didn't hear me and turned around.

Thank fuck, they didn't.

"Are you kidding me?" the blonde asked, shaking her head.

Alexandra shrugged. "I mean, I just don't get how he's only just *now* feeling like this. He knew I did Muay Thai when we met. I've been doing it for like eight years. And I've been a vet for five, again, well before we met."

"There's more to it," the other woman said, stepping forward and grabbing their drinks for them. "Let's sit. Our next patient isn't for thirty minutes. We have time."

Alexandra nodded and the two took the seat behind me, Alexandra taking the chair *directly* behind me. A floral and spicy scent wafted across my shoulder, and I fought the urge to close my eyes and inhale deeply.

I hated this woman, after all. I had to keep reminding myself of that.

"I'm just glad that I didn't put Cade on my insurance plan as I'd planned to," Alexandra said. "I mean, and the new plan is a good one."

I sat up a touch straighter at the mention of medical insurance, my interest piqued.

Just how good a plan were we talking?

I couldn't see their faces now, so I just had to make up what I assumed their expressions would be.

I figured the blonde was nodding while pursing her lips. "Really glad. Yeah, I'm happy with the new plan. East Coast Animals Veterinary Hospital is a big enough company, their pockets are deep enough that they can pay to take care of their employees. I nearly fainted when I saw how great the dental coverage is, too. My kid needs braces, so ... was not looking to pay for those puppies out of pocket. Xavier Blue Trust is by far the best insurance company out there. And the fact that ECA decided to go with the platinum package ..." She let out a whistle. "It's nice."

"Yeah, me, too. High premiums but great coverage all around."

I opened up a new browser menu on my laptop and typed in *Xavier Blue Trust Platinum Package.*

"I submitted inquiries for six different apartments last night. I've heard back from two so far and have plans to go look at them tonight after yoga."

"That's good. Onwards and upwards."

Alexandra groaned. "I just love my apartment. It's so perfect."

"I know. But you have complained more than once about the fact that your neighbor upstairs vacuums at like five in the morning. Maybe it's time to get something on the top floor?"

Alexandra snorted.

They talked about other things, but I didn't quite hear them since I was engrossed in what I was reading on the screen.

Xavier Blue Trust was one hell of an insurance provider.

Ninety-nine percent of other providers in the US were ab-solute trash and found loopholes and ways to deny people at every turn. Some of them even deemed pregnancy a pre-ex-isting condition and wouldn't cover certain things for a woman who was experiencing a difficult pregnancy. A co-worker of mine complained about that very thing since his wife was expecting twins and experiencing a lot of complications.

Her insurance provider denied her prescription coverage for her insulin since she developed gestational diabetes, as well as the medication she needed to treat her hyperemesis—the same thing that Kate Middleton had with her pregnancies that made her super sick.

And as roofers we didn't even have medical insurance, so we either went without or forked over nearly half our paychecks in premiums.

Which was why I was in the pickle I was in—in desperate need of surgery so that the benign tumor pressing on my optic nerve wouldn't one day, without notice, render me completely blind. The hospital had outright denied me, since they took one look at my seasonal job in the trades and deemed me essentially destitute and unlikely to ever pay them back for the surgery.

And with no insurance, I was royally fucked.

The surgery alone was close to two hundred thousand dollars. Add in recovery therapy, post-op appointments. That's more than some houses cost.

But the insurance package Alexandra had would cover a large chunk of such a surgery—or so said Xavier Blue Cross's website. And she had a killer, steady, reliable job. She was a partner in the practice even.

Hmmm.

I tuned back in to their conversation, the cogs in my brain spinning so fast, had they been the teacups at Disney World, every single person riding them would be wolfing their cookies.

"I honestly think you should just cancel and not go to this stupid wedding. The bride sounds like a monster," the blonde vet said. "You can't let what other people think of you rule the way you live your life. Especially not people from the past who don't matter."

"Says the woman who killed herself at the gym for five months so she would look, and I quote, 'hot as fuck' at her husband's high school reunion," Alexandra countered.

I was sure the blonde rolled her eyes. "That was for Howard, not for me."

"Sure, sure." Alexandra paused, probably to take a sip of her coffee drink. "It shouldn't matter. I know that. But I had a really shitty high school life. A really shitty school life, if I'm being honest. I didn't have a ton of friends. Just a best friend."

My chest tightened at the mention of her best friend. My sister.

"The rest of my *friends* were guys, but none of those friendships felt real. And as soon as they got girlfriends, they bailed on me and stopped talking to me because their girlfriends hated me. I hoped college would be different, and in some ways it was, but in some ways it wasn't." She let out a big sigh. "It was safer to be her friend than it was to be her enemy. Even though,   when you were her friend, she regarded you as a potential enemy anyway and was always on the offensive."

"Ugh. I hate those people."

"We had a lot of the same friends, and we were even roommates with two other girls for a year. And I just wanted this wedding to be an opportunity to show her—to show everyone from vet school—that I've made something of myself, you know?"

"I get it, honey. I do. But their approval of you shouldn't be your validation of worth. You're *so* accomplished."

Alexandra made a noise in her throat. "I just want a hot date for this wedding. I want them to see that I'm not some single loser like I'd basically been the entire time they knew me, since 'Men like girlygirls and women who are inherently feminine.'"

"Who the fuck said that?"

"One guess."

"I hate this bitch, and I've never met her."

Me, too.

"I'm thinking about putting out an ad for a boyfriend for hire. Just for the wedding."

"Dear God, no. You're better than that. And you also don't have time to weed through the plethora of losers who are absolutely going to respond to your ad. I also won't let you go anywhere with someone you barely know and I haven't properly vetted."

"Thanks, *Mom*," Alexandra said sarcastically.

"We should get back, though. Rufus is going to be here soon. The poor guy has no idea he's losing his balls today. I bet he's licking 'em real good on the car ride over here, thinking they'll be there to lick when he gets home."

Alexandra chuckled. "At least we're not putting anyone down today."

"Yeah, yesterday was rough. I hugged my Trixie extra hard when I got home."

"I need to come over and hug Trixie, too. I don't have my own at home to hug."

Their chairs squeaked as they slid them back and stood up. The back of Alexandra's chair bumped mine, and she said a murmured apology.

I waited for the gasp of recognition, holding my breath.

But it didn't come.

She didn't notice me.

Phew.

I kept my head down until I knew they had left through the door and walked past my window back toward the vet hospital.

I made sure not to be too early but also not to be too late.

If the studio was too empty, she'd notice me right away, but if it was too full, I might end up having to lay down my yoga mat right in front of her.

I needed to be strategic about this.

Yes, I planned to end my stalker ways and reveal myself to Alexandra. I just had to do it the right way. I wasn't sure what my end game was here, but ever since I saw Alexandra sitting in Linda's diner as upset as she was getting dumped by that douche Cade, I couldn't get her out of my head.

Which of course, had prompted me to follow her. I had no desire to harass her or anything like that, I'd grown up a bit since our high school days, but I was definitely curious about her, and that of course, led me to spend my entire day off yesterday following her.

The yoga class started at five-thirty, and if yesterday was any indication, Alexandra showed up at about five twenty.

I made sure I was there at five-fifteen to scope out the studio and lay my rented mat down in the perfect place.

Keeping my face down and doing some quad stretches, I kept my ears open to the door but my eyes away from the door.

The place was filling up, and luckily, I'd scored a spot at the back and behind a couple of really tall dudes.

"Good evening, everyone," came Alexandra's voice, though slightly breathier than I'd heard her speak this afternoon. "Please find your way into a *shavasana* that works for you."

What the hell was a *shavasana?*

I watched what the other people around we were doing and followed suit.

Oh, it was just lying on your back.

I could definitely do that.

She dimmed the lights.

"Today's practice will be all about letting go of the external struggles that bog us down. That bog down our minds, our hearts, and our bodies. We carry so much tension in our shoulders, so I want you to visualize, as we move through each posture, pushing those weights off your shoulders and letting them fall to the earth. Each time you come into downward dog, imagine the weights tumbling off. Close your eyes and don't let the fidgets consume you. Find your stillness."

Gentle spa-like music began to play in the background.

"Focus on your breathing. On your *prana*. In through the nose and out through the mouth. Begin to constrict the back of your throat and release your breath as if you were fogging up a mirror. Release it how you need to, whether it be in a moan or a sigh. This is your practice, nobody else's."

Her voice was so hypnotic and peaceful, I could literally feel the tension I didn't even know I had begin to dissolve away from my shoulders. My body was heavy and lay solid and comforting against the ground.

"Focus on your *oo-jay-i pranayama* or ocean breathing. Also called victorious breathing. Once you've let out your sighs and moans, close your mouth, drop your tongue from your teeth and constrict your throat to the point where your breathing makes a sound almost like you're snoring. Place your hands on your diaphragm if you need to and feel your chest expand with each breath, filling up the lower belly first, then the side ribs and finally the top of the chest. Keep your inhales and your exhales even. In for four, hold for four, and out for four."

Normally, I just breathed the way my body did it automatically, but being forced to focus on my breath made me realize just how shallow my inhales were. So when I had to consciously draw that air in and push it down into my belly and deeper into my lungs, the feeling of relaxation was almost euphoric. I was getting light-headed, and with each breath, my body sank deeper and heavier against the ground.

I'd never experienced anything like this before.

"Set an intention for today's practice. Focus on your *pranayama*. Allow your breath to guide you through each posture and to blow away all other thoughts. Leave them at the door. They don't belong in here. In here you are giving yourself over to your own peace and tranquility. You've come here today because you believe in self-care, you believe in self-improvement, so focus on yourself. Honor your commitment to show up, to come to the mat and take care of you. Don't let your practice be ruled by anyone else."

Various people around me released big breaths on sighs or moans, and enough women did it, and erotically so, that I had to tell my cock to go to sleep. Now was absolutely not the fucking time.

"Remember to constrict your throat and breathe out like you're fogging up a mirror. Like you're snoring. "

I did as Alexandra instructed.

"Begin to bring life back into your limbs. Roll your ankles and your wrists. Wiggle your fingers and your toes."

I did as I was told.

She took us through a few stretches while we reclined on our backs, most of them targeting the spine and hamstrings. Eventually, she had us come up to standing, where we had to lift our arms above our head for a "sun salutation," then drop them in prayer over our hearts.

Enough of the people around me knew what they were doing that I just followed the tall Swedish-looking guy in front of me.

We did a series of movements, one flowing into the other, then we'd end in downward dog, then hop up to the top of our mats, come up into sun salutation, and then go down into a push-up and what Alexandra called "baby cobra."

I got a kick out of all the animal names.

Camel, dog, cobra, cow, cat, pigeon, deer, sphinx.

Granted, I'd never seen a pigeon do what the pigeon pose looked like, but who was I to judge the ancient teachings of yoga?

All of her instructions were so polished. There was no hesitation in her words, no *ums* or *ahs*. She reminded us with each movement and posture when to breathe out and when to breathe in. She gave us options for those of us who were further along in our practice or for people like me who couldn't bend for shit and hadn't been able to touch our toes since we were in diapers.

"And come up into warrior two," she instructed. "Bend back into exalted warrior and hold it there. Reach back. I'm going to come around and check to see how everyone is doing."

Shit.

So far, she hadn't noticed me.

So far, I'd been able to successfully hide behind Sven or Lars or Bjorn or whatever. But as I held my pose, my muscles began to tremble as they engaged and tried to keep me stable, my eyes followed her.

She weaved her way among the other students, gently correcting postures or giving praise, smiling and demonstrating yet again how she'd perfected the art of hiding the soulless demon that resided inside of her.

My heart began to hammer inside my chest the closer she got to me.

I was sweating now and could feel the drips trickling their way down my forehead and temples.

I swallowed hard, unable to focus on my breathing any longer since my lungs had a mind of their own and I was practically panting like a dog in the sun.

She finished correcting the posture of the woman beside me, lifted her head, a beautiful smile on her face, but when her eyes found mine and recognition dawned, that smile dropped like that old lady dropped that necklace over the edge of the boat at the end of *Titanic*.

Fire replaced the calm that I'd seen in her eyes since class began.

Because she had been calm.

She'd been at peace.

Teaching yoga was obviously her happy place, and she enjoyed it. That was clear.

She was also very good at it.

A muscle began to tick her jaw, and her top lip curled into a snarl.

And then as if she suddenly remembered that she'd had us all in this posture for like two minutes, she blinked, turned away from me, and headed back to the front of the class. "Slowly make your way forward, breathing out as you shoot your fingers outward toward the back of the room and toward the mirror."

Her eyes locked with mine. Searing heat in beautiful blue.

"Umm ... extend your left leg back to meet your right, and ah ... come down into a low push-up if you can, or drop your knees to the floor. Be careful of your cervical spine."

The class followed her.

"Come into baby cobra or up dog, then join me in downward dog."

I did as she instructed, only when I tipped my gaze up toward her, as I held myself in downward dog, what I saw looking back at me as she glanced beneath her lifted body was the hot hate of a thousand suns.

Shit.

Yeah, convincing her of the plan I'd cooked up while trying desperately not to stare at her ass all class was going to be a hell of a lot harder than I thought.

CHAPTER FIVE

Alex

WHAT IN THE FOUR horsemen of the fucking apocalypse was Eli Evans doing in my yoga class?

What was he doing in Linley Park, Maine?

I couldn't concentrate on my breathing, let alone running through smooth teaching after that. My words were jumbled, I said *umm* and *ahh*, and I was pretty sure I made the class hold exalted warrior for like five minutes. Poor Gillian, the seventy-five-year-old who liked to practice to my left, was shaking like a leaf in a windstorm by the time I told them to breathe out of the posture.

Fucking Eli Evans.

What the actual fuck?

Class sucked after I saw his stupid face.

My entire day just got worse after I saw his stupid face.

I couldn't focus, I couldn't breathe, and I couldn't stop looking at that really hot motherfucker as hard as I tried not to.

Eli Evans had gotten really, really good-looking since I saw him eight years ago.

Like ridiculously hot.

His arms ... dear sweet lord.

I'm a total arm whore and will rub one out with my vibrator just staring at really nice arms.

And Eli had some very nice arms.

The definition in his deltoids and triceps was spank-bank fodder. And the pecs that popped even beneath his black, loose-fitting tank top were nothing to complain about.

He still had that floppy hair that tumbled down over his face to his cheekbones and facial scruff that made the lioness inside me start to purr.

But no fucking way.

Gross.

Eli Evans was gross.

Eli Evans was a jackass.

Eli Evans was my enemy, and I hated him.

"Namaste," we all said, sitting cross-legged on our mats with our hands at heart-center and our heads bowed.

I wanted to curl up into a ball or, better yet, for the Earth to open up and swallow me whole. Never in my six years of teaching yoga had I ever had such a rough class. Not even when I was a newbie and still finding my voice and my footing.

"That was great, Alex, thank you," Gillian said, placing a cool, bony hand to my shoulder, her rolled-up mat tucked under one arm.

I smiled at her in the mirror. "Thanks, Gillian. See you Friday."

A bunch of other students thanked me as well before they left.

I forced the corners of my lips up into a smile and told them they were welcome. But inside, my stomach roiled, my chest was tight, and a scream burned at the back of my throat.

I kept my head down as I rolled up my mat and went about turning off all the LED candles.

I preferred to practice yoga in minimal light, as it helped me find my center better and encouraged me to close my eyes when I was focusing on my breath. My students all seemed to like it as well, since my classes were always packed.

I didn't look toward Eli's mat, but I could still feel his snake-like presence. He was still here. He was still watching me. Like a serpent in the grass, beady-eyed and lying in wait until the perfect time to strike.

Why was he still here?

Why was he here at all?

Once I gathered everything and put it into my duffle bag, I stood up, exhaled deeply, and lifted my head.

"Can we talk?" he asked, standing right where his mat had been, only now his mat—a studio rental—was rolled up and under his arm.

"No," I said bluntly, heading for the door.

He followed me, but I didn't bother holding the door open for him.

"Alexandra!"

I slid into my flip-flops, waved goodbye to some straggler students who were chatting in the lobby, as well as to Savannah behind the desk, then opened the front door, again not bothering to hold it open for Eli, and headed at a brisk pace to my Jeep.

It was only six-thirty, and the air was still warm from a hot afternoon. The days were continuing to get longer, and from the way the sun hit my back, I could tell it had no plans of setting any time soon.

I tossed my bag into the back of my Jeep and yanked open the door.

"Alexandra!" Gravel crunched on the ground behind me.

Yesterday had been a super shitty day, then today we had a dog that was hit by a car brought in and we had to put him down. So today wasn't that great either.

I honestly didn't know why I thought we could go even one day without having to put down an animal because we rarely did. One can hope.

And now I was being thrown the wrench of all wrenches right at my face in the irresistibly handsome and evil shape of Eli Evans.

With my fists clenched at my sides, I spun around to face him. "What the fuck do you want?"

"To talk," he said, mildly out of breath.

I snorted. "You've never wanted to *talk* to me before. Just make fun of me and call me names. And I'm a little too tired to deal with that right now. But thanks." I turned to go, grabbing the oh-shit bar on the side of my Jeep to haul myself up.

His hand shot out, and he closed it over mine. "Just give me one minute of your time."

The man didn't deserve one second of my time, but curiosity, that cheeky kitten, had me wondering what on earth Eli had to say that would make him chase after me—his enemy.

Squinting, I turned to face him. "You have thirty seconds." I flicked my hand from the oh-shit bar so he was no longer touching me.

The tingle that his hand left on the back of mine was something I'd probably have to have a doctor take a look at. Could you get the clap from somebody just touching you?

I raised a brow at him when he hadn't said anything yet. "Tick-tock."

His simper was playful and I found myself pausing to stare at his mouth for a moment longer than was polite.

Had his lips always been that full?

Had he always had that one dimple on his left side?

He flipped his head, and that curl that came down over his face whipped back and stayed on the top of his head.

I refused to let myself gasp or for my body to begin to warm simply because the man had gotten hot in the last eight years.

Tons of hot people were assholes.

"Your boyfriend doesn't come to your class?" he asked.

Heat bubbled in my blood. I tamped down the growl, shook my head, and reached once again for the oh-shit bar, this time climbing up behind the steering wheel.

"I'd say it was nice seeing you, Eli, but we'd both know that was a lie. So it was *not* nice seeing you. I hope I never see you again, and maybe you should try The Zen Den over on Milford if you're interested in yoga. I don't think you're a good *fit* for this studio."

I shoved my key into the ignition and started the vehicle. I was about to throw my Jeep into reverse when the emotions from the last two days all rose to the surface. Gripping the steering wheel until my knuckles turned white, I looked down at him.

"You can't resist hurting me, can you? Even now, after we've been out of school for what, fourteen years, and haven't seen each other in eight, you haven't grown the fuck up enough to be a decent human being. You're still that asshole who put ketchup on my chair before I sat down in the seventh grade. Who put my finger in warm water when I slept over, who let your dog roll all over my pillow after he'd just rolled in cat shit. You're still an immature, lowlife weasel who finds enjoyment in hurting others. Because you knew exactly what your presence in my class would do to me. You knew it'd throw me off my game. And I hate to admit that you succeeded."

I clapped exaggeratedly.

"So bravo Eli Evans. You win again. Just like you did when we raced around the track." I held up a finger. "But just like that day, it wasn't an honorable win."

Tossing the Jeep into reverse, I made to move my foot off the brake, but he surged forward and held onto the side of the vehicle.

Normally, I loved my Jeep and having no top or sides on in the summer, but right now I was really wishing for some doors. For some space between us.

"You're not so fucking perfect yourself," he said. "You've got every one of those students fooled into thinking you actually have a soul, but we both know the truth." He scoffed. "I still can't believe you're a vet. Don't the animals bark and snarl at you since they can sense your true intentions, which is to hurt everyone in your path?"

How the hell did he know I was a vet?

Rage burned hot inside me. But I wasn't going to bite.

He was goading me.

Taunting me.

He wanted to see me break.

I wasn't going to give him the satisfaction.

With a smack of my hand, I batted his fingers off the side of my Jeep, pressed my foot into the accelerator and backed out.

Then I flipped him the bird and got the fuck out of there before he could revel in seeing my tears and the fact that once again, he'd won.

Eli

I shouldn't feel bad about making her cry.

I hated her ... right?

And yet the twisty sensation in my gut was painful and had me feeling like an absolute ass.

That hadn't gone how I wanted it to go at all.

But when she saw me and that glare made her blue eyes gleam, I was transported back in time to when we were kids and she'd scowl at me like that from across the classroom or across my dinner table when she'd have a sleepover with my sister.

And then when I asked her if we could talk and she blew me off, my ego spoke before my brain and I retaliated with something I knew would hurt her. I went for the jugular, which was something Alexandra and I always did to one another.

Even though we'd never been friends, we knew exactly which buttons of the other person's to press. Which buttons would cause the most amount of damage.

And so I pressed the boyfriend button since I knew that the wound there was still fresh.

She reacted just like I knew she would, immediately jumping to the defensive and dredging up even more old wounds. Picking off the scabs and letting them bleed so I could see how much my words still affected her.

Of course, at that point, all of my maturity had flown out the fucking window and I was no better than I was at thirteen, goading her, seeing just how far I could push until she snapped.

Fuck, I was an asshole.

She'd tried so hard not to cry in front of me. I saw it in the tightness of her face, the hard swallow in her long throat and the flare of her nostrils.

She flipped me the bird as she drove away, but I was watching closely and saw her swipe her fingers beneath her eye before she fled down the road.

In all our years verbally sparring with each other, Alexandra had never once cried in front of me.

She refused to let me know that I'd gotten to her, and today was no different.

Only today *was* different because today was the first day I saw her crying. Today was the first day I saw her break and realized that I'd pushed her too far.

You're not going to get what you want from her if you treat her like that.

Yeah, I knew that.

But the woman just did something to me, just brought out my inner asshole like nobody else.

I climbed into my truck and headed home, determined to try to make things some semblance of right tomorrow.

I wouldn't go back to one of her yoga classes, but I would wait outside of her work and get her to talk to me. Get her to *actually* talk to me and propose my plan to her. After all, there was something in it for both of us. I wasn't just trying to take.

I was supposed to be back at work tomorrow, so I'd have to figure out a way to leave the house we were roofing and get to Alexandra's work before she left.

She mentioned to one of the other yoga students that she'd see them again on Friday, and the online schedule indicated that she didn't teach tomorrow. So that left her work and possibly the Muay Thai gym as places for me to catch up with her.

And if she found out I knew she also went to Muay Thai, she'd think I was a stalker, probably get a restraining order against me, and then all hope for my well-thought-out plans would be gone.

I made myself a delicious kung pao chicken with extra chili peppers and cashews instead of peanuts because that was all I had. I sat out on my sundeck now that the sun had started to set behind the buildings to the west, and I brought up Alexandra's social media on my phone.

She went to Brown, which I knew, then from there, she did veterinarian school at Penn Vet in Philadelphia. From the looks of things, she'd been hired at East Coast Animals Veterinary Hospital—a big veterinary franchise with hospitals all up and down the eastern seaboard—right out of college and had been working there ever since.

The funny thing was, not one picture on her social media showed her boxing or doing yoga. There wasn't even a picture of her tattoo. There were just pictures of her and her ex and her and animals. And most of the time she was with animals, she was at work in those sexy dark blue scrubs.

Her social media was heavily curated to show the world a very specific version of herself, and in a lot of ways, it wasn't the real her at all.

It didn't take long for me to find out whose wedding she was invited to.

A Dr. Allegra Ruiz and a Dr. Ford Grady,

I blanched at their photos.

Very orange people.

Very plastic and very orange and very fake.

This was who Alexandra was trying to impress?

This was who Alexandra was in a big panty-twisted panic attack over canceling on?

I shoveled kung pao into my mouth and kept digging.

Allegra Ruiz came from money. So did Ford Grady.

Allegra and Ford owned a practice in Beverly Hills called Star Treatment Animal Hospital, but when I clicked on the website, the interior of the clinic looked more like a spa. Everything was white. There were jade plants and bamboo, a fucking fountain in the middle of the lobby, and every person on the staff member web page was blond, orange, and with near-horse-teeth-size veneers.

It was fucking creepy to look at.

I quickly clicked out of that page.

The hospital seemed to pride itself on not only its pet medical services but also its animal spa treatments, such as dental procedures, pet massages, doggy braces, doggy facials, chemical fur straightening, fur dying, manicures and pedicures—and yes, there were dogs with their nails painted—and something ridiculous called the "pet colonic" where they performed a colonic, which is essentially an enema on your pet to see how their insides are performing. But when I came to the neuticles—fake testicles for neutered dogs to help with their self-esteem and aesthetic—I nearly threw my phone off the balcony.

It was all just too much. I had to exit out of the window.

But I was already down the rabbit hole of terror that was Allegra and Ford, so I found them on social media and within seconds found their wedding website.

It was a lot.

Like super extra.

They were getting married at the Crown Elite Hotel on Coronado Island, which was just off San Diego. Something like two hundred people were set to attend. They reserved nearly the entire hotel, and the thing was supposed to be like a four-day event.

First, there was the cocktail party, then the following day was the rehearsal dinner party, then the next day was the wedding, and finally the day after the wedding was when they opened all their gifts at a pompous brunch and everyone got to puff up their chests or hide under their brunch crepes in shame over the expense of their gift.

I'd never been a big fan of weddings, but this seemed like something I'd rather have a bath with a billion fire ants than attend, let alone attend with Alexandra.

The vision in my left eye went super blurry, and black spots began to form around the corners. Keith was reminding me that I needed to make nice with Alexandra if I wanted to continue seeing things. Sight was worth going to this wedding, brunch crepes and all.

With a sigh, I put my phone in my pocket and took my empty bowl into the kitchen.

Back to the grind tomorrow.

I fucking hated my job.

My days off were Tuesday and Wednesday, which was why I was able to stalk-*not*-stalk Alexandra for the last two days.

But I had to pay the bills somehow, so up onto people's roofs I went.

Very few people knew that I'd flunked out of MIT after two years then took off traveling.

I just couldn't focus.

It's true what they say about the attrition rate and students in the engineering program. By sophomore year, like half of them switch majors or quit altogether.

The demands were just too much.

I saw more people cry in college in my engineering program than I ever did in thirteen years of school. Than I ever did in kindergarten.

It'd been a tough adjustment going from being one of the smartest guys in my graduating class to feeling like an utter moron in my classes with savant genius prodigy children who were building robots before their first pube sprouted.

I figured that since I got into MIT, I must be smart enough, but that just wasn't the case. I burnt out, left school and haven't looked back.

Of course, my mom knew and Eden knew, but I kept my social media presence pretty sparse and made sure to only post pictures of my travels—or my food because I am a millennial, after all.

I guess I couldn't really judge Alexandra for posting only certain aspects of her life on social media since I did the same thing.

I didn't want people to know that I'd flunked out of MIT or that I bounced around from job to job or that I was on the verge of going blind because of a douchebag tumor named Keith.

But those were all things I was ashamed of.

Alexandra was hiding accomplishments and things she was good at. I'd be posting that shit like crazy, not hiding it.

I pulled out my phone and scrolled through her social media photos again.

There were a lot of her with a lanyard around her neck and a badge that said *Linley Park Animal Shelter.* Did she work there, too?

Did the woman ever just sit the fuck down?

I googled the shelter and found out that you could volunteer to take dogs for walks. I immediately signed up.

I don't know why the fuck I signed up, since I knew that if Alexandra saw me there, she'd probably file a restraining order against me, then hit me with a right hook. But I signed up anyway. The pictures of the dogs got to me, and I hadn't had a good dog cuddle in way too long. I hadn't walked a dog since my own childhood dog Misty, and she died like fifteen years ago.

I signed up for next Tuesday, my next day off.

Then finally, I stowed my phone in my pocket, peeled my tank top over my head and went to go have a shower, knowing full well that I was going to beat off to the image of Alexandra's ass in those tight yoga pants—just like I had yesterday.

CHAPTER SIX

Alex

THURSDAYS I WORKED UNTIL ten o'clock at night. I didn't start until one in the afternoon, so I usually spent the morning at H&J sparring for an hour with whoever was around.

After showering at H&J, I grabbed lunch at a taco food truck not too far from work, then parked my Jeep behind the vet hospital and went inside.

I already knew that I had two neuters, a spay and three dental cleanings on the schedule for today. But more often than not when I worked the late shift, someone came running in around nine at night with their pet who ate something weird, or they ran over a cat in the street, and my ten o'clock end-time quickly turned into midnight or later.

It was six o'clock before I knew it, and I had a thirty-minute lull between clients. My stomach rumbled, reminding me that it'd been six hours since I'd eaten and that I'd most definitely burned more calories sparring with Hector than I'd eaten today.

The café where I usually grabbed my coffee would be closed, so that meant running down the road to the deli.

I was just telling Penny, the receptionist, that I'd be right back, choosing to walk rather than drive, when through the windowed front door of the hospital I recognized a face I'd hoped to never see again.

What was he doing here?

How did he know where I worked?

Shoving open the door until it slammed against the outside brick of the building, I stomped toward him. "Are you stalking me now?"

He climbed out of his truck, bringing with him a sub sandwich wrapped in wax paper. I recognized the emblem on the sticker. It was from Joe's Deli on Tillman and Jarvis. That place had the best sandwiches. "I thought you might be hungry." He offered me the sandwich, but I didn't even flinch, let alone reach for it. My stomach told me not to be an idiot, but my brain told me that he'd probably poisoned it with ipecac and I'd be vomiting for the rest of the night.

With a heavy sigh, he set the sandwich down on the hood of his truck. "I'm sorry for yesterday, okay? But can we just have an adult conversation?"

My jaw ached from how hard I was clenching it.

"Listen, I knew you worked here because I saw you and a coworker at that café over there a couple of days ago. I overheard your conversation about your boyfriend dumping you."

"So that's why you brought him up yesterday, because you knew it would sting. You always know exactly the right buttons to push."

He closed his brown eyes for a moment. "Yes. But I shouldn't have."

How much had he heard of my and Denise's conversation?

"Eavesdropping is rude."

He rolled his eyes, but his full lips lifted on one side in a lopsided smile. "So is flipping someone the bird."

"Not when they deserve it."

My stomach grumbled loud. So loud that he heard it and picked up the sandwich again. He held it out for me.

With a sigh and a head shake, he opened it up on one end and took a manly bite. "See, it's not poisoned."

I narrowed my eyes at him. "Maybe you're just willing to sacrifice having the shits and spits all night in order to know you've given them to me, too."

He lifted a shoulder. "Maybe. Or maybe I came with a peace offering."

"Eli Evans doesn't do *peace*. What's the catch?"

"You have something I need. And I can offer you something you want."

"I highly doubt that." I crossed my arms in front of my chest, then against my better judgment, I reached over, snatched the sandwich from his hands and took a giant bite. It was fucking delicious.

I moaned and allowed my eyes to close as I let my taste buds go on an adventure and have a couple of mini-orgasms.

When I opened my eyes, Eli was grinning at me in that cocky Eli Evans way.

"I need a surgery," he said. "I have a benign tumor in my brain, but it's pushing on my optic nerve and will eventually cause me to go blind."

I paused midchew. And, of course, my gaze drifted immediately to his eyes.

They were a beautiful, soft brown with dark flecks of copper around the irises.

Eden's eyes had been the same.

"Can you see okay right now?"

He nodded. "I can." He glanced at his truck. "I'm driving, aren't I?"

I refused to chastise myself for not thinking of that first. The hunger was messing with my brain. Besides, there were plenty of people who had driver's license   but damn well shouldn't. My grandmother, for one. The woman was blind as a bat and could barely see over the steering wheel, and yet every five years they kept renewing her license, no questions asked.

"And where do I come into all of this?" I reached the bottom of the first half of the sandwich, glanced at him, and he nodded his head to say I could eat the other half. I dove in.

"I overheard you talking about your insurance plan, and it would cover the majority of my surgery. And it wouldn't classify it as a pre-existing condition, unlike some plans. You guys are with a really decent company, which is difficult to say in this country."

I nodded. I couldn't disagree with that. Xavier Blue Trust was really great. I couldn't wait to go for massages and acupuncture and maybe even take advantage of some counseling, since I was apparently overly masculine and no man would ever love me because I could probably kick their ass.

"You want me to put you on my plan?" Where was he going with this? And then, before he said anything, the truth of it all came crashing down around me. I shoved the sandwich back into his arms. "Uh-uh. No fucking way. I am not *marrying* you. Are you out of your fucking mind?"

"You need a hot date for the Oompa-Loompa wedding. I need decent insurance so I don't go blind. I think it's a pretty decent trade."

"A decent trade?" I tossed my head back and laughed. "You want my insurance coverage, you want to *marry* me, and in return, you'll be my date to a wedding?"

"This wedding seems to be pretty fucking important to you. I heard you talking about taking out an ad for a boyfriend for hire and having him come with you on the road trip so you can take cutesy pictures to make the relationship believable. I can do that." His lips slid into another one of those sexy half-hitched grins, which I hated to admit made him look all the hotter. "I can be the most amazing, attentive, convincing boyfriend you've ever had in your life."

"But you'd actually be my husband?" I said snidely, glancing around the parking lot for the cameramen who were preparing to jump out, because this had to be a joke. Some horrible reality-show prank. No way on earth was Eli Evans asking me to marry him.

"For insurance purposes only."

"And once you get your surgery?"

"We get it annulled, obviously. Or divorced or whatever. Stating irreconcilable differences."

"The difference being, I think you're a total asshole and you disagree with me."

The smirk was back. "Precisely."

Heat raced through my body like a runaway train on fire. This proposition, this *proposal* was an absolute joke.

Right?

I mean, he *did* fit the part of a hot boyfriend. Those arms alone were … yum!

But that attitude.

His personality.

Besides his looks, the rest of him was one hundred percent crap.

Could I *My Fair Lady* his personality in ten days?

Ten days didn't seem like enough time for the total overhaul he needed.

The man needed a personality transplant.

I shook my head. This idea was preposterous, and furthermore, the thought of spending ten days with Eli made me want to vomit up the delicious Joe's Deli sandwich I'd just eaten. And anybody who was anybody knew that you did not waste Joe's sandwiches.

Which was why I said, "No fucking way." Then I turned around and headed back to work, not looking behind me but knowing by the reflection in the windowed door that he was standing there, watching me leave.

As I expected, a woman came in at nine forty-five with her black lab aka garbage guts, saying he'd just eaten a ton of chocolate.

We gave the dog something to make him vomit, then put him on an IV to pump him back full of fluids. So by the time the lab and his owner left, it was nearly eleven when I went to my Jeep. Penny and the vet tech George waved at me as they climbed into their vehicles and headed home.

I used every ounce of willpower I had to not look out the front window to see if Eli was still in the parking lot during the last hours of my shift. Every single ounce until I was using a spatula to scrape the bottom of the barrel.

He couldn't still be out there, right?

It'd been over five hours since I spoke to him. And yet something told me he wasn't going to back down. Desperation fueled him, and knowing how good my insurance plan was would keep him pushing for this cockamamie scheme of his to take shape.

The man was barking up the wrong tree.

With a heavy sigh, I put my key in the ignition and turned it over.

Nothing. Not even a sputter.

What the hell?

Did Eli do something to my Jeep?

With a growl, I unbuckled my seat belt, hit the lever for the hood and went to go see what the hell was up. It was dark out now, and I needed the light from my phone to see under the hood.

Thank God my dad raised me and taught me how to do the simple things like boost a battery, change my oil and change a tire. I could also check for simple malfunctions, too. I wasn't some damsel in distress who couldn't take care of herself or do what needed to be done.

Only staring at the engine and double-checking that everything on the battery was tight and no possum or feral cat had crawled up into my engine, I realized I had no idea what needed to be done.

"Need a hand?"

I jumped at the voice, even though half a second after I heard it, I knew who it belonged to.

I spun around. "What did you do to my Jeep?"

Eli's hands were shoved into his pockets as he sexily sauntered his way toward me. "What are you going on about?"

"What did you do to my Jeep? It was running perfectly fine this morning. And now it's not. The only difference I can think of is the fact that I've seen you between now and then and you want something from me. So you probably came out here, poured Kool-Aid into my transmission and are trying to play the hero so that I'll agree to marry you."

A giggle bubbled up inside me at the sheer ridiculousness of what I'd just said.

"I didn't touch your Jeep," he said with a deep, surly grumble as he nudged me out of the way and came to peer into the engine just as I was.

"Then why the hell are you still here?"

"Because I want to talk to you."

"You already talked to me. You told me the most hilarious joke I've ever heard in my entire life. And now you can leave."

His gaze tipped to mine. "It's your radiator."

I glanced down, and shit, he was right. It was completely fried. How the hell did that happen?

"You'll need to call a tow truck and have it taken to a garage."

"No shit," I grumbled.

"I can give you a ride home."

"No, thank you. I'll call a cab."

"You know as well as I do that no cabs run midweek in this town after eleven. And we don't even have Uber or Lyft."

I growled, slammed the hood, and then went to the front seat to grab my purse and gym bag. "Then I'll walk. It's only six miles." I headed to the sidewalk.

"Alexandra!" he called after me.

I ignored him and kept walking.

I refused to look back at him. Refused to acknowledge him.

The sound of running in gravel echoed behind me, then the revving of a truck engine. I still wouldn't look.

"Alexandra, get in the fucking truck," he said behind me.

I knew he was in his truck now, driving at the speed of a sloth with his window rolled down.

"I'm completely happy walking. It's a beautiful night."

"Alexandra, get in the truck."

I spun around on my heels. "It's Alex. My name is Alex. You know I prefer Alex and have preferred Alex my entire life, and yet for some stupid fucking reason, you refuse to call me that. It's just another way that you choose to taunt me. So no, I'm not getting in your truck, and I'm sure as hell not fucking marrying you." I turned back around and picked up speed.

"You think I *want* to marry you? I haven't been able to stand you since the day I met you. But this is a deal that can benefit us both. After the wedding, all I need is for you to put me on your insurance as a dependent and then once the surgery is done, we get it annulled. We don't have to live together. You'd be free to date and sleep with whoever you wanted. It would be purely business."

"And if we get audited or the insurance company sends an adjuster in to see if we're lying?"

"We say we're in an open marriage and this is what works for us. Trust me, I can be very convincing."

I scoffed. "Well, you're doing a shit job convincing me."

He murmured something behind me that I couldn't quite hear, but I was sure it was something extra assholey, so I kept walking.

"Get in the truck, Alex. You've had a long day, and you're not going to get home until like one o'clock. Let me drive you home."

"And in return, I have to marry you?"

"No, in return, you say thank you."

I came to a crosswalk at a red light. No cars were coming, so in an attempt to gain some space from him, I crossed anyway while he had to wait at the red light.

He caught up to me as soon as the light turned green.

"I understand how you feel," he said through the open passenger-side window.

Casting him some side-eye, I kept walking. "Yeah? And how's that?"

"Like a failure."

Now that made me toss my head back and laugh.

"*I'm* a failure? I'm a fucking doctor of veterinary medicine and an accomplished yoga instructor. How the hell do you justify calling me a failure? Or thinking that you know I feel like one?"

More importantly, how the hell did he know that was exactly how I felt?

"Because you're not living the life you want to be living right now. Otherwise, if you were, you wouldn't give two shits about having to impress the Oompa-Loompa dog colonic people with a hot boyfriend. You wouldn't even be going to their fucking Oompa-Loompa wedding."

I stopped and turned to face him. "How the hell do you know whose wedding it is?"

"You mentioned Allegra Ruiz at the coffee shop. You two really didn't drop your voices. I'm sure the baristas heard you."

I glared at him.

"Get in the truck, Alexandr—*Alex*. Get in the truck, Alex."

"Tell me why you think you understand what it's like to be a failure and maybe I will."

His jaw clenched, and I could see the war going on behind his eyes as he tried to decide whether he should tell me or not. Whether getting me into the truck was worth revealing something vulnerable about himself. He'd always been able to find the gaps in my armor better than I could find any of his, and it was for this very reason. The man shared nothing about himself, never let any one in.

Eli took a deep breath. "I flunked out of MIT my sophomore year. I've been traveling and working odd jobs ever since."

My eyes must have doubled in size because the color that bloomed on his cheeks beneath the sexy dark scruff was the shade of a poppy.

Without saying anything, I reached for the door handle and climbed into the passenger seat, placing my duffle bag and purse on my lap after I put on my seat belt.

He pulled off into traffic without saying anything.

We drove in silence for five solid minutes until finally, my curiosity got the better of me. "Do you even know where I live?"

More color filled his cheeks and this time traveled down his neck. "No."

I smiled, then looked out the window. "I just moved. Turn left at the next set of lights."

CHAPTER SEVEN

Eli

I PULLED UP TO the curb at Alexandra's building and turned off my truck, pivoting in my seat to face her. "Given any more thought to my *proposal?*"

She barely turned to face me, but the glare in her eyes was clear and the scowl on her face even more so. "You can't be serious?"

"As a fucking brain tumor named Keith."

Now she really turned to face me. "Keith?"

I shrugged. "A douchey name for a douchey tumor."

She shook her head and made a perturbed face before saying, "Are you not going to address the elephants in the room and just how much they're all saying that everything you're asking is a colossally bad idea?"

I squinted at her. Which elephants was she talking about? Because there were many.

She rolled her eyes and held up her hand. "Let's start with the most obvious elephant, shall we? The biggest and fattest one." I remained quiet. "You have hated me for our entire lives."

"I'm pretty sure you've hated me, too."

"Irrelevant."

"I beg to differ, but go on. Name those pachyderms."

Another eye roll. "Elephant number two." She stuck out another finger and tapped it. "Our parents are married."

I cringed. Yeah, I tried to forget that bit. "Do you speak to your mother?"

"No." Her head shake was tight. "She's dead to me."

I lifted one shoulder. "And I haven't seen my dad in eight years—he's dead to me too—so even though we're *technically* stepsiblings, I don't really think *that* Dumbo is exceptionally large."

She growled, and for some stupid reason it made my dick jerk in my jeans.

"You are someone I would seriously consider smothering with a pillow while they slept."

That comment made me snort and smile, which thankfully made her crack a small, obviously reluctant grin as well.

I nodded. "I'm not your favorite person, got it."

But her expression sobered quickly, and her scowl returned.

We both knew the next two things she could say, but I thought she was hoping she didn't have to say them just as much as I was hoping she wouldn't say them.

"I think that's enough reasons, don't you?" Her shoulders slumped. She was tired.

Saving puppies and giving hamsters hysterectomies all day was probably exhausting. But at least where she worked had air-conditioning. I was stuck outside in the blistering heat dealing with hot shingles and downwind from a guy who farted way too fucking much for me to not question his gut health.

Her fingers wrapped around the door handle, and she went to pull it open. "Thank you for the ride. What do I owe you for gas?"

I waved her away. "Marry me and we'll call it square."

Another eye roll. Another smirk. Another scoff.

"You need a ride to work tomorrow?"

I was surprised those shoulders could drop even more. She really was defeated.

"I'll call my co-worker. I'm on her way. But thank you."

I nodded. I didn't want to push—too hard.

Opening the door, she grabbed her purse and duffle bag, then slid out onto the sidewalk. "Thank you for the ride."

"Think about it, okay?"

She seemed less perturbed than a moment ago, and maybe it was just me being hopeful, but I could have sworn I saw her considering it. Her brow lifted slightly, her lips tilted just a touch. She was thinking about it. She was thinking about what it would be like to be married to me.

Now you're just being cocky.

She closed the door, but because the passenger window was still down, I knew she'd hear me. "I'll come to Monday's yoga class, and you can let me know what kind of cake you want at the wedding. I'm partial to vanilla with raspberry buttercream in the center, but I'm open to suggestions."

There was that smile. It was still small, but it was there, and it made her eyes sparkle under the flickering orange streetlight.

"I think The Zen Den is more your vibe. A lot of guys with giant egos and little dicks. You'll fit right in."

I sucked in a breath and touched my hand to my chest. "Ouch."

The ire was gone from her eyes, but the venom remained in her tone. "In all honesty, Eli, how can you see it working? You blame me, admit it. You blame me for all of it."

The amusement I'd felt, the excitement at having possibly turned a corner with Alexandra all evaporated, leaving all those long-indelible feelings of hate and resentment. My lips dipped, and my brows furrowed. Everything inside me grew dark and twisty, and an intense stabbing pain began to form in my gut and chest.

"I thought so," she said plainly. She turned to go, then glanced over her shoulder at me as she was halfway up the path. "So you can sleep a bit better at night, not a day goes by that I don't feel guilt and pain over what happened to Eden. Over not being there for her when she needed me. It's why I haven't left the country since. I loved your sister more than I loved my own, and I will never, ever get over her death and the fact that I could have prevented it." Then she showed me her back and walked toward the front door to her apartment lobby.

I watched every one of her moves.

"You could have lied, you know?" I called after her, instantly regretting it.

Her back stiffened and straightened. She knew exactly what I was referring to. She didn't turn around but called out, "The truth is always better than a lie. He would have found out eventually. What they did was wrong, and you know it."

The hot, charring flames of anger began to lick up the sides of my stomach and into the depths of my throat. "You broke up two families," I said, wondering why the fuck I wasn't shutting up.

"You know I didn't, Eli. And until you realize that, this will never work."

She struggled to find her keys in her purse, then couldn't figure out which key on her keychain went to the building. Maybe she was nervous because I was still there, or perhaps it was just fatigue. I couldn't tell in the dark.

She opened the lobby door, stepped inside, and disappeared.

And yet, I still sat there.

My chest rose and fell rapidly, like I'd just sprinted down the street. The pain and heat in my chest and stomach were so intense I thought I might puke, but my throat was so tight that even if I did puke, it wouldn't come out.

Of course, Alexandra was right.

I blamed her for Eden's death.

Because when Eden needed Alexandra the most, she wasn't there.

And neither was I.

When Eden's depression got so bad that the only way out she could think of was suicide, she called her best friend looking for help, and Alexandra was off in Thailand with her boyfriend and unreachable.

Eden felt unloved. Unwanted. Unworthy of life.

So she took her own.

I'd been in Mozambique on a safari at the time, so of course, I also felt guilty for not being reachable. She'd tried calling me, but I'd been in a place without service.

At the time, I'd been furious with Alexandra for not picking up the phone when Eden called. Equally furious with myself, of course, but it was so much easier projecting that anger outward than inward.

I'd said a lot of mean and hateful things to her, particularly after Eden's funeral, which had resulted in Alexandra leaving my mother's house not long after arriving, her face red and full of anger.

Deep down, I knew Eden's death wasn't her fault. That was just my pain and my own guilt looking for a way to make sense of what happened. I projected the guilt I harbored over not being there for Eden onto Alex, which she didn't deserve. She was hurting just as much as I was, but I'd been too blinded by the pain of losing my sister, I didn't see it that way. It was easier to blame someone else if it provided a reason for what happened. And the person it felt easiest to blame was Alexandra since she'd always been my target.

But traveling for the last decade and Keith in my skull had helped me come to terms with some of my rage. Blame and hate were poison for the mind and body. They took up the room in your soul that could otherwise be occupied by things that brought you joy.

So no, I didn't blame Alexandra for Eden's death—not any-more. She was hurting over not being there for Eden just as much as I was. It was one of the few things we had in common.

But ... I wasn't entirely reformed in my anger—we're all work   in progresses until we die. Because as far as breaking up our families went, well ... she was right about that.

I did blame her.

After my breathing returned to some semblance of normal, I turned the ignition over in my truck and shifted into drive. A quick glance up at the building showed a few lights on on the first, third and fifth floors.

Which one was hers? Did she overlook the street or the parking lot?

I was about to turn back to the road and hit the accelerator when movement on the third floor drew my eyes.

Drapes were pulled back, and a shadowed face peered through the window in a unit on the third floor. I ducked low to get a better look, and the head pulled away and the drapes dropped.

Fury simmered inside me. Fury at Alexandra, at myself, at my mother, at Alexandra's father. At everyone involved in the destruction and dissolution of my family that ultimately resulted in my sister's death.

Alexandra and her "the truth is always better than a lie" motto was why at the age of sixteen my perfect, suburban life came crashing down around me and Eden, destroying everything we ever loved.

This was not at all how I saw any of this going. I hit the ac-celerator and gunned it away from the curb, knowing full well that my engine was loud and my tires burned and squealed on the road.

I did not fucking care.

I needed to find a liquor store that was still open. Then I needed to drink until these feelings, the ones that made the darkness begin to close in around me, disappeared. I needed to pass out without the hateful thoughts that were like a branding iron in my brain.

I needed to forget Alexandra Hartford.

I needed to forget that I ever thought we could make this deal work.

And I needed to get the fuck out of Linley Park and the fuck out of Maine. Because even knowing she was here was too much.

Because everything Alexandra Hartford touched, she destroyed.

And fuck if I was going to allow myself to be the next victim on her list.

Alex

Friday Penny picked me up. I called a tow truck and they grabbed my beloved Jeep and took it to a body shop. It would be at least a week until I got the Jeep back, so I was driving a courtesy car for now. A silver Toyota Camry.

Ugh!

My dad had drilled it into my head that no vehicle should ever be the color or shade of fog. It made it impossible to see at night or on a foggy day and just increased the risk of an accident.

It was June, so I didn't really have to worry about fog, but either way, my resentment toward the sedan and its color kept rearing its ugly head every time I had to drive it.

But whatever, at least the Jeep was getting fixed. I only had to drive the mom-mobile in the death shade for a week. I was pretty sure I'd survive.

I'd also decided to just move the hell out of my old apartment and into my new one, so I'd hired a moving crew for Saturday to help me move into my new place.

Not that I had a ton of stuff, but it was just easier with people who knew what they were doing and had a cube van and dolly. Particularly since I couldn't fit shit in a Camry.

I could confidently say that the only upside to my new apartment was the fact that it was closer to work by a staggering five minutes.

The rest of it was crap.

It was west-facing—so getting alllll that daytime melt-your-face-off heat. My unit looked out onto the street, not the parking lot (okay, that was a second bonus, but it was minor), and I was on the third floor of five stories. But the biggest piss-off was that the neighbors below, above and on either side of me smoked.

I made sure to sign no more than a six-month lease because I was already on the hunt for something better.

Maybe, if the replacement radiator didn't pillage my bank account too badly, I could afford a chunk of property by the end of the year. Even if I just put a tiny house or an older model RV on it for a few years, at least it would be mine.

This was just a means to an end. A roof over my head and a place to do laundry.

I'd have to talk to my dad about looking out for a used, circa early 2000s RV for me. He was such a wheeler and dealer, could dicker like an American Picker.

So by Monday morning, I had spent a total of two nights in my new apartment, woke up to the smell of cheap cigarettes wafting through my window and what sounded like two silverback gorillas fighting for the right to mate with the females in the unit that shared a wall with my bedroom.

Only, I was pretty sure silverback gorillas didn't yell out, "Harder, Jerry, fuck me harder. Choke me. Choke me!"

Of course, Saturday, I made sure to volunteer for three hours at the Linley Park Animal Shelter, since I made that commitment and would not bail on the people there or the animals.

It was another reason why I hired a moving company, so that I could still help out where I agreed to help out.

It had actually been really therapeutic spending time with the animals. Some of them needed a couple of injuries looked at, but the majority of them just wanted the attention, and I was more than happy to sit on the grass and let the dogs swarm me like a hive full of happy honeybees.

One dog in particular, an elderly border terrier named Jill, had taken a strong liking to me. She curled up in my lap almost as soon as I sat down and didn't move until I had to get up to leave. Her snoring rivaled that of a Tibetan mastiff, but she was sweet as could be.

If only my apartment was pet-friendly and I had the time to dedicate to a needy dog, I would have adopted Jill on the spot.

Monday at work was uneventful, and I'm not going to lie that I half-expected to find Eli leaning against his truck waiting for me when I finished work at five, but he wasn't.

Had I finally scared him off for good when I reminded him Thursday night just how much he hated me?

I hoped so.

He needed to understand that what he was proposing would never work. It would never be believable by anybody with eyes, ears or two brain cells to rub together. Nothing about us screamed "believable married couple." Nothing about us even screamed, let alone whispered, "believable friends" or even "believable people who tolerate each other."

It was best if Eli Evans forgot about me entirely and found someone else with great insurance to marry and if I posted an ad on Penny Saver or Craigslist for a date.

I waved goodbye to Penny and headed to my courtesy car. I taught yoga at five-thirty and then was going to head to H&J for an hour. Hector texted me yesterday to tell me a new guy came by the gym and when he heard about my record, he wanted to spar.

I really disliked guys like this, but whatever.

I'd go a few rounds with him and get a cardio workout while I was at it.

I hit Joe's Deli on my lunch break, saving half of my sandwich for my drive from work to yoga.

I was just finishing my final bite when I pulled into the studio parking lot, only to see a familiar truck parked right out front.

Son of a bitch.

If I didn't have to teach, I would have pulled back out and just headed straight to H&J, but alas, I was the instructor for the five-thirty Yin yoga class, so I couldn't just bail.

Fucking Eli Evans.

Grabbing my mat and bag out of the back seat of the car, I stomped my flip-flop-covered feet toward the front door. He was in the lobby, and when his eyes snagged mine, he held my gaze—or should I say glare, because I was glaring at him.

Yanking the door open, I took a deep breath and tossed on the best smile I could muster, though anybody with even half an ounce of empathy would know it was fake as shit.

"Alex, hey," Savannah said with a wave.

I wiggled my fingers at her, didn't look at Eli, because fuck him, and headed straight for the studio doors. "Give me seven before you send people in, please, Savannah," I called behind me as I pushed open the door.

"You got it."

The moment the door closed behind me, I exhaled the breath that had gotten lodged in my chest.

I needed a few minutes to center myself. I needed a few minutes of deep breathing. When Eli showed up in my class last week, all those years of breath practice had flown right out the window. I couldn't let him do that to me again.

I laid down my mat and reclined into savasana.

I would not let Eli get to me.

I would not let his presence in my class affect my teaching.

I would not let his presence in my class affect my breathing.

He could blame me for Eden's death all he wanted.

I blamed myself, too. And I would until the day I died.

He could blame me for his parents getting divorced. We both knew that wasn't on me. But if he needed someone to be angry at, someone easy to hate, then he could have at it and hate me until the cows came home.

But I would not let his negative energy and all the hate that followed him around like an imprinted duckling to affect my yoga practice or my own energy.

I couldn't.

Closing my eyes, I toned the back of my throat and relaxed. I exhaled deep through my nose, then pulled the air back into my chest, filling up my belly and every corner of my lungs. I held it for four, then released, repeating this until a sense of calm, an almost hypnotic feeling of being half-awake, half-asleep took over my brain and body.

"You ready for people?" Savannah's gentle voice interrupted my trance, but I was grateful and nodded.

"Send them in," I said before getting up and going to the equipment corner to get a stretching strap and a couple of blue foam yoga blocks.

People began to file in through the doors.

Even though I was facing away from the door, I was in front of a mirror and could see the door and everyone who entered.

Was he deliberately hanging back?

Did he decide to leave?

I really hoped so.

Gillian took up her spot to my left like she always did. "How are you today, dear?" she asked.

"I'm okay. How are you, Gillian?"

"My grandchildren are coming tomorrow, so I'm getting in some Zen vibes before all hell breaks loose."

I chuckled. "A little chaotic?"

"There are just a lot of them, and they're all high-energy."

"Maybe you can get out the yoga mats and do some yoga on the deck with them, teach them what you know."

She chuckled. "Maybe."

"Please find your preferred version of savasana, everyone," I said, keeping my eye on the door. "We will begin in two minutes."

Where was Eli?

And almost just as importantly, why was the spot directly to my right still unoccupied? The rest of the spaces behind me were filling up. If he did come in, he would have to—

Shit.

The door opened and in strutted—because that asshole could strut—my nemesis. His brown eyes scanned the room, looking for a spot, but just like I knew, he wasn't able to find anything.

Except right next to me.

Our gazes locked in the mirror and stayed locked as he weaved his way through the reclined bodies, blocks, and mats.

His brows lifted as he unfurled his mat—this time. It wasn't a rented one. Did he actually go out and buy a yoga mat? Was this going to be a regular occurrence?

I might have to switch and go teach at The Zen Den.

Ugh.

Without saying anything, he took in the strap and two blue foam yoga blocks I had at the foot of my mat, then he went over to the equipment section and found what he needed. I followed him with my eyes the entire time.

Why was he here?

Why?

Whatever, it didn't matter. I was a professional.

I cleared my throat and reclined down to my mat. "If you haven't already, please find your version of savasana."

I closed my eyes.

If my eyes were shut, I could pretend he wasn't there.

Except for that fresh, manly smell that was now wafting over toward me.

Damn him.

Taking a deep breath, I shoved all thoughts of Eli out of my head—as best I could—and began. "I'd like to thank you all for coming today, for putting your health, strength, and well-being first for an hour. I honor the light that shines inside of all of you and would like to encourage you to make this practice your own. Your neighbor is not your competition. What he or she or they can do is not a yardstick for what you can do. We are all on our own journey here. We are all on different stepping-stones along our path. Nobody knows what injuries or disabilities others are facing, so please don't compare yourself to anyone. Push yourself for you and only you."

Against my better judgment, I opened my left eye and peered to the side. Eli's eyes were closed, and he was lying flat, breathing deeply.

He was such an asshole.

"Deep breath in through the nose; hold for a count of four if you can. Then out through the mouth for a count of four. When you're ready, close your mouth, let your tongue fall away from your teeth or the roof of your mouth, and begin to constrict the back of your throat. Create a sound with your exhale. Let your neighbor hear your breath."

Noises of people breathing out against the backs of their throats filled the room.

"We call this the ujjayi, or victorious breathing. It takes some getting used to, but with time and with practice it can help you move through your yoga practice, deepen your stretches and further relax your body."

The proper sound of ujjayi exhales echoed from Eli.

At least he was taking this seriously.

"Five more deep breaths, then turn onto your right side in the fetal position, with your cheek resting on your arm."

I led the class through five more inhales and exhales, then slowly, the class moved over to their right.

Again, I couldn't stop myself, and I opened my eyes.

Damn, he had a nice back.

And a nice ass.

A really nice ass.

Why did he have to get hot?

Like, why?

I glued my eyes shut and squeezed my inner thighs together, determined not to think about Eli in any way besides how much of an ass he was—

With a great ass.

Shut up, brain.

I was not going to think about him. Eli was a jerk, and that was all there was to it.

"Please set an intention for your practice today," I said to the class. "Whether it's just to push yourself to go a little bit deeper, hold your posture just a little bit longer, or just work on your breathing, leave all other thoughts and problems at the door and take this hour to focus on you."

I set my own intention: not let Eli muck up my class.

"Last week we focused on our solar plexus, the third chakra. Tonight we are going to work on the second chakra, which is our sacral chakra. The sacral chakra is associated with our emotions and feelings. Relationships. The expression of our sexuality and sensual pleasure."

Why, oh why, did Eli have to come to tonight's class? I always worked through our chakras each week during Yin yoga, and this week just happened to be the sacral chakra. Fuck my life.

I continued talking. "The sacral chakra is associated with the realm of emotions. It's the center of our feelings and sensations. It is directed by the principle of pleasure and is particularly active in our sexuality and the expression of our sensual and sexual desires. It allows us to feel the outer and inner worlds, creativity and fantasies. If you're new to my deep stretch Yin class and don't know where your sacrum or sacral chakra is, take your fingers and go about three inches below your belly button, in your lower belly. In the back, it is located in your lower lumbar vertebrae. For those of you with ovaries, the sacral chakra expands into the ovaries, and for those of you with testicles, your sacral chakra expands there.

"Three more deep cleansing breaths, everyone."

I heard Eli inhale deeply.

"The color of the sacral chakra is orange, so as you inhale, imagine breathing in a glowing orange energy and pushing it through your body, into your limbs. Envision that orange glow prying open your joints and pulling gently on your muscles and spine, helping them elongate and stretch. Allow this orange energy to help every cell in your body to awaken and rejoice. One more deep breath and then please make your way to a sitting position, where we will begin with our first posture for the class."

I kept my eyes closed as I gracefully pushed myself up to a sitting position, then brought my feet together in front of me.

With another deep breath, I brought my palms together in front of my chest at heart-center, and finally, at long last, I opened my eyes.

Eli was in the exact same position I was in, only his eyes were glued to mine in the mirror, and unlike my deer-in-the-headlights look, he was wearing a sexy smile, and holy crap, I couldn't decide if I wanted to kiss him or punch him.

CHAPTER EIGHT

Eli

SHE WAS CUTE WHEN she was pissed.

I was an asshole, I knew, but Alexandra was fucking adorable when she was angry, when she looked at me with that stunned, wide-eyed look, it was all I could do not to pop a half-chub right there in front of the mirror.

She led us through the practice, and unlike Wednesday's class, we held these stretches for way longer and they weren't nearly as complicated.

I could tell that she was doing everything in her power to avoid eye contact with me, so of course, that just made me try to catch her eye even more.

Yeah, I know. I was an asshole.

I nearly had a heart attack when she demonstrated plow pose, then took it a step further into snail, and then again into snail two. Her body was folded in half with her ass in the air, knees beside her damn head. She had to be doing that to me on purpose. She just had to.

Holy fuck.

Add in the sensual sound of her deep breaths, sighs and moans, and I was like a teenager in there. I would have to buy myself a congratulatory smoothie afterward for not popping a full stiffy after what went down in that class.

But two could play that game, so despite the fact that it wasn't a hot yoga class, I was getting pretty warm having to hold the poses, and I noticed a few of the other guys in the room had removed their shirts, and several women—including our fearless leader—were in sports bras, so in between held poses, I tugged off my shirt and tossed it next to my foam blocks.

Then I made damn sure to watch her and her reaction to seeing me shirtless.

I was not disappointed.

Her eyes widened, her pupils dilated, and her nostrils flared. She tried so hard not to look at me but continued to fail miserably. And every time I caught her looking, I either winked or smiled.

I was an asshole, I know. I know.

"Find your savasana once more," she said as the class came to a close, "then turn over to your left into the fetal position, cheek to arm, and complete the circle. Express gratitude to yourself for your practice today. You made it to the mat; you took time for yourself. Inhale all that you deserve, that you are worthy of, and exhale that which no longer serves you. Thank yourself for honoring your intention as best as you could and for taking time to focus on yourself and the care you require. I am honored to be a part of the energy in this room today and to lead you through this practice. When you're ready, meet me back up in a sitting position that is most comfortable for you. Please honor that which feels most true to you, and bring your hands to either heart center or your third eye." Even though I could tell she was frazzled with me being there and so close beside her, her voice never quavered. It was smooth, calm, and gentle the entire time. Props to her. I probably wouldn't have been able to do the same.

I knew she was staring at me, just like I had stared at her ass and back when she was demonstrating plow and snail.

I tightened my back muscles, giving her a show.

I couldn't tell if she gasped or not, but I could practically feel the laser beams from her eyes penetrating the back of my skull.

After a few deep breaths and recognizing that I did *not* in fact honor the intention I set for the practice—which was to not stare at Alexandra's tits or ass—I made my way back up to sitting position, crossed my legs, and put my hands in prayer in front of my heart.

In all honesty, up until I actually did the first class, I'd kind of thought all of this "heart center" and "harness your energy" and "honor the light that shines within each of you" crap was just that ... *crap*. But as Alexandra took us through the poses and my body stretched in ways that it'd never stretched before, I started to really understand how yoga could become addictive. It was a weird high and rush of endorphins that I didn't experience when I worked out in other ways.

It was also a lot more spiritual, and despite my extensive travels, I never considered myself a spiritual person.

"Thank you so much, everyone, for such a great practice today. Namaste."

The class—including myself—echoed her "Namaste," then everyone got up and began rolling up their mats, spraying their blocks and straps with disinfectant and putting them back in the equipment area.

I moved slowly, hoping that the room cleared out and eventually it was just Alexandra and I.

I needed to apologize for Thursday night.

I'd done a lot of thinking—and drinking—over the weekend, and I realized that yeah, I blamed her for shit, but at the end of the day, it was just easier to blame her. Someone I already hated—or thought I hated—than myself or anyone I loved. Like my father.

I also wasn't ready to give up on my proposition. It seriously seemed like the best solution to both of our problems.

The room cleared out quickly, leaving just Alexandra and I. I could tell by her movements, and the way she avoided looking at me at all costs, that she was pissed off.

Her pace was brisk as she went to the equipment corner and made sure everything was in order, then she gathered the LED candles and turned them all off, storing them in a small storeroom off the classroom.

"Alexandra ..." I said gently.

Her back stiffened.

"*Alex*, I mean. Sorry."

I'd known since kindergarten that she preferred Alex to Alexandra, and yet the asshole part of me continued to call her by her full name because I knew it was what she *didn't* want.

"I don't know what you're trying to do, Eli, but you just need to stop," she said, still not looking at me. "I thought on Thursday night that you'd come to your senses, so unless you're seriously taking up yoga—which again, can be done at The Zen Den—please leave me alone."

"How's your Jeep?"

"In the shop until Friday. I'm driving a courtesy car."

"How do you like your new apartment?"

"Every neighbor above, below and beside me smokes on their deck, and I woke up to my neighbor choking his wife during very animalistic sex." She hit me with a hard, sexy glare. "How do you think it is?"

My lip twitched. "Was she at least asking to be choked? Or should we be calling the police?"

"'Harder, Jerry, fuck me harder. Choke me. Choke me!'" she said in a breathy, porn-star voice. Then she cocked a hip out, tilted her head, and pursed her lips. "What do you think?"

My mouth dropped open. And not only from how blunt she was being but how fucking hot that made me.

"Did it at least turn you on?"

Her eyes became thin slits. She grabbed her bag and rolled up her yoga mat, then stalked past me toward the door, not saying another word.

"I'm going to take that as a *yes*, then," I said, following her out into the lobby.

Most people had left.

We slid into our flip-flops, waved at Savannah, and headed out the door. She didn't bother holding it for me.

That's when I realized I was still shirtless.

Whatever. It was almost summer, and I was hot.

I followed her to the parking lot, where her rental Camry was parked two stalls over from my truck. "Can we just talk?" I asked her. "I want to apologize for Thursday."

She hit the fob for her courtesy car and tossed her bag and mat into the back seat. "I think we talked plenty. I think we talked more on Thursday than we ever have in our entire lives—at least civilly, anyway. Let's not ruin a good thing, hmm?"

I rounded the front of her car so that we were standing directly in front of each other. Her chest heaved, and fuck me, it was impossible not to let my eyes caress her body and spend an extra second—or three—on her tits. That is until she growled.

"I'm sorry that I blame—*blamed*—you for what happened with our parents," I said, determined to look her in the eye when I spoke to her. "And for what happened to Eden. Eden's death was NOT your fault. I was an asshole for saying that it was. And an even bigger asshole for saying it to you at her funeral. For everything I said that day. It was wrong of me to do it, and I didn't mean any of it." I cringed at the memory of how I'd behaved that day. How the agonizing weight of grief in my chest had made me lash out at Alexandra so ferociously. Fuck, I was an asshole.

Her expression was blank. But she blinked several times, which let me know she hadn't fallen asleep standing up with her eyes open.

"And I'm sorry I called you a family-destroying super bitch when it all went down." Jesus fucking Christ I'd been a prick. "I don't deserve your forgiveness, but you do deserve my apologies." I raked my fingers through my hair, then glanced at her.

Her expression was still blank.

"And I'm sorry that I told Randy Baskin that you had crabs when everyone knew he was going to ask you to prom," I continued on a big sigh.

Her eyes went wide. "You did *what?*"

Oh shit! Did she not know about that?

Rage took over her features. Her bottom jaw jutted out, and she got this psychotic gleam in her eyes. "I thought you just spread a rumor that I liked to hotbox my bathroom with my own farts and *that* was why I didn't have a date. But you told Randy I had *crabs?*"

"I was angry," I said, holding my palms up in innocence. My yoga mat and keys tucked under my arm.

"You ruined my entire high school life, Eli. I was the laughingstock of the school for months."

"And I'm sorry."

She shook her head and pulled open the door to her car and plopped down into the seat, causing her ponytail to swing wildly behind her. "Get the fuck out of my face and away from my car before I run you over."

"I still think we can solve each other's problems if you just listen to me."

"I've done more than enough listening for a lifetime." She closed the car door and retracted the window. "Get away from me, Eli. I mean it."

The engine in the Camry started.

"I will run you the fuck over."

I backed up and lifted my hands in surrender. Then before I could even tell her that I'd see her soon, she pulled out of the parking stall and into the street, speeding away much faster than the speed limit allowed.

With a sigh, I walked to my truck, hit the fob and tossed everything into the back seat. Then I got behind the steering wheel and headed over to H&J.

I made sure to park up the street a little so that Alexandra had time to get out of her car and head into the gym before she saw me. I could only imagine the screaming fit she'd have if she thought I followed her.

Once she was inside, I gave her another couple of minutes before I got out of my truck, grabbed my duffle bag from the back seat, and headed toward the glass doors of H&J Muay Thai.

I'd met Jao (the *J* of H&J) yesterday and made sure to play up the ignorant, arrogant schmuck from the gym across town, looking to see who in this gym had the best sparring record.

Of course, Jao was quick to inform me that Alexandra was their reigning champ and always eager to spar with new people. I told him to let her know a new guy was looking to go five rounds with her and watched him text her right then and there.

None of that had been a lie.

I *did* practice MMA at the gym down on the water, Harbor Cat MMA, because it was closer to my apartment. So it wasn't like I was going to be stepping into the ring a complete novice and taking every punch Alexandra threw at me.

But I also knew she wanted to punch me. I saw that in her eyes. So I figured this was a good excuse to allow her to try.

I pulled open the door, and Jao behind the counter recognized me instantly.

His smile was wide as he came out and offered his hand. "She just got here. Good timing. I've told all the guys about you, so you might have a bit of an audience."

I shrugged. "Not a problem."

The man I assumed was Hector, Jao's business partner and the *H* of H&J, came over and offered me his hand as well. "Hector. Nice to meet you."

"Eli," I said, glancing around the place. "Very nice setup you have here. I'm usually over at Harbor Cat, since it's closer to my house, but figured I'd try something new."

"What the fuck are you doing here?"

Ah, she'd seen me.

Jao and Hector's eyes went wide, and they broke our little trust circle to turn and watch Alexandra stomping toward us, rage in her electric-blue eyes.

"Are you fucking following me?" she asked, coming to stand in front of us, her tape-wrapped hands on her hips.

A bunch of guys in the gym all turned their attention to us.

My body began to heat up.

I shook my head. "No. I'm here to spar with whoever has the best sparring record."

Her eyes formed thin slits. "Which is me."

I pretended to be shocked. "Is it? What a coincidence."

"You do Muay Thai?" The skepticism in her voice was thick.

"I spent a couple of months in Chang Mai, got into it there. But I tried capoeira in Brazil and started taking jiu jitsu lessons when I was in Japan. So I dabble." I shrugged. "I like it all."

She turned to Hector and Jao. "This is the guy who wants to fight the person with the best record?"

They both nodded, clearly suspicious and wondering how we knew each other.

Her face turned stony and back to me. "Fine. Let's do this. I've been wanting to punch your smug face for nearly twenty-seven years."

"Gotta get you to sign a waiver first," Jao said, ducking back behind the counter, then holding out a clipboard.

"I'll sign whatever," I said, keeping my eyes on Alexandra. I took the clipboard and quickly filled out what I needed to fill out, then I handed it back to Jao.

"I take it you two know each other?" Hector asked, wiggling his index fingers between Alexandra and I.

"Unfortunately," she said.

I followed her toward the vacant ring. One of the guys hanging around, a ripped blond dude with a full sleeve of tattoos, greeted her warmly and helped her with her gloves. I don't know why that pissed me off so much, but it did. I did not like the way he was looking at her or how his eyes kept zeroing in on her tits.

I yanked off my tank top and ditched my flip-flops, pretending not to notice the way her eyes widened when she saw me shirtless again.

Hector offered to help me with my gloves, and I thanked him for it.

"Care to make this a little more interesting?" I asked her as I pushed back the ropes and climbed into the ring at the same time she did.

She glared at me. "I win, you leave town and never come back. You win, you get to keep coming to my yoga class?"

I grinned. She had so much fire in her belly now compared to when we were kids. I liked it. "That's child's play. I win, you agree to the deal. You win, I leave you alone and you never have to see me again. I'll stop coming to your yoga class, never come here again, forget where you work and live. I'll stay on my side of town. You stay on yours."

The flames of fury burned bright in her eyes. Her nostrils flared.

I had her right where I wanted her.

The allure of never seeing me again if she won was just too grand of an opportunity to pass up.

Which, I had to admit, stung more than I thought it would.

I could see the cogs spinning in her brain.

Her lips curled up into a sinister smile, then she nodded and extended her right glove forward. "You have a deal."

Holy shit!

I bumped her glove with mine and grinned as I put my mouthguard in. She put in hers as well.

Jao climbed into the ring. "We'll do the first to fall. That's what we typically call a knockout here. Not a huge fan of people going unconscious. It's bad for business." He set the rest of the rules, told us to bump gloves again, then dropped his hand to tell us to start.

Alexandra came at me like a rabid badger. The woman was practically frothing at the mouth. Murder gleamed hot in her eyes as she kept her right hook tight. But I managed to block her and got her with an uppercut that sent her stumbling backward.

She regained her footing quickly and charged me again. She was all knees and elbows, dancing light on her feet and keeping me guessing constantly where the next assault was going to come from.

She was good.

Way better than I expected.

She had flexibility and agility that I didn't have. That I couldn't have because I'd only done two yoga classes so far. I could hear her breathing deep almost as she did with yoga with each swing and knee jab. She was focusing on her breath, using it to help guide her movements.

I'd never sparred with anyone who did that before.

It was also super distracting for me, and more than once because I was distracted, she got me good in the ribs with her knee or the front of the face with a jab.

She could kick her leg above her head, and her reflexes were quick.

Each round was only three minutes, but it felt like we'd been going at it way longer.

She had me against the ropes now, our bodies slick with sweat, tight up against each other in a clinch. Her forehead rested against mine while her arms held onto my neck. I had her in the same hold. We were both panting.

I shouldn't be turned on because I was fighting hard for something I desperately needed, literally *fighting*, and there were a bunch of dudes around us, and Alexandra hated me. But fuck, I was turned on.

Her strength, her power, her snark, it all revved my engine.

Jao blew the whistle, and she unlocked from me and stepped away.

We had a two-minute break.

She approached the ropes, and Hector handed her a water bottle.

The tattooed guy who had assisted Alexandra with her gloves handed me mine, and I thanked him. "You're getting hosed in there, man," he said with a chuckle.

I spat my mouth guard into my glove and squirted water into my mouth, then tossed him a glare. "Yeah, you ever fought her?"

He shook his head. "No fucking way. I don't want to get my ass handed to me. Have you seen how high she can lift her leg? And how pointy her elbows are?"

"I'm experiencing it."

"She's fucking good, man. Has taken down most of the guys here."

I grunted.

He reached for my water bottle, and I handed it to him, then put my mouth guard back in.

Alexandra was already bouncing on her heels, waiting for me.

She cracked her neck side to side and fixed me with a seriously lethal glower.

Jao whistled, and then she charged me again.

The woman was a machine.

A fighting machine.

Her kicks made contact. Her uppercut connected with my chin and had me seeing stars. Where was her strength coming from? I hadn't been to Harbor Cat in at least a week, since stalking and convincing my enemy to marry me had taken up a considerable amount of my time, but I was already feeling tired.

Whereas Alexandra seemed like she had like twenty more rounds in her.

She's that *determined not to marry you.*

That thought distracted me enough for her to find an opening and clock me hard across the right cheek. I flew back against the ropes and blinked away the little birds flying around my head.

"Y'all right?" Hector called from the side.

I blinked a couple of times, and even though those little birds were no longer spinning around my head, my vision, particularly that in my left eye, wasn't good.

It was super fucking blurry, and the edges were dark like I was looking through an empty paper towel roll.

"Hey, y'all right?" Hector called again, this time louder and firmer.

I shook my head and glanced at him, then at Alexandra. Even though things were blurry, I could see the unease and concern on her face quite clearly.

I tapped the top of my glove with the palm of the other. "Time out," I said through the mouth guard.

Jao blew the whistle.

Hector was suddenly under the rope and grabbing me by the elbow. "Hey, you okay, man? You don't look so good."

All I could see was a brown blurry blob in front of me with bushy bobbing eyebrows and a moving mouth.

Was this it? Was this the first stage of me going blind? Was Keith's ego growing again, and I'd wake up tomorrow unable to see a fucking thing? All before I secured any kind of insurance to pay for the fucking surgery.

"People live completely normal and happy lives without vision, sir," the representative from the hospital said. "Unfortunately, given the unpredictable nature and seasonal aspect of your job as a roofer, we're unable to help you without adequate insurance. You are not considered a necessary, life-threatening surgery."

Sure, being blind wasn't life-threatening, but what the actual fuck?

I sure as fuck couldn't continue being a roofer if I was blind. I'd fall off the roof.

Hector's hand landed on my shoulder. "You need to me to call it? No shame in bowing out, man. She's tough."

"Just need a minute," I mumbled, stepping away from Hector and jamming the "knuckles" of my boxing gloves into my eyes and rubbing and pressing as I growled in frustration.

Please, please, please let me see. I'll find another way to get the insurance coverage. I'll throw the fight so she wins. Please, just let me open my eyes and see properly.

I took a couple of deep breaths until I was calm, then I slowly, with my stomach in my throat, opened my eyes.

The blurriness began to recede along with the dark shadows around the edges.

I let out a sigh of relief.

Thank fuck.

"Y'all right?" Hector asked.

I swallowed and nodded, spinning back around to face everyone. At least eight faces stared back at me, all of them flooded with concern, including Alexandra's.

"Things just went fuzzy for a sec," I said, brushing it off.

Alexandra's eyes widened.

"Let's do this," I said, bouncing my gloves against each other a couple of times.

Alexandra grinned. "You gonna fucking fight me now," she yelled through her mouth guard. "Don't treat me like a girl. Fucking fight me."

"She yells that at everyone, man," the tattooed guy from earlier said. "Hates it when she thinks you're going easy on her. Just makes her madder. You're best to just give it your all and knock her out if it's what you can do."

A few of the other guys, including Hector, nodded in agreement.

Was I holding back?

I didn't think I was, but maybe I was.

I didn't want to hurt her, even though I knew she wanted to hurt me.

But I did want her to agree to marry me so that I could use her insurance for my surgery.

But I'd just promised the universe, or whoever was fucking listening, that I'd throw the fight and find another way to get my surgery covered.

Now what was I supposed to do?

She bounced back lightly on her toes, her hands up in the protective position. She kicked out with her right foot, but I blocked her and went in for a knee jab to her stomach, which she blocked and gave me the opening I needed for a swift left hook that she didn't see coming.

She stumbled backward, blinking in surprise.

Rage but also excitement flared in her eyes, and she came at me again.

She tried a couple more kicks and an elbow to my face before Jao blew the whistle.

We went two more rounds like this. She came at me hard. I blocked sixty percent of her shots. She blocked eighty percent of mine, but the twenty percent I did manage to make had her growling and her eyes smiling. She knew I wasn't taking it easy on her anymore. I was fighting to win.

"Final round," Jao said as I returned to the center of the ring after a quick sip of water.

Alexandra and I were both slick and glistening with sweat. The tops of her breasts practically glowed under the bright lights, and her chest heaved. She wasn't doing her pranayama breathing anymore. She was nearly as winded as I was.

I nodded at Jao. Alexandra nodded at Jao, and he blew the whistle.

She came at me hard once again.

But in the last four rounds, I'd learned her technique. I'd been studying her. She always came on the offense. Always struck first. She didn't hold back and wait for her opponent to make the first move, and this round was no different.

She was a tough fighter, but because she didn't hang back and always came out swinging, it meant she exhausted herself faster than I did. She had more energy at the beginning of the round, but I had more at the end, and I planned to use that to my advantage.

I blocked her as best I could, kept us from getting into another clinch, and barely threw any of my own punches or kicks. I could tell she was getting tired. I saw it in her eyes, felt it in the lessening impact of her kicks and punches.

Her breathing was ragged, and her grunts and growls became more intense.

It was time for me to up my game and send her to the ground.

Catching her off guard, because I rarely came at her first, I surged forward, rewarded by the surprise in her eyes. I went in with a hard left hook, a right uppercut, and a knee to the ribs.

She managed to block all but the knee and made a loud *oof* sound when I made contact. She stumbled backward.

But she caught her balance and lunged back at me.

She must have been storing energy somewhere because I was not anticipating the frenzy of punches and kicks and jabs coming at me from someone who, just a second ago, I thought was close to passing out from exhaustion.

I couldn't keep up.

This had to be her end move. It was too perfect, too wild not to be something she'd been honing for years.

It was like I was being mauled to death by a wolverine in a sports bra.

And because I was so busy deflecting her blows, I wasn't making any of my own or paying attention to when she pushed onto her left foot, leaped up, and brought her right knee right into my eye and cheek. Then it was a couple more well-placed punches to my face, and I was spinning around and falling to the mat before I could even blink.

The whistle sounded, and there was clapping.

The mat felt good against my face.

"And that's why I won't fight her," the tattooed guy said.

A few of the men chuckled.

I opened my eyes to find sexy feet with hot pink nail polish on them directly in front of my face.

Was it wrong that the first thought that came to my mind was how I'd like to suck those toes and watch her squirm? Probably.

"A deal's a deal," she said, bending over and giving me a great view down her bra. "Now leave me alone."

Then she walked away, climbed under the ropes, and I did not see her again ... that night.

CHAPTER NINE

Alex

DEAR GOD, I FELT good.

I was on cloud nine. Cloud ten if there was one.

After I kicked the shit out of Eli and sent him spinning to the mat, I went out and grabbed a couple of beers with some of the guys from H&J, including Hector and Jao.

Greg, the blond guy with the sleeve of tattoos, and his wife, Jenelle, owned a bar just a half a block away from H&J, so we all went there, and Jenelle wouldn't let me pay—she never did when I kicked another guy's ass.

I only had two drinks, but I also treated myself to some of Jenelle's amazing deep-fried pickled beans.

Jao and Hector said I didn't have to go back and clean tonight, since I'd earned a night off, given the way I took down Eli. I promised to be back tomorrow night to clean, but they just waved me off.

Salt of the earth, those two.

So by the time I got home around eleven, I was tired but really fucking happy.

I'd not only kicked Eli Evans's ass—something I'd wanted to do since I was five—but he would now officially leave me alone for good. I didn't have to worry about finding him back in my yoga class or waiting outside my work, leaning all sexy-like up against his truck.

I was Eli-free, and it felt good.

However, my elation at kicking his ass and being rid of him was only slightly deflated at the memory of him rubbing his eyes and blinking repeatedly.

He didn't say anything at the time, but I would hedge to guess something was going on with his vision, only he was too proud to say anything. Did everything go blurry? Did he lose sight in one eye?

A big part of me wanted to take pity on him and call the match, but an even bigger part of me kept saying that if the roles were reversed, he wouldn't have shown me an ounce of mercy, so why should I show him any?

Then he regained his vision or decided to use the sight he had left and let the rest of his senses guide him, and we resumed the fight. He also seemed to fight harder. But I fought the hardest. I'd wanted to kick his ass since we were kids. Since he put my Teenage Mutant Ninja Turtles lunch kit on the top of an anthill in the fourth grade but only after smothering it in honey. Yeah, I've wanted to deck him for a long fucking time. And today I finally got that chance.

I'd showered at H&J, so when I got home, all I did was set up the portable speaker in my living room, put on some top forty, then I tackled the kitchen and started unpacking.

I liked to consider myself a minimalist. Marie Kondo was my hero, and about twice a year, I went into purge mode and chunked out. If it didn't bring me joy, into the trash or off to the second-hand store it went. Sure, sometimes I ended up needing more than one spatula, but when that happened, I just washed the one I was using or made do with a different utensil.

However, despite how little I had, I still had a lot of stuff. I decided to tackle and unpack a room a night. Saturday I'd done my bedroom, Sunday the bathroom and storage closet in the dingy, terrifying apartment building basement, and now today was the kitchen. The living room would be easy since it was mostly just books needing to be put on a bookshelf and some art on the walls.

I was just unraveling my cutlery from a dishtowel when an alert on my phone interrupted the latest Ed Sheeran song playing through the speakers.

An acidic taste formed on my tongue when the notification was revealed to be from Allegra. I was about to dismiss it until I reread the subject line. *URGENT NEWS, ALEXANDRA.*

This one was direct to me.

Why?

Curiosity was a persistent cat, so I brought up the email, wandered into my living room, pushed a box to the side, and sank down onto the couch.

Dear Alexandra,

Your social media status hasn't changed, but your boyfriend's has. Or should I say, ex-boyfriend? *I checked. If this is the case, please let me know ASAP. You will, of course, still be charged for his meal and party favor, since all of these things are past their date of refund. I suppose I can try to make room for you at the singles' table. Though it's mostly just old divorced and widowed aunts and uncles.*

Let me know ASAP if your boyfriend dumped you.

Adios,

Allegra Silvia Ruiz

That bitch.

What the hell?

No, I hadn't gotten around to removing Cade from my social media, because ... I had a life, a job, and I was in denial—obviously. I was also hoping that my date-for-hire could look similar to Cade and I could just tell people that it was him. He'd simply lost/gained weight, grown/shrunk a few inches or whatever. I would've figured it out when I had to.

I brought up Cade's social media.

His status said: In a relationship with ... *Rachel McGuire.*

WHAT?

Who was Rachel McGuire, and how the hell did he rebound so fast?

Unless ...

Was he cheating?

A thousand angry thoughts pinged around in my head. My fingers trembled as I scrolled through his social media, then through Rachel's. It was hard to tell how long they'd been together.

Did he dump me so he could be with her?

And where the hell did Allegra get off telling me to tell her if Cade dumped me?

None of this felt real.

I pinched myself.

I grabbed a book out of the box beside me and knocked it against my forehead six times.

"Wake up. Wake up. Wake up!" This had to be a nightmare. There was no other explanation for it.

Clearly, Eli had actually won the fight and I was passed out on the mat dreaming of Allegra emailing me and Cade already having a new girlfriend who—was also apparently a swimsuit model.

Lovely.

"WAKE UP!"

A pounding on the wall behind my head echoed through my apartment a second later.

Shit.

I could not let Allegra win.

I could not go to her wedding alone.

But I also couldn't cancel and not go at all.

That would be even worse.

Like a desperate idiot, I brought up Eli's social media.

The man had been all over the world.

And the photos were gorgeous. Landscapes, people, markets, skies, forests, oceans, statues, and animals. Every single shot was professional quality and stunning.

He's hot. He's available. He's willing.

I scrubbed the heels of my palms into my eyes.

Yeah, but he was also painfully annoying, an asshole, cocky, and he blamed me for his parents—and my parents—getting divorced.

All those cons vastly outweighed the three measly little pros.

And yet, those pros were making it more and more difficult for me to turn down his offer. Especially after Allegra's email and finding out that Cade was already dating someone else. Someone who probably made less than he did and also probably couldn't kick his ass.

But maybe Eli didn't want to go to the wedding with me anymore since I'd kicked his ass.

Was he home licking his wounds? Cursing my name and proclaiming that I somehow cheated? There'd been a few of those guys at the gym after I beat them. They said I cheated.

How the hell did you cheat at Muay Thai? Particularly when there were at least half a dozen Muay Thai connoisseurs watching the entire match.

I didn't even help Eli up after I knocked him down. I'd grabbed my stuff and went and showered. He promised that if I beat him, I'd never have to see him again, and I intended to make good on that promise the moment his face hit the mat.

And now I was sitting there contemplating asking him to drive with me across the freaking country, stop at major tourist attractions and take lovey-dovey couple photos so that by the time we got to San Diego, we were a convincing couple in love for Allegra and all our other vet school friends.

The whole thing sounded ridiculous, and if my dad had any say, he'd tell me to forget all of it, tell them all to fuck off, and tell me to move back home so I could be closer to him.

But moving home meant being closer to my mom, too. Closer to Eli's dad. Closer to all the memories that still messed with my sleep.

I just couldn't.

Zooming in on a picture of Eli smiling, I chewed on my bottom lip. When we were kids, Eden had told me that I should just get over my feud with Eli and that he and I should date. She said it would be the best thing ever because if Eli and I got married, then Eden and I would be real sisters.

I'd snorted, scoffed, and laughed at her joke. She'd always been a hopeless romantic. This was probably another reason why she took her parents' divorce as hard as she did. To her, they'd been a fairy tale come true.

My finger hovered over his face, and I gently slid it along his cheekbone. But it suddenly slipped and, oh dear God, no!

I hit *like* on a photo from like five years ago.

What did I do?

I unliked it as fast as I could, but the deed was done.

He probably already knew I'd hit *like*.

Heat spread through me, and my gut did a big flip.

Tingles prickled along my arms.

Ugh!

I waited for the instant message taunting me. Teasing me over liking one of his pictures, let alone one from five years ago.

But nothing happened.

Maybe he's sleeping like a normal person?

Perhaps ...

He'd never let me live it down if I turned around and asked him to be my date to the wedding. He'd lord it over my head for eternity.

However, I'd already hit emotional rock bottom. My boyfriend, who dumped me a week ago—not *even* a week ago—had already moved on, and my friend nemesis, my fren-emesis? Was making sure I knew just how much better her life was than mine by demanding I tell her if I was dumped and saying if I came alone, I'd be put at the singles table with divorced aunts and handsy uncles.

I hit *message* on his profile page.

Worst-case scenario, he becomes so unbearable, I leave him at a truck stop somewhere near Chicago.

I needed wine for this.

Thankfully, I'd unpacked the corkscrew.

I got up from the couch, found the fifty-dollar bottle of red I bought a couple of weeks ago—Cade and I were going to drink it in celebration of moving in together—and poured a big glass.

With a couple of gulps of liquid courage down the hatch, I bravely typed. *Even though I won the match, I accept your offer. My insurance in exchange for you accompanying me to the wedding.* I hit send. Took another sip, then immediately followed it up with another message. *We will establish some ground rules. Separate hotel rooms every time. The moment your surgery is over and you are in the clear, we get it annulled.*

The three little dots that indicated his response was on its way were dancing up a storm.

I drank more wine. My fingers got brave. *Did something happen with your vision during the fight?"*

OK. Followed by *Yes.*

That was it. That was all he texted.

Ooh, he was a wily one, that Eli Evans. He was probably smiling so damn hard, his cheeks hurt right now, but he knew that if he showed me even an ounce of that triumph that I'd lose my shit.

Which I would.

I don't know how I'd lose my shit, but I was one snide remark away from doing it.

I couldn't drive over to his house, because I had no idea where he lived. Or worked. He knew all of those things about me. He knew precisely where I spent about ninety-five percent of my time. Work, the yoga studio, H&J and home.

And yet, I had absolutely no idea where he was or what he did.

The three dots danced some more.

I drank more wine.

Let's meet some time this week to draw up an agreement and plan the road trip.

That wasn't an unreasonable request.

In fact, he was being extremely agreeable.

There had to be a catch.

He was playing me.

With the liquid courage of a fifty-dollar bottle of malbec coursing through my veins, I let my fingers—and my anger—do the talking.

If I find out you've played me in any way, Eli, so help me God, I will kick the ever-loving shit out of you. Just like I did today. There will be no mercy. I will make your life a living hell, just like you did mine for over thirteen years. You need me more than I need you. Just remember that.

The dots wiggled.

I drained my wine glass, got up, and returned to the kitchen to pour myself more.

The dots continued to jump.

OK.

I growled. Even without doing anything, he was doing something, and what he was doing was making me really fucking mad.

He knew my buttons better than anybody, and he was pushing all the ragey ones right now.

Do you have a suit? There were a thousand other snarky things I wanted to say to him, but I didn't have nearly enough wine in my bloodstream for the true bitch to come out. Give her time, though. She was just sharpening her talons.

*I can buy a suit(s), tie(s) and dress shirt(s) in whatever shade
and style you like. Send me links or pictures, and I will do my
best. Or we can go shopping together and find what is needed.
You're the boss.*

I couldn't figure out how to react. He was being SO GOD-
DAMN NICE, and yet the Eli I knew was never this nice without something else up his sleeve. He was not an appreciative
person. He was not a *nice* person.

This is Eli Evans from Greenfield Connecticut, right?

I had to ask. Maybe somebody had hacked into his account
and was just catfishing me or whatever this was.

Yes.

I still wasn't convinced. *Tell me something that only Eli and
I would know. I need to verify your identity.*

I waited for the sarcastic "You can't be serious?" reply, but
it didn't come.

The little dots jiggled. And jiggled. And jiggled.

I took a sip of my wine and held it on my tongue.

*Your mother and my father had an affair. You caught them
on April 19th, the day before my sixteenth birthday. They're
now married, and I haven't seen my father since my sister's
funeral eight years ago.*

I swallowed hard.

Yeah, it was the real Eli.

The dots bounced.

*Can I keep coming to yoga class? I really enjoyed it. If you
prefer, I can not come to your class, but Savannah was right
when she said you're a great instructor. I understand why your
classes are always full.*

I threw my phone across the room before I had a chance to
think about what I was doing. Thank God I had one of those
LifeProof cases that could withstand just about any kind of
torture.

Who was I talking to?

This was not the Eli Evans I remembered. Or the Eli Evans I'd sparred with earlier today or practiced yoga beside even earlier today.

Drawing my knees up to my chest and holding my stemless wine glass in both hands, I wedged my thumbnail between my teeth and stared over my knees at my phone lying lifeless on the ground next to a box marked "throw blankets."

I sat there for what was probably a good five minutes before I drained my second glass of wine, got up, and approached my phone like it was a coiled snake ready to bite. Why anybody would approach a coiled snake, I have no clue. That just seems stupid, but so was my grabbing my phone to see what else Eli had said.

Think about it. You don't have to answer me right away. But thank you, Alex. I appreciate your agreeing to help me out. I promise to be a convincing and attentive boyfriend at this wedding. I won't let you down.

My phone number is 207-998-6987 if you want to text me or call me.

Good night, Alex, and talk soon.

A chill raced down the length of my spine as if someone had just scraped the tip of an icicle from the base of my neck to just above my ass.

I shivered and dug a throw blanket out of the box, draping it around myself.

Reading and re-reading this message, I tried to come up with something to say in return, but I came up with nothing.

I still couldn't tell if he was being sincere or if this was just all part of his elaborate ruse to once and for all humiliate me.

By the time I went to bed, I decided that I was going to remain on guard with Eli every step of the way. I would drive. He would never get the keys to the rental car, and I'd never leave him alone in the car without taking the keys with me. I would always look down at my seat before I sat down, I would control the music, and no way in hell was he getting my phone.

This was a business transaction, for lack of a better description. He had a service I needed—his hot singleness—and I had a commodity he required—a kick-ass insurance plan.

That was it.

That was all it ever would be.

Once we returned to Maine and he got his surgery and was given the thumbs-up by the doctors, we would get the marriage annulled and never see each other again.

Easy peasy.

So then why that night did I dream about Eli in a three-piece suit looking hotter than any man I'd ever seen, leading me onto the dance floor, spinning me around and looking at me like he loved me, like he was my husband and I was his wife, and we wanted nothing more than to be together forever?

CHAPTER TEN

Eli

TUESDAY WAS MY DAY off and my first day volunteering at the animal shelter. To say I'd slept like a baby last night would be the understatement of the century. Last night had been the best sleep I'd had in close to eight years.

I wasn't sure what came over Alexandra or why she contacted me out of the blue on social media, but when her message popped up, I literally dropped my drinking glass to the floor, causing it to shatter and send orange juice everywhere.

I tried to be as agreeable as I possibly could in order to assure her that I would do whatever it took for her to hold up her end of the bargain. I didn't even mention the fact that she had liked a picture of mine from five years ago. And boy oh boy did it take a lot of willpower for me to *not* rib her about that.

But I managed. Because the stakes were extremely high.

When she asked me to verify my existence, it'd caught me off guard, but then, she'd always been a suspicious person. And since I was being nicer to her than I'd probably ever been, it made sense.

I thought at first about telling her something about Eden, but I didn't want to shut down the lines of communication. Then I thought about bringing up something about how I'd tortured her in school, but that didn't really shine me in a very positive "marry me" light. In the end, I chose to mention our parents and the devastation that we shared there.

She changed the subject quickly, thankfully.

I hadn't *thrown* the fight, but I also didn't give it my all. I promised the universe that I wouldn't push for her insurance anymore in exchange for being able to see. And the universe had obliged. Now I was stuck trying to figure out if I was still kosher with the universe because Alexandra had kicked my ass, only to come to me saying she'd marry me after all. After I took my loss and my wounds and went home.

How was this arrangement sitting with the powers that be?

I didn't think about it for long and abandoned my broom and dustpan to go check out my closet.

I had nothing in the way of formal dress wear. So I would let her play Barbie and dress me up like a good Ken doll. Only this Ken had junk in his boxer briefs, unlike that smooth eunuch plastic doll my sister used to play with.

I opened the door to the animal shelter and was immediately hit with the smell of dog and pet food. There was also an obnoxious amount of barking.

Wincing at how loud it was, I smiled at the woman behind the desk. Her name tag said Yolanda. "Hi, I'm Eli Evans. I signed up as a volunteer to walk the dogs."

She grinned at me. "Hi, yes, we've been expecting you. Follow me." Getting up from her chair, she walked through an open door behind her, and I followed.

Since it was a warm and beautiful day, the big garage door out into the yard was open, allowing the warm, fresh air to flow in.

Each dog's personal space was behind a chain-link gate, but the back of their space had a smaller door out into the yard.

Most of the dogs were out in the yard, but there was one who was curled up in "her" bed, since her name plate said "Jill."

"Is this one okay?" I asked, pausing in front of Jill's gate and pointing at her.

Yolanda smiled. "That's Jill. She's quite a bit older than the rest of the dogs we have here. And although she's not aggressive, she just prefers people to other dogs, so she doesn't go out into the yard with them. Finds it too overwhelming."

Crouching down, I put my fingers into the holes, and Jill pried herself out of her bed and slowly walked over to me. "Hey, girl," I said softly.

She licked my fingers.

"You're welcome to take her for a walk," Yolanda said. "Not too far, since her hips aren't great. But she'd love to go to the park up the road, sit under a tree and just get a good ear scratch."

I glanced up at Yolanda. "That sounds perfect." Then I turned my attention back to Jill. "What do you think, Jilly Bean? Want to go for a walk?"

Jill's tail wagged, and she sniffed my hand.

"I'll go get you a leash," Yolanda said, heading back out to the front desk.

I stayed with Jill until Yolanda returned, then she opened the gate and clipped the leash to Jill's collar. "Take her for as long as you like."

Nodding, I led a bouncy-footed Jill out the front door.

She was an easy dog to walk. She didn't pull. She didn't need to sniff at every tree or stop and mark every bush. She just seemed content to be out with somebody and not cooped up in her pen having to listen to all the other dogs demand attention.

We didn't walk for long, since I could tell that even the fifteen minutes to the park down the road was taking its toll on her old bones. Luckily, she only weighed about eleven pounds, so I could easily carry her back to the shelter when we decided to head back.

Yolanda gave me a couple of poop bags, a small bag of treats, and a portable dog water bottle and bowl. It all fit easily enough in the big pocket on my cargo shorts.

Once we stepped onto the grass at the park, Jill's spirits seemed to lift even more. The earth was softer than the concrete, which probably eased the pain in her joints.

We made our way over to a big oak tree and sat down in the shade against the trunk. She plunked her little wiry-haired butt right next to my hip, leaned back against me, and looked up with those enormous brown eyes.

I rubbed her belly. "You're just a big suck, aren't you, Jilly Bean?"

She didn't say anything—obviously—but I could tell in her eyes that she was agreeing with me.

We sat there and watched the kids at the playground play for a while. People with their own dogs walked by, but Jill paid them no mind. Unlike my childhood dog Misty, who developed a one-track mind to socialize and greet all other dogs she came across, Jill didn't give a crap that there were other dogs around. She just closed her eyes and started to snore as I continued to rub her belly.

I closed my eyes and leaned back against the trunk of the tree.

I needed to do something to show Alexandra that she could trust me not to fuck this up. That I was committed to our arrangement and would be the best damn pretend boyfriend she'd ever had and convince everyone at that wedding that we were madly in love.

It helped that we grew up together, so I legitimately knew a ton about her. We wouldn't have to give each other our biographies on the road trip, at least not anything between the ages of five and eighteen.

I might need to learn a bit more about what she'd been up to since then, though, besides becoming a vet, a yoga teacher and a badass Muay Thai enthusiast.

I opened my eyes and rubbed at my cheek. She'd gotten me good. I woke up this morning with some bruising around my left eye. But the fact that she agreed to my proposal made the discoloration and tenderness worth it.

Could I go to her yoga class tonight? I wanted to. But she hadn't responded when I asked her if I could.

I honestly didn't think I'd enjoy the class, but not only did the postures challenge me and my body, the way she spoke was hypnotic. Yesterday, she'd had us hold a forward fold for four minutes, and even though my hamstrings and groin were in significant discomfort, the way she spoke, the way she told us to surrender to the discomfort, expand with our inhales and push ourselves deeper into the stretch with our exhales had me almost falling asleep.

And not in an "I'm bored" kind of way. In an actual hypnotic kind of way. It was crazy and addictive.

I reached into my pocket and pulled out the treat bag. Jill popped open one eye and watched me suspiciously.

"What nice thing do you think I can do for Alexandra that will show her how much I appreciate what she's doing for me?" I asked Jill, handing her a treat. She took it from my fingers so gently.

"I already bought her a sandwich."

Jill rolled over onto her front and sat patiently beside me, staring at the treat bag.

"Can you do any tricks? Can you shake?" I held out a hand. She placed her paw in it, and we shook. I gave her another treat. "Can you lay down?" She lay down and rested her chin on my thigh. I treated her again. "Can you roll over?' To my surprise, she did just that. I gave her another treat. "You're a clever little thing. I mean, obviously, I'll buy my own suits and dress clothes and stuff. Pay for my own hotel room and food. But what else can I do?"

Jill shook her entire body like all dogs do, and a glint of something shiny on her collar caught my attention. She allowed me to nudge her head to the side so I could get a better look.

Her dog tag, which said "Jill," was in the shape of a heart, but on the entire outside of the stainless-steel heart were pretend diamonds. Cubic zirconia maybe?

That was it!

I ruffled Jill's head affectionately and gave her another treat. "That's it, Jilly Bean! I'll go get her a ring. Like a real engagement ring. One she can wear and show off at the wedding."

Jill licked my fingers, then settled down and rested her chin on my thigh again. We were both about to close our eyes and doze off from the pleasant warm breeze and fresh air when my phone vibrated in my pocket, directly beneath Jill's chin, making her leap up.

"Sorry," I said, fishing the phone out.

It was a text message.

And it was from Alexandra.

You can come to yoga. I think we should discuss the parameters of this arrangement. I'm not going to H&J tonight. Can we talk after yoga? If you're coming.

I grinned, then ran my hand over Jill's head again. "She's warming up to us, Jilly Bean." I texted back. *Thank you. I will be at yoga tonight, and we can definitely talk. Dinner?*

Her reply was almost immediate. *No. Drinks.*

Fair enough. Smith's?

Yes.

OK. I will see you at yoga and then Smith's.

OK.

The texting ended.

Having decided that the vibrating beast in my pocket was not going to try to attack her, Jill had settled back down, resting her chin on my thigh. She glanced up at me, curiosity in her eyes.

"Tell me, Jilly Bean, if you were a stubborn, infuriating, annoying, successful, beautiful, strong, fierce, and educated human woman with fire-engine red streaks in your hair and a huge tree tattoo on your back, what kind of engagement ring would you want?" Jill made a quiet *boof*. "I'll also add that you wear a sleek black leather jacket and drive a white Jeep. You're also ridiculously suspicious, incapable of lying and have a great rack and ass." Jill looked up at me, and I could have sworn she dropped one eyebrow in disapproval.

I tossed my head back and rolled my eyes.

"I didn't *lead* with the thing about the great rack and ass. I said she was smart first."

Jill groaned.

"A black diamond to match her black heart?"

Jill growled.

"Okay, okay, that was mean. Sorry."

I googled jewelry stores in the area on my phone, and the list popped up. I clicked on the most highly rated one, then went to their website. For a small-town jewelry store, their website was pretty impressive. Most of their inventory was online.

I brought up the larger image of a simple white gold band with a princess-cut diamond in a tension setting. The diamond was flush with the band. It was beautiful, but it wasn't flashy. It didn't scream, "Look at me! I'm getting married!" It also seemed very practical, and if jewelry could be sporty, I'd call this ring sporty. Like, it wouldn't snag on clothing or knock into stuff. When she went to put her hands in her pockets, the ring wouldn't get caught on the outside of her pants.

I turned the phone toward Jill. "What about this one?"

Jill made another *boof,* but she sat up and pressed her nose to the screen, sniffing.

"I like this one, too. It seems like something that Alexandra would wear, don't you think?"

Jill *boofed* again.

"Do you know Alexandra? Have the two of you met?"

Jill sniffed my screen a bit more, then glanced up at me, lifted her paw and tapped it against the phone.

"I'm going to take this as your approval. You've got good taste, Jilly Bean."

Jill *boofed* one more time, then turned away from me, wandered to the end of her leash and squatted for a pee.

"I'm going to give you some privacy and call the jewelry store to see if they have it in stock." Then, giving the lady some space, I turned my back and called Prestige Jewelers. Because I now, technically, had a fiancée, and she needed a ring.

CHAPTER ELEVEN

Alex

"NAMASTE," THE ENTIRE CLASS replied, all twenty-four of their heads bowing at the same time.

I lifted my gaze and found Eli looking at me in the mirror.

Thankfully, he'd taken a spot closer to the back of the class and hadn't made a peep for the entire hour.

But that didn't mean his eyes didn't say a million things as he worked through his practice and each posture.

Even for this only being his third class, he was showing improvement.

I hated to admit that I was impressed.

The class began to roll up their mats and file out.

I steeled myself for him waiting for me like he had the last two times, but when I stood up, my own mat under my arm, he was nowhere to be found.

I gathered all the candles, tidied the blocks and straps, then headed out of the studio.

He wasn't milling around in the lobby with the other stragglers.

Was he bailing on drinks?

I waved goodbye to Savannah, then headed to my Jeep.

Thank God it was fixed.

Not that there was anything wrong with the Camry—besides its color and uncoolness—and my dad would argue until he was blue in the face that a Toyota was a far superior brand than a Jeep, but I loved my Jeep and had missed it.

Scanning the parking lot for Eli's truck, I came up empty.

He was bailing.

What the hell?

Go to Smith's. If he's not there, then he's bailed. Give him the benefit of the doubt.

I needed to listen more to that little voice in my head. She was right more often than she was wrong.

Tossing my mat and duffle bag into the back seat, I climbed behind the steering wheel and turned over the ignition. She purred like a beauty.

I stroked her dash. "Good to have you back, baby girl." Then I pulled out of the parking lot and drove the three blocks to Smith's bar, a local favorite that was known for their live bands on Fridays and Saturdays, as well as a beautiful backyard patio complete with a koi pond with turtles and a gazebo.

The pond had to be heated or covered over or something in the winter, though, otherwise those poor fish would get frozen like fish sticks.

There wasn't much parking, but I managed to snag a spot just as someone else was backing out.

I climbed out and grabbed the loose white T-shirt out of my duffle bag and pulled it down over my sports bra. My phone vibrated in my bag.

Grabbed us a table in the garden next to the pond.

So he hadn't bailed.

Why was I angry that he had proved me wrong? That he hadn't bailed and was living up to his word?

With my wallet, phone and keys in my hand, I headed for the front door. Music filtered out, along with the sound of laughter and utensils on plates.

I heaved open the heavy wooden door and stepped into the dark Tudor-style pub or bar or whatever you wanted to call it. The walls were real wood paneling and the rafters hung low. The sign outside said this place had been established in 1968, and by the looks of things, it hadn't had an update since the day it opened.

It was a seat-yourself kind of place, so I waved at the bartender and headed through the pub toward the back patio.

As always, the garden was beautiful.

It was still too light out for the tiki torches and LED candles, but soon, when the sun went down, the oasis would become even more magical.

I found Eli at a two-top round table, right next to the pond, as he said. He smiled at me, and holy freaking Twilight Zone, the man stood up when I approached the table.

"Why are you standing up?"

Color bloomed in his cheeks. "Isn't that what you're supposed to do when a woman approaches or leaves the table? Isn't that proper manners?"

I gave him a disgusted look and took a seat. "Since when do you have proper manners?"

He exhaled and rolled his eyes as he reclaimed his seat across from me. "I wasn't sure what you wanted to drink, so I told the waitress to come back for our order." He picked up the menu off the table and started reading it. "I'm hungry. You?"

"I said no to dinner."

"I don't think soup is dinner. Or calamari. Those are just starters. Or appetizers, or whores de oovres."

I nearly dropped my phone. "What?"

"What part do you want me to repeat?"

"The thing you said after appetizers."

"Whores de oovres?" Slowly his mouth spread into a big, cocky smile.

I rolled my eyes and smirked. "You're such an ass."

"And you were about to make fun of me for mispronouncing something. Who's the bigger ass?"

I glared at him over the menu. My stomach grumbled. I'd skipped dinner, since I was running later at work and had to speed way too freaking fast to get to yoga on time.

"Want to split the nachos?" he asked. "I promise to eat most of them so that you don't feel like you ate enough food for it to be considered dinner and therefore can go home feeling good about *not* having dinner with me."

Who the fuck was this guy?

"Hello," a very sexy waitress with red hair in two plaits down over her tits said as she sidled up next to our table. "What can I get you guys tonight?"

"I'll have the pilsner that's on special and the nachos," Eli said, handing her his menu and then looking over at me.

I watched him intensely, waiting to see if he ogled the waitress.

Because she was very ogleable—was that a word? Her black miniskirt was short, her black Smith's tank top showed off an awful lot of cleavage, and she was probably a good eight years younger than us. Which was probably the most important part out of all of that, because she was still high on life, enthusiastic about her future and believing that her Mr. Right was out there just waiting for her.

Poor, innocent, naïve little thing.

"I'll get the tuna steak, rare with the sesame dip. And can I get a side arugula salad?"

She nodded. "Anything to drink?"

"I'll get the summer berry mojito that I saw on the specials board out there."

She grinned and batted thick lashes. "Perfect. I'll bring your drinks right out." Then she took my menu and skipped off. Okay, well, she didn't *skip*. But in my sarcastic and cynical mind, she skipped.

I looked up at Eli, fully expecting his eyeballs to be glued to our waitress's ass and ready to give him a piece of my mind, but to just add on to the stack of surprises, he wasn't looking at her. He was looking at me.

"Thank you for letting me come back to yoga," he said. "Tonight's class was really good. I can't hold tree pose for more than three seconds to save my life, but—"

"You'll get there," I said, shocking myself with my encouraging words.

He smiled. "I hope so. I see everyone around me, and so many of them are so flexible and accomplished. I feel like a bumbling, inflexible fool."

I reached for my water glass and took a sip. That's when I noticed the slight bruising around his left eye. "How's your cheek?"

He touched the spot I was referring to. "Tender, but I'll live."

"I'd apologize but ..."

"It felt really good to kick the shit out of me."

I snorted and smiled. "I can't tell a lie."

"Yeah, I know."

Damn, he looked really good right now. Carefree and so casually sexy, it was mind-boggling. He'd changed out of his board shorts from yoga class and was now in khaki cargo shorts and an olive-green T-shirt. It worked well with his coloring and brought light into his brown eyes. And that neatly trimmed scruff along his jaw, chin and upper lip. Something inside me purred ... probably my clitoris.

His throat moved on a swallow as he glanced down into the pond.

"If this is one of your pranks, Eli ..." I focused my gaze down into the pond as well. I hadn't realized how tense I was until now. All that bending and destressing from yoga hadn't done a lick of good for how tight my shoulders were at the moment.

I cocked my neck side to side until it cracked.

"It's not," he said quietly, drawing my attention away from the fish and back to his face. "I'll admit that when I first saw you, I was filled with hate. Because honestly, that's the first emotion that comes to mind when I think of you ..." He managed a hangdog expression. "Or at least it was. I was thinking of ways to pay you back for all the pain you caused my family, but then—"

"Then you found out I have an awesome insurance plan," I said plainly.

He shrugged. "Well, yeah, but I also started talking to you and realized that my perception of you for all of these years is not who you really are." Scratching the back of his neck, he broke our eye contact and started playing with the stubby stem of his water glass. "Traveling the world and this stupid fucking tumor has really helped me gain some perspective. Hate is poison. And that's something I forgot when I first saw you. All my old feelings came flooding back and I was blinded by the past."

"But you remember now?" I lifted a brow. This could all still be part of his schtick. He has been known to get elaborate and creative with his pranks.

Eli nodded. "Yeah, I do. I don't hate you. You're not a bad person. You have a soul—" I snorted at that comment which made him crack a small smile. "And I'm willing to follow your lead on this whole thing. You just tell me what you need from me. I don't want to fuck this up." His eyes found mine, and the sincerity behind his gaze made a gasp snag silently in my throat. "I really am sorry for the shit I pulled when we were kids. For how I treated you. You didn't deserve it."

I took another sip of my water. "Thank you." This was a start, but after the shit he'd put me through for thirteen years—the things he'd said to me at Eden's funeral—he wasn't completely off the hook. Yes, he'd apologized for saying that stuff, and blaming me, but he also wanted something from me, and people said things they didn't believe or mean when they were desperate.

And Eli was desperate for my insurance.

So, no, as much as his apologies helped ease the pain that had been lodged like a barbed hook in my chest for all these years, all was not forgotten or forgiven. Eli wasn't an idiot either. The way he was looking at me right now, said he knew he'd have to work hard at earning my trust, because right now he didn't have a shred of it.

This could all still be a game to somehow humiliate me. I had to keep up my guard with Eli every step of the way, no matter how charming he might turn out to be.

His fingers fidgeted in front of him on the table, and his eyes darted around the garden.

"Here we are," the waitress said, returning to our table. "One pilsner and one summer mojito. Your food shouldn't be too long either."

We thanked her for our drinks, and once again, I watched Eli closely to see if he stared at her ass.

He didn't.

Reaching for my mojito, I brought the straw to my lips and took a long sip.

Ahhh, liquid courage.

"Do you have a rough idea of where you want to stop along the way for pictures?" he asked, taking a pull off his beer.

I shook my head. "No, Cade and I were just going to wing it. See what struck our fancy and pull off the highway when something intriguing came along on a billboard."

"So you didn't book any hotels?"

I shook my head again. "We didn't want to be constrained to a timeline and *have* to be anywhere for a certain day. We basically just need to make sure we're in San Diego two days before the wedding. The rest is up in the air."

"And you want to keep to that spontaneity?"

I narrowed my gaze at him. "What are you getting at?"

He shook his head, a mask of innocence on his face. A dark lock of hair fell over his forehead, and I shoved down the groan in my chest. "I'm not getting at anything. I'm just asking about the trip. I'm happy to do some research or book hotels or whatever. Put me to work."

"Are we getting married in Maine? If so, we'll need to go get a marriage license together." A fought back the urge to make a face of disgust. I did not want to be having dinner with Eli Evans let alone going to get a marriage license with him. What had my life become?

He shrugged. "We can get married in whichever state you like. Want to get married by an Elvis impersonator in Vegas?"

I lobbed a sigh. "I don't know. Let me think about it. So, you don't have any suits?"

"No. Nothing that will work for the kind of wedding the Oompa-Loompa twins are having."

I snorted again, then sighed again. "Yeah, me either."

"We could go into the city and go shopping."

"Maybe." I glanced into the pond and watched the big orange, black and white fish swimming around.

"Whatever you want. I'm following your lead on this."

I was quiet for a moment. So was he. The silence between us wasn't awkward, but it was tense. And that tension was doing all kinds of weird and frustrating things in my lower belly and between my legs.

"Separate hotel rooms," I said, after almost a full two minutes of neither of us speaking.

"Obviously."

"And you pay for your own meals."

"Of course."

"I'm driving."

"I assumed as much."

"I control the music."

His lips twitched and hitched up halfway on his face. "We'll see. What about kissing?"

"What? What the fuck are you talking about?" Heat prickled along my arms.

His brows nearly shot off his head. He leaned back in his chair and held his palms toward me in surrender. "Whoa! Don't get the wrong idea. I mean PDAs. If we're going to be convincing, I'm *going* to have to touch you. Possibly even kiss you on the cheek or something. Hold your hand. I'm just trying to get a sense of what my limits are and what will get me clocked in the jaw with a swift left hook."

Oh!

Yeah, I supposed he was right.

"I ... I hadn't thought that far."

He lifted a broad, sculpted shoulder. "Well, give it some thought and let me know."

"All right, the tuna steak with sesame mayo and a side arugula salad and the nachos." The waitress slid our food in front of us, along with cutlery and napkins. "Can I grab you guys anything else while I'm here?"

I shook my head, once again watching Eli.

He shook his head as well, smiled up at her, but not in a leering kind of way, then she was off.

I glared at him.

"What?"

"Is she not your type?"

"What the hell is that supposed to mean?"

"Why didn't you check out her ass and tits and flirt with her?"

He looked at me like I had just sprouted another head. "Because I'm sitting here with you."

"But otherwise you would have?"

He opened his hands as if asking for a clue. "What the hell are you getting at here, Alexand—*Alex?*"

"You didn't leer or ogle her at all. Is she not your type?"

"Forgive me if I prefer my women to be old enough to rent a car," he said, dipping a chip into the ramekin of guacamole.

"Also, never do I *ogle* or *leer* at another woman when I'm with a woman. Whether that woman is my girlfriend, fuck buddy, or fiancée who wants to stab me in the back of the hand with her fork. I'd like to think that regardless of the company I'm with or even by myself that I don't ogle or leer. I have more class than that."

"Wait, what?"

He rolled his eyes. "Which part do you want me to repeat this time?"

"Your *fiancée?*"

Popping a black olive into his mouth, he shrugged. "I mean, you are, aren't you?"

Was I?

I *had* agreed to marry him. Although this was purely a business arrangement, but still ...

We were going to get married, so ... that meant that Eli Evans was my fiancé. My brain swirled and my stomach flipped, then flopped.

He cleared his throat. "And since you're my fiancée and you should probably at least *look* the part in pictures and at the wedding and stuff, I got you this." He slid a small blue velvet box across the table at me. "If you don't like it or it's not your style, the guy at the jewelry store said we can exchange it."

My mouth was completely dry.

My eyes would not blink.

My heart was beating at an alarming speed.

Was I having a stroke?

I glanced up at him, and what stared back at me was absolutely terrifying.

Eli Evans was looking at me with hope.

My breath escaped my nose in ragged pants as I continued to stare at him.

The hope on his face quickly began to fade, being replaced with unease and worry.

He swallowed and gently nudged the ring box closer to me. "Can you at least just look at it? You're starting to freak me out."

My arms began to prickle, and a comforting, familiar heat started to whip up into a froth inside me. How fucking dare he?

How dare he *not* be who I had known him to be for the majority of our lives?

How dare he show me the awful side of himself for all those years, the mean and spiteful side, when this guy existed as well?

This was the guy that I actually would have thought about dating, like Eden had suggested, had he actually been present when we were younger.

But no. I only got the evil Eli. The mean prank king.

I gnashed my molars together, snatched up the box, and opened it.

I couldn't hide the growl in my throat.

It was stunning and so perfectly me, I wanted to spit.

I lifted my eyes back up to Eli. He shifted uncomfortably in his seat. "Can you say something?"

My lip curled up. "Why?"

His brows knitted. "Why what?"

"Why didn't *this* guy exist back when we were kids? Why did you only give us asshole Eli? Or is *this* guy just a façade?" I wiggled my finger up and down in front of him. "Because I don't recognize you."

His wide, muscular shoulders slumped a bit. "I'm not a big fan of who I was back then, either. I was a jerk. I did and said some really horrible things. But I assure you, this isn't a façade." He looked back down at the ring box. "Do you like it?"

I glared at him. "I fucking love it, you prick."

His face lit up, and his smile damn near knocked me back in my chair.

Fuck.

This guy in front of me, if he was the real deal, was someone I could see myself ... *liking*. Tolerating and not having a terrible ten days with. If—and that was a big if—he wasn't playing me and I was finally seeing Eli for who he really was.

Either way, I was still super pissed off that this nice guy was lurking inside him all along.

Like what the fuck?

"I guessed on the size," he said, having relaxed enough to take another sip of his beer. "But we can get it sized. The guy said we could get it sized in time before we leave."

I pulled it out of its soft satin bed and, with shaking fingers, slid it onto my ring finger.

Son of a bitch, it was the perfect fit.

I tipped my eyes to Eli.

He was grinning again.

My glare softened.

"I work Saturdays and Sundays," he said, dipping another chip into his guacamole, "but I messaged a co-worker and asked him if he could work my Saturday this weekend and I'd work his Wednesday next week. He agreed. So if you want to go into the city to get some dress clothes this weekend, we can."

"I volunteer at the animal shelter for four hours every Saturday, but I can move my time and be done by one." I pushed the prongs of my fork into the flesh of my tuna steak and then dipped it into the sesame mayo. The sun caught the diamond on the ring, and it glowed, distracting me like a magpie to a piece of tinfoil.

I brought the tuna to my mouth, but my eyes were on the ring.

"I'm glad you like it," he said. "I thought it was practical but not flashy. Kind of sporty, like you." It was all those things. It was beautiful. It was perfect. It was exactly what I would have picked out if the man I wanted to spend my life with had taken me ring shopping.

Then it hit me: This was a real engagement ring. He'd mentioned the jeweler a couple of times, but the angry rushing sound of my pulse in my ears drowned out his words. Or at the very least, stopped them from sinking in.

I gaped at him. "This is *real?*"

He seemed taken aback. "Yeah. Why wouldn't it be?"

"Because we're not actually *engaged,*" I said with a hiss, dropping my voice to a whisper like it would be a travesty if the strangers around us or the turtles in the pond knew the truth of our sham.

"But we are," he said, mimicking my whisper and hiss. "Because we're actually going to get married. And you want our relationship to be believable, right? So you need a real ring."

"Can you afford this?"

He got his back up at that question. His smile fell, and he sat back against his chair. "Just because I need your insurance to pay for my surgery doesn't mean I'm destitute. I'd rather *not* go into debt paying like a hundred grand for surgery if I can help it. I'd like a house one day, maybe some land. I shouldn't *have* to pay to survive and receive medical care. I shouldn't have to pay to be able to see."

No, he shouldn't. The healthcare system was definitely broken in this country.

"I'm sorry," I said. "But either way, we can return it or sell it or whatever when we get the marriage annulled."

He shrugged and sipped his beer. "Whatever."

What did that mean?

I was really confused. And still pretty damn angry, too.

I wedged off another piece of tuna and shoved it into my mouth.

Maybe I was just hangry, not angry. Maybe if I quietly ate my tuna and salad, I could make sense of what was happening.

I finished my tuna without saying anything else to Eli, then moved on to my salad, using the leftover sesame mayo as dressing. He ate his nachos and drank his beer without pushing me for more conversation.

In a lot of ways, I felt like I was meeting Eli for the first time tonight. Seeing the real him ... or the *new* real him. Because truthfully, since that first night in my yoga studio when I saw him, he'd been nothing but cordial, bordering on kind toward me.

And yet, no matter how much I ate, the fact of the matter was that him being nice just made me mad.

"How is everything tasting?" the waitress asked, having returned to our table without me noticing.

"Nachos are great," Eli said.

I nodded. "Tuna and salad, too."

"Can I get you guys anything else to drink?" she asked.

We both shook our heads. And yet, even though he said he didn't ogle women, particularly when in the presence of other women, I watched him like a hawk again as our waitress left.

"Is she your type?" I asked, instantly regretting my snarky tone.

He finished chewing, then took a sip of his beer. When he tilted his head back, that roguishly sexy lock of hair that was usually over his forehead fell back and clung to the top of his head. "I don't really have a *type*. I like who I like. And I've liked all kinds. And I think, as I get older, my 'type' or the women I'm attracted to has changed."

I brought the straw of my mojito to my mouth. "And what kind of women are you attracted to now?"

His smile was cocky and impish. "Why do you want to know?"

That was a very good question. Why *did* I want to know?

I rolled my eyes and scoffed. "Forget it."

He lifted his chin. "I'll tell you my type if you tell me yours."

If I thought about it hard enough, I also didn't really have a "type." I liked who I liked. My last three serious boyfriends had all looked very different, been built differently, had different jobs and educations. And yet I'd been attracted to each of them.

"No type?" he asked, his half-cocked smirk back, making that single dimple on his left cheek get extra deep.

This man was infuriating. Particularly when he was reading my mind.

"I guess not," I said reluctantly.

"My type is ..." He tapped his finger to his chin. "A confident woman. Someone with drive. Passion. But she also has a kind heart and a soft spot that she only shows to certain, select people. But she's also a badass and wicked smart."

Tingles raced through me.

"And the redhead doesn't fit that bill?" I asked, hating that my voice cracked at the end.

He shrugged. "I just think she's too young. She doesn't know what she wants in life, and that's okay. But I want a woman who does. Whether that's to dominate her industry, raise a house full of kids, or retire on a houseboat by the time she's fifty, my 'type' is the kind of woman who knows what she wants out of the next thirty or forty years of her life."

Why was I panting?

Also, why was I staring at his lips when he spoke and wondering what it would feel like to have those lips pressed against mine?

I swallowed, but my mouth was dry. I reached for my mojito and drained it.

Why was he looking at me like that?

Like he wanted to ... I don't know, kiss me and eat me alive.

Or was that all in my head?

Was it me who wanted him to kiss me and eat me alive?

Was I thinking he was looking at me a certain way because I wanted him to look at me that way?

"So should we discuss the road trip?" he asked casually, loading up a single nacho chip with so much sour cream, the sheer weight of it was surely going to cause the chip to snap.

I watched as he shoveled the chip into his mouth and chewed.

Dear God, was I jealous of a tortilla chip? What was wrong with me?

I was clearly under the weather and needed to get home immediately.

I stood up. "I have to go."

He stood up too.

Because he was a gentleman? What the hell was going on right now?

"Why?" he asked. "Have I done something wrong?"

I shook my head. "No. Yes ... no. I don't know. But I have to go."

I reached into my wallet.

"I've got it," he said.

Shaking my head furiously, I pulled out two twenty-dollar bills. I knew it was more than enough for dinner and a tip. "No. We're dutch the entire way, remember. I pay for me. You pay for you."

He held up two hands in surrender. "Okay. Sorry." Unease slid across his face. "Are we still on for Saturday?"

I glared at him.

He looked worried.

Now I felt like a bitch.

"Yes," I said. "We're on for Saturday. I'll text you." Then before I could fall any further under his spell or whatever the hell was going on, I grabbed my phone, wallet, and keys and ran out of the pub as fast as my legs could carry me.

I did not stop panting and my heart did not even begin to slow down until I was back inside my apartment, behind my door and with the deadbolt flipped.

It was like the thoughts and feelings I'd been having for Eli had chased me all the way home, and I'd only just evaded them in the lobby, taking the steps two at a time and slamming the door in their face.

But those sneaky little bastards found the crack under the door and came in through the draft.

Eli Evans was hot.

Eli Evans was nice.

Eli Evans bought me a fucking engagement ring.

I held my hand up in front of me and stared at the diamond and white gold.

Holy shit!

Eli Evans was my fiancé.

CHAPTER TWELVE

Eli

AFTER THE WAY ALEXANDRA ran out of Smith's on Tuesday night, I made sure to steer clear of her for the rest of the week. Yes, I went to yoga on Wednesday, but I stayed at the back of the class and didn't stick around to chat her up at the end. I rolled up my mat, got in my truck, and went home.

What was Eden thinking right now? Not only were Alexandra and I civil with each other, but we were planning to get married. If I glanced up at the clouds would a pig whizz by?

I went to Harbor Cat on Thursday after work and grappled with a couple of guys I'd gotten to know there. Then Friday, I went back to yoga, but again, I stayed at the back and let Alexandra do her thing.

I thought about approaching her and trying to finalize plans for Saturday then, but I didn't want to push. She said she would text me, so I had to wait patiently and believe she would.

Even with that expensive ring—which I did not see on her finger at yoga on Wednesday or Friday—I was still worried that she'd get cold feet and call the whole thing off.

Which was why I was on my best behavior. Not something that came easily to me, particularly when it came to Alexandra, but I was trying.

I still couldn't figure out what made her run out of Smith's like that on Tuesday. I fully expected to get a text from her later that night bailing on the entire arrangement, but thankfully, no text came through.

After my shower and dinner, I sat on my deck with my tablet and drew.

Ever since Eden's death, I'd been dabbling and doodling, writing and illustrating. It was my way of dealing with her death and also keeping her alive.

"The Evans Twins Chronicles," a graphic novel that I was not only writing but illustrating as well, was already halfway through its fourth volume.

I hadn't shown it to a soul, of course, but maybe one day I would.

It starred Eve and Elliott Evans, two mild-mannered twins who at age ten stumbled upon a radioactive meteor in their grandfather's pasture. At first, it made them both very sick, but then once they recovered—very quickly, I might add—they developed superpowers like superhuman strength, the ability to heal rapidly, and lightning-fast reflexes.

But what was the most interesting thing about their powers was that the closer the twins were to each other, the stronger their powers. When they were far apart, their powers diminished. But when they were together, they had the strength of a construction crane and could lift collapsed bridges off trapped cars.

It was my way of staying close to Eden. Of keeping her present in my mind on a daily basis. I also felt that she was feeding me story ideas and helping fine-tune the series.

When we were kids and would go and visit my grandfather, who lived on a farm, we would have to share a room. I took the top bunk since she got up to pee at least twice a night and said she didn't want to break her neck climbing down.

It was a bit of an adjustment for the first few nights every time we went. The different nighttime sounds—all the crickets, frogs, owls, and cows mooing in the barn. So when we couldn't sleep, we'd come up with Evans twins stories.

Eden didn't want to use her own name, so she chose Eve—to stick with the whole biblical theme, *Eve and the garden of Eden*—so I just went with Elliott, even though my full name is just Eli.

She was a much better storyteller than I was, but I was a better artist.

We had plans to create this series together and maybe one day publish it.

But then we got older, our grandfather died, our parents got divorced, and it felt more like we were just trying to make it through each day and get to the next. When our mother turned to drinking after the divorce, Eden and I kept our heads down and powered through school as best we could, avoiding going home as much as possible. We wanted nothing to do with our father, and his side of the family abandoned us because we wanted nothing to do with him, so in a lot of ways we felt trapped.

Eden spent even more time with Alexandra.

But school had been my only safe haven.

And tormenting Alexandra had been a sick outlet for me. It was a place where I could channel my anger and my frustration at a target who, in my mind, deserved it.

If only she'd kept her mouth shut and not run to her dad.

Maybe our parents would have ended the affair on their own and my mom and her dad would have never been the wiser?

Up until recently, I'd been illustrating by hand with pencil and paper, but last year I splurged and bought a tablet and taught myself an illustration program. Now it was way easier to draw and color, and I could do it anywhere.

I was just shading in Eve's hair when my phone vibrated.

I'll pick you up at 1:30 tomorrow. Address?

Well, at least she wasn't texting to bail.

OK. 9076 Cormorant Avenue. I'll be out front waiting.

OK.

Was that it?

Fuck, she was infuriating. And so damn stubborn.

I'd bought her a goddamn engagement ring, for Christ's sake, and yet I could tell she still thought I was playing her.

Do you blame her? You pranked her a lot in high school. Treated her like the enemy. You were Jim, and she was your Dwight.

But Jim and Dwight ended up as friends in the end, right?

I set my phone down and continued sketching.

Five minutes later, my phone pinged, indicating something new on my social media.

I set the sketch pen down, picked up my phone, and nearly had a stroke.

Alexandra had gone and set her relationship status to: *In a relationship with Eli Evans.*

Wow!

Again that surreal feeling, like I was living someone else's life, hovering above as a spectator or something, began to creep into my brain.

Since we were not social media friends, I had to accept her friend request, then I updated my own status.

I honestly rarely posted on social media anymore and didn't stay in contact with people from high school, but that didn't matter.

The eighteen-year-old inside of me who knew how serious it was to change your relationship status—at least back in the day—was having a mild panic attack.

You did just spend like four grand on a ring and yet THIS is what is making it feel real?

Touché. But! Up until now, the "relationship" between Alexandra and I was only known by us. Now we were telling anybody and everybody who was on our social media.

My mom would probably call in the next two days asking if I'd lost my mind, and if Eden were still alive she'd ...

No, Eden would probably love this. She'd always wanted me and Alexandra to get along. She'd even suggested once that we date and that if we got married, then Alexandra would be her sister. I'd told her that we had a greater likelihood of actually finding a radioactive meteor in grandpa's field than Alexandra and I ever dating, marrying or even being civil to each other.

And yet ... here we were. Fake dating. Really engaged and somewhat civil with each other.

Maybe I needed to go ask the people who bought my grandfather's farm if I could go scour the field for meteors.

I was just about to set my phone back down when it vibrated and a text from Alexandra popped up.

It's official. No backing out now, Evans. Figured we'd take a picture of the ring and my hand at the Grand Canyon or something, pretend you proposed there.

I grinned and texted back. *I'll get down on one knee and stare at you like you're the most amazing woman in the world if that's what you want.*

Radio silence.

Fuck.

I went back to sketching.

It was getting dark, so not wanting to strain my eyes, I packed it all up and headed inside.

Tired from the day and working in the sun since nine in the morning, I decided to head to bed.

I hadn't planned on rubbing one out, but when Alexandra texted me just as I was about to close my eyes, with a link to a suit and a message that said *I think you'd look really good in this blue suit*, all I could envision after that was me in a suit, with her in some slinky thing with no back and that tattoo out for everyone to see, on her knees right in front of me, looking up with pure defiance in her eyes as she slid my cock between her lips, the same shade as those candy-apple chunks in her hair.

Fuck.

Was I falling for my fiancée?

I beat off to that exact same image twice more on Saturday morning before Alexandra came to pick me up. Well, the first time the image was the same, her red lips wrapped around my cock, but the second time I was picturing my cock sliding back and forth between her tits while she reached down with one hand and touched herself.

Why I tortured myself this way and put these thoughts into my head, right before I had to spend several hours with her in the confined space of a vehicle, I had no fucking clue.

But we really couldn't control our thoughts, at least not our filthy ones. Our proclivities were our own. Our attractions were primal.

And as her Jeep careened around the corner and her hair trailed behind her as ombre-hued aviators covered her eyes, every feeling I had was primal.

As she jerked her chin at me when she pulled up to the curb, I realized she told me to get in. I only had a water bottle with me, so I just climbed in beside her.

She had on a white tank top, low-rise jeans, and flip-flops. Those hot-pink-painted toes looked extra sexy today.

"Figured we'd head to the Rutherford Mall in Underwood. What do you think?

I nodded. "You're the boss."

All I got from her was an eyebrow lift.

She pulled away from the curb and headed for the highway.

Underwood was only about a thirty-minute drive south from Linley Park, but it was where everyone went to shop. It had all the major retailers, as well as all the major retailers like Costco, Walgreens and Walmart.

But it also had a bunch of strip malls, so hopefully we'd be able to find what we needed within the day.

"So what do you need to buy?" I asked, glancing out the ... well, there were no doors or windows, so I just looked beside me to the side of the road whizzing by. But if I kept looking at her, I'd remember those dirty thoughts I'd had last night and this morning and surely say something to fuck it all up.

"Dresses. Shoes. Makeup."

Then she dropped the conversation.

This was going to be a painful day if we couldn't find some common ground and at least be civil with each other.

"Have you had any responses to your status change?" I asked.

"My dad thinks I've lost my fucking mind."

"Yeah, my mom, too."

"My sister doesn't *do* social media, so ..."

That's right. I often forgot that Alexandra had an older sister, Sidney. Sidney was six years older and had already been living out of the house and in England when shit hit the fan with their parents. She might have come back for Eden's funeral, but I honestly couldn't remember.

From what I knew, she and Alexandra were not close, given the age gap (their parents had experienced several miscarriages between the two), and Sidney was also a bit of an ... *odd duck*, to put it gently.

If the rumor mill could be believed, she lived in something of a commune in England. She and a bunch of friends had bought a chunk of property, built a house, and sold things they made and grew in order to sustain themselves. But the rumor mill also suggested that there was some poly love going on. Like everyone who lived there also slept together.

I honestly didn't know what to believe these days, but my fuzzy memories of Sidney made me want to believe that these rumors might be true.

"Allegra—the Oompa-Loompa bride, as you've called her—messaged me to say that your personalized party favor will say *Cade*, so you're just going to have to live with it, since she hadn't anticipated me getting dumped and finding someone new so quickly."

"Tell me again why we're even going to this bitch's wedding?"

She rolled her eyes.

"No, seriously, tell me."

She was quiet for a moment, but then her shoulders dropped, and even though I was only looking at the profile of her face and she was in sunglasses, I could still see her resolve begin to crumble. "She's just *that* girl. A frenemy. I don't want to be like this. I don't want to care what she thinks or what any of them think, but I do, and I hate that I do. I just wanted to, for once, not feel self-conscious or insecure around them. Around *her.*"

"And you have in the past?" What in the fuck did she have to be self-conscious or insecure about? She was smoking hot, smart, and could kick nearly anybody's ass.

"I have no idea how to do my makeup. I've always been a tomboy. They're girlie girls. Men gravitate toward them like they're fresh water and the guys have been wandering around the desert for weeks. And Allegra was always just a *little* better than me in class. When I got ninety-five percent, she got ninety-six, and she never let me live it down."

"Hmmm, I remember someone very similar to that in high school." I shot her a grin.

She rolled her eyes. "I was not that bad."

"You made sure I knew you did better than me. Which was why, when I beat you at that race, I made sure *you* knew I'd won."

"You played dirty. You made me believe I'd leaked my period through my shorts." Her head shook. "How the hell did you even know I had my period?"

I shrugged. "I saw you ask Eden for a tampon earlier that day."

She scoffed. "You know I would have beaten you had you not done that."

I mirrored her shoulder lift. "We'll never know."

"You play dirty, Eli Evans."

Oh, if only she knew just how dirty we played in my mind over the last twenty-four hours. She'd pull over onto the side of the highway and kick my ass out into the ditch.

I needed to reassure her that I was going to play clean this time, though.

"I'm sorry," I said, only half meaning it. "If you want to race again, I'm up for it. We can even wait until you're not on your period."

That got her smiling. Her chest lifted when she made a laughing noise. But she only graced me with a bit of side-eye. "Not worried you'd get your ass kicked by me *again?*"

"I'm secure enough in my masculinity to not let it bother me. I'm not the kind of guy that gets bent out of shape about a woman being strong." I reached over and gently squeezed her bicep. "I mean, I can still probably bench press more than you. Maybe even do more chin-ups. But when it comes to being able to put my legs over my head, well, I'm willing to concede when I know I've been beaten."

"Oh, you think you can do more chin-ups than me?" There was no snark in her tone now. It was all playful. She took the off-ramp.

"Don't know. Just guessing."

She was still smiling.

It wasn't long before we were at Rutherford Mall and she was finding a place to park. She grabbed a cardigan out of the back seat and slung a small purse across her body. But all that did was settle the purse strap between her tits and draw my attention.

I looked skyward. If she caught me checking her out, I'd be done for.

"Should we do me first or you?" I asked, realizing the second the sentence came out of my mouth how it could be interpreted.

Innuendos and double entendres had never popped into my head with Alexandra before—at least not this quickly—and now they were the first things to arrive, no matter what she said or I said. I immediately took it to the gutter.

"We can do each other at the same time," she said innocently. "Unless we go to a men's or women's only store."

My chest tightened. I bit my tongue.

She was ahead of me now, and like a fucking preteen boy and NOT a thirty-two-year-old man with some self-control, my eyes zeroed in on her ass.

She pulled off jeans. Holy fuck, did she pull off jeans.

And that small peek of skin between the hem of her shirt and the top of her jeans. I damn near wanted to kiss my fingers like a French chef. Fucking perfection.

Which was ironic, considering I'd seen her in less. She did yoga and boxed wearing a sports bra and yoga capris. But right now, the simple outfit she had on was perfection.

"You coming?" she asked, glancing at me over her shoulder.

Nodding, I caught up with her like a dopey puppy.

"Now if we plan to go to *all* the events, we'll need at least four outfits each. The cocktail party, the rehearsal dinner, the wedding, and then the day-after brunch. Obviously, a suit for you for the wedding, and I'd like a long dress. But I think we can get away with dress shirts, dress slacks, and a sport coat or suit jacket for the rest of the days."

I held the door to the mall open for her, and we were instantly hit with the cool air-conditioning.

"Do you own dress shoes?" she asked.

I shook my head. "None that are very nice. Always wanted a pair of wingtips, though."

She nodded. "I like wingtips. There's a great shoe store here. We'll go there, too. I need a bunch of fucking heels, as well." She made a face as if she'd rather eat glass than put her foot in a sexy strappy sandal.

I snorted a laugh. She shot me a look, but there was a smile attached to it before she rolled her eyes.

I followed her lead through the mall. She seemed to know exactly where she was going. After a couple of minutes, we came to a formal wear store, and she walked right in.

She wasted no time hitting the men's section.

I was checking out some shirts at a table when her warm hand on my shoulder made my entire body stiffen. Then, with her other hand, she reached for the back collar of my shirt.

"What are you doing?" I asked. I inhaled, pulling in her spicy, floral scent and fighting the urge to close my eyes.

"Checking to see what size you are."

I cleared my throat and pushed out the invading, inappropriate thoughts. "I'm a tall-athletic. Chest: forty-two, forty-four. Neck: sixteen and a half to seventeen and a half. Sleeve: thirty-five to thirty-six."

She nodded. "Okay. Thanks."

I exhaled when she lifted her hands away from me and turned toward the wall of hanging shirts.

Yes, I found her attractive, but it was only in the last week that I was having more and more of these intrusive and inappropriate thoughts. We'd been locked in a clinch during our sparring match. Forehead to forehead, arms locked around each other's necks, bodies slick with sweat, chests heaving with shallow breath and exhaustion. And yet that hadn't affected me the way her touching the collar of my shirt did just now.

However, now that my cock thought back on our clinches, it was waking up.

A salesman came over to us, offering assistance.

Alexandra was all business and pointed to the dark blue suit on the mannequin. "Can he try that on, please? And the dress shirt beneath it. Tall-athletic." She turned to me. "What's your inseam?"

"That's an awfully personal question," I replied. "What's your bra size?"

She rolled her eyes.

Grinning at her, I approached the salesman, leaned in, and brought my voice down. "Thirty-four long, thirty-two waist."

He nodded. "I'll see what I can find."

Alexandra continued to browse the shirts, grabbing a few that she liked. Then she moved on to dress pants and ties. By the time the salesman arrived with the suit in tow, she had my arms loaded with stuff she wanted me to try on.

"All right, head on in, and let's see how everything fits," she said, pointing me in the direction of the changing rooms.

I shook my head, tossing her a cocky smile. "Nope."

Her brows narrowed, and anger flashed in her blue eyes. "What?"

"Not before we see what we can find for you."

I asked the attendant if he could put all my clothes in a changing room, then reserve the one beside it for Alexandra. I'd seen the dollar signs in his commission-making eyes when we asked about the suit, so he was happy to oblige.

Alexandra followed me into the women's section, where I started browsing through the racks.

"I can find my own dresses," she said haughtily, adding a scoff to the end of her words.

"I'm sure you can. But this is a team effort. You did me. Now I do you." I stacked a boulder on top of that groan that wanted to break free of my chest. I definitely wanted to *do* her. And for her to *do* me.

This was dangerous territory I was entering.

Shark-infested waters.

A small cage filled with hungry tigers.

I stopped on a sexy gold or champagne or beige or whatever the fuck color dress. Grabbing the hanger, I pulled it off the rack. "This one. Find your size. I won't look if you're self-conscious. But just know, you have no reason to be. You're fucking hot." Then I kept walking, not giving her any room to negotiate. Though I really wished I'd seen her face.

I grabbed another dress. This time, it was royal blue and looked like a bunch of bandage-style straps all sewn together. It was also strapless. I yanked it off the rack.

"This one, too."

She huffed behind me but didn't object.

I kept moving.

I ordered her to grab a total of seven dresses, plus a skirt and a crop-top type thing. She didn't say *no* once, but I could feel her ire as she trailed behind me.

I didn't look back at her at all, since I couldn't keep the smile from my face and knew that it would just incite her.

With her arms loaded, I returned to the changing rooms, where Jamie, our kind salesperson, had hung up all of my clothes.

"Come out with the first dress on," I told Alexandra before I closed the curtain, blocking out myself from the rest of the world.

I had to stifle my chuckle when I heard her murmur, "Bossy prick."

CHAPTER THIRTEEN

Eli

I REALIZED IN ABOUT a quarter of a second that there was only half a wall separating Alexandra and I from each other. I saw her feet and those sexy hot-pink-painted toes and could hear her moving next door.

The quick *zip* of the zipper on her jeans had my own jeans getting uncomfortably tight.

Do not get a boner in the dress pants. Do not get a boner in the dress pants. At least wait until you've bought them.

I pulled my T-shirt off over my head, then let my jeans drop to the floor. The half-chub in my boxers was noticeable, but if I thought about men's butts in baseball pants for a solid minute, it should deflate enough for me to pull back the curtain.

Hopefully.

First, I was going to try on the suit. I went with a crisp, white dress shirt, then the slacks, followed by the vest and finally the jacket. She'd picked out an on-the-thinner side black tie, and I put that on, too. Thankfully, my dad had taught me a proper Windsor knot before he decided to throw away his family and have an affair with Alexandra's mom.

The sound of the curtain in her changing room being pulled open echoed into my changing room, so I made sure my dick wasn't visible, then pulled back my own curtain.

Jamie was zipping up Alexandra's dress—the royal blue bandage strapless one—but she whipped around to face me when Jamie was finished.

Her eyes widened, pupils dilated, nostrils flared. It was a primal reaction that I would have to be an idiot to miss.

I had a primal reaction of my own—in my pants.

"Holy fuck," I breathed.

She glanced away, but the smile that lifted one side of her mouth was dead sexy.

"You're getting that one," I said.

She smoothed her hands down the sides, turned on one foot, and glanced at herself in the mirror. "Yeah, I like it, too."

"You can't wear those two together, though," Jamie said. "The blues are too close in color, but not close enough. If you know what I mean?"

Alexandra and I nodded.

"He should just wear a dress shirt and maybe dark gray pants when you wear that dress."

"I have dark gray pants in the room," I said, hooking a thumb toward my changing room and a stack of pants on the bench.

I stepped out and away from my room to get a better look at myself in the mirror outside the changing rooms. "What do you think?"

"I think it's a perfect fit," Jamie said. "Doesn't even look like you'll need tailoring."

Alexandra nodded. "Looks good." I caught her checking out my ass and grinned, but when she saw me see her, her eyes whipped up to the ceiling as if a flock of geese had just flown overhead.

"You guys got any brown wingtips?" I asked, focusing my gaze on Jamie.

He nodded. "Sure do. Size?"

I glanced back at Alexandra and smiled as I said, "Thirteen."

I did not miss the flare of her eyes or the way they drifted down to the front of my pants.

"Eyes up here, lady," I said, catching her gaze back in the mirror.

Startled, she ditched the surprised look and went with a glare before returning to her changing room and dramatically pulling the curtain closed again.

"What is the dynamic of your relationship?" Jamie asked, glancing back and forth between me and the closed changing room curtain.

"She's my fiancée," I said chipperly. "But she'd rather not be."

Alex

Oooh, that Eli Evans was a wily bastard.

A wily bastard with exceptional taste in dresses and whose ass could fill out a pair of dress slacks like nobody's business.

What the hell?

And size thirteen shoes?

Was he packing an anaconda in his damn trousers?

For the rest of the day, I found my eyes drifting to the front of his pants WAY too often for my liking. What was wrong with me?

Our time with Jamie, our very helpful salesman, turned into a bit of a shopping spree movie montage. We'd duck into our changing rooms, then come out, spin around, make yay or nay faces, thumbs up or thumbs down, then head back behind the curtain.

Eli also made a second trip out into the women's section, only to return with another six dresses for me to try on.

All of them were beautiful, but not all of them were right for me.

But at the end of the day, I bought four dresses, a skirt, a crop top and three different pairs of strappy sandal heel-things. My credit card was crying.

Starved, because trying on clothes is nearly as exhausting as Muay Thai boxing—joking—we swung into Taco My Taco on the drive home.

"This is amazing," Eli said as he held his lobster fish taco in his hand and a bit of sauce dribbled out over his fingers. "Like I'm ordering another one." He lifted his chin at the teenager behind the counter. "My man, order me up two more of these delicious lobster tacos, please. I'm just going to finish this one, then wipe my hands, then I'll come pay."

The kid nodded. "You got it."

"Like seriously, Alexan—*Alex*, you need to try this." He turned the taco around and held it out for me to take a bite.

I was happy with my own ceviche taco, so I made a face and waved him off. "I'm fine."

"Take a bite." There was that tone again. The one from earlier today when he was picking out dresses for me. It left zero room for negotiation, and my body rebelled against my brain and got all hot and turned on by it.

What the hell?

Before I could tell him to go shove the lobster taco up his ass, I leaned forward and took a bite. Our eyes locked.

Then I shut my eyes, sat back, and moaned.

I moaned as if someone had just licked my clit and not like I had a big piece of lobster and delicious sauce and homemade tortillas in my mouth.

My cheeks heated.

I swallowed, then opened my eyes.

His grin was cheeky, sexy and something I wanted to kiss but also punch right off his face.

"My man," he called to the kid behind the counter again. "Make that three. My fiancée wants one, too."

"You got it."

"You're an ass," I said, biting back into my own taco.

"I'm going to argue that I'm not."

I sat back in my chair. I hadn't been expecting that response.

He finished the taco and licked his fingers. I pushed down my groan, resisted the urge to close my eyes, but crossed my legs under the table and squeezed.

"How's your taco?"

I know he was asking about my dinner. But my first instinct was to say, *"Wet, pulsing and craving dick ... or tongue ... or a couple of long, calloused fingers. Can you help me out?"*

What the hell was wrong with me?

I cleared my throat. "It's good."

"Can I have a bite?"

I glared at him for a moment, then rolled my eyes and held it out. He leaned forward across the table and took a bite.

Damn it all to hell, even that was sexy.

Holding up a finger, he tilted his head toward the counter to tell me he was going to pay. I watched him walk away, hating how damn good he filled out a pair of jeans and that even his T-shirt fit him like a glove. A glove I wanted to tear off of him with my teeth.

Besides his whole bossy, demanding, and thirst-trap side today, Eli had been a perfect gentleman. He opened doors for me, he was polite, and he tried on everything I picked out while selecting appropriate shirts, pants, and ties. And when he slid into those wingtips, I was pretty sure my vagina made an *mmhmm* noise.

I will reluctantly admit that if I ignored the fact that we were enemies, I actually had a good day.

"So what's on the docket tomorrow?" he asked, returning to our table, sliding back into his side of the booth, and taking a sip of his coconut water. "It's your day off, right?"

I bobbed my head. "Yeah. I think I'll head back to the shelter. They're really short on volunteers, and being around all the dogs makes me happy."

"Do you have a dog?"

"No. I want one so badly, but my life is too busy. It wouldn't be fair to a pet like that. Not even a cat. Plus, I haven't lived in a building that allows pets. Cade's building does, so we were going to get a dog when I moved in since between the two of us, we could be there enough for a pet. But then that dream died, along with our relationship."

"Did you think he was your Prince Charming? The one?"

Where did that question come from?

I wrapped my lips around the straw of my lychee water and took a sip. I had to think about it for a minute. When I was *in* a relationship with Cade, yeah. I thought he was the one. I mean, we planned to move in together. And yet now I can see so many reasons why it never would have worked out.

Finally, I shook my head. "I did think he was. But now I realize that he wasn't. And not just because he ended it. But because we were just so different."

"But don't opposites attract?"

"Yeah, but you need to share a few interests, even just a favorite television show. But I don't watch a lot of TV. He was always trying to get me to read these books, like Vonnegut and Hemingway, and I just couldn't get into them. Nothing against the writers because I can understand why they are the classics that they are, but they just couldn't hold my attention. He wanted me to read them so that we could discuss them. Or to watch a documentary so we could discuss it."

His lip curled up. "So he just wanted to argue?"

I nodded. "Pretty much. Because it was never a 'discussion' for long. It quickly turned into him telling me all the reasons why I was wrong for thinking something about the book or documentary. That my subjective opinion was incorrect. Maybe that's why I couldn't get into the books, because I was too busy thinking about how I could 'match' Cade's interpretation of the book in order to just avoid an argument. Or being told that I was wrong." I shook my head. "It's all so stupid. He wasn't my knight in shining armor, that's for sure. Not now that I am removed from the relationship and can analyze it without rose-colored glasses." I picked up a piece of scallop that had fallen onto my plate and popped it into my mouth.

"Not that you *need* a knight in shining armor. Because you sure as fuck don't."

My head snapped up from where I'd been looking at my plate.

"And a lot of knights in shining armor are just douchebags wrapped in tinfoil, anyway. What you want is an equal. Someone who challenges you but doesn't disregard your opinion. Someone who is open to your opinion and being changed by it, if they agree. Cade just sounds like a narrow-minded tool."

Why was my breathing suddenly ragged? Why was my body warm, especially my neck and cheeks? And let's not forget about the way that space between my legs was practically pulsing with its own heartbeat.

I swallowed. "Yeah."

"I think you're better off. You dodged a bullet with ol' Cade the Cad."

"Here we are. Three lobster tacos." The kid from behind the counter set three plates down at our table. "Enjoy."

"Thanks, my man," Eli said with a smile as he reached over and grabbed a taco off the plate. He pointed with his index finger at one of the other ones. "Dig in. We both know you enjoyed it."

I grabbed one. "You just can't resist, can you?"

"Can't resist what?" he asked, shoving the food in his mouth into his cheek.

"Being all flirty and ... and ..."

"And?"

"I don't know ... flirty and *extra* flirty."

His smile turned wicked. *"Extra* flirty?"

"Changing your tone when you say certain words, putting a *sexual* or suggestive inflection on a word. Bobbing your eyebrows like two caterpillars doing push-ups. That's *extra* flirty."

His free hand touched his brows. "Caterpillars doing push-ups? Like how bushy are we talking?"

I rolled my eyes. "You're impossible."

He finished that taco and reached for the second one. "Lighten up, Alexa—*Alex.* I'm just trying to have fun. Trying to make you laugh. We're in this nightmare of an arrangement, for better or worse. Literally, in fact. We might as well make the best of it, right?"

I grumbled.

"So what time do you want to leave Wednesday?"

I licked off the sauce that had dripped onto my thumb. "Huh?"

"Well, you planned to leave ten days before the wedding, right? That's Wednesday."

Oh my God. The days were just flying by. He was right. I was leaving on the twenty-fifth, and that was Wednesday.

"I guess early in the morning?"

He nodded. "Sounds like a plan. I'll be waiting on the curb with my suit bags, sexy smile, and a sweet-ass road trip mix tape. Your Jeep has a cassette player, right?" He snorted at his own joke.

I took another bite of my taco. Holy crap, this was good. My ceviche taco was good, but this was better.

He grinned slyly like he knew exactly what I was thinking. Then he looked over at the counter again. "My man?"

"Yeah?" the kid called back.

"Four more of the lobster tacos, to go."

"You got it!"

CHAPTER FOURTEEN

Alex

I GREETED YOLANDA SUNDAY morning as I grabbed my volunteer vet name badge off the hook behind the front desk and made my way back toward the kennels where the dogs were kept.

As soon as the dogs saw me, those who weren't at their gate doors barking and wagging their tails already were up out of bed and joining the chorus.

Another volunteer, a woman by the name of Sharon Abrams, was already there and feeding the dogs their breakfast.

"Morning, Sharon," I said, opening up the back garage-style door into the dog yard.

"Morning," she said with a wave. "Watch out for land mines."

I grinned at her as I grabbed the shovel and the bucket. "Thanks for the reminder."

After I was done scooping up all the poop, I started opening up the kennels from the outside so the dogs could come into the yard for some exercise. Yolanda would have a list for me of which dogs—if any—needed medical attention. I managed to treat five dogs yesterday, all of them new rescues. As well as four cats. Then I took my girl Jill for a walk to the park before I picked up Eli.

The majority of the dogs raced outside, then demanded my attention as soon as their door was opened. But a few moseyed out like they were the sheriff in town and hadn't a care in the world.

Then there was dear sweet little Jill.

She stayed inside her kennel because, well, she wasn't fond of too many other dogs all up in her space.

But she wouldn't snap at them or snarl. She just avoided them.

I understood her sentiment. I got overwhelmed when there were too many people in my personal space, too. I could never understand how people could go to these multi-thousand-person concerts and stand in the mosh pit right by the stage. The sheer thought of it gave me mental hives.

Once the rest of the dogs were out and I gave them some attention, I went to check on Jill.

Apparently, we had a new volunteer at the shelter, and he'd taken a shine to Jill as well, taking her for a walk on Tuesday.

Not getting to adopt Jill was probably the most disappointing part about not moving in with Cade, now that I thought about it.

Crouching down next to the open door that led into Jill's kennel, I tilted my head to look inside. "Hey there, Jilly Bean. How you doing, old girl?"

Her ears perked up at her name, and when she saw it was me, she pried her old bones out of her bed and slowly walked toward me.

She had no qualms with me picking her up, and she started to lick my hand and tried to lick my face.

"No face kisses," I said, turning my head with a laugh.

I'd checked her out yesterday, but her left hip felt inflamed so I wanted to check on it today, now that she'd rested overnight. The swelling seemed to have gone down but not enough for my liking.

Sharon wandered out into the yard, and I grabbed her attention. "I'm going to put Jill on some anti-inflammatory medication, okay? Her hip is worrying me. And we'll add some turmeric to her food, too. I'll let Yolanda know."

Sharon nodded. "Yeah, old girl was hobbling a little yesterday after you left. I think even these short jaunts to the park are too much for her now."

I kissed the side of Jill's head, which prompted her to turn and try to kiss me back. "Maybe we need to start carrying you to the park, hmm, Miss Jill. Just let you walk on the grass for a bit but no more hard sidewalks."

"Probably a good idea," Sharon said.

Melancholy settled inside my heart when the realization that I wasn't going to see Jill for two weeks dawned on me. I knew there were another couple of vets who volunteered their time with the shelter as well, but it wasn't nearly as routine as I did. Francesca only came twice a month, while Robert made an appearance once a month or once every month and a half. I was the only on-the-schedule, never-failed-to-show-up vet. The shelter relied on me.

The animals relied on me.

Plus, I enjoyed coming here.

Yes, I got to spend time with animals every day with my job, but it was different coming here. Work didn't afford me the opportunity to just sit and let the animals climb all over me, to get smacked in the face with a thick, excitedly wagging tail.

I came here to remind myself of my dream, which was a rescue shelter like this but on a huge chunk of land, where dogs could come and live out the rest of their days running for hours, chasing balls, digging holes, and loving life. I was living in a shitty apartment, working long hours, cleaning at H&J, and teaching yoga so one day—before I was too old and tired to do it—I could fulfill my dream and take care of animals.

With Jill still in my arms, I went over to a bench and sat down. A few dogs came to sniff at me and check out Jill, but for the most part, they left us alone. Jill settled onto my lap, and I poked and prodded a bit more at her hip. She yipped once when I pressed a little harder, so I backed off. "Sorry, girl."

As the clock approached ten o'clock, a few Sunday morning dog-walk volunteers showed up. A lot of times it was families who, like myself, lived in no-pet apartments, so in order to get their dog-fix, they came here and walked some.

There were also a few elderly people, and some teenagers looking to fill their volunteer-hours requirement for high school.

Unlike yesterday, I carried Jill to the park down the road, rather than allow her to walk. Once we were on the grass, I put her down and let her walk on the leash. She pulled me over to the same big oak we'd sat under yesterday, and as soon as my back was against the trunk, she sat down beside me, leaned against my thigh, tilted her head back, and looked up.

I rubbed her chest and belly. "You're a sweet thing, Miss Jilly Bean. And I'd take you home with me in a hot minute if I could."

Keeping one hand on her chest, I brought my purse onto my lap, opened up a small compartment on the inside, and pulled out the ring from Eli.

I slid it onto my finger and held my hand out. "What do you think, Jilly?"

Jill leaned forward and sniffed the ring, then let out a *boof.*

"I know, right? It's so perfect. So me. I just ..." I shook my head and glanced out at the playground full of children and families. "I can't figure him out. I want to believe that he's not playing me. I want to believe that this will all work out. But I'm also afraid to let down my guard around him, you know? Add in the fact that he is ridiculously hot now, and it's all just messing with my head."

Normally, I didn't wear the ring. I kept it at home while I was at work, yoga and H&J, but for some reason today, I put it in my purse.

I had two more days of work, then I was officially on vacation for two weeks. I hadn't taken that kind of time off in eight years. Not since I went to Thailand with my old boyfriend, Owen. We were gone for a month, and it was three days before we were set to return home that Eden killed herself.

I hadn't gone anywhere since.

I also hadn't made a friend as close as Eden.

Jill and I sat at the park for another half hour or so, then I scooped her back up and carried her home to the shelter.

As much as I loved her, I really hoped someone adopted her. But the likelihood of that happening was small. Not very many people adopted old dogs. They wanted puppies that could grow with their family, that they could train and name themselves. Nobody wanted an old dog who might only have a year left, who was on medications and couldn't even go out for a walk.

I kissed the top of Jill's head as I carried her down the sidewalk under my arm. She seemed pleased as punch to be toted around like a clutch purse and not forced to walk on the sidewalk.

She was such an agreeable little thing.

Once we were back, I put her back in her kennel, and she went crazy drinking water from her bowl.

I found Yolanda and Sharon chatting at the front desk. "I'm leaving Wednesday morning for two weeks, but I want to pop by Tuesday night after work. I'll leave the hospital early so I can come check on Jill before I leave." I glanced at the calendar behind Yolanda. "It looks like Francesca will be in next weekend, so that's good. She can follow up on things with Jill."

"Where are you going?" Sharon asked, tucking a strand of her brown wavy hair behind her ears. Her diamond studs sparkled under the fluorescent lighting.

"San Diego," I said with a sigh. "But I'm driving. Turning it into a road-trip-style vacation. Gonna hit tourist traps along the way. Then I have a wedding to attend on Coronado Island on the fifth."

Both women made *O*'s with their mouths.

"You and Cade going together?" Yolanda asked.

I winced. "No ... we're actually not together anymore."

Their eyes turned sad.

"It just didn't work out. To be honest, I'm most bummed about the fact that his place was pet-friendly and we were going to get a dog but now I can't."

Their chuckles were meek and didn't last more than a couple of seconds.

"So who are you going with now?" Sharon asked. "Do you have a date?"

I nodded. "I do. He's a ... childhood friend. His sister and I were best friends all through school. So he's agreed to be my date."

"Ooh, maybe something will come of it," Sharon said, bobbing her dark brows. "A friends-to-lovers kind of romance. I love those. Almost as much as I love enemies-to-lovers tropes."

That made me laugh. "Well, we actually are enemies. We hated each other all through school. Now we're just ... *tolerating* each other. He's doing me a favor I suppose you could say."

Sharon's brows shot nearly clean off her forehead.

I swatted her upper arm and gave her a look. "Not *that* kind of favor. This arrangement is strictly platonic. Get your mind out of the gutter, woman."

"I love where this is going," Sharon snickered, her brown eyes gleaming.

"Uh, no. It's not going anywhere. There will be no happily ever after with this guy," I said, shaking my head. "No riding off into the sunset. No two-point-five kids and a picket fence. We've declared a truce, and he's helping me out." I didn't dare tell them the rest of the deal, since if they knew that we were getting married and it was only for insurance purposes, Eli's claim for coverage could be denied if we got investigated.

"You know who you should meet?" Yolanda asked. "There's a new guy who comes in on Tuesday afternoons. The guy who took Jill for a walk. He is *very* nice to look at. You two would make a cute couple."

I shrugged and lobbed a sigh. I wasn't ready to start dating again, but the way these two women were looking at me with their hopeful matchmaker glasses goggles on, it would be easier to just play along. "Well, when I'm back from San Diego, I'll have to sneak over on an early lunch break one Tuesday and check him out."

They both nodded eagerly. Such hopeless romantics the both of them. Didn't they know that fairy tale love stories didn't exist in real life? That there were no such things as white knights, they were all just douches wrapped in tinfoil.

"In the meantime, make sure that Jill gets the turmeric powder on her food, along with the anti-inflammatory drops. I'll check on her Tuesday night." I tapped my knuckles on the desk twice, then waved goodbye.

"I want pictures of you and this *enemy* not *lover* at the wedding," Sharon called after me. "I'm crossing my fingers it turns into more. Like only one bed at the hotel, so much sexual tension you need a damn machete to cut through it."

I rolled my eyes at her, fighting the smile that tried to curl the corners of my mouth. "Your romance novels are giving you an unrealistic expectation of life and men, Sharon."

"Or are they giving me a new standard men need to reach?" She tilted her head and eyed me questioningly. "If more men got over themselves and read romance books written by women the world would be a much happier, more orgasm-filled place. I'm sure of it."

"Not sure anything would get done, we'd all just be orgasming all the time," I quipped before shooting them both a wink. "Bring in your favorite book for me when I get back and I'll give it a whirl, see what's got you so hellbent on believing fairy tales still do exist."

Sharon pointed at me with determination in her eyes. "You're on. Prepare to be aroused."

With a snort and a head shake, I smiled, waved at them both, then I was gone and off to go buy makeup I had no idea how to wear. Hopefully, the girl at the counter would take pity on my inept ass and give me a few pointers. Otherwise, I could very well end up going to the party looking like it'd been Eli who won the sparring match and gave me a knee to the eye and not the other way around.

I left work at four on Tuesday. I needed to swing by the animal shelter before I went to yoga. I went and sparred with Jao at H&J last night, then stuck around and gave the gym a very thorough cleaning. Not that it would last until I was back in two weeks, but it left my conscience clear that I was earning my keep and my free membership.

Members at the yoga studio were not happy that I was going to be gone for two weeks, but they wished me a relaxing vacation nevertheless. I took their playful frustration as a sign that they liked me and my classes, which I already knew they did, since my classes were always full. But it was still reassuring to hear things like, "I like Celine's class, but yours is the best, Alex. Come back soon."

As I walked into the shelter, I smiled and nodded at Yolanda. "How's our girl today?"

"A bit lethargic," she said, her expression grim. "But she's still eating, which is good. Sharon's in there with her now."

I thanked Yolanda and walked into the row between the kennels. Several dogs were outside in the yard but not Jill. Sharon was sitting with her in her kennel, Jill's head on the woman's lap.

"She's still eating and drinking, so that's a good sign, right?" Sharon asked when she saw me approach the chain-link gate.

I nodded. "It is. Yolanda says she's been lethargic?"

"Yeah, just a little bit. Extra snuggly."

"Let's take a quick look. Can you bring her into the exam room?"

Sharon nodded and groaned slightly when she unfolded herself from her cross-legged position on the ground. She picked up Jill, then followed me to the exam room.

I poked and prodded at Jill gently, but the little thing didn't want to stay standing, so I let her lie down.

Sharon and I exchanged worried looks.

"Could it be the anti-inflammatory meds making her tired?" Sharon asked, stroking Jill from head to tail along her back.

I shook my head. "They shouldn't be. But we'll reduce her dosage a little and see if that helps. I'll write down the new dosage before I leave." I pressed lightly around Jill's neck, checking out her lymph nodes. They were mildly enlarged, but not in a worrisome way.

"It might just be the heat getting to her," I said, grabbing a treat from the jar and placing it on the exam table directly in front of Jill's face. "I know we encourage volunteers to take them for walks, but in this heat, it's not necessarily such a good idea. If the new volunteer could come in the evening when it's cooled off or maybe stick to some shadier places, that might help. But we may just have to resign ourselves to the fact that Jill is not a dog that needs—or wants—to be walked anymore."

"The new guy is going on vacation for a couple of weeks, so Yolanda or I can let him know when he gets back."

I nodded absentmindedly. "Okay."

Scooping Jill up off the table, I held her against my chest like you would a baby so I could see directly into her gentle brown eyes. "You're a good old girl, Jilly Bean." I kissed the top of her head.

"You leave for your trip tomorrow?" Sharon asked.

Nodding, I walked out of the exam room and back into the rows of kennels. "Yeah. Bright and early."

"Well, have fun. I'll be sending out the romance vibes for you and this 'enemy' of yours."

I shot her some cynical side-eye, but she just smiled.

"Enemies-to-lovers is one of my absolute favorite tropes. And there is a reason it's so popular. The sexual tension manifesting as hate, but then it becomes too much and suddenly you just attack each other with your mouths, clothing magically disappears, and then it's just sweaty bodies, a lot of grunting and teeth and—"

"Sharon!"

Her cheeks went bright pink, but her smile was wicked.

"I appreciate your enthusiasm, and you do you, girlfriend, but that will absolutely NOT be happening here. I hate to burst your bubble."

Her pout was hilarious and had me laughing as I set Jill back down in her bed and ran my hand over her back.

I said goodbye to Jill, then made my way back out to the front desk.

"If you have any questions or concerns about Jill or any of the other dogs, just give me a call. I might be on vacation, but I'm still a vet and I care about these animals. I can always video chat with you and guide you through an exam."

They smiled.

"You've got a pure heart, Alex," Yolanda said. "Enjoy your vacation."

I waved to both of them as I headed out the door.

Next stop: the car rental company, then the grocery store, and finally home to pack for tomorrow. For tomorrow, I would be embarking on the greatest challenge of my life. Ten straight days in a vehicle with my enemy—who was now frustratingly gorgeous and also technically my fiancé.

This was going to be my Everest.

I only hoped that I could make it to the top without losing a limb to frostbite or pushing my climbing partner off the side of a mountain.

CHAPTER FIFTEEN

Alex

I WAS AWAKE, DRESSED, and completely packed by six o'clock on Wednesday morning. Eli texted me at six-thirty to say that he was ready when I was. So with my stomach in knots, I climbed into the white rental SUV and headed over to his apartment.

I was five minutes from his place when my phone started to ring.

The caller ID said it was the shelter.

Dread in the shape of a fat, black snake began to coil around my insides and squeeze my heart.

I put the phone in the dash holder and hit the green button. "Hello?"

"Honey ..." It was Yolanda.

"What happened?"

I braced myself for her answer, even though, deep down, I already knew what it was.

"It's Jill, sweetie."

No.

Ice filled my veins.

"I came in early this morning to check on her and found her unresponsive in her bed. I checked her pulse and ... she's gone."

I pulled up to the curb at Eli's building.

"I'm sorry to call you. I know you're probably heading out of town right about now. But I figured you'd want to know."

"I'm still in town, just picking up my date for the wedding. I'm going to come by on my way out of town, okay? I want to see her."

"Of course. "

We disconnected the call just as Eli came out of his building's lobby. He smiled and waved at me, but when I didn't return the greeting, his expression faltered and concern filled his eyes. He had a lot of stuff. Like *a lot*. Why?

I didn't get out of the vehicle but rather let him sort out where to put his suitcase, other bags, and suit bags. Why did he have so much stuff?

A couple of minutes later, he climbed into the passenger seat. "Morning."

"Morning," I said stiffly.

"What's wrong?"

I shook my head. "Nothing."

"Alex ..."

Sniffling, I pulled away from the curb, wiping a tear from beneath my eye. You'd think after being a vet for all these years and having to deal with animal death on almost a daily basis that it would get easier. But it didn't. Each death affected me. Each death took a piece of my heart.

And Jill's death was going to take a bigger piece than most.

"Did something happen?" he probed.

I shook my head. "It's fine. I just have to make a stop at the shelter quickly."

I kept my eyes on the road, but I could tell that he was watching me. His expression was stony.

"Pull the fuck over now, Alexandra."

My body responded without giving my brain a chance to argue with his demand. I pulled over to the curb.

"Look at me."

Swallowing, I looked at him.

"What happened?"

As bossy as he was being, the concern in his eyes was unmistakable. I searched his face for a moment, and then for some reason, the dam broke and the tears just started to fall. "Jill died."

"Jill died."

It wasn't a question. The way he said her name was as if he knew her.

I lifted my head. "A dog that I'd grown attached to at the shelter, she ... she had a stroke or something last night. Yolanda found her this morning, and she didn't have a pulse."

He nodded, and pain creased his face. "I know Jill. I've been walking her on Tuesdays."

My mouth dropped open. *"You're* the new volunteer?"

He nodded again. "I fell in love with her immediately."

"Me, too."

"Can I come in to see her with you?"

My head bobbed stiffly. "Yeah."

"Okay."

We didn't say anything else. We didn't need to. I pulled back out onto the empty road and drove the ten minutes to the shelter. Besides Yolanda's car, the parking lot was empty. The door was also locked since the place didn't actually open until eight-thirty, but after I knocked, Yolanda came and let us in, her gaze curious as she took in Eli and I together.

"Where is she?" I asked.

Somberly, she led us through to one of the exam rooms where little Jill lay on the stainless-steel table, covered gently with a blanket. I pulled the blanket away from her face. She simply looked like she was sleeping. I reached for a stethoscope from the wall, put it to my ears and then pressed the chest piece against her little chest.

No heartbeat.

"How was she last night after I left?" I asked, taking the earpieces out and draping the stethoscope around my neck.

"Still lethargic. But okay."

I squeezed my eyes shut. The backs of them burned.

"She was old, honey. Really old." A hand landed on my shoulder.

"I know."

"You gave her so much love. We all did. She didn't go into the next life not feeling loved."

"I know." I just wished I could have shown her more. She didn't deserve to die without a family. Without a true place to call home.

She'd been dropped off at the shelter because the old lady who owned her died, and her kids didn't want Jill since they had pets of their own to take care of.

"I just want a minute to say goodbye," I said to Yolanda.

"Me, too," Eli added, stepping up beside me.

Yolanda nodded. "Of course. Take all the time you need."

Tears dripped down my cheeks unchecked, and my nose was now completely plugged. But that didn't matter. I picked up one of her velvet-soft ears and ran my thumb over it. "You're such a good girl, Jilly Bean. Such a sweetheart."

"That's what I called her, too," Eli said softly.

Our elbows touched, we were so close. He pulled the blanket away from her body a little more and stroked her back.

"She helped me pick out your ring. I showed her pictures of rings, and this was the one she approved of." He tapped the engagement ring on my finger.

I glanced up at him. "She's got good taste."

"I took her to the park up the road, and we would sit under that big oak tree and just talk and watch the kids at the park."

New, fresh tears flooded my eyes. "We did the same thing."

He smiled and with his free hand reached up and wiped away the tears that were rolling down my cheeks. "I would like to pay for her to be cremated, then when we get back, we can go to the tree at the park and sprinkle her ashes. What do you think? It seemed to be her favorite place. Or at least, I'd like to think it was."

My bottom lip trembled, and I swallowed past the impossibly hard lump in my throat. I nodded. "I like that. Thank you."

"We didn't know each other for long, Jilly Bean, but you made a lasting and unforgettable impact on my life. I will be forever grateful." Eli rested his hand on her back. "And I won't ever forget you."

I turned back to Jill. "I won't ever forget you either, and I'm sorry that I couldn't bring you home with me. I'm sorry that you died alone in your kennel. You didn't deserve that."

Eli's free hand found mine and squeezed. I squeezed it back.

Then we just stood there for probably ten or fifteen more minutes, petting and staring at Jill, giving her the love that she deserved, that she should have felt when she passed on into the afterlife.

We were just leaving the exam room, both of us wiping our eyes, when Sharon entered through the side door. She stopped in her tracks, and her eyes went saucer-size.

"*Eli* is Alex's wedding date," Yolanda said with a teasing tone to her voice.

I could see every single dirty-minded cog spinning in Sharon's head like her forehead had a big picture window in the center of it. She smiled in a self-satisfied way, but then when she took in our upset faces, her expression sobered. "Jill?"

I nodded.

"I'm sorry." Her eyes drifted from me to Eli and then back again. "To both of you."

"I'm going to pay to have her cremated, then if you can hold on to the ashes until we're back, I'd appreciate it. We'll sprinkle her at the oak tree in the park. Apparently, that's where we both took her." He glanced down at me. "I think she'd be happy there."

I nodded. "I think so, too."

"We can make that happen," Yolanda said.

Eli and I both thanked her.

"Don't let this ruin your trip," Yolanda added.

I was avoiding Sharon's gaze at all costs since I knew exactly what that hopeless romantic was thinking.

That's when I realized that Eli and I were still holding hands.

I released his fingers like they'd turned into worms and took a step to the side, away from him. Stupidly, I looked at Sharon. Her smile was small but incredibly smug.

I shot her a glare.

Eli was making arrangements for the cremation with Yolanda, so he paid me, letting go of his hand no mind at all. But I could still feel the warmth and comfort of his palm in mine. Like a brand but not at all painful.

A few minutes later, Eli finished up with Yolanda, and we said our goodbyes.

He was completely oblivious to the knowing smirks of the other two women, but I wasn't.

I made sure he was outside before me, then poked my head back into the door. "Knock it off."

Sharon smiled wider. Yolanda started to laugh.

"It's not like that."

"Sure, it's not," Sharon said innocently. "And that ring on your finger came out of a gumball machine."

With a growl, I closed the door and stepped back into the empty parking lot. The morning air was still cool, but there was no breeze, and the clear sky and glow to the horizon said it was going to be a hot day ahead.

I hit the fob, and Eli and I climbed into the SUV.

"Need a minute?" he asked softly.

I shook my head. "No."

But I took a minute anyway.

"Thank you for coming with me," I said.

"Thank you for letting me come." I felt the weight of his words and all the meaning behind them. He was thanking me for Jill, for the road trip, the engagement, insurance. All of it. And I felt his sincerity.

I tipped my eyes up to his. "Ready to go?"

His smile was only half-cocked, but it was sweet and real. "Let's get this show on the road."

CHAPTER SIXTEEN

Eli

WE DROVE FOR THE first couple of hours in silence. It wasn't an awkward silence though, more a silence of reflection. A silence of respect for the recently departed Jill.

I didn't know the little dog for long, but I'd fallen in love with her instantly.

Alex hadn't asked me how I started or why I started volunteering at the shelter, but if she did, I would be honest. I'd say I stalked the shit out of her on social media, saw that she volunteered at the shelter and decided to do it, too.

But she hadn't asked, so I wasn't going to volunteer that information.

The sun was climbing in the sky, and even though we were comfortable in our air-conditioned rental vehicle, it was easy enough to see the heat already starting to have an effect on the day.

Thankfully, we were driving west, so the sun would be chasing us.

Since where we lived in Maine wasn't too far from New Hampshire, we were passing through New Hampshire before lunchtime.

Alex decided that we'd take the more southern route to bypass the Canadian border and the Great Lakes, then make our way north and take the northern route the rest of the way.

I said that I was just the arm candy and along for the ride. She was the captain. That'd gotten a snort and a smile out of her.

"Let me know when you see a sign for a gas station," she said, breaking the silence after nearly two and a half hours.

"Yes, ma'am."

"And any attractions that pique your interest."

"You got it."

She glanced at me out of the corner of her eye.

"Can I help you with something?"

"Did you cut your hair?"

I grinned. "I didn't, but a barber did. I tend to leave these kinds of things up to the professionals, you know? Got him to trim my beard, too, though I'll probably see if the hotel has a barber to tidy things up again before the wedding."

Her eyes rolled.

Unease wormed through me like creepy tentacles. "Do you like it?"

She was quiet for a moment, which of course just made more tentacles begin to coil and twist. "Yeah, it looks good."

Phew.

"But I also liked that little floppy curl thing you had that fell over your forehead."

I smiled. "Yeah?"

She shrugged. "I mean, it was unruly and made you look like you'd just rolled out of bed—"

"Doing wondrously filthy and fun things, right?"

Her eyes became thin slits. "I didn't say that."

"I just finished your sentence for you."

"You presumptuously assumed I was going to say something that I was in fact *not* going to say."

"Gas station!" I pointed to the right up ahead.

She swerved, then righted the vehicle, but not before a car behind us honked.

"What the hell?" she said, looking at me like I'd just told her that I invented the color blue.

"You told me to tell you when I saw a sign for a gas station."

"Yeah, but you didn't have to yell it at me like it was a dead deer in the middle of the road and I was about to hit it."

She put on her indicator, switched lanes, and pulled into the gas station, giving me a glare the entire time.

Once she pulled up to a pump, I climbed out. So did she.

"I'll pump my own gas, thank you," she said snidely.

"Wasn't going to offer. I'm going to get snacks. You want anything?"

Still glaring at me, she shook her head.

With a shrug, I jogged toward the convenience store.

By the time I returned to the rental, she was back sitting behind the steering wheel. My arms were loaded with bags of food.

"Road trip food," I said, plunking my butt back down in the passenger seat.

She glanced over at me and what I had in my hands, then made a disgusted face.

"What?" I asked, offended by such a look.

"Doritos? Cheetos? Fritos? What, no Funyuns?"

With a big grin, I reached under my arm and held up a bag of Funyuns. "No, they're right here. Your favorite? You want them?"

She blanched. "No. Gross."

I rolled my eyes, pivoted and put all the junk food behind my seat, except for the Funyuns. "You can't tell me you eat avocado, salad, nuts, and chicken every day all day. Live a little. We're on a road trip. And what is supposed to be a *romantic* road trip. And I'm the kind of guy who doesn't care what his woman eats so long as she's happy."

She reached into the center console between us and pulled out a bag of trail mix. However, this bag didn't appear to have any M&Ms or chocolate chips in it.

I made my own disgusted face. "Bird food."

She opened the bag, shook some out onto her hand, then tipped the mound into her mouth.

Defiantly, while still maintaining eye contact with her, I opened the bag of Funyuns, mimicked her actions and shook some out onto my hand, then tipped my hand up and shoved the pile into my mouth.

I may have flown a bit too close to the sun on this one, though, and overestimated how much my mouth could handle. I stared at her, my cheeks inflated like a chipmunk as I struggled to chew, moisten and navigate my tongue around all the crunchy onion-flavored goodness in my mouth.

The corner of her mouth jiggled upward slightly. Then she rolled her eyes, turned over the ignition and vacated the gas station.

I swallowed down the globular mass in my mouth and reached for my water bottle from the cupholder. "Are we powering through New Hampshire straight on to Vermont?"

"I figured we would, yes. I would like to hike The Long Trail on Mount Mansfield. I think we could get some good pictures up there. I've found a hotel outside of Burlington that has vacancies."

"Okay. That sounds like a plan."

"Yes."

What the fuck was up her ass now?

The woman wasn't even hot and cold; she was scalding or frigid. I'd only gotten some lukewarm temperatures a handful of times. The rest she was either wanting to freeze my nuts off or burn them.

"What have I done now?" I asked, not sure I could bear ten days of this. We'd only been on the road for a few hours, and the respectful silence we had over the loss of Jill was now silence fraught with tension and the cold shoulder.

"Nothing."

"For fuck's sake, Alex. Don't be one of those women. I didn't *think* you were one of those women."

"What kind of woman are you referring to?"

"The 'it's fine' or 'it's nothing' kind of woman, meanwhile inside you're plotting the best way to kill me and get away with it. Just fucking tell me. I'm not a mind-reader. I'm not a head-game player. If I've done something, I deserve the right to either make it right or defend myself."

It looked like she was struggling to keep the words in. Her jaw was clenched, her lips pinned tight.

"Just spit it out."

A muscle in her jaw pulsed.

"Tell me now, Alexandra." I kept my voice calm but put that authoritative edge to it that she seemed to respond to.

"Why did you hold my hand?" she blurted out.

What?

"Huh?"

"When we were with Jill, why did you hold my hand?"

Oh my fucking God, was that what this was all about?

"Because you were sad and it felt like the kind and nice thing to do. I was also hurting—*am* also hurting—and I thought it was a moment where we could comfort each other. You squeezed my fingers back, you know. And held onto them as we went to speak with Yolanda and Sharon."

"I ... I forgot that we were holding hands. I was too consumed by grief."

Riiiiight.

"I see you're wearing the ring."

"I didn't want to forget it at home."

Riiiiight.

"Don't hold my hand again."

I held up my hands in surrender. "Don't have to worry about that. I will not. Not even if you're about to fall over the edge of a cliff, I will not reach for your hand. Even if you're drunk off your ass and stumbling around in four-inch heels, I will not take your hand. Even if you need emergency dental surgery because you spontaneously grow another set of wisdom teeth in the next ten days, I will not take your hand. I will allow your heavily medicated ass to make your own way from the surgeon to the hotel. You're on your own, sweetheart." I crossed my fingers over my chest. "Cross my heart."

"You're an ass." Her lip twitched. She was trying not to smile.

"And you're grieving, so I'm going to let this bitch switch you just flipped stay on for a little longer, but once we reach our destination in Vermont, I'd appreciate it if you turned it off for a bit. I'm not the enemy, Alex. I'm trying here."

"I know," she whispered. "I'm sorry."

We drove another two and half hours in silence. No music, no chit-chat, but the tension wasn't there either.

She was thinking. I was thinking.

However, I highly doubted that we were thinking about the same things.

I doubted she was thinking about how much she liked holding my hand. Or how nice it was to have someone else there with her to say goodbye to Jill.

Or how since moving to Maine, she hadn't found anybody to really connect with and spend time with or banter with like this and didn't realize until now how much she missed having a friend.

She was probably thinking about how badly she wanted to leave me at the next gas station.

Not how much she wanted to take my hand again and drive in companionable silence with our fingers intertwined.

She probably wasn't thinking about any of those things.

Neither was I.

Alexandra did tell me to pack hiking boots, so I dug around in all my travel gear and brought out the boots that had taken me all around the world.

I hiked Machu Picchu in these babies. Put sole to the ground on the Appalachian trail, and made it to the top of Mount Kilimanjaro. These boots had seen it all, trod on the same dirt as the Incas, and had more beer spilled on them in Vietnamese streetside bars than any pair of shoes ever should.

We reached the trailhead around one thirty, having stopped and grabbed lunch at a food truck in the center of town.

Alexandra wasn't nearly as frosty toward me as she had been, but I could tell that her bitch switch wasn't fully off yet, either.

Like me, she chose to drive in comfortable clothing, which ended up being very similar to her yoga attire. Tight, ass-hugging capris—this time in a navy-blue color—and her sports bra was covered by a loose-fitting gray tank top thing that twisted in the back but otherwise had no back and showed off her tattoo very nicely.

I wore khaki-colored linen shorts and a white T-shirt. Once we switched footgear, we headed out onto the trail.

"Says here that it's a steady two-point-three-mile climb to the top. We'll cross route 108," I said, reading about The Long Trail on my phone.

She nodded. "Yeah, I know. I googled it all last night."

She was ahead of me, and I didn't mind it one bit. I could stare at that ass all day.

But I was trying to be a gentleman here, and she was clearly not developing disconcerting feelings for me the way I was for her, so I jogged to catch up with her.

We passed a few people coming down in the opposite direction.

The sun was high overhead and very hot. In no time, I was a sweaty mess, and my shirt was becoming rather see-through.

We were nearly at the top when Alexandra stopped and tugged her tank top off over her head. She handed me her water bottle. "Here. You look like you're about to die."

I took it from her and said "Thanks" cynically. "How long did it take to get your tattoo?" I asked, squirting water into my mouth.

"About ten hours. I went in two stints."

"Where'd you get it done?"

"A place in Baltimore. Guy books out like a year in advance. But I love his work, so it was worth the trek and the money."

"It's really nice."

She contorted her body in such a way so she could sort of look over her shoulder. "Thanks."

I handed her back her water bottle, and she squirted some into her mouth. The sun caught her in such a way that when she dropped her head back down, the rays shone into her eyes, making them glow. Her face was illuminated, and her skin glistened with perspiration.

She was honestly, painfully, the most beautiful woman I'd ever seen.

"Ready to keep going?" she asked, not waiting for my answer but moving forward, her thick ponytail of dark, almost black chunks, mixed with fire-engine-red streaks, swishing behind her.

Once again, I jogged to catch up.

We reached the summit, and although the walk along the ridge had lent us an incredible view, the summit did so even more.

"Wow!" she said, standing at the highest point with her hands on her hips. "This is beautiful."

"Yeah," I said quietly, even though I was looking at her.

"Shall we get a picture of our super sweaty faces?"

"If that's what you would like."

She brought her phone out of the pocket on her leggings and showed the scenic view below her back. I sidled up beside her and looked into the camera part of her phone.

We both smiled. *Click.*

"That's crap," she said. "It's so fake."

"Because it *is?*" I replied.

She grumbled. "Let's try again. You hold it this time. Your arms are longer."

"Yes, ma'am." I took her phone, held it out in front of us, and we both looked at it and smiled.

Click.

"Better," she said with disappointment.

"Here, let's try again."

She nodded, got into position, and at the last second, I turned my head, closed my eyes, and kissed her cheek. *Click.*

Then I was shoved to the side—thankfully not off the damn top of the mountain.

"What the hell was that?"

After I regained my footing, I looked up at the crazy person who was also my fiancée. "I was making it look realistic."

"The fuck you were."

I rolled my eyes, glanced at her phone and the REALLY GOOD FUCKING PICTURE, then held it toward her. "Look for yourself, you psycho."

She stalked toward me, a big angry storm cloud, and snatched her phone from my hand. She looked down at the picture.

I waited.

Her expression softened.

The gray clouds turned white and fluffy. "This is better," she said, reluctance evident in her tone.

The clouds disappeared altogether, and the sun came out. She smiled and lifted her gaze to mine. "Sorry."

"It's okay. Just try not to shove me when we're on the edge of a cliff, okay?" I looked down below, then took a cautious step back. "I won't look nearly as good in my suit all beat to shit from tumbling down a mountain. Would look even worse pasty, dead and smelling like embalming fluid."

She snorted, rolled her eyes, then graced me with another smile. "Consent, buddy."

Grinning, I nodded. "Consent is key."

We milled around the top of the mountain for another twenty minutes, then made our way back down. By the time we got back to the vehicle, it was nearly four o'clock.

"We can check into the hotel now," she said as she filled up her water bottle from the ten-gallon jug of water in the hatch. "Should we head there and shower?"

"Sure. Where did you book the hotel?"

"In Burlington. But I thought we could quickly drive to Barre, which is home to the world's largest zipper. You know, social media photo fodder and all that crap."

"The world's largest zipper?" I scratched my head. "Why is that a thing?"

"Why do people grow their fingernails into twirls that resemble three-feet-long rotini noodles? For the fame, of course."

I shrugged and climbed into the passenger seat as she climbed into the driver's seat. "Fair enough." I pointed dramatically toward the windshield. "Onward to Barre, then, and the world's largest zipper."

She chuckled and turned over the ignition. "Onward."

I brought up my phone and typed in "things to do in Vermont."

"In Waterbury, which is kind of on the way to Barre, there is the Ben & Jerry's Flavor Graveyard. Might I suggest a detour? I see you have a cooler in the back with ice packs. I bet we could buy some dessert."

Her eyes gleamed, and when she turned to face me, the most genuine, excited and beautiful smile glowed back at me. "I love that idea."

CHAPTER SEVENTEEN

Alex

OVER THE COURSE OF the day I loosened up a bit and finally started to relax. Or, as Eli had put it, I'd flipped off my bitch switch.

I could have let him have it for calling me a bitch, but the reality of it was, I was being a bitch.

The man was just infuriating.

And yet he wasn't.

That was the thing.

I was just angry because the man I thought I knew, the man I expected him to be because that was who I'd known for practically my entire life, was not the man I was driving across the country with or sat on a bench outside the Ben & Jerry's store swapping pints of Americone Dream and Karamel Sutra Core with.

Eli was a nice guy.

A really nice guy.

And I was crazy-attracted to him and it scared the crap out of me, because I couldn't tell if he was attracted to me, too, or simply putting on an Oscar-worthy performance as my boyfriend slash fiancé.

"Swap?" he asked as we sat on a bench outside the Ben & Jerry's Flavor Graveyard with our ice cream pints and plastic spoons.

I nodded and handed back the Americone Dream while accepting the Karamel Sutra Core.

Scooping some of the soft caramel onto my spoon, I shoveled it into my mouth and hummed in delight.

"That's exactly the noise you're supposed to make when you're doing the Karamel Sutra," he said, pulling the spoon free from his mouth. "Maybe a little more panting. And some heavy gasping. Maybe an *oh God, yes.*"

I rolled my eyes. "Is that why you picked this flavor, so you could make the jokes?"

"Absolutely. My favorite is actually Chocolate Peanut Butter Split, but I couldn't think how I could work in dirty jokes with that one, so I went with the obvious flavor." He bobbed his brows at me and smiled. "Now don't forget to stick your leg behind your head when you eat that next bite. That's the Karamel Sutra way, you know."

Feeling cheeky, I got up from the bench and went over to the grass, where I sat down, lifted my leg behind my neck, left it there, then proceeded to pick up the pint and spoon again and take another bite. "You mean like this?"

His mouth gaped and his eyes grew wide.

I smirked.

It took him a moment to regain his composure, but eventually, he did. Then he sniffed, sat back and put another spoonful into his mouth. "Give me five more classes and I'll be doing that, too. You make it look harder than I'm sure it is."

Laughing, I slowly lifted my leg and got out of the posture, then stood up and rejoined him on the bench. "I have no doubt." Without saying anything, we swapped pints again.

He dug into the Karamel Sutra. "Oh God, yes. Just like that. Yeah, baby. Just like that. Good girl. Daddy likey."

My spoon hung in midair, and my head snapped around to look at him.

That stupidly sexy smile was back. "What? I can't do the Karamel Sutra poses yet, but I can make the appropriate noises."

That *good girl* comment had my body on fire. Good thing I had ice cream to cool it down.

I'd never been interested in being called a *good girl* in bed, but hearing it now from Eli, even when he was just joking around with ice cream, had me craving to hear it from his lips as I wrapped my lips around—

"Ready to go?"

Shaking the thoughts of insanity from my head—because I'd have to be insane to go there—I nodded and stood up.

He finished the Karamel Sutra and I finished the Americone Dream, then we tossed them into the trash can.

After visiting the Ben & Jerry's Flavor Graveyard and mourning the loss of great flavors from our past, like Dublin Mudslide and Turtle Soup, we quickly drove to Barre to see the world's biggest zipper.

Turns out, the world's biggest zipper wasn't actually a functioning zipper at all but rather a concrete art piece between two buildings. Regardless, we did the tourist thing and got a picture in front of it. Eli took one of me standing at the bottom of it, then I took one of him, and then we did the iconic scrunch selfie as we had on the top of the mountain and both got into the shot.

Then it was a little over an hour to Burlington.

Thankfully, the hotel had two rooms vacant. They were right next door to each other and had an adjoining door. Whatever, we didn't have to use the cheater door.

After we showered off the sweat from the day and got dressed, we reconvened outside our rooms in the hallway and headed into town.

Church Street in Burlington was known for its Italian piazza vibe at night. And I had to admit that I got that vibe, too. Not that I'd been to Italy, but apparently Eli had, and he said it gave him the same sort of feel.

We strolled through the four-block marketplace taking in the local vendors, entertainers and different restaurants. Despite having eaten an entire pint of ice cream, my stomach rumbled.

"I heard that," Eli said with a grin. "There's a bear in there. We need to feed it before it flips the hangry switch."

Smirking, I shook my head and rolled my eyes. "It's a very sensitive switch."

"Yeah ... are all your switches that easy to flip?"

What was he getting at now?

"Could *Cade the cad* fuh-lip your switch?" He over-enunciated the word *flip* and made a little *pop* sound with his mouth when he articulated the *p*. And for some really stupid reason, it made my insides clench.

This conversation had taken a quick hairpin turn.

I swallowed, then pointed. "Hey, it's a tasting room. Want to get a flight of beer? Says they have food." I needed to distract him—and me—and get us onto a much less dangerous path.

His amused smirk said he knew exactly what I was doing. But he didn't press, just nodded, grabbed my hand, and tugged me into the taphouse.

At first, I was pissed he grabbed my hand and was about to wrench free of his grasp, but he released it before I could get mad, smiling brightly at me as we slid into opposite sides of a booth. "They advertised yam fries and deep-fried pickles on the sandwich board outside. I think this place decided for us that we needed to come here."

"As long as the yam fries come with chipotle mayo."

His eyes glimmered. "Oh, they better."

I took pictures of him sitting behind his flight of five beers. Each glass, going from left to right, held a slightly darker beer, until the last one, a stout, was nearly black and opaque.

We were slightly buzzed and laughing our asses off by the time we stumbled back to the hotel sometime around eleven.

Luckily, we were staying at Burlington Garden Inn, which was only a block from Church Street, so we just walked home after dinner and many drinks.

I fumbled in my purse for my key card. "Oh God!"

"What?" His worried expression was exaggerated, just like my exclamation.

"I can't find my card."

"Oh no!"

We stared at each other for a moment, mirror images of panic, then we both burst out laughing.

"But seriously. I'm going to have to go sleep in the garden if I can't find my key card."

"The concierge is open downstairs, you weirdo."

"Yeah ... but I don't want to bother them."

I kept searching in my purse but couldn't find the card.

"Can you just like ... run and then kick it down?"

"Who do you think I am, woman? Jackie Chan?"

"No," I said with a pout. "He's a better actor."

A warm hand fell to my hip, and he turned me around, then something slid from my pocket along the cheek of my ass. "You mean this card, you drunk nut?"

I exhaled in relief. "Yeah. Thanks."

He shook his head and chuckled. "Bit of a lightweight, huh?"

"Not always ..." My eyes drifted down to where his hand still rested on my hip. I was wearing dark blue jeans, a cute gray crop top, and my leather jacket. I'd only just put on my jacket on the walk back when the breeze picked up, but otherwise, I'd kept it off, since the night air had been warm.

But his skin was touching mine and sending small electric pulses through my entire body.

Swallowing, I stepped forward, dislodging his hand from my hip, and waved the key card in front of the security panel. The light flashed green and it clicked.

I turned the handle, then faced him.

"What time do you want to get on the road tomorrow?" he asked. Something was passing behind his eyes that I couldn't place. Disappointment?

"I dunno ... like eight? It's just over four hours to Camillus, then almost three from Camillus to Niagara."

He nodded. "Sounds good. I'll meet you right here at eight."

We stood there for a moment, awkwardly staring at each other.

My gaze fell to his lips.

The man had nice lips.

The man had nice everything.

That's when I realized that he was staring at my mouth, too. And when I also realized that I was licking my damn lips.

Dear, God! What was wrong with me?

"Have a good night," I said quickly, opening the door, dashing inside and closing it, only to plaster my back against the hard wood, my chest for some reason lifting and falling as if I'd just run up six flights of stairs.

His door opened, then closed.

Squeezing my eyes shut, I shook my head back and forth. "Bad idea. Bad idea. Bad, bad, bad idea."

My head was kind of spinning. I wasn't normally this much of a lightweight. It had to be the heat.

I needed some water.

I also needed to brush my teeth.

I took another thirty seconds to just stand there, with the door propping me up, to let my senses and body find some balance again, then I turned on a few lights as I made my way to the bathroom. I filled up the drinking glass in the bathroom sink six times and chugged before my head finally started to clear.

I hadn't bothered with makeup, just a little lip gloss, so I just did a quick splash of water on my face before I reached for my toothbrush and toothpaste from my toiletries bag.

Where was my toothpaste?

Don't tell me I forgot to pack toothpaste.

You forgot to pack toothpaste.

Mother ducker.

Like an idiot, I checked my back pocket, since my key card had been there, so maybe I'd put my toothpaste back there, too. I was definitely drunk. And my toothpaste was not in my pocket.

My mouth tasted like beer and pulled-pork sliders. I couldn't go to bed with this on my tongue. I also didn't want to bother the people at the desk downstairs.

Did I knock on his door and ask to borrow his toothpaste?

Your parents spent good money on braces, and you've never had a cavity. Don't let your pride ruin your hygiene habits now.

The voice in my head was a confusing bitch.

With a grumble, I took my toothbrush to the door that connected our rooms, lifted my fist and, with a deep breath, knocked.

I held my breath.

I couldn't hear footsteps or anything on the other side.

Had he already fallen asleep?

I knocked again, then waited.

Still nothing.

I was about to walk back to the bathroom when the door swung open. "Everything okay?"

My mouth dropped open.

He was in black boxer briefs AND NOTHING ELSE.

I swallowed. "I ... I, um ... I forgot toothpaste."

Nodding, he left the door open and walked into his room and to the bathroom, returning a second later with the tube.

Determined to look anywhere BUT the front of his thighs, or his stomach, or really anywhere that was the very sexy Eli Evans, I focused on squeezing the toothpaste on the tube as if I was defusing a bomb with only seconds to spare.

Looking beyond him into his room, I handed him back the toothpaste. "Thank you."

"Hold on to it. I just squeezed some into a glass, so I'll be good for morning, then you can buy some."

"O-okay." I nodded. "Thanks."

"That everything?"

I nodded again, still refusing to look at his body or his face. I couldn't. I was sure my cheeks were the color of a cherry tomato.

"Have a good night, Alex," he said, his voice almost a purr.

I swallowed, nodded for the third time—or maybe it was the same initial nod and my head just hadn't stopped moving. I didn't know for sure. Then he closed the door but didn't engage the lock.

My breathing was back to that just-sprinted-up-the-stairs panting.

I needed to fix this.

I needed to have some sense knocked into me.

Right there, in front of the adjoining door, I stripped down to nothing, then stalked into the bathroom, set my toothbrush down on the vanity before I turned on the faucet for the shower. I deliberately didn't turn it on to warm. Because the thoughts I was having at the moment needed to cool the fuck down.

I jumped in under the freezing spray and screamed.

Then there were some weird shuffling noises, the sound of a door and heavy, quick footsteps, and the curtain was being pulled open. "You okay?"

It was Eli. And he was standing there with a pure look of panic on his face.

And I was naked.

"Sorry!" He quickly averted his eyes. "I heard you scream. Thought you fell. Sorry. Sorry."

Mortified, I pulled the curtain back in place. "The water was cold," I said. "I—I wasn't expecting it to be cold."

And yet, I was. Because I was trying to bring down the temperature of my rampant, steamy thoughts about Mr. Black Boxer Briefs, the scream came out regardless.

I buried my face in my palms. "I'm okay. Thank you."

"I'm gonna go."

"Yup. Thanks. Have a good night."

"You, too."

I reached out and adjusted the temperature of the water to NOT that preferred by a penguin, then stood there under the spray until my toes and fingers were prunes and not a single hot, sexy thought about Eli had vanished down the drain, as hard as I tried to wash them away.

I fell into bed, far less drunk than when I'd arrived at the hotel but still with a very muddled and murky mind. I needed to set some clearer boundaries with Eli if I was to avoid doing what my libido and clitoris were telling me to do. Which was to throw myself at him and fuck him as well as the consequences of such actions.

But there would be none of that.

I was going to stay sober from now on.

There would be no more hand-holding, no more kissing me on the cheek.

This was a business transaction, nothing more.

I turned over onto my side and held my left hand out in front of me to look at the ring. My right hand caressed my cheek on the spot where his lips had been. I didn't have to think very hard to remember what even that innocent kiss felt like.

A beautiful buzz. A heated caress. A promise of so much more.

Closing my eyes, I went back to that moment on the mountain, then I took it a step further, and a step further, until my left hand, the one with the engagement ring on it, traveled down my body and beneath my pajama shorts.

I needed the release to fall asleep, and try as I might, I couldn't conjure anyone else for my fantasy but Eli.

Which made me realize that there wasn't anybody else I wanted to be with but Eli.

Fuck.

CHAPTER EIGHTEEN

Eli

I WOKE UP RIGHT before six the next morning, rubbed one out to the image of a wet, naked Alexandra in the shower, because how the fuck could I not? Then I made myself a hotel room coffee and took it out onto the deck to enjoy the rising sun.

I brought my tablet outside with me and did a bit of sketching, too.

At first, I hadn't heard her knock on the adjoining door. I'd thought the knock was elsewhere in the hotel, and I'd been washing my face in the bathroom. But then I realized it was her and didn't have a chance to put on anything else. Not that I was naked when I answered the door, but I could tell my lack of clothing made her uncomfortable.

Like an asshole, however, I'd enjoyed watching her squirm and look anywhere but my face or body. Her cheeks grew pink, and the flush traveled down her neck and chest.

Then, when she screamed, I truly thought she'd fallen in the shower since I heard the water engage, so I rushed to help.

Only the drunk nut hadn't fallen. She'd just stepped into cold water and decided to scream at eleven at night.

I shook my head and chuckled. At least she'd loosened up over time yesterday. Had turned off her bitch switch so our time together wasn't being strangled with tension and anger.

Though, in all honesty, the tension was still there. It was just a different kind of tension. The kind of tension that I felt in my pants.

After about thirty minutes of drawing, the call of writing and a specific scene popped into my head, so I switched to my writing program and began to type.

The sliding sound of the glass deck door for Alexandra's unit carried over to where I was, and I froze.

A small lattice partition was our only offer of privacy.

Keeping still, I watched her out of the corner of my eye. She unfurled a yoga mat, did some stretches, then turned toward the rising sun for a sun salutation. She went through probably fifteen poses, doing the ujjayi breathing and even binding.

At some point, I abandoned the creepy side-eye I was watching her with and just turned to watch her.

Even though I'd watched her several times now in yoga class, I was no less impressed now. And the fact that she was only in a pair of underwear and a sports bra was a little different than the leggings and sports bra she usually wore. Her underwear didn't cover her ass at all, and when she lifted her leg, I could see through her sheer panties.

Though I knew after last night that she had a landing strip and nothing else.

That was fucking hot.

Her moves were graceful and flowing. When she was in practice, she was at peace, unlike the rest of the time, when her shoulders seemed full of stress. Her body was on constant edge.

I wasn't sure if she knew I was there, but I didn't make a move or a sound just in case she didn't. The last thing I wanted to do was disrupt her. Besides, watching her was like watching a flower bloom. Plus, she had a rocking ass, and when she bent down into downward dog and pointed those two bare peach halves my way, what happened in my pants was beyond my control and not something I wanted to stop.

She ended her practice with a final sun salutation, then leaned over the railing with her forearms on top and gazed off into the distance.

Maybe it was the way the sun was hitting her, combined with the shadows from the deck above, but right there, at that very moment, I didn't hate the idea that Alexandra and I were going to be married. That for all intents and purposes she was going to be my wife.

How fucked up is that?

Less than a month ago, I hadn't given the woman an ounce of my energy. I hadn't thought about her in eight years. Then I see her through a diner window and am compelled to follow her. To learn everything I could about her.

And even then, I clung to the belief that she was evil, and I vowed to take her down a peg for the havoc she'd caused in my life over the years.

Now I was engaged to her, and the idea of waking up next to her every day for the rest of my life didn't sound like something I'd choose being quartered and drawn over anymore. Because I was pretty sure if you'd asked me back when we were seventeen if I'd rather marry Alexandra Hartford or be quartered and drawn, I'd have picked the latter.

Now, not so much.

She wasn't the heartless, soulless bitch I'd convinced myself that she was. The way Jill's death affected her proved that she had a heart—and a big one. It was like I was finally getting to see the real Alexandra Hartford. Or at least, I was seeing her out from behind the veil of hatred I'd thrown over her for all those years.

She turned around to head back inside and paused. "How long have you been there?" The embarrassment was clear in her voice.

"Since before you came out."

"And you didn't feel like saying anything?"

"Didn't want to ruin your chi. Besides, I've watched you do yoga loads of times."

"Not in my underwear."

"True. But after last night, I didn't think that mattered."

She growled.

"Who screams like that when they get into the shower?"

"Somebody who has had too much to drink and didn't turn on the hot water. That's who."

"Well, I thought your drunk ass fell in the tub and perhaps you cracked your head open. Forgive me for trying to be a gentleman."

The funny thing was, despite the fact that we were bickering, there was no venom in either of our tones. I could tell she was smiling as she spoke, and so was I. We were bantering, not bickering, and it was refreshing.

"Well, next time, if you hear me scream, just leave me to bleed out, okay?"

"Can do."

"Much appreciated."

"You about ready to hit the dusty trail?"

"Sure am, grandpa. Who the hell says *dusty trail* anymore?"

"Grandpas, I'm sure. I look forward to being one, one day, and getting to use such lines authentically."

She chuckled. "Meet you in the hallway in thirty?" She turned to head inside.

"You know it. Though, Alex?"

"Hmm?"

"Maybe put some more clothes on, hmm?"

"You're an ass." But the smile was in her voice, and that was what mattered.

We grabbed breakfast to go in Burlington, then got back on the highway and continued west. Our rough plan was to stop in Camillus and go to the hot sauce tasting place, then on to Niagara Falls and make our way to Erie for the night.

Although she was much friendlier and chattier than the day before, I could tell that Alexandra had erected a wall around herself and she was determined not to let me in. She would not let me penetrate that wall. HA!

"Do you even like spicy food?" she asked me as we climbed out of the rental in the parking lot for the hot sauce tasting room.

"Fucking love it," I replied. "Anything spicy I could get my hands on when I was traveling, I tried it. The hotter the better. Of course, I pay dearly for it later, but it's worth it in the beginning." I held the door open for her. "It's kind of like unprotected sex. Feels so good when it's happening. The risk seems to outweigh the consequences, but then the next day when your balls start to itch and it hurts when you pee, you realize maybe you shouldn't have had the chef add that second ghost pepper."

"Your metaphors are terrifyingly mixed here," she said with a snort. "Has it ever burned when you peed?"

I shook my head. "No. Never. I always wrap it up, but I know people who have not and felt the burn later."

She shook her head, still smiling. We paid for our tasting fee, then took a seat with two other couples at a big, long table. One of the staff brought us a tasting journal so we could record the flavor profiles of their hot sauces.

Thankfully, they started off mild with jalapenos and serranos, then we worked our way up to the cayennes, habaneros and ghost peppers.

After that last ghost pepper, I glanced over at Alex. She was flush and had tears in her eyes.

"How you doing?"

Her chest heaved. "This is a lot."

Yeah, it was. My throat burned, and my tongue was asking me, "Why?"

"Next, we have the one million scoville"—the scale used to rate the heat levels of peppers—"ginger reaper sauce made with the Carolina reaper pepper," said the woman who was running our tasting. "Who wants to give it a go?"

I glanced at Alexandra. Her eyes turned fierce. Determined. She nodded.

I smiled and nodded, then looked up at our tasting host. "We'll do it."

We were trying each sauce on chicken wings, but there were also cheeses, veggies, and crackers on the platter. Alexandra and I each took a couple of pieces of cheese to help temper our palates.

They also offered craft beer, but since it was the middle of the day and this was just a stopover for us, we didn't drink. We still had to go to Niagara Falls and then get to Erie.

The woman poured a dollop of the one million scoville sauce into a divot on our tasting tray. I picked up a chicken wing. Alexandra picked up a chicken wing.

We dipped.

I held my chicken wing out toward her, and without me having to prompt her, she knew what to do and knocked her wing against mine in a "cheers," then, with our eyes locked, we took bites.

Holy fucking red flames of hell.

It was like someone had literally poured gas on my tongue, then struck a match.

My nose was stuffed, tears streamed down my cheeks, and I had this uncontrollable urge to cough, but my throat was too tight to let me do it.

I was going to die.

I glanced over at Alexandra, and she wasn't doing any better.

Lifting my fist, she bumped hers with mine in solidarity.

At least we wouldn't die alone.

Milk was brought out for us, and we both chugged.

She used the hem of her shirt to wipe her eyes, so I did the same.

The red streaks in her hair were the same shade as her face. *Click.*

I dropped the hem of my shirt from wiping my eyes to find her, looking like a gorgeous mess, with her phone out. Then she leaned in toward me. I leaned in toward her, and like idiots who would be living on the toilet tomorrow, we smiled into the camera.

Click.

"You guys are too cute," the woman from the tasting room said.

"I think I should kiss your cheek," I whispered, turning my face and speaking into her ear. I felt her shiver beside me.

But she nodded.

"Here, why don't I take one for you," the woman said.

Alexandra nodded and handed her the phone.

We got close. I wrapped my arms around her, my mouth and lips still on absolute fire, and kissed her cheek.

Click.

Click.

"These are great," the woman said. "I can tell how much you're in love." She pointed to Alexandra's ring. "And engaged, too. Congrats."

We both murmured a thank-you and drank more milk.

In addition to the tasting, they also played trivia games for prizes. Alexandra and I got pretty competitive with that and were tied for first until she answered the last question wrong, and I stole the lead with the right answer.

"What sauce are you choosing?" Alexandra asked after we'd cleaned ourselves up a bit and were getting ready to leave. Every participant got to pick one bottle of their gourmet sauce as a take-home souvenir.

"Definitely the Ommegang Beer sauce," I said, grabbing a bottle of it off the shelf. "You?"

"Cucumber gin. And I'm going to buy one of their monthly subscriptions for my dad for his birthday. He'll love it."

We left the hot sauce house with full bellies and singed esophagi but for the most part in high spirits.

It was two and half hours from Camillus to Niagara Falls, but we filled that time singing to my super-awesome playlist, complete with some NSYNC, Backstreet Boys and Britney Spears.

In the parking lot for the Niagara Falls boat tour, we filled up our water bottles from the ten-gallon jug in the back, then headed off to go and get super wet by the large volume of falling water.

Much like when we were at the hot sauce tasting place, eager and generous strangers offered to take our picture for us.

I was sure she had loads of social media fodder by now, and we were only on day two.

The boat was as close to the falls as it could get, we were in our blue ponchos, and our faces and heads were drenched.

She looked beautiful.

Looking out over the railing, I was reminded of that scene in *The Office* where Jim and Pam run off to get married by the boat captain when everything with the church wedding begins to go awry. How cool would it be if I went and waved down the captain and had him marry us right here?

We'd planned to get married in Vegas, but a part of me just didn't want to cheapen it like that, even though this entire thing was supposed to be a sham.

Wherever we got married, we'd need to get a marriage license in that state first.

Resting my hand on her shoulder gently to get her attention, I inhaled deep. She spun to face me, smiling bigger than I'd ever seen and looking so gorgeous. Her hair was stuck to her head, and long, thick chunks clung to her cheeks.

"This is so cool," she yelled, still smiling, her blue eyes twinkling. "I'm so glad we stopped here."

"Me too."

Water droplets hung off her lashes like drops of dew, and the way she was looking up at me had my entire body heating up. If this was anybody but Alexandra, I would swear her eyes were telling me to kiss her. But I couldn't get a read on this woman, and I didn't want to push or do something to undo all the progress we'd made. She'd flipped shit on me yesterday for kissing her on the cheek, so ...

But she let you kiss her on the cheek today with your hot pepper lips.

That was true.

But I didn't want to just kiss her on the cheek. I wanted to kiss her everywhere.

Abandoning the idea of getting married Jim and Pam style, I smiled down at her, then tucked the hair that was stuck to her face behind her ear. She continued to smile and glow and be gorgeous as she looked up at me.

A second later, the spell between us was broken and she turned back to look out into the mist and raging water. I blinked through the water drops and wrapped my hands around the railing in front of me. Because if I didn't do that, I was going to wrap them around her waist, draw her back to my chest, and never let go.

CHAPTER NINETEEN

Alex

WE DROVE FROM NIAGARA Falls to Sandusky, Ohio, arriving at almost midnight and to the only hotel with a vacancy. A one room with twin beds vacancy.

Shit.

I'd tried so damn hard to keep a wall up around myself, blocking out Eli. To set a firm boundary, but the man was making it impossible.

Between him being adorable at the hot sauce tasting to giving me some serious Jim and Pam vibes on the boat at Niagara Falls, I was a more confused and mixed-up mess than ever before. And this time I was sober.

We thought about stopping in Erie, but when it was still light out as we drove through, we decided to press on. Then when we reached Cleveland, we couldn't find a hotel in our price range or up to our standards with a vacancy since there was some gigantic concert going on that had all the hotels full.

So we pressed on.

I'd heard of a food truck in Sandusky, Ohio, run by an Argentinian man and his American wife, so I wanted to try it. All their reviews and the fact that everything was organic, grown in their garden, and their beef was grass-fed and sustainably and humanely raised just added to the appeal. Whether we stayed in Sandusky or not, I planned to find this food truck and eat at it.

We found a hotel last-minute in town, albeit only one room. But it had two beds, so thank God.

I could just hear Sharon cackling as her romance trope predictions began to take shape.

Not quite, Sharon. There might only be one room, but there are two beds, so HA! In your face.

"Do you have the key card?" Eli asked as we approached room number 314.

I pulled it out of my back pocket. "In fact, I do."

"Good, because I haven't done the calf stretches required to Jackie-Chan the door."

Waving the key card in front of the lock, I snorted and shot him some side-eye.

We rolled into the hotel room, dead on our feet after a long but fun day.

He flicked on the light behind me, and I let out a sigh of relief at actually seeing two beds.

If Sharon had her way, there would have been a mistake at the front desk and they would have given us a room with one bed—a double no less—and not the room with the twins like they said.

You strike out again, Sharon!

"Left or right?" Eli asked.

"I'll take the one on the right," I said. "Closer to the bathroom and deck so I won't bother you when I get up to pee or do yoga in the morning."

"I was awake before you were today," he pointed out, plopping his suitcase on the bed on the left. "I also sleep like the dead and never get up to pee in the middle of the night, so you don't have to worry about me."

I didn't say anything but rather opened up my suitcase and went on the hunt for my toiletries bag. "Mind if I shower first?" I asked, the knot in my stomach growing tighter the longer we were together, alone, in a hotel room.

"Go for it. I'm going to step out onto the deck and grab some fresh air."

He walked past me with a smile, but I could see the fatigue in his eyes.

I headed to the shower, using the complimentary hotel shower cap to keep my hair from getting wet, since the heavy mist of Niagara Falls did that for me.

The warm water pummeling my back, no matter how long I stood beneath it, did nothing for the tension in my shoulders. I'd locked the bathroom door at first but then, against my better judgment, unlocked it.

If I fell and knocked my head on the tile, I WOULD want him to barge in and save me, despite my earlier instructions of leaving me to bleed out.

Eventually, I was clean and rosy pink. I still had his toothpaste, so I brushed my teeth, then stepped out into the hotel room.

Eli was still on the sundeck.

"All yours," I called.

"Thanks."

Pretending to pay him no mind, I went about organizing my suitcase, but I was actually keenly aware of when he reentered the room, when he walked behind me with his long-legged stride, and the way his nimble fingers unzipped his suitcase. My lower body clenched at the thought of him unzipping something on me.

I closed my eyes. Dear God, this was going to be impossible.

The bathroom door closed, and I released the shallow breath that had trapped itself in my lungs.

The water engaged, so I quickly finished what I was doing in my suitcase, put it on the floor beside my nightstand, along with my yoga mat, then climbed into bed and shut off my bedside light.

I turned away from his bed and squeezed my eyes closed.

I was still awake when he turned off the shower. Still awake when he brushed his teeth, still awake when he used the toilet. Still awake when he opened the bathroom door, turned off the light, and walked heavy-footed to his bed.

There went my breathing again.

You'd think I didn't do a shit-ton of cardio and breathing exercises every week and I was some two-bit hack with the resting pulse of a hamster.

He put his suitcase on the floor, pulled back the covers and slid beneath them. Then the light went out and we were bathed in darkness.

"Alex?"

I swallowed. "Yeah?"

"Can I join your yoga practice in the morning?"

"Yeah."

"'K, thanks."

"You're welcome."

"Good night."

I sighed. "Good night."

Narrator of one of Sharon's romance books: But it wasn't a good night, for despite her debilitating fatigue, with Eli just feet away, sleeping in probably no more than boxer briefs, Alexandra found sleep to be impossible. Every time she closed her eyes, thoughts of Eli, of him sliding into her bed and treating her like a scoop of Karamel Sutra on a spoon, plagued her. It wasn't until she heard his gentle snoring that she could finally find peace. But then she was at the mercy of her dreams, and those turned out to be even dirtier than her fantasies.

"More. Deeper. Oh, Eli. Yeah, just like that." I bowed my back on the bed, bit my bottom lip, and exploded as Eli's thumb rubbed my clit and his fingers pumped inside me. His mouth found mine and he took what was his without apology, dragging my bottom lip between his teeth. I moaned when he pushed his tongue into my mouth. I sucked it like I would his cock.

I moaned again as the orgasm spooled through me, my mind and body melding together into one euphoric wave of ecstasy.

When the climax began to wane, he broke the kiss and looked down at me, smiling. I blinked up at him, mirroring his smile and marveling at the gold and copper flecks in his eyes.

"You're beautiful."

My cheeks heated. "So are you."

He tucked a strand of wayward hair behind my ear. "What time do you have to be at work?"

I stretched beneath him. "One."

"I'm working on the railroad today. Hauling cows from Madagascar to Detroit."

I blinked at him. "What?"

"Or maybe it's manatees today?"

"Huh?" Unease replaced the warm feelings of bliss that occupied my body.

"Don't you love working at the Ben & Jerry's factory, making new ice cream flavors? You really scored the best job in the world, babe."

I blinked. Then blinked again, then shoved him off me. His fingers slid out of me, but I barely registered the sensation. "What are you talking about?"

He cocked his head. "Your job? Working at Ben & Jerry's. Are you okay?"

With ice in my veins, I sat up in bed and opened my eyes.

And that's when I realized I'd been dreaming.

The hotel room, bathed in the dusty light of dawn outside, was around me. Eli was *not* in my bed.

I glanced over to his bed.

He wasn't there either. But he had been because it was unmade.

Oh my God, I'd been having a sex dream. A sex dream about Eli.

A finger-bang dream.

And it'd been good.

I'd moaned. I'd said stuff.

What all did I say?

Did I say it out loud?

DID HE HEAR ME?

About to lose my fucking mind, I leaped out of bed and went to the drapes that covered the sliding-glass door to the deck. I pulled them aside. The sun hadn't even broken past the horizon yet. Eli wasn't outside. I checked my phone on my nightstand. It was five minutes to six.

Where was he?

I stood in the middle of the room and took deep, calming breaths. I was a yoga instructor, for Christ's sake. I needed to calm my damn breathing.

In through the nose, out through the mouth.

Deep breaths.

Once my pulse no longer thundered in my ears, I could hear more, and what I heard was coming from the bathroom.

We *did* just eat a bunch of hot sauces yesterday. Was he experiencing the ring of fire?

I hesitated to put my ear to the door but then went and did it anyway. Whatever, everybody poops. No need to make a big thing about it.

I sidled up to the door. The light was on.

There was groaning and grunting and a weird, faint, slick sound. That's the only way I could describe it. Like something wet was being rubbed or stroked or ...

I leaped away from the door like it was on fire.

My hands landed on my head, and I began to pace.

Eli was jerking off.

Eli was jerking off in the bathroom.

There was but a door, a piece of wood maybe two inches thick, separating me from a masturbating Eli.

Another grunt.

And I was back beside the door.

What was wrong with me?

This was so hot. Did he wake up from my moaning, get turned on, and need to go jerk off? I should be more embarrassed than I was. But I wasn't. I was turned on.

Standing there leaning against the wall, I slid my hands down my pajama pants and found myself wet.

Well, what do you expect from the dream you just had?

I ran rough circles over my clit, feeling it swell beneath my fingertips.

I could tell by the sounds Eli was making that he was close.

I needed to make this quick.

Closing my eyes, I leaned my head back against the wall, bit my lip, and pictured what was happening on the other side of that door.

I grabbed more wetness from my pussy and returned to my clit.

I went double-time on my clit, and just as I heard Eli coming, I came, too. As if I were back in my dream, the heat in my lower belly exploded outward as my mind and body became one and the pleasure consumed every part of me.

I slouched against the wall until the climax receded, and I heard the toilet flush. The sink ran, and that snapped me out of my post-orgasmic fog.

I scurried back across the room and jumped into bed, pulling the covers over me just as the door opened.

He didn't return to his bed, but he did grab something from his suitcase, then he went to the drapes, pulled them back just a touch, and even though my eyes were closed, I could tell he was looking at me.

I didn't move.

I didn't breathe.

I waited until he opened the deck door, stepped outside, and closed it again.

Then I counted to sixty in my head before I got out of bed and went to wash my hands.

I counted to sixty three more times as I finished up in the bathroom, then went back out into the room to change into yoga pants and a sports bra.

I needed to compose myself.

I could not let him know that I knew he'd gone and jerked off in the bathroom.

I also couldn't let him know that I knew he knew I'd had a sex dream.

A few deep breaths and a little pep talk about the fact that we were two adults, this was all hilarious and natural and I had nothing to be embarrassed about, and I was pulling open the sliding-glass door with my yoga mat under my arm and stepping out onto the deck.

"Morning," he said, not bothering to look at me.

"Good morning." I stepped to the side and unfurled my mat. "Do you still want to join me?" I hedged a glance at him out of the corner of my eye. He was wearing board shorts, not just his boxers. *Phew.*

"If you're okay with that?"

I nodded. "Of course."

Even with the cool morning air, my body was reaching volcanic temperatures.

He was also avoiding eye contact with me.

He slid the deck chairs as far away as possible to give us both enough space.

"You're welcome to share my mat," I said, determined not to let the events of this morning mess with my head any more than they already were.

"Thank you."

He joined me on the mat, and even though we were on opposite ends, we might as well have been elbow to elbow given how much his presence, scent and heat affected me.

"We'll begin with a sun salutation," I said, hating that my voice cracked.

He followed my lead all the way through.

It was a little awkward trying to organize ourselves on opposite ends of the mat for downward dog, but poses like baby cobra, sphinx, child's pose, tree, and warrior were easy. Mind you, when I lifted my head and came face-to-face with Eli, all deep breaths escaped me and my lower body began to tingle.

My hips were tight from all the sitting and driving, so I made frog pose our second to last pose. However, I told him he didn't have to stay in that pose for as long as I planned to since it wasn't an easy one.

He merely grunted and stayed in the pose as long as I did. We finished with an opening pose—camel—then rounded out our practice with a final sun salutation. At that point, the sun was beginning to creep up into the sky, blanketing the dawn with a muted yellow glow.

"Namaste," I said out loud. Though normally, when I practice alone, I just say it in my head.

"Namaste," he repeated.

We turned to face each other, smiling. But just like mine, his smile was small, and he refused to meet my eyes.

"Since we're awake, should we get on the road?" he asked, his voice sounding deeper and more gravelly than normal. Sexier, too.

"Sounds good."

He stepped back so I could enter the hotel first. His heat radiated into my back, and my nipples peaked beneath my sports bra. I sucked in a breath and took larger strides and moved over to my suitcase to create more distance between us.

We worked in silence, getting dressed and gathering our things.

I didn't bother with makeup. I rarely do. So after we brushed our teeth and double-checked we left nothing behind, we were rolling our suitcases back down the hall to the elevator.

The elevator felt mighty small.

Between Eli, myself, our suitcases, and the giant elephant that was our mutual masturbation, the air was stifling, and I could barely move.

When the elevator reached the lobby, I practically lunged out of the car and gasped for fresh oxygen as if I'd just been underwater way too damn long. I also picked up the pace so I was ahead of Eli.

You're going to be in a car with him in half a minute, dumbass.

I ignored the bitchy voice in my head and just kept trucking.

We put our stuff in the hatch of the rental, then we were on the road. He was my navigator as we tried to find the food truck, which was apparently open a few mornings a week for breakfast, and Friday—today—was one of those days.

Eventually, we found them, then got in line.

"So is there anything you want to do while we're here?" he asked after we'd stood in line for ten minutes without speaking.

You mean like get another hotel room and ride your face like it's the damn Tilt-a-Whirl?

I cleared my throat, then shook my head. "I'm good."

"So I say we head to Chicago, hang out there for a day, then drive like crazy through Iowa and Nebraska until we hit Colorado. What do you think?"

I nodded again. "Mhmm."

Dammit. As hard as I tried, the thoughts of this morning were creeping in and affecting how I was with him. Crap.

"Hey." He gently grabbed my elbow. "You okay?"

I nodded and turned away from him. "Yep. Totally fine."

"I'm okay to drive, too. I know you were all '*I'm driving because I don't trust your ass,*' but I'm hoping we're past all that. Aren't we?"

I nodded again and stepped forward with the line, disengaging his hand from my elbow and immediately mourning his touch. Crap. Crap. Crap. "Yep. You want to drive, you can. Sure. Sounds good."

"Alex ..."

I shook my head.

"Alex."

I shook my head again.

"Alexandra, look at me."

I looked at him. What was with this alpha tone he had that made me disobey every feminist bone in my body? I fought the urge to drop to my knees in front of him right then and there.

"What the fuck is going on?"

"Nothing," I said with a hiss.

"Bullshit."

"What can we get you?" the pretty blonde woman with the bicep tattoo asked from inside the truck.

I stepped forward and placed my order. A breakfast empanada with egg, chimichurri and gouda. Eli placed his, too, then we stepped to the side.

I could tell that he was upset that I'd re-erected my walls.

But I wasn't about to tell him, at least not in a line of like thirty people, that I knew he'd heard me having a sex dream, which then prompted him to go jerk off in the bathroom, which then prompted me to jerk off outside the bathroom.

Yeah, no.

So we stood in broody silence as we waited for our order.

Then, when our order was ready, we sat on a bench and ate in more broody silence.

We were in the vehicle and on the road an hour later, broody silence having replaced the nineties playlist we listened to yesterday.

Maybe twenty minutes had passed since we left Sandusky before he abruptly pulled over to the side of the road, threw the vehicle in park, put the hazards on, unbuckled his belt and turned to face me. "What the fuck is up?"

I shook my head and crossed my arms in front of my chest. "Nothing."

"The fuck it is."

I couldn't take the stifling tension—or the flashes of what I thought he might look like as he pleasured himself—out of my head. Not to mention how real my dream had felt until it wasn't. I unbuckled my belt, flung open the door and stalked to the back of the SUV, leaning against the back bumper sucking in fresh air like a madwoman. I needed air that didn't smell like Eli. Air that hadn't passed through his lungs first.

He was slamming his door twenty seconds later, the crunch of gravel under his shoes an angry grate mixed with the zoom of traffic.

"What did I do?" he asked, his voice stern but not altogether unkind.

"You didn't do anything," I said. Which was the truth. Because he didn't. Not anything to offend me anyway.

"Obviously I did because you've been distant with me all morning."

"You haven't done anything, Eli, I swear."

"Then what the fuck is going on?"

I shook my head and crossed my arms over my body again, looking down at my shoes.

He invaded my space, casting a shadow and placing his feet on either side of mine. A knuckle came under my chin, and my breath hitched as my heart began to beat wildly in my chest. "Talk. Now." The last word was said with such an edge, I blanched inside and then immediately melted.

My face was hotter than the surface of the sun.

"You heard me," I finally whispered.

His brows scrunched in confusion for a moment and then understanding quickly dawned in his brown eyes.

Slowly, he nodded.

"And then I heard you."

His eyes widened. "Oh."

CHAPTER TWENTY

Eli

WELL, SHIT.

I hadn't been expecting her to say that.

Yes, I absolutely did hear her.

I sleep like the dead, but when someone is basically having sex next to you, it's not exactly something you can sleep through.

I tried so fucking hard to just lay there and not react. The number of times I woke up with a wet bottom sheet during my teen years was more than I'd care to count. And most mornings, I still woke up with a tent in my drawers after a rather steamy dream. I couldn't say I moaned and groaned the way Alex did, but maybe I did.

I thought I was doing a pretty good job just pretending to be asleep while she and whoever she was with in her dream did their thing. But when she cried out, "Oh, Eli." Well, there wasn't much I could do about the tent in my shorts after that.

It got so bad that I just had to go take care of things. Otherwise, I'd wake her up and ask her if she wanted to turn that dream into a reality, then shit would surely hit the fan.

But I never expected her to wake up and then hear me giving myself the old five-finger squeeze.

How long did she stay to listen?

I stepped out of her space with no idea how to respond.

"Let's just pretend it didn't happen, okay?" she said slowly. "That's what I've been trying to do but obviously failing miserably at it. I'm sorry."

I nodded.

"We're both adults. Sex dreams are completely normal, as is masturbation. We have nothing to be ashamed of."

"Right." I nodded again but only because I had no idea what else to do.

"You heard me moaning or breathing heavy or whatever as I was having a ... *adult relations* dream. And then I woke up from that dream and heard you having ... *adult relations* with yourself in the bathroom. Two perfectly natural things. Right?"

She left out the part where she said my name. She was having sex with ME in that dream. It wasn't just any *adult relations* dream.

"Right," I finally said. "Nothing to be ashamed about. Perfectly natural."

She nodded and attempted to compose herself. "I say we just pretend it didn't happen. I will stop acting weird, and we can just continue on this road trip as if this morning never happened."

Oh, but it did happen, and even though I could try to *pretend* that it didn't, I wasn't about to forget that it did. She'd called out my name during her dream, and that meant something. It had to.

"We'll make sure that the next hotel we stay at has two rooms so I don't wake you up and you are free to ... have adult relations with yourself any hour of the day and with the bathroom door open, if you prefer."

"Can you stop fucking calling it *adult relations?*" I spun on my heel and took four paces away from her. "You called out my name, for Christ's sake." Shit, I hadn't planned on saying that. And by the look on her face, I really fucking shouldn't have.

She went beet-red.

Dammit.

We were so close to getting back to where we were yesterday, *friendly*. And now I went and fucked it all up.

"I ..." she started.

"I'm sorry," I said, stepping back toward her. "I shouldn't have said that. I want to pretend it never happened, as well. I didn't mean to embarrass you. Just forget I even said that."

Her throat bobbed hard, and all I wanted to do at that moment was run my tongue along the delicate line, feeling her pulse, which I was sure was raging.

She sucked in a sharp breath, which made her tits lift high in her black figure-hugging tank top. "I'm sorry that I said your name."

Fuck. Fuck. Fuck.

Back out four paces I went, this time pulling on my hair and growling. But I was back in front of her five seconds later, invading her space, my feet on either side of hers. I tilted her chin up with my finger. "I don't care, and it's not something you *ever* need to apologize for, got it? You can have all the sex dreams about me you want."

Her lips twitched.

I smiled.

She smiled.

Thank fuck.

"We're making progress, you and I," I started. "We're on the road to friendship, or at least I thought we were. I don't want to ruin that. I don't want to backtrack and have you hate me again." I made sure I was looking directly into her vibrant blue eyes when I said this.

Her throat moved again. I hammered down the groan in my chest, along with the urge to step farther into her space and claim her mouth, which was only twelve inches from mine.

"I don't hate you anymore," she said softly.

I exhaled.

Our gazes were still pinned, and even though I could see the tension and upset begin to fade away, there was still a reservation left inside her. She was holding something back, and the longer I looked into those deep blue pools, the more I could see the flickering flames. She was burning to tell me something.

But what?

Did I take a stab and ask her? Or was that risking ruining the moment, as well as sliding backward in progress? We agreed to pretend it didn't happen. That meant *not* talking more about it, right?

"I say, as soon as we step back into the car, we pretend it didn't happen. But out here, we can say whatever. If something else happened and you want to share ..." I nodded in encouragement. "Then you can. No judgment."

Goddammit, my groans were beginning to build up. I wasn't going to be able to keep them all at bay for long. Particularly when she bit her bottom lip on one side like that.

I lifted my brows. "Anything else to share?"

Unsaid words burned in her eyes. She was desperate to share something with me. I could tell.

"We should get to Chicago," she said softly, "if we want to make a day of it there." She blinked, then looked away, breaking eye contact with me and, in turn, the spell between us.

I stepped out of her space, nodded, then headed back to the driver's seat and behind the wheel.

She buckled herself in the passenger seat, and I merged into traffic.

"Music?" she asked a minute later, reaching for my phone from the holder on the dash.

I nodded. "Whatever you want."

She put on some Jack Johnson.

Then we sat in silence.

Dear God, I was an idiot. Why did I tell her that she said my name?

Why?

Because you want her, and you want her to want you back.

I glanced over at her out of the corner of my eye. That holding-back-something look was still there on her face.

But I'd established that the car was a safe space where we were going to pretend that this morning hadn't happened, so if I went back on my word, things between us could get dicey again.

"I was reading up on things to do in Chicago, and they have a combo architecture, food, and history tour," I said, throwing out an olive branch.

"That sounds good," she said. "I know they have a really eclectic food scene."

Then we fell into silence again.

This was painful.

I cleared my throat. "So uh ... what got you into yoga?"

A serene smile settled over her face. "I was a stress-cadet in college, so it was either burn out my sophomore year or find something to help me calm the fuck down."

"And you found yoga."

"I found yoga. And it became a bit of an obsession. What started out as a couple of times a week quickly became six days a week, sometimes seven. But it helped me so much. It seemed like a no-brainer that the next step in my practice was becoming an instructor, so since my final semester my senior year was actually the lightest of my entire undergrad, I did the yoga teacher training at the same time."

Thank God she was talking again. The awkward tension that had hung like a suffocating fog in the vehicle was slowly getting sucked out of the vents.

"How long have you been at the studio in Linley Park?"

She wrinkled her nose in a cute way. "Since I started at the hospital. So five years. I love it there. I wish I could teach there more, but you know, work-life balance and all that. Though I'm still shit at that balance despite not teaching there more."

I chuckled. "All work and no play—"

"Helps Alex pay off her student loan debts faster."

"True. But you also need to enjoy life while you're living it."

"And I do. I would just rather enjoy life debt-free. I would rather enjoy life on my own property with a pack of rescue dogs."

"Is that what you want to do?" As if this woman could get any more appealing.

She smiled wide and nodded. "I want acreage so I can rescue dogs that nobody else wants or that are at the end of their life—like Jill—and they can live out the rest of their days digging holes, chasing wild rabbits and rolling around in the grass. Even if I live in an RV or a tiny house, I want land for the dogs."

"Where would all these dogs sleep if you're in nothing more than a tiny house?"

She laughed. "I'd build a big, insulated and heated barn with a sleeping space for each of them. I'd love to get some horses, too, one day. I actually did an equestrian veterinarian practicum for four months and loved it. Dr. Chu is our primary equestrian vet at our practice."

"How close are you to your goal of buying land?"

"Not close enough," she said with a frown. "I would be closer if Cade and I moved in together and split the rent, but since that's not happening now ... at least a few more years."

"Right."

"What about you? What made you decide to start coming to yoga?"

Well, that was a loaded question. Did I tell her the truth? That I followed her to work, then the yoga studio, and finally H&J?

"I was super stiff from work, particularly all the hunching over we have to do as roofers, so I thought maybe yoga might help with the back pain."

She nodded.

And thank fuck, she didn't press any further and ask why I chose *her* studio over all other studios like The Zen Den.

"And how about Muay Thai?" I asked, eager to keep the conversation going since the more we talked, the less tension there was between us. It was when we were quiet that things began to feel awkward.

"I went to Thailand with a boyfriend eight years ago, and we went to a couple of fights, then we went and tried it ourselves, and I was instantly hooked. Came back here, found a Muay Thai gym, and have been practicing ever since. It's a good balance since it's so much cardio and ab work, while yoga is all strength and balance training."

"I get that. I'm enjoying the fitness combo, too."

She glanced at me out of the corner of her eye. "When did you get diagnosed with Keith?"

I grinned at her use of the douchebag's name. "About sixteen months ago. I was in India and started having some vision issues. My travel insurance covered an optometry visit while I was over there, and the optometrist found the tumor. I came back to the US immediately, was referred to Dr. O'Shea, then moved up to Maine to be closer to him. All within the span of about three months. And I've been shelling out money to him ever since. We've been monitoring it. It's growing faster than we would like, and my vision issues are getting more frequent, which is why I need the surgery sooner rather than later."

"It's benign though, right?"

I nodded. "Yeah, no cancer. Just a big fucker moving into a place he's not welcome."

Her hand shot out and pointed straight ahead. "Pie stand!"

I laughed. "I take it you want pie?"

"When there is a pie stand sign, advertising homemade pies by what is most likely a white-haired grandmotherly type person, you stop for pie."

Still laughing, I got into the right lane, then took the next off-ramp. It was only a quarter of a mile down the road, where sure enough, Harriet's Homemade Pies stood as a little roadside stand, complete with a checkered tablecloth and chalkboard signs.

We parked on the side of the road since there was no curb and hopped out.

It was a scorcher of a day.

Only one other patron was there, buying pies from Harriet, but they paid for their pastry, got in their vehicle and left as we sidled up to the stand.

SO MANY PIES.

I'd never seen so many damn pies.

And so many different kinds.

Harriet had apple, peach, pumpkin, rhubarb, cherry, blueberry, something called Saskatoon berry, bumbleberry, apple caramel, and last but not least, the *pièce de résistance*, lemon meringue.

Alex's eyes went wide. "I don't know what to choose."

"Oh, lemon meringue all the damn way," I said, picking up the second to last lemon meringue pie and handing it to the white-haired grandmotherly-looking Harriet.

"Do I want apple caramel, or do I want blueberry?" Alex said, tapping her finger to her chin.

"Is that the dilemma?" I asked. "Just those two?"

She nodded. "Yeah. I mean, they all sound great, but I've narrowed it down to those two."

"We'll take the apple caramel and the blueberry," I said to Harriet, grabbing the other two full-size pies.

Alex looked at me, but the amusement and excitement in her eyes were what made my chest tighten.

We took a couple of pictures, including a few with Harriet, then I paid the lovely woman before we took our bounty of pies back to the car. We'd grabbed fresh ice before leaving Sandusky, so the pies had a nice cool place to rest before they became our lunch.

We climbed back into the rental car and were back on the highway in no time.

Alex was beaming.

Which made me beam, too.

She glanced over at me, still smiling. "Thank you."

I nodded. "We're on vacation. If you want two pies, get two pies. No regrets on this trip, right?"

She smiled even wider. "No regrets."

CHAPTER TWENTY-ONE

Alex

WE STOPPED FOR LUNCH, which consisted of pie and water, just outside of Chicago. We both had to pee, so Eli found us a rest stop with picnic tables in the shade. I was so glad he got both the blueberry and the apple caramel pie because had I only picked one, I would have been sorely disappointed. They were both amazing.

His lemon meringue was also delicious.

Harriet knew how to make a damn good pie.

I made sure to take pictures of us eating our pies, as well as Eli with his meringue mustache.

We got to Chicago and immediately found a hotel with two rooms, this time across the hall from each other, and unloaded our stuff. Then we went to meet up with the architecture, history, and food tour that I booked for us on the drive.

Eli kept his word and did not bring up the incident this morning at all. He scared me a little when we were standing at the back of the car and he asked me if there was anything else I might like to say before we went into the safety of the vehicle.

How did he know?

How did he know that I was burning up inside with the need to tell him that knowing he was masturbating in the bathroom prompted me to do it outside the bathroom? I don't know why I wanted to tell him, but I did. It felt like a lie—in fact, it *was* a lie—and I wasn't a liar.

"The truth is always better than a lie," my father used to say, which was why when I found my mother and Eli's dad together, I ran and told my dad.

It was also why. When Eli demanded I tell him what was up, I couldn't hold it in any longer and had to tell him that I knew he heard me and that I heard him. The truth was eating away at me.

So was the rest of the truth. Because I knew something he didn't, and to me, that felt like a lie.

I needed to keep my wits about me. I needed to stay sober—because who knew what drunk Alex might say—and convince myself that *not* telling him that I pleasured myself as he pleasured himself wasn't a lie. It was just an omission of fact.

But he flat-out asked you if you had anything else to say, and you shook your head and said no. That was a lie.

The voice in my head had morals the color of bleached ivory. Sometimes I really hated her.

We met up with our tour group and had a fantastic time. I probably took close to a hundred pictures, and despite the heat, Eli looked amazing in all of them.

Me, not so much. By the time the tour was over, I was a melting hot mess and my feet hurt, but I was happy, so whatever.

We were full from the food portion of our tour, but Eli insisted that we swing into a liquor store and take some drinks up to the hotel's rooftop garden.

I told him I wasn't drinking, but that merely earned me a rakish brow lift.

He opened the door after climbing six flights of stairs, and out we stepped into the most incredible center-of-the-city garden oasis I'd ever seen.

Trees and grass, benches, and even a small pond decorated the hotel roof. There were twinkling white lights strung in the trees and through the gazebo and pergola. The place was magical.

A few people milled about, but there was enough space and privacy for all. Eli led me over to a bench that was tucked away and on the edge of the pond. Fish and turtles swam around, reminding me of the pond in the garden at Smith's.

He opened the reusable fabric shopping bag he'd brought with him and pulled out two bottles of sparkling white wine.

"Champagne?" I asked, unease starting to prickle along my arms.

Without saying anything, he deployed the cork on one like a sommelier, then turned to me. "I wanted to do this the other night, right after we lost Jill, but didn't get the chance."

"Huh?"

"The old girl deserves a toast."

Aw.

He lifted the open bottle. "Jilly Bean, I didn't know you long, but in our short time together you stole my heart. You were a lovable little furball who loved nothing more than a good belly rub, and I'm a better person for knowing you. I won't forget you or our short but sweet time together. I hope that you're in a better place now with no aches or pains, other dogs are giving you the space you need, and you're getting all the belly rubs you could ever ask for."

A lump formed in my throat, and my eyes grew wet.

"Here's to you, sweet Jill. We'll see you on the other side." He lifted the bottle a little higher in front of him, then brought it down to his mouth and took a sip.

Was it wrong that I was jealous of the bottle?

Yep.

When he was done, he passed it to me.

Is it also wrong that I got a thrill at the thought of putting my mouth where his mouth had been? That in a sick, stupid, pubescent way, it felt like I was kissing him?

Yeah, it was wrong.

And stupid.

But I got a thrill nonetheless.

Clearly, I was losing my mind.

"Jill," I started, taking a big swallow to compose myself, "You were the closest thing I've ever had to my own dog. You listened, you comforted and you didn't ask for anything but love in return. I wish I had been able to bring you home with me, give you more and what you deserved for your final days, but I hope you know that you didn't leave this world unloved." A tear slid down my cheek as I lifted the bottle into the air, then brought it down to my mouth. It was dry, cool, and bubbly. It was perfection.

I passed the bottle back to Eli, only just becoming aware of the fact that we were sitting close enough that our knees were touching. I glanced down to where we were connected. So did he.

Neither of us moved to fix the dilemma.

He took another sip.

We sat there quietly, passing the bottle back and forth, enjoying the gentle gurgle of the small slate-rock waterfall that spilled into the pond and the hum and buzz of traffic below.

I glanced skyward, but there were too many city lights for us to be able to see the stars. They were up there, though, along with Jill and Eden.

"Why do you think we were enemies growing up?" I asked, after taking another sip of the wine when he passed me the bottle. "I don't even remember how it happened."

He finished the bottle and reached for the other one, deploying the cork in seconds. "I remember."

I sat up straight and looked at him. "When? How?"

An uncomfortable expression crossed his face. "It was the first day of kindergarten, and we were told to partner up. For what? I don't remember. But I remember we were told to pick a partner, and Eden chose you over me. She was my twin and my best friend. All through preschool when we were told to buddy up, she picked me or I picked her. And then, all of a sudden, she stopped choosing me and started choosing you. I was jealous."

My eyes must have been the size of dinner plates.

He shrugged and took a sip from the new bottle of sparkling wine. "Stupid, I know, but she made friends easier than I did. I didn't like to roughhouse and be wild like so many of the other boys. My sister and I never wrestled. We weren't assholes, and to be frank, a lot of the boys in our class were little assholes."

"I know they were. Damien Shapiro."

He nodded. "Joey Fic."

I nodded. "Cody Thornton."

He nodded again. "Dustin Manseth."

"Oh, he was a real troublemaker."

"And I just didn't subscribe to their kind of shithead fun. I love my sister, and when she started choosing you over me, I got mad."

"And took it out on me."

"Yeah."

"And then I retaliated with my own meanness, and so the feud was born."

"And so the feud was born."

He passed me the bottle, and I took a long pull, then held it on my tongue for a while, letting the bubbles tickle the insides of my cheeks and allowing my thoughts to settle. I swallowed and passed the bottle back to him. I was starting to feel the effects of the wine. My head was a little cottony, and my feet felt extra heavy. "I didn't tell her to choose me over you," I finally said. "I wasn't trying to come between you."

"I know that now. But at the time, I blamed you. I saw you as a usurper. Someone who was trying to come between me and my sister. Between me and my best friend." He tipped back the bottle, and I watched his Adam's apple bob in his throat as he swallowed. I wanted to chase that movement with my tongue.

"And when did you realize that I wasn't the enemy?"

"When we were so thick in our war, there was no way to dig myself out of the trench, even if I tried. We hated each other, and that was that. You were my academic nemesis. My athletic nemesis. And then when things with our parents went down, you were an easy target and became my emotional nemesis, too."

I sucked in a breath, then leaned against the back of the bench, tilting my head to the black sky. "Yeah, I often wondered why you hated me. My mom—in her stupidity, because she's chock full of it—said it was because you liked me. She said that boys who like girls but don't know how to tell them often turn their attraction into meanness." I scoffed. "I told her she was out of her damn tree."

"I did," he whispered.

I sat up and whipped my head to face him. "What?"

"I hated you, but I also liked you. It was super fucked up. I think that's why when everything with our parents went down, I just got so damn mad. I was super confused. How could I hate someone I liked? How could someone I liked do that? I felt betrayed, which doesn't really make any sense. But it's the only way I can describe how I felt. I thought that it was just stupid hormones, and while my brain was saying, *no fucking way,* my dick was saying *yes fucking way.*"

My mouth opened and closed several times, but no words came out. What words could I say? After a moment, words finally took shape. "Is that why you spread all those rumors about me just before prom?"

His eyes closed. He tipped up the bottle and drank more, then leaned against the bench and draped his arms over the back. When he opened his eyes again and pinned me with his gaze, everything inside me clenched.

"Yes," he finally said.

My mouth went dry. My heart beat wildly.

Kiss me.

Where did that thought come from?

I was definitely losing my mind!

"Spending time with you on this trip is putting a lot of our past in perspective. Honestly, I probably would have denied liking you—ever—until we started this road trip. But I realize now that a lot of my anger and confusion and the things I said and did were done because I liked you. And I'm not proud of that."

"I had no idea."

His lips pursed together, and he hinged forward, resting his elbows on his knees and staring down between them. A moment later, he lifted his head and pinned that soulful gaze on me. "I'm really sorry, Alex. For everything I did, for all the hurt I caused you. I'm not that guy anymore, I swear."

My nod was small. "I believe you."

He passed me the bottle again. I put it to my lips and took another sip. The wine was warm now, losing its sparkle, and there wasn't much left.

"Finish it," he said, lifting his chin lightly.

I did.

We sat there for a while longer, our knees still touching, the heat from his body flowing into mine. I was sure when I got back to my hotel room my panties would be an absolute puddle.

Looking around the rooftop, I couldn't see another soul.

Were we the only ones left?

"Does this place close at all?" I asked.

He shrugged, then checked his phone. "It's almost midnight."

I brought up my phone, then checked the hotel website. Sure enough, the rooftop garden closed at ... eleven.

Shit!

"It closes at eleven!" I bolted up from the bench and raced to the door for the stairs.

Eli was on my heels.

I wrapped my fingers around the handle and tugged, praying to Jill, Eden and all other angels that we were not locked on the roof of the hotel for the night.

To my surprise and delight, the door opened, but I'd pulled with such force that I went stumbling backward, hitting the solid wall of delicious-smelling muscle that was Eli's chest.

His hands fell to my waist to stabilize me. "Whoa, you okay?"

I nodded. "Yeah."

He let go of me on one side, reached over and pulled the door open again. "We're lucky. Thought I might have to make us a nest of tree branches for the night."

I laughed, but my heart wasn't in it. "Yeah, me, too."

"Seriously, though, we would have just called the front desk. Or tried the elevator around the corner."

We made our way down the stairs, but my feet were full of wine, and my thoughts were racing. I wasn't ready to say good night to him. I wasn't ready for the night to end. I wanted to go back to that bench, stare up at the starless sky and hear more about how he liked me.

We reached our floor and walked down the hallway side by side. He had the fabric bag over one shoulder with the empty wine bottles clanking together in it, but as we walked, he kept looking down at me, smiling.

I started smiling up at him, then those smiles turned into giggles.

"You sure get giggly when you've been drinking," he said, coming to a stop at our doors.

My face hurt from smiling so much. "Sometimes."

"Let's go grab breakfast at that place we passed on our tour today. The one that advertised those enormous breakfast platters with haystack hashbrowns and free-range fried eggs on sourdough and bottomless mimosas. I can drive so you can get the giggles."

I nodded and giggled just as my stomach grumbled at the mention of food.

His brows shot up. "You hungry?"

"I shouldn't be after the amount of food we ate today. Particularly how much pie I have consumed, but ... yeah."

Without saying another word, he whipped out his key card, flashed it in front of his lock panel so it blinked green, then he opened his door and stashed the bag and empty bottle.

"Come on," he said, grabbing my hand and hauling me down the hallway toward the elevator, his hotel-room door clicking shut behind us.

"Where are we going?"

"We CANNOT come to Chicago without trying a Chicago deep-dish pizza. It's sacrilege, I'm sure."

We got in the elevator.

"You think there's anything open at midnight?"

He scrunched his face and looked at me like I'd just asked him if the sky was blue. "Of course there is. This is Chicago. Besides, we walked past a pizza joint like a block from here, and their hours said open until 3 a.m. So we're going."

He hit the button for the lobby, and the doors closed.

We were standing so close, our shoulders touched.

Well, more like my shoulder touched his arm, since he was a good six inches taller than me.

He reached up and lifted a strand of my dyed red hair. "What prompted these?"

I smiled but cast my eyes to the ground. "I started doing them a few years ago. I hit a real low point in my life. Random shit, really, and I just needed a pick-me-up. So I went to the salon, started flipping through the magazines, and saw a woman with the same dark brown color as me, same thick waves, too. But she had these super cool thick bright red streaks, and she rocked them. I said I wanted them, too, and then I fell in love with the look and have kept them ever since."

He twirled the chunk around his fingers. "I like them. They're edgy and hot."

You're hot.

The elevator doors opened, and he grabbed my hand and tugged me out and toward the front door.

And he did not let go of my hand until we were standing in the pizza place giving the guy our order, and when he finally did let go, I wished he hadn't.

CHAPTER TWENTY-TWO

Eli

"ANOTHER ROUND OF BEERS, my good man," I said with a mouthful of pizza as I waved and smiled at the guy behind the counter.

"Coming up," the guy said, reaching into the cooler behind him.

"This is really freaking good." I tipped back my craft lager—my second since we arrived at Go Deep or Go Home—and washed down the pizza.

Alexandra nodded. "So greasy but so good."

I grinned at her. She had a speck of pizza sauce on her cheek.

"You got a little—" I tapped my cheek.

Her brows lifted. "Here?" She touched her cheek but in the wrong spot. The woman was definitely drunk. Her eyelids were at half-mast, and the placid, goofy smile on her face was adorable.

I shook my head and chuckled.

"Here?" She dabbed at the wrong spot again.

Laughing, I reached across the table and gently wiped the sauce off, bringing my finger to my mouth. "Got it."

Her eyes flared.

"Two more beers," the pizza guy said, setting them down in front of us.

"You're the bomb, Danny, the absolute bomb."

He chuckled. "I try."

Alexandra had ditched her leather jacket onto the booth seat beside her and was wearing just a cute black crop top, which gave me ample view of her tattoo and ripped torso.

I finished the first beer, then grabbed the second, allowing the fresh one to wash away the warm monkey-piss flavor of the first. Lifting a finger off the bottle, I pointed at the part of her tattoo that came out across the back of her shoulder. "What's the story behind the tattoo? You don't get something that big without meaning."

She finished her beer, made a face that I understood well since it was probably warm like mine had been, then dabbed at her mouth with a napkin. "I got it shortly after Eden passed, actually. We'd been talking about getting matching tattoos. We liked the cherry blossoms and the gray mixed with pink. Feminine but strong, we thought. We were going to get opposite sides of our bodies done so that when we stood side by side, with our arms around each other, it looked like a whole tree. Branches growing across each of our backs and the trunk down our sides."

She swallowed and took a deep breath.

"We liked the idea of the blossoms because they're such a fleeting beauty in this world. People wait for them and go on trips and walks and journeys just to see them. And yet a big wind storm, or even just time and the change of the season, and they're gone. Then the leaves come, the tree stands tall, grows a little closer to the sun. The roots keep it grounded in the earth. We just loved the symbolism of it all. We sketched it up one night when she came to visit me at college and we'd had too much to drink.

"Of course, she never got hers, but I wanted to honor our plan. Honor her, so I went and got it. I changed it a bit, but the meaning behind it remains."

"I think she'd love it," I said after a pregnant pause. "I think she'd be glad you went and got it done."

"I put her name in one of the branches and the words *soul sister* in the roots, since that's what we called each other." She chuckled. "And when we'd pass notes back and forth to each other in class, we always signed it with a little drawn bird. Hers faced left; mine faced right. We never put our names, just our birds. I found some of our old notes and had the birds put on one of the branches, facing their respective ways. Hers is drawn by her and mine is drawn by me."

Now was not the time or place to be having such thoughts, but the idea of running my tongue along every inch of her popped into my head and wouldn't go away.

She brought the beer to her lips and took a sip. "I should not be having more to drink. This beer is going to push me over the edge from tipsy to full-on drunk."

"I think tipsy has been in your rearview mirror for a while now," I said with a laugh. "But how drunk do you feel right now? Pukey, pass-out drunk? Should I be taking it away from you?"

She pouted and sat back in her seat, cradling the bottle like it was a baby. "No. I'll be fine."

I laughed and reached for another slice of pizza. "Eat more. It'll help."

She nodded and grabbed another slice of the shiny deep-dish pepperoni pizza we'd ordered.

We finished our pizza and beer in the next fifteen minutes, then handsomely tipped our man Danny, waved goodbye to him, and headed back to the hotel.

The woman was definitely drunk given the way she walked—or more like staggered.

With a chuckle, I looped my arm around her. "Come here. We don't want your cute drunk ass getting skinned knees."

She grinned up at me. "Thanks."

I laughed again. "Are you still going to rise with the sun and do yoga tomorrow morning?"

She hummed in thought as we stepped onto the elevator in the hotel. "Maybe not with the sun. Maybe with the afternoon rooster."

"The afternoon rooster?" I hit the button for our floor.

"The rooster that crows for the afternoon."

"Never heard of such a bird. But I think we should be out before eleven, otherwise we'll be stuck paying for another night."

"Right!" She held up a finger. "I'll be up around nine or so, maybe ten." She pulled her phone out of her pocket and unlocked the screen. "Can you set the alarm for me for nine? Then another one for ten?"

"I can, since you're probably too drunk to do it and will set it for p.m. and not a.m."

She leaned into me. "Yep!"

I set the alarms on her phone, then handed the phone back to her.

The elevator door opened, and we stepped out into the hallway. She went to go left, but I steered her right. "This way, you drunk nut."

She giggled. "Whoops!"

We came to a stop in front of our doors, and I let go of her. "I've thoroughly enjoyed today," I said. "Every aspect. The pie, the tours, seeing drunk Alex."

She giggled again. "Me too."

"You sure you're going to be okay?"

She nodded. "Yeah. I'm not pukey drunk."

"Okay. I'm just across the hall if you need anything. Tooth-paste, someone to hold your hair while you send Danny's incredible deep-dish to the fishes."

She giggled. "It was good pizza."

"Really good pizza."

I turned to go when she called out, "Hey."

"Yeah?"

"Are you drunk?"

"Tipsy but not nearly as gone as you. Why?"

Her lips twisted. "I hate lying."

"I know."

"Like it makes my insides get all twisty and hurt."

"Okaaaay ..." Where was she going with this?

"When you were in the bathroom this morning, I got super turned on and I ... I got myself off standing outside the door listening to you."

My jaw dropped.

"I've been holding that in all day. You asked me if there was anything else I wanted to say, and I said no, which was a lie because I wanted to tell you. I felt like I was keeping something from you. Keeping an aspect of what happened from you. So ... anyway." She exhaled. "That's off my chest. Okay. I'm going to go to bed now." She showed me her back, and waved the key card in front of the lock. It flashed green, then she opened the door and stepped inside.

I was speechless and paralyzed in the hallway.

She turned to look at me. "Hopefully we forget this conversation tomorrow, huh? Since we're both super drunk. Good night."

Then she closed the door, leaving me, my boner and my total state of shock standing like idiots in the hallway.

How in the fuck was I supposed to go to sleep after Alexandra dropped that fucking bomb on me?

Well, I didn't right away. I went into my hotel room, took my cock in my hand and rubbed one out—possibly a little too roughly—because I was still trying to make sense of it all.

Did she think that by telling me when she was drunk that I would just *forget* this news tomorrow? I did tell her I wasn't as drunk as she was.

I mean, she was an absolutely adorable drunk, and I enjoyed every minute of her immense inebriation, but just because we drank drink for drink didn't mean I was as plastered as she was. I still had my wits, and I would abso-fucking-lutely remember her telling me this tomorrow.

However, if she didn't remember, I would have to play dumb.

Fuck.

But getting back to the issue even bigger than trying to act normal around Alexandra tomorrow after her admission was what she'd admitted.

She got turned on hearing me jerking off, and then she stood outside the bathroom door and got herself off, too.

Jesus. Fuck.

She could have just knocked on the damn door, told me what she wanted, and then neither of us would have been forced to abuse ourselves. We could have just fallen into bed and taken care of business properly.

I slid my fingers along my cock, squeezing the head slightly as the tension in my balls and lower belly began to build.

Did she tell me this for a reason? Besides the fact that she said she felt like she was lying and the lie was eating away at her from the inside? Was this her way of telling me she was into me? Was this her way of telling me she wanted something more?

We'd made so many strides over the last few days, had some amazing laughs and memorable moments, I didn't want to ruin things by assuming this was more than harmless flirting. But the way she sat up and looked at me when I told her that I'd had a thing for her when we were kids made me think she *did* want more. She was looking at me differently.

A few more strokes, and I was coming into a tissue. The release was instant but also fleeting, and by the time I finished my shower and climbed into bed, all those endorphins had faded away.

How was I supposed to face her tomorrow?

Like a man. Wait for her to bring it up, and if she doesn't, assume she doesn't remember telling you and leave it at that. If you bring it up, you could embarrass her and set your relationship back beyond repair.

Yeah, that was what I would have to do.

Even though it was almost three in the morning, I wasn't tired. Rather, I was wired from what Alexandra had said.

I brought up the pictures I'd taken of her and me today and smiled at the goofy faces she was making. When she relaxed, when she let her hair down and didn't take things so fucking serious, she was a lot of fun.

A photo of her she didn't know I'd taken popped up. We were on the river cruise and she was leaning against the railing, the wind in her hair, her sunglasses on, and a serene and beautiful smile on her face.

My chest grew tight, and of course, my cock got stiff again, too.

I lifted the covers and glared at it. "Really?"

There was no denying him, so I rubbed another one out, this time ashamedly, staring at that picture of Alexandra.

CHAPTER TWENTY-THREE

Alex

I WORE MY SUNGLASSES as Eli and I took the elevator down to the lobby the next morning. Our suitcases rolled behind us when we walked across the tile to the front desk and handed in our key cards.

We'd parked in the underground parking, so we took our stuff to the rental car, then drove to the breakfast place.

We barely spoke to each other when we met in the hallway at ten forty-five, but I was guessing it was because we were both hungover.

We'd had a lot to drink.

My head hurt.

Thankfully, though, I didn't puke.

I just felt like shit today.

"I'm in no condition to drive," I said, rubbing my temple as I buckled my seat belt and leaned against the door. "Can you drive?"

"Yep."

He turned over the ignition and backed out of the stall. We were at the restaurant in ten minutes, but then finding parking was a beast of a task and took us another fifteen.

There was also a bit of a line for the restaurant, which normally I would never join since I considered standing in line for a restaurant—no matter how good—to be a giant waste of my time. But I was hungover and on vacation, so whatever.

"How are you feeling this morning?" I asked, taking a big gulp of the water bottle I was toting around like a lifeline.

"I'm okay."

"Your head's not pounding?"

"No."

I wrinkled my brows and looked up at him. "You're acting weird."

"Pot, kettle, darlin'," he said with a smirk.

I snorted. "Touché." But then my expression turned serious. "Did I say something last night to offend you? 'Cause I honestly can't remember much past Danny nodding at us when we asked for extra cheese."

His eyes bulged for half a second, and had I not been looking directly into his eyes, I would have missed it.

Shit, what did I say?

He shook his head. "Nope. You didn't say anything. I asked you about your tattoo, then I had to keep you propped up as we walked home, then we said good night."

I narrowed my eyes even more. "You sure?"

He nodded. "One hundred percent."

I blew out a breath, which made the hair around my face flutter. "I can't decide if I'm too hungover for food or so hungover I need all the food."

"The struggle is real."

"So real."

We moved with the line. We were next to head into the restaurant.

"So I've been thinking," I said after a moment. "Maybe—now just hear me out—maybe we just get one hotel room from now on but we splurge on a *better* suite, with two king-size beds. I still think it'll be cheaper. But like, we can buy some earplugs and whatever. But I don't, like, *hate* you anymore, and you don't *hate* me, right?"

His gaze found mine, and it was penetrating. Alarming. Exhilarating. "I don't hate you."

I swallowed. "So then we just get one room?"

"We'll see what the places offer when we go to book something. Sometimes two rooms are still cheaper than an upgrade."

The waitress led us to our table.

I ended up ordering the breakfast platter, with two poached eggs, Swiss cheese, sourdough, avocado, turkey bacon, and haystack hashbrowns. I also went hair of the dog and ordered a mimosa.

Eli just got a coffee and the same platter as me.

Although we didn't eat in silence, he was distant, and I felt it. Like an entire ocean lay between us, even though he was sitting beside me at the bar as we watched the bartender make fancy boozy brunch drinks.

We were on the road by one o'clock with a plan to zoom through the rest of Illinois, Iowa, and hopefully stop in Nebraska for the night.

Eli said he was fine driving.

We drove for an hour before he pulled over for gas and bathroom breaks. That also gave him an opportunity to go stock up on more road-trip snacks, since he'd depleted his stash of Funyuns, Doritos, and all other *itos*.

I decided that I wasn't going to let whatever weird mood he was in mess up our day. While he was buying snacks, I googled fun things to do in Iowa, and when Ledges State Park with its river, cliffs, and stone bridge popped up, I knew it was just the detour we needed. Plus, I didn't wake up with enough energy to do yoga this morning, so I was feeling off-balance and in need of some grounding. In need of some exercise.

He stopped at the passenger door behind him and unloaded the bags of snacks, besides the Funyuns, then he slid in behind the steering wheel, bringing his bag of onion-flavored fried corn rings.

"We're making a detour," I said.

"Okay, where?"

"Ledges State Park. I really liked our hike in Vermont, so let's go on another one."

He put the car into gear. "You're the boss."

It was another four hours to Ledges State Park, which meant we were getting there just around dinnertime. I read online that it also had a campsite, so the scent of campfire and meat over flames filled the fresh air as we climbed out of the rental and went around to the hatch to change into our hiking boots.

We loaded up a small backpack with water and some snacks and headed out on the stream walk.

It was a nice change of scenery from the skyscrapers of Chicago. The fresh air was welcome, too.

Eli started off down the trail without me, and I jogged a bit to catch up, the hangover from earlier that morning no longer plaguing my brain the way it had earlier. I'd popped a couple of Tylenol and chugged some water, so I was feeling better. The tall maple and oak trees lined our path, the sun breaking through their leaf canopy and casting long, mottled shadows along the ground. We stopped to read a map and some information about the park and trail.

"Oooh, let's go check out the sandstone cliffs," Eli said.

I nodded and together we took off down the trail.

"You used to camp a lot with your grandpa, right?" I asked. "You and Eden."

"Yeah, every summer."

I wrinkled my nose. "We didn't do much camping as kids. Mostly *glamping*, where we rented a motorhome or a cabin somewhere."

"I remember. Eden loved it when you would invite her camping with your family. I was jealous that she got to go and I didn't."

My smile fell. "I'm sorry."

He shook his head. "Don't be. We were twins but not *conjoined* twins. We didn't have to do everything the other one did. Took me a bit more time than her to realize that, though. Probably because she made friends easier than I did."

We walked more but didn't speak. He'd been off all morning.

I really hoped I hadn't said anything to offend him last night. He told me that I didn't, but now I wasn't so sure if I could believe him.

Kids were playing in the creek, splashing and having fun. At first, I wondered why there were so many people, but then I remembered that it was Saturday. My days were all blending together without work and teaching at the yoga studio to keep me organized.

In a way, I kind of liked the freedom.

We hiked some more, stopped and took some pictures, then found a quiet spot on the creek to sit, take off our socks and shoes and dip our feet.

I was munching on some baby carrots that I'd pulled out of my cooler when I turned to Eli. "Why didn't you ask me to prom?"

He looked genuinely shocked. "What?"

"Well, if you sabotaged other guys from asking me, why didn't *you* ask me?"

"Because I hated you."

"But you said you also liked me." Now I was confused.

"I hated you for breaking up my family, Alex. For all the crappy things you said and did to me—"

"Because you started it. You started the war."

He nodded and those full lips I couldn't stop staring at dipped into a frown as he stared down at his feet in the water. "I know. I did. But I was still ..." He exhaled a deep sigh. "I was still attracted to you. Still ... *wanted* you, but I also hated you. So I didn't want anyone to have you or take you to prom. I didn't want to go with you, but I also didn't want anyone else to. And as sick and horrible as it sounds, as ashamed of myself as I am now, I wanted you to hurt. I wanted you to suffer." His face fell, then he looked away. "I'm sorry I did that."

I glanced away from him and focused on my toes in the clear stream. I wiggled them and thought about what he'd just said. He'd been a really angry kid, I remember that, but not destructive like some of the other boys in our classes. He seemed to keep most of that anger locked deep inside, only bringing it out when I was around. Then, when our families imploded, his anger quadrupled and I felt that hate the moment we were in the same breathing space. Even when we were on opposite ends of the school, I could feel how much he hated me.

But we'd both changed since then.

I offered him a baby carrot. "Carrot?" An olive branch.

Again, he seemed genuinely shocked. He took a carrot.

We crunched in silence.

"You don't seem angry now," I said after almost five minutes of neither of us talking. "Did traveling and Keith really change you that much?"

His chest expanded on a deep inhale, and he closed his eyes when he breathed out. "Yeah, they did. I was still really angry when I went to college. It took flunking out of school to humble me and going traveling to realize how trivial and first-world so many of my problems were. I needed to let that shit go. I made friends, connected with people, and as cliché as it sounds, I found myself. I came back a lot calmer, a lot less angry, and a lot more self-aware." His lip lifted on one side into a delicious smirk, and a laugh huffed from his nose. "I'm still a work in progress, though. I'm not saying I've reached any kind of enlightenment. I've just dropped a lot of those heavy sandbags of rage that were stacked up like shoulder pads for over twenty years."

"Which was why you made that mean comment about Cade coming to my yoga class," I said softly.

His expression became grim. "Yeah." His eyes lifted to mine. "Again, I'm a work in progress. And I'm sorry I said that." Pushing his fingers through his hair, he exhaled again. "I've been doing a lot of apologizing on this trip. All necessary, but it's just making me realize how big of an asshole I was to you. Keith has also done a lot to help me—as much as he is a giant douchebag. I don't take shit for granted the way I used to."

I nodded, then stared back down into the crystal-clear water. "I'm glad traveling helped put life in perspective for you and allowed you to slough off some of that rage. Anger is necessary in life, but it's not healthy hanging onto so much of it."

Maybe take your own advice and reach out to your mother? Ha!

I delivered a knee jab to the voice in my head, hard enough that she seemed to get the message and was over in the corner sulking.

There was letting go of anger, and then there was letting go of toxic people. I was no longer angry at my mother. I was over that. I was over her. I released her from my life, from my mind and from my heart. She was pure poison and did not deserve space in my world. But I wasn't angry with her anymore. I refused to use up the energy within me to be mad at her anymore. She was dead to me. And it was pointless being mad at a dead person.

"We could camp here," he said after another long, quiet pause between us.

"We don't have any camping gear."

"Yes, we do."

Now was my turn to seem genuinely shocked, because I was.

"I brought a small tent, sleeping bags, blow-up mattresses, a camp stove, and I see you have blankets in the back."

"Why on earth did you bring camping gear?" That explained all the shit he brought with him and that giant-ass bag that covered nearly the entire back seat. I thought he was just one of those people who packed a month's worth of clothes for a weeklong trip and packed for every season. I should have asked what all that stuff was. That reminded me, we needed to find a laundromat.

"You never know when you might need it. We could have hit a roadblock, a landslide. Our rental could break down. We need to be prepared."

"A regular Boy Scout."

He grinned. "So you want to see if they have any campsites? I saw that they have a few first-come-first-serve walk-in ones that you don't have to reserve. They also have some hike-in sites, but I don't think we want that."

I made a dismissive face and shook my head. "You really want to camp?"

He shrugged. "Worth a shot seeing if any sites are available. It might be fun. We could build a fire, roast Doritos like the pioneers did."

I snorted. "Like the pioneers."

He seemed to be loosening up from earlier. He was back to the fun, joking Eli from last night. Maybe this was just how he got when he was hungover. Real broody and quiet.

"If they have any campsites left, I'm not against it," I said cautiously. "Barring there are toilets nearby. I'm not going off to dig a hole somewhere with a shovel."

He chuckled. "I would never ask you to. I'd dig the hole for you, then supply you with a map to find it."

I leaned over and bumped his shoulder with mine. "Such a gentleman."

They had one campsite left when we went to investigate. It required us to "stay" for two nights, but we just paid for two even though we only intended to stay for one.

We didn't have a lot in the way of food, but we also wouldn't starve.

After we parked in the camp spot, Eli went about setting up the tent while I did inventory on our food situation. I really did not want to be roasting Doritos over the campfire.

We had half a blueberry pie left, six apples, another bag of baby carrots, a bag of Doritos, a bag of Fritos, a bag of Cheetos, three lemon poppyseed muffins, four protein bars, and two mushy and bruised pears.

No, we wouldn't starve, but dinner was going to be an eclectic smorgasbord.

Since it was only the end of May, there was no fire ban in effect, and campsites around us had gray-blue smoke billowing up into the ether.

"Need a hand?" I asked him, wandering over to where he knelt on the ground beside a bunch of tent poles and a spread-out tent. I plopped my hands on my hips. "Have you ever set this tent up before?"

"Not for a while. But yes." His brows scrunched in a cute way, then he tipped his head up to look at me. "I could use a hand."

Grinning, I crouched down and waited for instructions.

We made a good team and had the tent erected in no time.

I gathered all the blankets I had from the rental and brought them over to where he was blowing up the mattresses.

It was nine o'clock. The sun had just gone down and twilight was setting in.

"Do you know how to start a fire?" I asked him, holding the blankets against my chest and watching as his cheeks puffed out adorably before he blew the air into the mattress.

He put the plug into the mattress. "Not only can I set fire to kindling and scrunched-up newspaper, but I've been known to set ladies' loins aflame as well." He ducked into the tent and put the mattress down next to the other one.

That's when I realized that we were going to be sleeping RIGHT NEXT TO EACH OTHER. Like RIGHT next to each other.

Shit, maybe this wasn't such a good idea after all.

When he suggested roughing it in a tent, like Daniel Boone, for some reason I envisioned a big tent with multiple rooms where you could stand up. This was not the case.

I was pretty sure a Saint Bernard would have trouble turning around in this damn tent.

Heat and tingles and prickles and flutters began to take over my body.

I swallowed.

"Blankets," he said, on his knees and halfway in the tent.

I handed him the blankets.

"We don't have any pillows, but a rolled-up hoodie can do in a pinch."

I nodded. Then my eyes found his ass and decided to just take up residence there.

How on earth was I going to be able to lie next to this man for an entire night? Smell him. See him. Hear him.

I masturbated to the sounds and knowledge of this man pleasuring himself, and yet I was expected to just sleep next to him without those thoughts running like a hamster who'd just taken a hit of speed through my brain.

I couldn't do enough yoga or deep breathing in the world to keep my mind clear of such wanton thoughts.

"All set," he said, zipping up the tent and standing in front of me. "Now for the fire."

I stood there like a complete tool, watching him transform into this sexy, rugged mountain man.

Okay, maybe that was a bit of a stretch, but his ability to just take charge and handle any situation that came to him was seriously hot.

He'd also located a flannel shirt in his bag, and although a little wrinkled, it was just adding to this lumberjack, camping-man image he was personifying nicely.

My mouth was dry.

My panties were not.

"Got any camping chairs or a beach blanket or something so we have somewhere to sit?" he asked as he crouched down next to the fire, struck a match and started blowing on a small pile of dried grass, leaves, sticks and what looked like—Doritos?

"Are you burning Doritos?"

"They're great fire-starters," he said. "Super greasy."

And sure enough, a flame took shape, and he started to build a fire with the kindling and firewood we purchased from the same place we paid for our campsite.

I went on the hunt in the back of the rental for something to sit on but came up with nothing. Nothing besides the Coleman cooler that was about three feet long. "Will this do?" I asked, heaving it out of the back.

He nodded. "Sure will. Just can't put it too close to the fire. Otherwise, it'll melt."

Once the fire was going, we went about "making" dinner.

First, he heated up the pie in the metal pie plate on the grate over the fire pit.

The warm pie was freaking delicious.

Then he roasted some carrots, apples and pears in the pie plate over the fire, which ended up not tasting as weird as I feared they would.

We each had a protein bar, and I broke down and ate a couple of handfuls of Funyuns, which delighted Eli immensely.

We also both sat on the cooler, squished together, thigh to thigh, elbow to elbow. He'd thrown a black vest over his flannel, and when he finished his Cheetos and dusted his hands off, he reached into the inside pocket of his vest and drew out a worn silver flask with leather inlay. He unscrewed the top, brought it to his lips and took a sip.

I finished my roasted pears and carrots and set the metal pie plate down on the ground, keenly aware of the warmth his thigh against mine was sending into my body.

"Want some?" he asked, passing me the flask. "It's whiskey."

I took the flask from him and swept my thumb over the soft, worn leather. "This is old."

"Was my granddad's."

"I only met your granddad a handful of times, but he was a real character." I put the mouth of the flask to my lips and tipped it up. It was smoother than I was expecting, but I rarely drank whiskey, so even though it was no Wild Turkey, it still made my taste buds and palate get a bit of whiplash, and I coughed as I swallowed.

He chuckled. "Yeah, Gramps was a real character. A straight shooter if ever there was one."

We stared into the flames.

Darkness had settled in completely now, and we could hear the other fires crackling and small groups of people in the surrounding campsites.

"What time is it?" I asked, wanting so badly to turn and look at him, to watch the flames dance in his eyes and make the gold stand out like polished ingots, but we were sitting so close, I wasn't sure I'd be able to control myself and not lunge out and kiss him if I did.

My phone was charging in the rental.

He brought out his phone. "Almost eleven. Tired?"

I yawned. "Yes and no. My body feels tired, and I know I should sleep, but my brain is wired." I took another sip from the flask before handing it back to him.

"I think I'll hit the hay, but you're welcome to stay up later. I have those earplugs I bought yesterday, so I won't hear a thing."

Like me having another sex dream.

My face got hot.

I didn't say anything for a moment, then nodded. "Okay."

He pried himself up from the cooler and went to the rental to go and rummage around in his suitcase.

I stared into the flames, wondering if I should just recline the passenger seat all the way back and sleep in the rental or risk sleeping next to Eli and the mental and physical repercussions that might have on my body and brain.

We lucked out and scored a campsite close to the bathrooms. He took off toward them.

I continued to stare into the fire.

The crunch of gravel behind me told me he was back. His hand fell to my shoulder, and parts of me started to melt. "Good night," he said.

I swallowed. "Good night."

The tent zipped open. Zipped closed. Then he shuffled around in there for a bit.

I watched the fire die down, and when it was nothing but glowing embers and I was sure Eli was asleep, I got up and started my own bedtime routine.

My phone said it was nearly one o'clock by the time I climbed into the tent.

It took a few moments for my eyes to adjust to the darkness, but eventually I could see well enough.

My clothes smelled smoky, so I changed into my pajamas in my sleeping bag, then, because I was an idiot, I rolled over to check to see if Eli was sleeping.

He was beautiful.

His long lashes fanned out over his cheeks, and his scruff was getting a little unruly. I missed that roguish lock of hair that tumbled over his forehead before he got a haircut. My insides clenched.

I will not have sex dreams about Eli tonight.

I will not have sex dreams about Eli tonight.

I closed my eyes, and even with my lids closed, he was all I saw.

My dreams were fucked.

I was fucked.

CHAPTER TWENTY-FOUR

Eli

DESPITE THE FACT THAT I went to bed over an hour before Alexandra, I didn't sleep. I was too busy worrying about her outside by herself. Yes, it was a full campsite and there were rangers and staff, but there were still bears and weirdos.

When she entered the tent, I pretended to be asleep.

Then she lay there watching me. I was so tempted to open my eyes, but I didn't.

We had a good day together. Even if it had taken me a little while to get over the bomb she dropped last night, I eventually didn't let it rule my behavior and regained some of my composure.

But sleeping beside her like this, my cock was a steel pipe.

She was beautiful.

Beyond beautiful.

I wanted nothing more than to reach out and tuck the strand of wayward hair that had fallen across her face, but I couldn't. I wasn't that type of person to her, at least not when we were sleeping.

I swallowed. Why the fuck did I suggest we camp? I knew the size of the tent I had packed. Why did I think this was a good idea when I was having these feelings for Alexandra? The tumor was obviously pressing on the dumb decision part of my brain and causing me to make even dumber mistakes than normal.

When I figured she was actually asleep, I let out a sigh and rolled over onto my back.

"I didn't wake you when I came in, did I?"

Shit!

"No," I said sheepishly. I hadn't put in my earplugs yet. "Having a harder time falling asleep than I thought."

"Me, too."

She rolled over onto her back as well.

"Did you date at all in high school?" she asked, after a moment of quiet.

"Not really. I was pretty nerdy in high school. I had one girlfriend in my junior year but otherwise, not really."

"But you had a prom date."

"Yeah, Ashley Wilson"

"And you went to Sully Davis's party at his parents' lake house after prom."

I nodded. Not that she was looking at me. "Ashley got the invite, not me."

"Eden went, too. With her date, Mike Townsen."

"Yeah, we all shared a limo."

"How was the party?"

"You didn't go?" I glanced at her out of the corner of my eye. Her head shook. "No. I didn't go to prom. I didn't have a date and after the rumors about me ... I just didn't want to go."

Fuck.

I rolled over onto my side, which prompted her to do the same. "I'm really sorry. I didn't know it got that bad. I thought you went."

She shook her head again. "No. I didn't."

I squeezed my eyes shut. No wonder she was still so guarded with me. I'd hurt her so much when we were kids. I wouldn't blame her if she never took off all of her armor when she was around me.

"If it's any consolation, Ashley ditched me. She ended up making out with Terry Kramer, said she only went to prom with me to make him jealous."

She snorted. "It does make me feel a little better, actually."

"Eden's date got super drunk and puked all over her, so we both left early."

"I heard."

My eyes had adjusted to the dark, so I could see her now. There were maybe two feet between us, max.

"I really am sorry, though, Alex. Truly. For everything."

"And I believe you."

But I didn't believe her.

"You could make it up to me ... sort of," she said, a smile in her voice.

"Yeah? How?"

"Tell me something that nobody else knows. Something that you've never told a soul. It doesn't necessarily have to be a deep, dark secret, but tell me something that you've never shared with anyone else."

I stared into her eyes, though it was impossible to see the beautiful blue in the dark. "Stays in the tent?"

She swept her arms out of the sleeping bag. "Cone of silence. The vault. What happens in the tent, stays in the tent."

My cock twitched.

"I mean, what is *said* in the tent *remains* in the tent," she quickly corrected.

I was quiet for a bit, thinking about what I could share with her that nobody else knew but that would also be impactful and show her not only how much I had changed, but just how sorry I was for who I'd been back then.

I reached beside me into the small bag I'd brought into the tent with me and grabbed my tablet. I turned it on. "I've been working on this for almost four years. It was Eden's and my dream. We cooked it all up together when we were kids sleeping in bunk beds at our grandfather's farm." I brought up the graphics first, then opened the window with the words as well, then I passed it to her.

She flipped over to her belly and sat up on her elbows, the blue light of the tablet illuminating her face.

Her eyes were wide.

My nerves had my stomach in a tight knot.

"I have never shown any of this to a soul. Nobody. You are the first."

Her finger flipped through a bunch of the illustrations, and some of them where I'd written the dialogue and narration into the picture boxes.

I couldn't get a read on her.

Her mouth opened slightly.

After a full five minutes of her not saying anything, just blinking and swiping her finger and me about to lose my damn mind, she turned to me. "This is incredible."

Thank fuck.

"Eli, this is amazing. You're going to publish this, right? Like you're going to publish this." That last bit wasn't said as a question.

I took back the tablet, flipped the cover back over the screen and tucked it away. "I dunno. I'd like to, one day. But ..."

"But what? That was amazing. The artwork, the story, the concept. Original and brilliant. I had no idea you could draw."

I nodded. "Yeah, it's always been something I kind of kept to myself. Eden knew, but that was about it. The plan was that I would draw and she would write. But we would publish it together—if we ever published it. It was a childish pipe dream. But I started putting it together as a way to keep her memory alive. As a way to stay close to her. Sometimes, I feel like she's helping me with the plot, whispering ideas into my ear."

I glanced over at her. She was on her stomach, still, propped up on her elbows, and even in the dark, I could tell she was crying.

Shit.

"That's beautiful," she whispered. "And you absolutely have to publish it."

I shrugged. "We'll see."

"Can I read everything up until this point? I'd love to read it all."

"I have three novels done—I mean they're rough, but they're done. I'm halfway through the fourth right now."

Her eyes glittered with unshed tears, but her smile was wide. "That's amazing. I want to read it. To feel Eden's presence the way that you do."

Only one side of my mouth lifted up.

She turned to face me. "I think she'd be really happy that you're pursuing the dream even though she's gone."

That was what I thought, too.

For the first five years of our lives, Eden and I had really only had each other as playmates. Yes, we went to preschool for one year when we were four, but before that, it was just us. We lived in a small rural town in West Virginia where it took our mom thirty minutes to drive each way to the preschool. We lived down a dirt road with no neighbors, no other kids to play with. It was just Eden and me. It was when we moved to Connecticut and the suburbs that we finally started playing with kids besides each other. Eden adapted to it faster than I did, but then, she just had that sweet, easy-going personality that drew people in like flies to honey.

I was quieter, and although I made a few friends over the years, it took me a while to warm up to people.

Until I started traveling, that is. Once I started traveling, my wings finally spread and I was no longer afraid to jump into the unknown or hang out with people I just met an hour ago. I didn't shy away from singing karaoke with complete strangers in a bar until two in the morning, then hopping on a boat to a rave with them the next day, all of us hungover and ready for the next adventure.

And I brought that mentality back with me.

Eden hadn't had a chance to spread her wings and fly, so in a lot of ways, I felt like I was experiencing the world for the both of us.

Caught up in my thoughts, I shook my head and glanced over at Alex. She was watching me.

"I miss her, too," she whispered.

I don't know why I did it, but I reached out for her hand and laced my fingers with hers. She smiled and looked down at our clasped hands, squeezing my fingers.

As much as I was enjoying this moment, it was a little depressing. I wasn't ready to say good night to Alex, so I needed to come up with a way to lighten the mood.

"Two truths and a lie?" I asked.

Her smile turned wry. "Truth or dare."

My dick perked up as he'd been falling asleep. "How about just truths?" If my dick had fists, he'd have punched my nuts for that suggestion.

She smiled and nodded. "Okay. I'll go first."

I lifted a brow at her. "Let me have it."

"How old were you when you lost your virginity?"

Whoa, she was going straight to the meaty questions.

I pouted and made sure my eyes were extra puppy-doggish, then I drew my answer out with a sad, pregnant pause. I knew when her eyes narrowed that I had her. "I'm still a virgin actually."

Her mouth opened. Shut. Then opened again.

Then it split into a beautiful smile. She untangled our hands and shoved me in the shoulder. "The fuck you are."

I burst out laughing. "I had you for a second, though. Admit it."

"Half a second, maybe."

"Okay, my turn. Same question."

"You didn't answer my question, though."

"Oh, right. Eighteen, the third week of my freshman year of college. Your turn." I was eager to learn who had the privilege of being with Alexandra first. Then I wanted to hunt the fucker down and punch him. Not really, but the primal beast in me was fantasizing about it.

Her lips twisted. "Derek Sharpe, the summer before our junior year."

"Of high school?" I had to blink, otherwise my eyeballs were going to pop out of their sockets.

She nodded.

"Who the fuck is Derek Sharpe?"

"I went to The Hamptons with my aunt's family for most of the summer that year. I think you and Eden were at your granddad's a lot. My dad went on a boys' fishing trip, so I went to my aunt's beach house. Derek was with his family for the summer staying a few houses down the beach from my aunt's. We started hanging out and ..."

"And ..."

Her brows scrunched. "And we had sex."

Why was my heart beating so wildly?

I'd had plenty of sex, been with plenty of women, and Alexandra had most likely been with other men since Derek. She was about to move in with Cade the cad a few weeks ago. So why was hearing about the guy she lost her virginity to bothering me so much?

Because if you'd played your cards differently in high school, that could have been you. You're also jealous that she lost her virginity before you.

"I mean, in reality, virginity is just a social construct," she went on. "The hymen is not a *thing* you break. So I didn't really look at it like I was *giving* Derek anything or *losing* anything to him. We hung out, we had fun, he was really hot and also a virgin, so we just decided to do it."

I bunched my fist beneath the sleeping bag at her mentioning Derek being *hot*.

"Did Eden know?" I asked. Not that my sister would have told me about Alexandra having sex, but maybe she would have. Though, I already knew that if I found out about her summer sex fling I'd have just been enraged and taken it out on her in some way. So it was probably best that I didn't know at the time.

"Of course," Alexandra said, her tone incredulous. "I told Eden everything. And of course, she wanted *all* the details." She snorted. "As much as she was the extrovert and I was the introvert in our friendship, she lived vicariously through me that summer. But she got hers the following summer with that ranch hand at your grandfather's farm."

"What?"

"Oops. I thought you knew?" She blanched and the cords of her neck stuck out. "Yeah, she hooked up with that hot ranch hand ... Clint, I think? Up in the hayloft and everything. Said it was the best first, second, third, fourth, and fifth times she could have ever imagined. He was like twenty-one and so fine. She sent me pictures and boy was I jealous."

"Granddad would have killed Clint if he'd found out," I murmured, still getting over the shock of all of it.

"Well, it's a good thing he didn't find out then, huh? I'm surprised you didn't know, though."

Yeah, so was I. That made me sad. I thought that Eden and I had shared everything with each other.

Alexandra shrugged, seemingly unaware of just how blown my mind was at the moment. "What about the girl you first slept with?"

"Huh?"

Her head tilted. "The first girl you were with your freshman year. Was it love at first bone?" She snickered.

I needed to get ahold of myself. The jealousy I felt over this Derek guy and the fact that he was Alexandra's first was wild and came out of nowhere. Not to mention the news about my sister and Clint the ranch hand. How did I not know what they were up to?

I cleared my throat. "Jenny French. We were in the same calculus class and started studying together. She came to my dorm to study and ..."

Mimicking me, she leaned in and went, "And ..."

I rolled my eyes, the angry heat in my body beginning to dissipate. "And we had sex."

"And then were you guys college sweethearts?"

I shook my head. "No, she realized she hated calculus so dropped out of MIT a week later and enrolled at another college, I think she switched to an English major or something. She also started dating one of the guys on the football team." I shrugged. "It is what it is."

Alexandra pouted.

I wasn't enjoying this game as much as I thought.

Glancing over at her, I smiled weakly. "I'm actually pretty beat. Probably going to turn in."

She nodded, though, even in the dark, her eyes seemed sad, disappointed. "Okay."

I rolled away from her, hating myself. "Good night."

I heard her get comfortable and roll over, too. "Good night."

I wasn't sure how long I lay there awake, listening to the gentle sounds of Alexandra sleeping and the quiet night around us. But I can say exactly how hard I berated myself for not only my behavior back when we were kids and teenagers, but also now. I had no right to be jealous of a guy I'd never met. I had no claim on Alexandra then, and I had no claim on her now.

Technically, she's your fiancée, so you kind of do.

What I needed to figure out was whether I wanted to claim her, wanted to make her mine more permanently than an arrangement for insurance and a hot date to a wedding. And after that, I needed to figure out how to help her see that it was what she wanted as well.

CHAPTER TWENTY-FIVE

Alex

WE WERE ON THE road by eight in the morning. A quick gas fill-up and some fast-food breakfast burritos and we were on the interstate headed for Nebraska. We decided to just drive like crazy people and blow through Nebraska as fast as possible, only stopping for more gas, food, and bathroom breaks. One of our rest stops had a giant head of Abraham Lincoln, so we made sure to take pictures in front of it.

I was jokingly reading from a website boasting some of the best roadside attractions on our route and about to ask Eli if he wanted to stop and check out a marble and collectibles place—apparently, it boasted the world's largest collection of marbles—when he swerved hard on the road and let out a "Holy Fuck!"

A car honked its horn as it whizzed past us.

"What?" I asked, gripping the dash in front of me and dropping my phone to the floor.

"My left eye. Fuck!"

"Huh?"

"I need to pull over."

Everything was happening so fast. There was no curb, no berm or anything for him to pull over onto on this stretch of highway.

Traffic was moving fast.

"Are you blind?" I asked, my voice coming out shakier than I intended it to be.

With a calmness I did not feel in even one cell of my body, he guided the SUV off the interstate and down the off-ramp. A moment later, he found a pullout and parked.

"Wh-what just happened?" I asked, my throat tight and the backs of my eyes burning.

Why was I close to tears?

Eli squeezed his eyes shut and his grip on the steering wheel tightened until his knuckles were white. I ignored the way the movement made his forearms flex and his biceps pop.

"Eli!" I shook his shoulder. "What just happened?"

"I'm hoping that when I open my eyes in a second that I can see out of both, because when I closed them, I could not see out of my left."

Oh my God.

"Like at all?"

"Like at all."

"Fuck," I breathed.

"Yeah."

"Has this ever happened before?"

"Not a complete blackout, no. Just blurriness."

"Oh my God." My hand flew to my mouth as I studied his profile.

His throat moved hard as he swallowed. The fear etched across his face was something I felt deep in the pit of my stomach.

I was scared, too.

This could be it. The beginning of the end of Eli's vision.

He did say that Keith was growing fast and he needed the surgery sooner rather than later. Maybe we needed to go find a chapel now and get it over with. Get him on the list for surgery the moment we got back from California. Or maybe we needed to forgo San Diego entirely and just fly home? If that was what he needed, then I'd do it.

I reached for his hand and gently pried it off the steering wheel, lacing my fingers through his and squeezing. He squeezed back.

"It's okay," I said. "We'll figure it out. If we need to fly back to Maine from Denver, then we'll do it. If you're blind, I'll help you."

"It's just the left," he said through gritted teeth.

"I know ... but that fucks with depth perception and peripheral vision. It can take some time to adjust."

His grip on the wheel loosened, and with his eyes still closed, he turned to face me. His throat moved again, and I studied his face and shoved down a groan as I stared at those full, suckable lips that always seemed halfway between delicious and an infuriating smirk and a growl.

Beneath the sexy scruff, his jaw was like an ice sculpture, and although his cheekbones weren't nearly as round or pronounced as mine, at least he had some.

"I'm going to count to three and then you're going to open your eyes, and we'll deal with whatever the outcome together, okay?" I said softly, though truthfully, I could stand just staring at the man and the way his lashes fanned out across his cheeks for a little while longer. The index finger on my free hand itched to trace the line of his thick brows.

A muscle ticked in his jaw.

"Okay?" I probed. "On the count of three."

His throat moved as he swallowed. "Okay."

"One ..." I squeezed his hand. "Two ..." I moved my face in a little closer until we were nearly nose to nose. "Three. Open."

He opened his eyes, and beautiful chocolate and gold leaf stared back at me.

"What's the verdict?"

"You're beautiful," he said softly, the breath of his words hitting my lips and making heat sweep through me. "But I can only see you with one eye."

My own eyes closed. "Shit." I released his hand and unbuckled my seat belt. "I'll drive. Let's head to Denver and book a flight home."

He lunged across me and pulled my hand from the door handle. "No."

I released the handle and faced him as he sat back in his own seat. "Eli. You're blind."

"In one eye. And the sight may return in a little bit. But I can still see. We're not going home."

"You. Are. Blind."

"And I made a promise to you, and I'm going to see that promise through. I owe you at least that much." There was a hint of anger in his tone, but I didn't think that anger was directed at me. "I do think you should drive, though. At least for a bit. You're right about the depth perception and peripheral vision. I need some time to adjust."

"Your sight is more important than this wedding," I whispered after a long moment of quiet between us.

"I think everything is more important than this wedding," he said. "But it's important to *you*, and therefore, it's important. So we're going, Alexandra. No arguments."

My back snapped straight when he said my full name.

Why did it keep doing that? And why did I want to purr like a kitten when he said it? And why did I want him to say it like that again?

"At least let me take you to a hospital in Denver," I said.

"Why?"

"To get checked out?"

"I already know what they'd say. They'd send me for an MRI and then come to me and say, 'Mr. Evans, we're afraid you have a Keith pressing on your optic nerve. We recommend surgery. Here is the price tag. Would you like us to remove your arm and leg with a chainsaw or an ax? A local anesthetic *does* cost extra.'"

I rolled my eyes. "It feels irresponsible *not* to take you to the hospital."

"I'm not going to the hospital, Alexandra. End of discussion. Now get out of the car and come around to the driver's side," he said. "And don't you fucking dare take us to the airport or hospital." He opened his side and got out. We met around the back of the hatch, and a look that sent butterflies into a frenzy in my belly passed between us before we kept walking and got back into the car.

He buckled his belt.

I buckled my belt, keenly aware of how fucking wet my panties were and trying to figure out why.

He pointed ahead. "There's the sign to get you back onto the interstate."

Nodding, I turned the key in the ignition, and with my heart in my throat and my nerves almost completely shot, I pulled back into traffic and toward the on-ramp.

We were quiet for a long time.

Eventually, Eli closed his eyes and tipped his head back against the headrest. I couldn't tell if he was sleeping or not, but I operated under the guise that he was and didn't put the music on.

We drove for five hours without saying a word to each other. Three of those, his eyes were closed and I was basically alone with my thoughts.

Cannoning, plaguing, worrying thoughts.

It was almost seven at night, and I was hungry. My stomach grumbled furiously and apparently loud enough that Eli sat up in his chair and opened his eyes. I didn't know why I breathed a sigh of relief to see his eyes again, but I did.

I had no idea if he had vision in either of them now, but I hoped that he did.

"Take the next exit, and we'll find something for dinner," he said, his voice a deep, gravelly grit like he'd just woken up. Perhaps he had?

"Can you see with both eyes?" I asked, my voice quiet.

He shook his head stoically. "No. Left one is still out."

I swallowed and took the next exit. The town was small and sleepy, but it boasted a Subway, so I swung in, and we got out to go and grab some sandwiches.

Again, we were quiet as we stood in line to order our dinner. We took our sandwiches back out to the car and once again sat in silence as we ate.

I knew he was dealing with his fate, and I didn't want to push, but at the same time it felt like he was pushing me away even though I'd done nothing wrong. I offered to forgo the wedding and just head back to Maine so he could get the surgery sooner, but he declined.

I didn't want to get frustrated with him, but sometimes, as hard as we tried, we couldn't control our feelings and they just took us over, even when we didn't want them to.

After we finished our sandwiches, we got back on the road, the sun chasing us as we headed west. I stayed quiet until the sign on the interstate said DENVER 105 MILES. I didn't know why that sign was my trigger, but it was.

I waited until there was a spot for me to pull off the highway and did. Twilight had started to set in, and I hated driving at this time of night, but I knew I had to, so I wasn't going to say anything—about that.

I was going to say something else, though.

"Need to pee?" Eli asked, turning his head to face me so he could see me out of his right eye. The strings of my heart tightened.

I shook my head. "No. But we need to clear the air."

His thick brow lifted. "About?"

"All of *this.*"

"And *this* is?"

"You being a dick. I haven't done anything wrong. And yet your silence and sullenness are making me feel like I have. I'm really sorry that you have a douchebag tumor in your brain and he's decided to fuck with your eyesight right now. But that's not my fault, and yet you've totally shut down and shut me out and it's not fair."

I exhaled, crossed my arms over my body, and stared straight ahead.

There. I said what I wanted to say. What had been burning like acid, unsaid, on the back of my tongue for the past several hours.

"Not a bit of this is your fault," he said quietly after a long, awkward pause between us. "And the fact that you have offered to fly home or take me to a hospital, removing my end of the bargain while keeping yours, has just made me feel like an even bigger dick. You're ..."

"I'm what?" I snapped, regretting my venom as soon as I spat it out and wishing I could take it back.

"Amazing," he breathed, his shoulders slumping. "Selfless. Strong ... and incredible. And even though we're only getting fake married, I don't deserve to be married to someone like you."

My mouth opened, then closed, then opened again. I turned to face him. Sadness was painted all over his face, but even with his turned-down mouth and the pain in his eyes, I could see something else flickering in the depths of his irises. Something burning. Something hot and ... dangerous.

It made my body ignite and my stomach did a big somersault.

"I'm sorry if you felt like I was upset with you. I'm not. At all. I'm upset at myself and just trying to process things. I also keep hoping and maybe even praying a little that my vision might return." He reached across the console and took my hand in his warm, calloused one. "I'll do better. I promise. I can still see, and I shouldn't have made things so tense in here for the last several hours. That wasn't fair to you."

I hated how good my hand felt in his. How badly I wanted that hand and the other one all over my body.

I cleared my throat, squeezed his fingers, then pulled my hand free and placed it back on the steering wheel. "Thank you for your apology. I accept." I turned over the ignition, turned off the hazard lights and, when it was all clear, pulled into traffic once again.

Eli leaned forward and turned on the stereo, then brought up some Linkin Park on the app on his phone and then linked it with the Bluetooth.

Before too long, we were both bobbing our heads and singing "Numb" like nothing had happened. We made it to Denver just shy of midnight.

CHAPTER TWENTY-SIX

Alex

I SCORED US A kick-ass deal at a really nice hotel using some promo code that popped up in my email. The only thing was, it was for one room with two king-size beds and a massive Jacuzzi tub.

To say I didn't take one look at that tub and start having thoughts about taking a sexy bath with Eli would be a bald-faced lie.

The hotel also had an outdoor—*and* indoor pool. Apparently, the outdoor pool was up on the roof. But we were too tired by the time we checked in, and the pool closed at ten, so we just retired to our room.

"Feel free to have a shower first," Eli said, plunking his suitcase down on the suitcase rack next to one of the king-size beds. "I can wait."

"Thanks," I said, yawning and peeling my tank top over my head.

"Uh ..."

I glanced behind me at Eli, who had paused what he was doing and was now just staring at me.

"What?"

"You're just going to get undressed right here?"

I rolled my eyes at him. "Not naked—though you *have* seen me naked. But I wear a sports bra at yoga."

His cheeks had turned a ruddy shade, and he averted his eyes. "Fair enough."

Chuckling, I took my pajamas with me into the bathroom and shut the door.

The shower was also huge. Big enough for two.

We'd had a great drive through Nebraska, the vast fields of corn and soybeans on either side of us for miles as we sang along to music and chatted, but ever since last night and our conversation about when we lost our virginity, I'd felt a shift with Eli. And it wasn't necessarily that he was distancing himself from me. I couldn't quite put my finger on it, but there was this weird, almost possessiveness about him now. And it wasn't even the way he spoke to me, which hadn't really changed. It was the looks he gave me, particularly those he gave me when he thought I wasn't watching.

I kept telling myself that it was all in my head, but when our conversations in the car came to an organic end and I just sat there looking out the window, I could see his reflection sometimes, and the way he was looking at me sent delightful shivers all through my body and shook a tree full of butterflies in my belly.

He seemed a little ... angry when I told him I'd lost my virginity just before my junior year of high school.

"Who the fuck is Derek Sharpe?" The venom in his tone had me laughing when I thought back to how much fire was in his eyes, even in the dark tent.

I hadn't had a crush on Eli in high school, but I could have. If he hadn't been so mean to me, if he hadn't taunted me, I definitely could have. And then it would be him who I would have lost my virginity to—maybe.

I turned on the water and after the room started to steam, stepped into the shower and closed the glass door behind me.

I washed the campfire smoke from my hair, shaved my legs and let the water sluice over my body.

My hair was full of shampoo when there was a knock at the door. "Alex, I need to pee."

"Uh ... okay, just let me rinse out my hair."

"I won't look. Can I just come in? I'm going to piss my fucking pants. That Gatorade is hitting me hard."

I snorted and shut my eyes, tipping my head back. "Fine."

The door opened. I opened my eyes and watched through the mottled glass and steam-covered shower door as Eli, holding his hand over his eyes, walked past me toward the toilet.

"I told you not to drink that whole thing," I said. "Besides the electrolytes, that shit is poison. And you can get electrolytes by adding a little bit of pink Himalayan sea salt to your water."

He started to pee. "Enough lecturing. I've learned my lesson."

I laughed. "Just saying. If your pee is Day-Glo yellow, maybe you should cut back on the sports drinks. It's not like you spent the morning shooting three-pointers, then ran a half-marathon. We sat in a car for ten and a half hours."

The toilet flushed. The sink ran.

I opened my eyes and screamed to find him standing right next to the shower door. But even through the steamed glass, I could tell his eyes were closed.

"You done?" he asked, that commanding alpha tone that he sometimes used making my nipples pebble.

I swallowed. "Just need to rinse the conditioner out of my hair."

"No, I mean, are you done haranguing me?"

I grinned. "But it's so much fun."

"What would you do if I opened my eyes right now?"

I swallowed again. "The glass is mottled and all steamed up. I doubt you could see much. And you've seen it all before, remember? When you thought I'd fallen and smacked my head on the tub."

"So you're saying I can open my eyes?" His words and the way he was talking were doing things to me. I wanted to open the door and drag him into the shower, take his mouth and let him do anything and everything he wanted to my body so long as he kept talking to me the way he was now.

I was breathless. How was I breathless? I was standing still, barely moving. And yet my heart was beating wildly and my chest rose and fell like I'd just finished an uphill jog. I swallowed again and stared into his face through the glass, into his eyes, or where his eyes were, except they were closed. "I'm saying there's no point to you opening them, since you've already seen everything. There's nothing new to see."

He opened his eyes.

My breath snagged in my throat.

His eyes held mine. They didn't travel south at all.

And somehow, I felt even more exposed, even more *seen* than if he had let his eyes caress the rest of my body.

"Booked us a whitewater rafting tour for tomorrow," he said, breaking the trance I was in. "We leave at eight, so hurry up and get your cute ass into bed."

Dear God. My pussy clenched at his mention of my "cute ass" and the way he was telling me what to do.

WHAT WAS HAPPENING TO ME?

I nodded. "Okay."

Eli held my gaze for another second, then turned and left the bathroom.

I waited until I heard the door *click* shut before I exhaled and leaned my back against the wall, blinking and blinking and blinking because I just couldn't make a lick of sense of what just happened. It had to be another dream.

But it wasn't a dream.

What kind of game was he playing?

I finished rinsing my hair, then shut off the water. I probably took more time than I needed in the bathroom, brushing my teeth and getting dressed, but that was the time required to compose myself.

When I finally opened the door, Eli was standing in the middle of the hotel room wearing nothing but a pair of black boxer briefs, and an amused look on his face, holding his toiletries bag.

I averted my eyes from the front of his boxers immediately.

"'Bout time you got your ass out of there," he said, walking past me. "Into bed, Alexandra. We have a big day tomorrow."

I gaped at him.

"Oh, and I called the front desk and scheduled laundry service for tomorrow, so make a pile of clothes you want to be washed and it'll get done while we're rafting." He closed the bathroom door.

I stood there staring at the door he just closed for at least two full minutes.

My body tingled. My pussy pulsed, and my nipples were hard as rocks beneath my tank top.

I wanted to open that bathroom door and do what he'd done to me, only I already knew that I wouldn't be able to keep my eyes from drifting downward. I didn't have that kind of self-control.

I shook myself free of the rebellious, wanton, increasingly filthy thoughts that were cannoning around my head and got into bed.

But the longer the shower ran, the more I thought about Eli covered in soap, with his hair wet and water droplets clinging to his whiskers.

You cannot masturbate right now! You CANNOT!

I bunched my fingers into fists, then rolled over onto my side, away from Eli's bed. Squeezing my eyes shut, I tried to think of other things.

But not one other thought could penetrate my brain and the dirty, dirty things I was thinking about.

Like how much I would love to just take Eli in my mouth the second he stepped out of the shower. How the pain of my knees on the tile floor as I sucked his cock would only add to the thrill of it all. How I wanted him to grip me by the hair as I took him to the back of my throat and controlled of the speed and cadence at which I pleasured him.

The shower shut off.

I squeezed my eyes closed even harder. Like that would do something.

He wasn't in the bathroom for much longer, and even though I was entirely prepared for it, when the door opened, I jumped where I lay.

"This your pile of dirty clothes?" he asked. "In front of the dresser."

"How did you know I wasn't asleep?"

"I know you pretty damn well, Alex. I can tell when you're asleep and when you're not. Is this the pile?"

"Yes."

"'K. Now get some sleep. For real."

And like a good, obedient thing, I closed my eyes, and with very questionable and arousing things going on in my head, I willed sleep to come while at the same time praying that I didn't have another vocal sex dream about Eli.

We grabbed breakfast on the way to our rafting trip.

Eli didn't say whether or not I woke him up moaning and groaning in mid-dream orgasm last night, so I was going to err on the side of relief and believe that my sex dreams were silent. Because there was no denying the fact that I'd indeed *had* sex dreams about Eli. I woke up practically in a puddle of my own arousal.

We didn't have to drive far out of Denver. The rafting and ziplining place was near Lakewood.

We met with our rafting guide and all the other people on our boat.

I'd never been rafting before—Eli had, of course; what hadn't the man done?—but he didn't play the arrogant expert and listened to the instructions and rules.

With our life vests on and our paddles in hand, we walked side by side down to the raft.

Before we left the hotel, Eli pulled out a baseball cap and plunked it on his head, then he pulled out another one and plopped it on my head. "Figured you might need one, too," he said. "Grabbed them at the last gas station in Nebraska." Both of our hats said, "I've been to Nebraska. I can't deny it."

I snorted but thanked him.

"You excited?" he asked, glancing down at me as we approached the water.

"Excited and nervous," I said.

"You'll love it. I promise."

I lifted my brows. "I hope so."

We sat where we were told to sit on the side of the raft. Eli was positioned in the back behind me, while I was the third person from the front.

A family—a mom, husband and their twelve-ish-year-old son—was on the raft with us, along with our two guides.

It was a "full ship," according to Stefan, our guide.

I glanced over at the only other woman in the boat, Ana. She smiled at me. "Have you ever been rafting before?" she asked me. She had an accent, but I couldn't place it. Italian? Greek?

I shook my head. "You?"

She shook her head as well. "No. We are on vacation from Portugal, visiting family. Manuel"—she pointed to her son—"wanted to go rafting. It was the one thing he asked to do when we came here. So we are here." She said something in Portuguese to her husband and son. "You nervous?" she asked, turning back to me.

"A little," I replied with a shrug.

Fingers gripped my shoulder and squeezed. "You got this," Eli said behind me, his warm fingers a boon of comfort.

Ana's brown eyes glittered as she smiled. "Where are you from?"

"Maine," I said, glancing behind me at Eli. "Well, Connecticut, originally, but we live in Maine now. We're on a road trip to San Diego."

Ana's eyes widened. "Oh, how fun."

"All right, let's go find some rapids," Stefan said, pushing us off and into the middle of the river before hopping onto the back of the raft. The other guide, Julian, was at the front. "Left!"

Those of us on the left—Julian, Eli and I—started to paddle.

"Right!" Stefan called out a moment later. "Paddle hard, all!" And so it went for our entire rafting adventure. Every time Stefan yelled, "Left!" we paddled like our life depended on it. When he yelled, "Left back!" those of us on the left paddled backward. And when he yelled, "Paddle hard, all," we all paddled until we thought our arms might fall off.

It was a workout I hadn't anticipated but was really glad to have. I'd been feeling rather sedentary on this trip, despite our short hikes. I knew I'd feel it in my arms tomorrow and welcomed the aches.

We stopped midway through our rafting trip, pulling over to a small, calm beach area where the guides brought out lunches of turkey sandwiches and juice boxes for all. Eli, because Eli was Eli, took off his shirt and went swimming where the water was calm. Which prompted Ana's husband, Sérgio, and son Manuel to join him. The three of them acted like goofballs doing handstands and seeing who could walk the farthest underwater on their hands. I'd dipped in a toe and deemed it way too cold.

Ana and I sat on the rocks, enjoying the sun on our faces, chatting. She showed me pictures on her phone of their nine-year-old pug Buddy, back in Portugal, and asked me about my favorite part of being a veterinarian.

"How long are you in Colorado for?" I asked, sipping from my grape juice box.

"A total of three weeks. We have been here nine days so far. Had to adjust to the jet lag and all of that. You?"

I nodded. "A couple of days. We raced through Nebraska, but we don't have to be in San Diego until Thursday, so we have a few days. We'll stop in Utah one day as well as Vegas."

"Sérgio and I want to go to Vegas, but Manuel doesn't want us to go without him." Ana laughed. "Maybe another time. Though I do want to see the Grand Canyon."

"Me, too."

She gently touched my ring finger where the engagement ring was and smiled warmly. "When is the big day?"

I shrugged. "We're just going to do it when we're in Vegas. Probably the only reason we're even going—besides the Grand Canyon."

Her eyes went wide, almost in horror. "What?"

"It's really not that big of a deal."

She shook her head, *tsking* me. Her brown ponytail swished behind her head.

We watched the guys splash in the water for a bit. The guides were beginning to pack up.

"What are you two up to tonight?" Ana asked after a moment of quiet between us.

"No idea. Probably find a restaurant to grab dinner, then back to the hotel. I'm sure after today—the rafting and then ziplining—we'll be exhausted."

She shook her head again. "No. You will come to my family's house for dinner. The game between Benfica and Sporting will be on."

"I have no idea what that is," I said, laughing.

"Football teams in Portugal. We root for Benfica."

Eli, Sérgio and Manuel emerged from the water and thanked the guides for the towels they offered them.

My mouth grew dry as I stared at Eli's wet, glistening torso. I also wasn't listening to a damn thing Ana was saying.

His eyes snagged mine, and right away he knew what I was doing. What I was thinking. Which, of course, prompted a cocky smirk from him, and I was pretty sure he tightened his abs so they popped even more.

The bugger.

"You have to come. We'll have Portuguese food, Portuguese wine, Portuguese desserts." Ana's hand gripped mine, drawing me out of my Eli-ogling trance. "So you'll come? Cab to the house. It's not far. That way you can drink all the wine."

I laughed. "All the wine?"

"Yes, of course. All the wine."

Sérgio came to stand next to his wife. She said something to him in Portuguese, then he smiled and looked at Eli and me.

"What's going on?" Eli asked, drying his hair.

"Apparently we're going to a party tonight," I said, extending my hand so he could help me stand up.

His brows lifted. "Are we?"

Ana and Sérgio both nodded.

"You are!" Ana said. "No arguments."

By the time we reached the end of our journey, I was completely drenched and unable to wipe the smile from my face.

My arms ached, but my heart was full.

We rode back, sitting on towels, in the transport van, back to where we started, and changed into dry clothes, then it was off to the ziplining course.

I wasn't exactly afraid of heights, but let's just say when I go up to the top of skyscrapers—not that I go up very often—I'm not one of those people looking over the edge at all the antlike people scurrying around below.

"Have you ever zip-lined—never mind," I said with an eye roll as Eli and I followed our new ziplining guides to the first platform.

He grinned. "Yes. In Costa Rica through the cloud forest."

"Right." I nodded. "Not much you haven't done, huh?"

"I've lived," he said with a chuckle. "If that's what you're implying." He nudged my shoulder. "You never know when you're going to be diagnosed with a brain tumor."

"Benign," I said, my expression turning serious.

"It's still trying to make me go blind."

We reached the first platform, and he stopped me with his hands on my shoulders, then he went about double-checking that my helmet straps were tight enough.

Just like our rafting guides had, our ziplining guides were very thorough in demonstrating where to put your hands, how to stop, and how to slow down.

The first guide—Anton—climbed onto the platform, then with an enthusiastic *whoop*, he ran and leapt off the platform and let the harness around his waist and between his legs keep him safe as he flipped upside down and "flew" down the line, overtop the trees to the next platform.

My stomach did its own flip upside down. I glanced nervously up at Eli.

He just grinned down at me. "You got this."

"I'm not so sure," I said, nibbling on my lip as I watched Sérgio climb up onto the platform with zero fear in his eyes.

Sérgio went, echoing Anton's *whoop* and adding his own *yeehaw* afterward as he zoomed down the cable.

Manuel went next, and just like his dad, the kid had zero fear in his brown eyes. Ana didn't look as confident, but like a trooper she stepped up onto the platform, gave me a huge smile and took off.

Then it was just Eli and me.

Eli stepped away from me for a moment to speak with Kendrick, the other guide.

My heart was in my throat, my stomach was threatening to unleash the turkey sandwich from lunch, and my hands were getting clammier and clammier.

Eli turned to me and rested his hand on my upper arm. "We can go together."

My brows knitted. "Is that safe?"

He nodded. "Completely. You can just sit between my legs. I'll loop my legs over yours, and then we'll go down together. Sound good?"

I nodded. "Yeah. Sounds really good."

His smile warmed me, and instantly my stomach began to settle and my breathing started to even out. We climbed up onto the platform, and Kendrick got me hooked up first. Then he helped Eli.

Eli hopped up, allowing himself to just hang there by the cable, and he spread his legs, inched forward until my butt was nestled against his crotch, then he lifted his legs over mine and crossed them. I was locked in.

"Ready?" he asked, his mouth right next to my ear.

A shiver raced through me, but it wasn't from fear. The warmth of his breath on my neck had my belly doing a new kind of flip-flop.

Swallowing, I nodded. "Yeah."

Kendrick pulled us backward, up the platform a bit, then when my feet could no longer touch, I gave him the nod, and he let go.

And away we went.

I squeezed my eyes shut, but as if he could see me, Eli said, "Don't close your eyes, Alexandra. Open them. Look down. See the forest below."

I did as he said, and sure enough, what I saw was nothing short of incredible.

We were flying right through the tops of the trees. Evergreens to the left and to the right, with the ground so far below.

"Amazing," I breathed.

"Yes," he said, his legs tightening around mine, the heat of his body a reassuring presence behind me. I could easily get used to this. Get used to being with Eli like this, wrapped up in his arms, in his strength.

And just as quickly as the ride began, it ended and Eli was squeezing the brake and we were slowing down as Anton waited for us on the platform.

We stopped, and Eli released his grip on my legs, putting his feet back down. I did the same.

"Good girl," he whispered, his tenor deep and gravelly.

I sucked in a breath, and my body started to buzz. My pussy clenched.

Anton unclipped us from the cable, and I took a moment to regain my composure before I turned around to face Eli. "Thank you."

His smile was half-hitched, unleashing that lone dimple, and one hundred percent sexy. "Happy to do it. You need me to do it again?"

I didn't think I *needed* him to, since it wasn't as terrifying a ride as I thought. But I certainly *wanted* him to. I wanted to be wrapped up in Eli as much as possible ... possibly forever.

CHAPTER
TWENTY-SEVEN

Eli

I WAS HESITANT AT first to head to a party with people we just met, but Sérgio was a great guy, and Ana and Alexandra seemed to get along quite well.

At Ana's encouragement, we cabbed to her relative's house from the hotel, which was only about six miles. That way, as Ana put it, we could "drink all the wine."

I wasn't sure that I was going to drink *all* the wine, but I was looking forward to drinking *some* of the wine. I also needed to distract myself and the fact that I could only see out of one eye. Since yesterday, I'd adapted to the lack of depth perception and having to turn my head so I could see better what was to my left, but it still fucking sucked. I'd definitely felt the handicap when we were rafting, particularly since Alexandra and I were on the left side of the boat.

So I needed this party to keep me from slipping into a bout of deep depression and dwelling on the fact that tomorrow I could wake up and not be able to see out of either eye since

Keith was obviously getting bigger and putting more pressure on my optic nerve.

Keith was such a fucking douchebag.

Back at the river, Sérgio asked me if I played football, and I said a little, then he insisted that I play with him and his cousins in his uncle's backyard.

Our conversation basically went like: "You play football, or what you Americans call *soccer?*"

"A little."

"Why do you not call it *football?*"

"Because we have a different kind of football that you hardly touch with your feet."

He laughed. "You can call it football."

"No, sir, I cannot. Because when Americans call things by their proper names and use the proper pronunciation, we end up sounding like pretentious douchebags. Like I cannot pronounce bruschetta, *broos-ketta,* as it is supposed to be said because I will sound like a pretentious douchebag and deserve every flogging I receive."

Sérgio laughed again and nodded. "Okay, okay. But you will play soccer with us. The game between Sporting and Benfica starts at six. You come for that?"

I'd simply laughed and splashed him with water. "I'll try, my man."

The tires of the cab crunched on gravel as it turned down the long driveway that led to Sérgio's uncle's house. To say the place was palatial would be an accurate description. I got a real Mediterranean vibe from it, particularly with the Spanish archways and fountain in the middle of the circular driveway.

"Oh my," Alexandra said beside me in the back of the cab. "Now I feel underdressed." She glanced down at the super sexy, very *not* underdressed white dress that she was wearing. It wasn't one of the ones that I had picked out for her on our shopping spree, but it was hot nonetheless. It was figure-flattering, had a deep but not plunging neck, and the back on it was hot with a cutout and a bow. Plus, that bit of lace that was kind of see-through beneath her tits was ultra hot.

"Shut your face," I said playfully. "You look hot."

Her smile was small, and she tried to hide it, but she couldn't hide anything from me. Tucking a strand of her hair behind her ears, she glanced down at her purse and whispered, "Thank you."

I'd gone with a pair of chinos and a short-sleeved button-down shirt with a dark blue and white check pattern.

I paid the cab driver. We climbed out of the cab and walked up to the front door. Alexandra had only just lifted her fist in the air, preparing to knock, when the door swung open.

"You made it!" Ana exclaimed, smiling brightly. She leaned in and hugged Alexandra, kissing her on both cheeks, then she did the same to me.

I lifted up the bouquet of flowers we'd bought before hopping in the cab. "I thought these might be better than a bottle of wine since you said we would be drinking *all the wine.*"

Ana chuckled and accepted the flowers. "Yes, no need to bring wine. We have so much. Portuguese wine also. The best."

Alex and I followed her through the vaulted-ceiling mini-mansion to where voices and laughter echoed from the back patio and yard.

A big-screen television was on in the living room with a soccer game playing, and Sérgio and two other men stood with beers in their hands, watching the game.

When Sérgio saw me, he extended his hand. I clasped it and shook, thanking him for inviting us. The man had a long beard and mustache that he styled so the ends twisted upward. It was quirky, but he pulled it off. He introduced me to his two cousins, Diogo and Estevo.

Ana took Alexandra off outside to introduce her to more people.

"Who's winning?" I asked, thanking a man with a thick black mustache for the ice-cold beer bottle he pushed into my hand.

"Sporting," Sérgio said with a grumble. "Fucking pussies." He gestured toward the screen, showing off the long tattoo on the inside of his left forearm. "Fucking ref is playing the favorites. He's getting money or blowjobs or something. Should have been at least two yellow cards, and he didn't give even one."

Sérgio stroked his beard with his free hand while his eyes remained glued to the screen.

The center fielder from Sporting flopped to the ground in what was obviously a fake-out, and the living room erupted into angry cries and a lot of men swearing in Portuguese.

"Motherfuckers!" Sérgio said. "Motherfuckers!"

I patted him on the shoulder. "I'm going to go find Alex. Be right back."

He nodded.

Manuel and some other kids were in the backyard kicking the soccer ball around while Ana, Alexandra, four other women, and two men sat around a big glass table on the enormous patio, a wine glass in front of each of them.

My hand fell to Alexandra's shoulder, and she glanced up at me, smiling. "Did your team lose?"

I grinned down at her. "Other team is being a bunch of motherfuckers."

"They always are," Ana said with a chuckle.

Something was cooking on the grill. I glanced over to see chicken thighs and drumsticks being kissed by flames, as well as a bunch of skinny little fish. Definitely sardines. The Portuguese loved their sardines.

"Everything good here?" I asked her, dropping my voice low enough so that just Alexandra could hear me.

She nodded and patted my hand with hers. "Everything's great." She lifted her stemless wine glass. "I'm drinking *all* the wine."

"As you should. You were a trouper today."

"Took me a moment to find my bravery, but once I found it—"

"You were a zip-lining machine," Ana added.

Alexandra beamed. "It was a lot of fun."

I squeezed her shoulder once more, then went to rejoin Sérgio and the other men in the living room.

It was almost ten o'clock, the backyard and deck were filled with twinkling lights, and the full moon was high in the sky and casting shadows across the yard.

I was half fucking snapped on beer and wine, as well as something else Sérgio's uncle Ricardo had called *Medronho,* which was a fruit brandy from Portugal and about forty-eight percent alcohol.

He'd passed around shots of that after dinner, and I had to say, it went down mighty easy.

With a full belly, fuzzy head and smile on my face, I sat next to Alexandra at the big glass table while Ricardo told stories that brought tears of laughter to most of his family's eyes.

Alexandra looked over at me and grinned. "Glad we came?"

I nodded. "Totally. You?"

She nodded. "Definitely. This is what a family is supposed to be. Not our messed-up version."

"Agreed."

But we didn't let that comment get us down. I sipped my wine and settled deeper into my chair. I would have loved to drape my arm around Alexandra's back and pull her into me. Even though I couldn't, it felt inherently natural to do it.

I could practically feel her fear earlier today, regarding the zip line. And since this trip was all about no regrets, I made sure to do everything I could to help her push past her nerves and accomplish what I knew she wanted to accomplish. And as I figured, she was stronger and braver than she thought and conquered those cables. I wasn't going to lie, though. Having her nestled between my legs on that first zip line had been heaven.

The family was speaking Portuguese, so I turned back to Alexandra. "Whenever you want to get out of here, just say the word. I'm on your clock."

She smiled shyly. "I'm okay. This is a lot of fun."

"What is so special about a Las Vegas wedding?" Ricardo said loudly, shaking both Alexandra and I out of our stupor.

"Huh?" I asked.

Ricardo was gesturing wildly. "Why do you go to Vegas to get married? So cheap, so gaudy." He swept his arms around his patio and yard. "Here, it is beautiful." He pointed at the moon. "You have the moon."

My eyes widened, and my mouth opened. "Are you suggesting we get married *here?*"

Ricardo nodded. "Here. Now. I am a minister." His hands continued to gesture. "Among other things."

I turned to face Alexandra. "Did you know about this?"

Her expression was as shocked, if not more, than mine. She shook her head. "Nope."

We both looked at Ana and Sérgio. They were grinning like a pride of lions planning their attack on a couple of unsuspecting antelope at the watering hole.

I shook a finger at Sérgio. "Oh, Sérgio, you are a wily bastard."

He tossed his head back and laughed wildly. "It's all my wife." He looped his arm around Ana and drew her close to him, kissing her on the side of the head. "She is a hopeless romantic."

Ana's eyes sparkled beneath the strings of lights over the table. "Why get married in Vegas, alone, where Russian mobsters marry strippers, when you can get married here ... in paradise. And with friends."

I glanced again at Alexandra. She was definitely drunk. And most definitely beautiful. I lifted a shoulder. "We were going to do it in Vegas."

"We were," she said slowly, her smile casually coasting across her face.

Ricardo slammed his hand down on the table. "Then it is settled."

"We don't have a license," Alexandra argued, though the fight in her voice was weak.

Ricardo waved his hand dismissively in the air. "Go tomorrow. Twenty minutes in and out. Tonight is the ceremony—what matters. Tomorrow you make it legal. Come back here when you get the license and I will sign it. No problem at all." He turned to Ana. "You take Alexandra upstairs to fluff her up. Eli, you come with me. Thirty minutes, everyone. We meet on the grass, under the arch."

"They have an arch!" Alexandra whispered to me as she stood up and slightly stumbled out from the nest of chairs to where Ana was already waiting for her.

"And I guess I'll meet you under it in thirty minutes," I said, suddenly feeling like I was the one getting ready to do a zip line for the first time. Only I had no harness, the cable was made of snakes, and it was a million-foot drop to the bottom.

But what—rather *who*—waited for me at the bottom platform was Alexandra. So no matter how terrifying the ride, I had to get to her no matter what.

CHAPTER TWENTY-EIGHT

Alex

ANA GENTLY SWEPT THE blush brush over my cheek. "I can see how much he loves you."

All I did was smile. I didn't have the heart to tell her this was all a ruse. A marriage of convenience. A business transaction.

"You'll be my maid of honor?" I asked, closing my eyes so she could apply a bit of eyeshadow.

"Of course. That is what friends do."

I smiled again. "Ricardo's yard is beautiful."

"There. Open your eyes."

I did as I was told.

"*You* are beautiful." She gestured to my dress. "And you are wearing white. It was meant to be."

Laughing, I stood up from the vanity.

"And you brought a bouquet of flowers. Double meant to be."

Blinking at the gorgeous woman with curly brown hair and kind eyes standing in front of me, I was overcome with emotion and practically lunged into her arms, hugging her. "Thank you."

Chuckling, she patted my back. "You are a little drunk."

"Maybe a little."

She laughed again. "It's okay. Almost all weddings in Vegas are done when people are drunk. At least here, the wine is good, the venue is good, and the company is the best."

I stepped out of her arms and wiped the tears from beneath my eyes. "The company *is* the best."

"Maybe you can come and honeymoon in Portugal? We are in the Algarve. The most beautiful place."

I nodded. I was too caught up in the moment, in the fairy tale of it all, to say anything besides, "I would love that."

A knock at the door had us both turning.

"Ready?" Ricardo's wife, Fatima, asked.

Ana and I nodded.

Fatima smiled, then disappeared.

Ana's hands landed on the sides of my arms. "The most beautiful bride I have ever seen."

I sniffled and laughed. "Probably the drunkest bride, too."

She took my hand and led me to the hallway. "Oh no. You should have seen my sister at her wedding. She was so drunk. Drank so much champagne the morning of. Puked right before she went down the aisle."

"Oh my God."

We descended the stairs.

"Missed her dress by a centimeter. And she'd had pesto canapes at the brunch as they got ready for the wedding, so the puke was green."

We both laughed.

"Well, I just ate sardines and piri chicken, along with enough wine and Medronho to make a whole frat house drunk, so I bet my puke would be a lovely color."

Fatima stood at the door with a clump of flowers made from the bouquet we brought for her and Ricardo. She'd wrapped a ribbon around the bottom and handed it to me as we passed her.

Ana let go of my hand, nodded at me, and as the music started—something beautiful on a mandolin—she walked down the makeshift aisle that was the stairs from the patio onto the lawn.

Manuel appeared at my side, his arm out. "I am to walk you down the aisle."

Smiling, I took his arm. "I couldn't imagine anyone else."

He beamed back at me.

We waited for five deep breaths, then on the sixth deep inhale, Manuel and I stepped forward.

I knew that Sérgio was standing beside Eli and Ana was standing where I would stand, and Ricardo was standing in the middle, but all I saw was Eli.

His eyes found mine, and for the entire procession down the lawn, under the lights, and with the moon directly overhead as I made my way to the archway covered in wisteria, I only saw Eli.

His throat moved on a swallow, and his smile faltered slightly for half a second, but his eyes held strong. His eyes never wavered.

I knew this was a real wedding and a sham of a marriage, but so much of this moment felt real. Felt right.

His gaze seared me. I felt it straight to my toes.

But where I felt it more than anywhere else was in my heart.

My chest tightened, and warmth spread through me in a rush.

Step by step, Eli's eyes held mine, and before I knew it, Manuel was pulling his arm from mine and stepping to the side while Eli reached for me.

I went to him, holding his hand with mine.

He smiled at me.

I smiled back.

Ricardo began to speak, but I barely heard him over the pounding sound in my ears.

"Do you have the rings?" he asked after what felt like half a second but was probably closer to two or three minutes. Time was standing still as I stood beneath an archway, under the light of the full moon and before a minister, marrying Eli Evans.

The mention of rings had me snapping out of my stupor.

I shook my head at Ricardo. "No. No ri—"

"Right here," Eli said, opening his palm to reveal two white-gold bands, one thinner and one thicker and bigger.

My mouth opened. "How?"

He shrugged. "I bought them when I bought your engagement ring. Been carrying them in my wallet so when we went to get married in Vegas I wouldn't forget them."

Blinking away the threat of tears, I smiled and shook my head. "Full of surprises."

Ricardo motioned for me to hold out my finger, which I did.

Eli slipped the ring on. Just like my engagement ring, it fit perfectly.

I took the ring from Eli's palm and slid it onto his finger.

Ricardo said a few more things, but again, I wasn't really paying attention. Not until he made me repeat after him, that is. Which I did, like a damn robot.

I was just too swept up in the magic that was Eli looking at me the way he was, and the fact that he had rings and we were actually getting married, in a gorgeous backyard surrounded by new friends. It was the wedding I never knew I wanted until I was in the middle of it. It was perfect.

It was Eli's turn to repeat after Ricardo.

His voice was deep, hypnotic and very, very convincing. I believed every word. I was lost in his eyes, falling further and further under his spell the longer he looked at me, the longer he vowed to honor and cherish, for better or worse, in sickness and in health.

I believed it all.

"You may now kiss the bride," Ricardo said.

I blinked and lifted my head to Eli's face, only just realizing that my gaze had drifted down to his mouth.

"We don't have to," I murmured, shaking my head.

His brows pinched and an angry expression took over his face. "The fuck we don't." Then he tugged my hand until my body was plastered against his. He cupped my face with his free hand and took my mouth with a possession I felt in every cell of my body.

His thumb tugged at my bottom lip, encouraging me to open for him as his tongue wedged inside. I acquiesced, allowing him to lead the kiss, to take complete control.

He could probably feel my pulse rapidly pumping through my veins where his little finger lay against my jaw.

My eyes were closed, and my body melted into his.

I'd never been kissed like that in my life. Never in such a way that I knew if my knees buckled, he'd hold me up, keep me standing as he continued to plunder my mouth, claim me as his and show me just what he could do with that tongue.

I vaguely registered the whoops, hollers and cheers around us.

It wasn't until Sérgio put a hand on Eli's shoulder and said with a chuckle, "Save it for the wedding night," that we finally broke our kiss.

My lips tingled, and I immediately touched them with my fingers.

Ana turned me around and drew me into a big hug. "Congratulations, sweetie," she said. "Now we celebrate with champagne!"

The cab ride back to our hotel was very quiet.

Eli and I sat on opposite ends of the back seat and both looked out our windows into the dark night.

I imbibed on a lot of champagne in celebration but was beginning to sober up on the drive.

I had no idea how drunk or sober Eli was.

We were at our hotel in no time, inside the elevator, shrouded in more silence.

I spun the now *two* rings around my finger. I wasn't used to having one ring on, let alone two, and despite the fact that they fit perfectly, my body and brain both knew they were there and refused to leave them alone. I risked a look at Eli out of the corner of my eye. He was playing with his ring, too.

The elevator door opened, and we exited, walking shoulder to shoulder down the hallway to our room.

I dug out my key card, and when the light turned green, I turned the handle but glanced over my shoulder at him. "Tonight was fun."

He cleared his throat. "It was."

The door closed, and we were standing in the dark of the entryway to the hotel room. Our eyes found each other.

The air was thick, making it difficult to breathe. The tension between us became tangible, an essence I could practically hold in the palm of my hand.

A thick muscle ticked in his jaw, and his tongue darted out and slid between his lips.

"I hated you for most of my life," he said.

"I hated you, too," I whispered.

"But I also really fucking wanted you."

I breathed out through my mouth, then swallowed. "The two do not have to be mutually exclusive. And we don't hate each other now, right?"

A storm brewed behind his eyes, and it made my pussy clench in longing.

"The need to be inside you right now is making my brain short-circuit."

Holy shit.

My mouth was dry. But my panties sure as hell weren't.

"You're my wife." The way he gritted out the words was as if each syllable caused him immense pain. But it was a pain he relished. A pain he wanted more of.

"And you're my husband."

"How drunk are you?"

"Drunk enough to have *a lot* of dirty thoughts parading around in my head. Sober enough that you wouldn't be taking advantage—and to know with immense certainty that we'd regret *not* doing this in the morning."

"We'd regret *not* doing this?"

I nodded. "You said that we should have absolutely NO regrets on this trip. Right?"

"Alexandra ... believe me, I want nothing more than to—"

"I've been thinking of nothing else since I found out your damn shoe size. Now I need to know, does the carpet match the drapes?"

He chuckled. "I think you're mixing your metaphors."

"Am I?"

"Yes."

"But am I?"

"Yes."

"But AM I?"

"YES!"

"But you still understand what I mean."

"I happen to be fluent in drunk chick."

He was quiet for a moment, but the heat coming off him, the power he exuded made me need to reach out to the wall for support.

"If we do this, then there's no annulment. We'd have to get a divorce."

I shrugged. "So?"

"You're okay with that?"

"Annulment Ashmullment. It's only dissolving a marriage in the eyes of the church, and we didn't get married under any pervy church eyes. Besides, *your* parents got married in a church, and look how that marriage turned out, huh? And my parents got married in a freaking Catholic church with cherubs and Jesuses and Marys all over the damn place, and they're sure as hell not celebrating their fortieth wedding anniversary this year. So church smurch. Divorce shmivorce. Fifty percent of people in the world get divorced."

"I think that's fifty percent of marriages end in divorce. But not all people get married." There was amusement in his voice.

I made a "so what" face.

"A church wedding does not a marriage make. People have gotten married underwater and stayed together longer than fools who knelt down on velvet and had dumb little crowns placed on their heads. So we get a divorce. Big whoop."

The word divorce suddenly tasted bitter on my tongue. And the idea of divorcing Eli made my stomach hurt.

"Stop talking about divorcing me." The fingers of one of his hands dove into my hair, cradling my scalp possessively, while the other hand held onto my waist.

He pushed me up against the door, the hand on my waist moving up to cup my breast. I moaned into his mouth, parted my lips more for him, and met his tongue with mine.

My fingers had a mind of their own and grappled and grabbed at the fabric of his shirt, desperate to remove it so I could feel the hard muscles of his body beneath my hands. Something I'd been dreaming of doing since the first time I saw him with his shirt off.

Grabbing both my wrists, he pinned them above my head against the door and dropped his mouth to my neck. "I hated you so fucking much," he said, biting my shoulder.

"I hated you, too."

"But I also really fucking wanted you."

"You said that already."

With a growl, he let go of my wrists, stepped back for a moment, and quickly unbuttoned and shed his shirt. I slid the straps of my dress over my shoulders, allowing it to pool at my feet. I hadn't bothered with a bra. His eyes lasered in on my bare breasts. "Fuck."

His mouth dipped, and he claimed a nipple, dragging it between his lips and sucking. His teeth tugged, and I cried out as the pleasure and pain mixed and shot right down to my clit. I moaned when his other hand found its way into my panties.

"Fucking wet," he murmured, switching to the other breast.

He rubbed my clit until I was mewling and grinding down on his hand. He cupped my mound, pushed two fingers inside me while his thumb went to work on my clit.

I bucked into his hand, and within a minute, I was coming.

He surprised me when he lifted his head from my breast and took my mouth as I climaxed, swept his tongue across mine as I panted through my nose, and let the ecstasy envelop me.

When I finally descended from my high, he pulled his finger free, then reached for the sides of my panties and tugged them down over my thighs.

"You on the pill or something?" he asked.

I nodded. "IUD."

"I'm clean."

"Me, too," I practically whimpered as my eyes drifted down the length of his ripped torso and watched with fascination as he unbuttoned and unzipped his shorts. "Got tested right after Cade dumped me."

"I don't have any condoms," he said. "Didn't expect this road trip to result in a fuck. Least of all a fuck with you."

"A hate fuck," I corrected.

His eyes found mine, and even in the dark room, I could see his pupils dilate. "*Former* hate, current *like* fuck."

He pulled his cock free from his shorts and boxers, kicking them both to the side. My mouth dropped open. A string of precum was dangling from the tip, and for some animalistic reason, I licked my lips. That did not go unnoticed by him.

With another growl, he lifted me up by the hips and slid me back down so I rested on his hips and he rested inside me.

Our groans echoed around the room.

Our eyes locked.

With one hand cradling my ass, his other hand found my wrists again and he pinned them above my head. My back was to the door, and my breasts were right at the level of his mouth.

We weren't moving, but our chests heaved.

There was nothing I could do but take. He had me helpless against the door as he mercilessly pounded up and into me, over and over again. His mouth found the other nipple, and he sucked hard enough a gasp snagged at the back of my throat. I tilted my head against the door and moaned.

Every thrust had his pelvic bone grazing my clit. Every thrust had me seeing stars. Every thrust catapulted me closer to another sweet, glorious release.

He lifted his head from my breast and took my mouth again, his tongue pushing possessively inside.

God, this felt so good. So right. As if something broken inside me had finally, at long last been healed. Something that I never thought could be repaired and I had since forgotten about. Older than most of my childhood memories, our feud had been going on for over half our lives, our hatred for each other an almost living, breathing thing. A splinter that was so deeply embedded, it became a part of me. A sore spot I just learned to live with.

Yet, as he kissed me, as his body claimed mine, I finally began to heal.

My heart pushed the splinter out and began to repair itself.

His mouth moved over to my cheek and jaw, and he dragged his teeth up the side. My pussy trembled around his cock. "That's right, Alexandra, squeeze my cock."

I hadn't realized it until now, but he called me Alex when we were being normal and having conversations like regular humans. But when he wanted me to do something, when he adopted that alpha-dom persona, he called me Alexandra. Even if he just wanted me to look at him, he dropped his voice, made it extra gritty and called me by my full name.

And I obeyed.

Because I really fucking liked it. Holy fuck, did I like it.

Normally, I corrected people when they called me Alexandra. I preferred to be called Alex and had since I was a kid. Eli had called me Alexandra when we were children because he knew I hated it. But now, he was calling me Alexandra for another reason, and I didn't hate it one bit.

It was almost like Alexandra was his pet name for me. *His* name for me.

And I was okay with that.

I was actually really okay with that.

"Do you want to come?" he asked, planting warm, wet kisses down my neck. His voice was a gravelly rumble in my ear.

I nodded, whimpered, and bit my lip as he hit a new spot inside me that had me seeing stars.

"Do you need to come?"

I nodded again.

"Are you going to soak my cock?"

Holy fuck, the dirty talk.

"I asked if you are going to soak my cock, Alexandra. Answer me."

I nodded again. "Yes."

"Good girl."

I groaned at his praise and the way it may my body throb.

He pumped harder, faster, and my body began to tremble as if I'd just touched an electric fence.

"Come when I tell you to. Not before."

"Okay."

His tongue circled a sensitive spot below my ear, and his grip on my wrists tightened. Is it wrong I hoped for bruises? For reminders of how he made me feel, of his controlled force, his intoxicating passion. Something I could look at tomorrow and instantly get wet from as the memories flooded me.

The fingers of his other hand dug into my ass, and he pulled himself harder against me. Deeper.

I wasn't going to be able to hang on much longer.

"When I take your mouth, you're going to come," he said, dropping his mouth and swiping his tongue across my peaked, tender nipple. "Got it?"

I whimpered and nodded.

"Answer me, Alexandra."

"Yes," I breathed.

He moved over to the other nipple, did the same thing, tugged it between his teeth for a second, then lifted his head. "Open your eyes. Look at me."

I did as he demanded.

He was still moving. Still bucking into me with deep, measured thrusts. My body was a riot. A maelstrom of sensations I struggled to collect and gather into me. They flew wildly inside my body, like leaves in the wind on a perfect autumn day.

We held each other's gaze.

He kept moving. Pushing me closer and closer.

A smile curled his lips. He knew I was struggling to abstain. Struggling to do as he demanded. But oh, how I wanted to.

He pulled back, and I moaned from how good it all felt, biting my lip as my breathing began to grow wild.

He paused.

I gasped.

Then he slammed home, took my mouth, and my body exploded.

CHAPTER
TWENTY-NINE

Alex

THIS ORGASM WAS BIGGER than the first one where he had his fingers inside me. This one I felt from the top of my head to the tips of my toes. Every inch of my body became electrically charged, hot, and rigid as the pleasure swept through me. I tightened around him, waiting for him to find his release so he could experience the pleasure that I was experiencing, but I didn't feel his cock pulse. He paused his movements so I could just be in the moment, but even in my state of euphoria, where my body and mind momentarily became one and I could hear the blood rushing through my veins and arteries, I knew he didn't get off.

My orgasm began to wane, and I went about collecting my thoughts and checking in with my faculties.

He broke our kiss and lifted his head.

I opened my eyes. "Did you not ...?"

His smile was absolutely wicked, and my pussy clenched around his cock on instinct.

Eli shook his head. "No."

Defeat was an intrusive bitch, and she began to wedge her way into my heart, kicking the high from my orgasm and all the happy dancing endorphins in the shins.

"I like to edge, if I can," he said. "It's all about the delayed gratification for me. Getting yourself almost there, then pulling back, and doing it over and over again. Makes the orgasm, when it finally happens, really intense."

"Oh."

That smile was back. He stepped away from the door, still inside me, and walked into the hotel suite to his bed. Gently, he set me down, and I had to stifle my whimper from us no longer being connected.

Calmly, confidently he climbed onto the bed, lay down, and with one hand, called me over. "Sit on my face."

I must have looked like a deer in headlights.

His brows narrowed. "Sit on my face, Alexandra."

I scrambled to obey, feeling a little self-conscious as I put his head between my thighs and hovered over his mouth.

Eli's tongue flicked out and hit my clit. My knees wobbled.

He did it again. My knees wobbled again.

A hard smack landed on my left ass cheek. "I said sit, not hover. Now fucking sit, Alexandra." The sharp sting from where his palm struck me quickly bloomed into a decadent heat. I lowered myself a little more. His tongue pushed into my pussy and began to thoroughly fuck me, just like his cock had.

I wasn't sure which was better.

Did there need to be a winner, or could I hand out gold medals to every part of his body that made me feel this good?

Of course, I could. I made the rules here. This was my award ceremony. Gold stars, blue ribbons, and gigantic trophies to his tongue, cock, and fingers.

His tongue plunged in and out like a piston.

I squirmed and bucked, worried only slightly about cutting off his breathing but even more so about hovering and disappointing him. He'd told me to sit, so I was sitting.

Just as I was about to lose my mind, he pulled his tongue free, flicked it over my clit a bunch of times, then sucked like a damn Hoover vacuum on the hood of my clit and I detonated harder than the last two orgasms.

I had no control over how my body responded. I was at the mercy of his mouth, and when I fell forward and screamed "OH MY GOD" into the pillow, it barely registered in my brain that I was even speaking.

My legs spasmed, my pussy pulsed, and all the while, the man just sucked and sucked and sucked to the point where I thought he might suck my clit clean off.

Even when the orgasm started to ebb and the waves of bliss coursing through my body began to recede from my extremities, he was sucking.

I jerked and went to pull away. But he held me in place with his hands on my hips.

"It's too much," I said, sitting up and tapping his head. "I need a minute. Please."

He released my hips, and I sat up enough so he could slide out from under me.

Flopping to the bed on my back, I draped my arm over my eyes. "Dear God."

I didn't have to see him to know he was smiling that smile I loved. The cocky one. The almost smug one. I hated it just as much as I loved it.

A dip in the mattress and a second later, the sink was running in the bathroom. I simply lay there with jelly limbs and a pulsing pussy, utterly satiated and yet hungry for more.

This had to be the work of Sharon. She'd put it out into the universe that this would happen with Eli and I. She probably had a pentagram made out of old Harlequin paperbacks in her living room right now. Or had sacrificed a hardcover Danielle

Steele novel, throwing it into the middle of a double bed and setting it aflame.

I'd have to get her something special from San Diego as a thank you.

The sink turned off, and I lifted my arm from my eyes just in time to see him sauntering back into the room, his cock hard, thick and veiny. I could practically see it throbbing. A bead of precum shone on the tip.

His eyes followed mine, and he flashed me another one of those smiles. "Oh, you will."

My brow lifted. "I will what?"

"Suck it. But not yet. I want to come inside you before I come down your throat."

Oh my God.

He climbed back onto the bed, and with a gentle but firm hand to my elbow, he encouraged me to roll over onto my belly. Then he tugged the duvet down so we were on the sheets. They smelled like him as I pressed my nose into his pillow and inhaled deep.

"I've wanted to run my tongue from your clit to the nape of your neck since I saw this tattoo," he said, crawling up the bed behind me and hovering. "Trace the ink."

I swallowed. "Yeah?"

"Yeah."

His warm, calloused hands gripped my inner thighs and spread my legs wide. I wasn't sure I was ready for more, but I also wanted everything he was willing to give me. Everything he wanted to do to me was welcome, encouraged, and I would not say no. I couldn't at that moment even dream of denying Eli a thing, least of all my body.

His tongue snaked between my legs from behind, and he flicked my clit. I jolted on the bed.

He did it again.

I jerked again.

Then his tongue began to work north. Or was it south? Technically, it was south on my body, but given that I was facedown, he was working north.

He spread my cheeks and flicked my tight hole. I puckered on instinct.

Nobody had ever licked me there.

"Don't," he said, leaving zero room for argument.

I relaxed.

"Good girl." He did it again.

I melted into the mattress.

Slowly, he circled my rosette with his tongue, which drove me absolutely bonkers. The slower he did it, the more I writhed and wriggled on the bed. My clit pressed and rubbed against the mattress, the friction a welcome extra bit of pleasure, not that I needed any more since what Eli was doing with his tongue was pretty magical.

Just as I thought I might lose it again, he licked me once more, then lifted his tongue and slid it up my crease to my lower back.

"These little dimples," he said, swirling his tongue around the two dips on either side of my spine, known as the Venus dimples.

His tongue continued on its journey, doing just as he promised and tracing the ink of my tattoo, swirling around the knots on the trunk, following each branch, each tiny twig. At each blossom, he'd plant a kiss, then continue on until he reached my shoulder.

His teeth sank into the top of my shoulder, and I sucked in a breath. "Again," I breathed, surprising myself with what I'd just said.

He kissed the place he bit, and I could feel him smile against my skin.

"Of course." He bit me again.

"Harder."

He bit me harder.

I ground my hips down against the bed, rubbing my clit harder against the mattress.

His tongue skimmed along the top of my arm to the final blossom that was inked across my tricep muscle, then he ended his quest with another kiss.

His body hovered over mine, and as he lowered himself, I spread my legs wider. He slid between my legs, and his cock found my center.

I sighed into the mattress and squeezed him, hugging him tight inside me, as if he'd just returned home, having been away for far too long.

Because when Eli was inside me, when Eli kissed me, when Eli worshipped my body, when I was WITH Eli, I was home.

And that thought wasn't nearly as terrifying as I expected it to be.

CHAPTER THIRTY

Eli

I'D GOTTEN PRETTY GOOD at edging over the years. I often did it when I was using my fist. It took a bit longer than just a quick jerk-off, but the orgasm was that much better, so when I could, I did it. Get yourself almost to that point of release, then stop, let your body settle and then go again. And again. And again, if you can.

And not that I was a one-trick pony or anything, but I wanted to give Alexandra all the orgasms I could before I finally came. I wanted her to soak my fingers and my face before she finally soaked my cock.

Although she'd already soaked my cock once, I knew that with Alexandra, once would most definitely not be enough.

I slid inside her and it was like coming home. She squeezed her hot, wet pussy around me and I groaned, dipping my head and biting her shoulder. She liked it when I bit her.

And when she begged for me to bite her again, I nearly came on the spot.

That was when I knew I needed to be back inside her, because no fucking way was I going to come on her back when I had the option of her tight cunt to take me instead.

I nearly nutted when she sat and came on my face.

Drinking her down unceasingly was the best fucking thing in the damn world.

I loved her like this, with her body pliant beneath mine, her walls down. Still soft but demanding, while at the same time acquiescing like a good girl to all my demands. She was muscular but soft, angular but curvy.

There wasn't an inch of Alexandra I didn't want to touch and make mine.

I slid my hands over hers, and our fingers intertwined.

She tightened her muscles around my cock, and I squeezed her fingers until my knuckles were white. She squeezed right back, our bodies locked in a union.

I moved gently in and out of her, but every time she pushed up with her ass, burying me deeper in her heat, my resolve to withhold my orgasm chipped away.

A tremor moved through her body and into me, turning quickly into an earthquake.

I began to fuck her faster, scrape my teeth over her shoulder again, loving the sharp suck of breath she drew in from her nose when that snap of pain from my teeth began to bloom into a pleasure I knew she already wanted more of.

It was a surreal moment and one I'll admit I dreamt of and jerked off to more than once as a teenager. The thought of eating Alex and fucking her with my fingers and sliding my cock into her pussy filled my rampant virgin fantasies from the age of thirteen to eighteen, and possibly beyond.

I abused myself to the mental images of fucking her face, coming all over her tits and taking her ass.

Never in a million years did I think any of those depraved scenarios I'd cooked up as an angry youth would actually come true. And yet, there I was, on top of her as she clenched my cock in her fist of a pussy, our fingers tightly tangled and my balls about ready to explode.

And not an ounce of anger or hate resided inside of me.

A new sensation, a new feeling was beginning to take shape, and I wasn't at all prepared to fight it.

I was having sex with my wife.

Alexandra Hartford was my wife.

And I was falling in love with her.

She was close. I could feel her pussy rippling and quivering around my cock, and it was pushing me closer to the edge, too. An edge I was finally ready to jump off. An edge I wanted to jump off with Alexandra.

I brought my mouth down next to her ear, sweeping her hair away from her face and tracing my tongue around the shell. "You're close. I can feel it."

"Mhmm," she said on a whimper, which only made my balls cinch up tighter against my taint.

"You're going to come again for me, Alexandra. Then we're going to have a shower, you're going to drop to your knees, and I'm going to let you take me in your mouth."

"Yes," she breathed.

"You want that, don't you, Alexandra? You want to watch me watch you fill your mouth with my cock."

"Yes," she said again on a pant.

The heat and pressure in my lower abdomen was more than I could take. I tightened my hold on her fingers, gave one final deep, hard pump, felt her clench around me, and then together, we let go.

My orgasm was intense, ripping my body completely in half as my balls drained and my cock pulsed inside her tight, trembling cunt. She squeezed and squeezed with each wave of her own orgasm, milking me for everything I was worth, then demanding I give her more when I had given her every drop.

She shouted my name into the mattress like a wild jungle woman as I buried my face in her neck, inhaling her scent in an attempt to ground myself. She smelled of sex, flowers, spice, and champagne. I licked her neck, wanting more of her.

Of her flavor on my tongue.

When she sat on my face, I couldn't stop eating. She was the best fucking meal I'd had in weeks, and even when I struggled to breathe, I couldn't stop.

Our breathing began to return to normal, her pussy released its vice grip on my cock, and I loosened my grip on her fingers.

We lay there for a moment, connected, satiated.

Then her body started to jiggle, and I realized she was laughing, which prompted me to start laughing. I rolled off her, and she flipped over to her back, her smile brilliant and beautiful.

I was on my back, too, my chest still lifting faster than normal, my body covered in a thin layer of sweat.

After another moment and the laughter had died down, I stood up, went to the bathroom, and ran a clean washcloth under warm water, then I returned to her and cleaned up between her legs.

She watched me with intensity but never said a word.

I went back to the bathroom, filled up a drinking glass, then brought it to her. "Sit up and drink some water, Alexandra."

She did as she was told.

"Good girl."

Fire burned in her blue eyes as she accepted the glass and put it to her lips. I'd figured out pretty quick that she had a praise kink. The way she reacted when I used her full name and gave her an order was something that made me instantly hard. And when I called her a *good girl*, I could see it in her eyes how much she loved it.

I didn't think she was aware of her kink though, which in some ways made it more fun.

When she finished the water, she handed me the glass, and I set it down on the nightstand. I reached for her hand, and she gave it to me, allowing me to pull her up to sit and eventually lead her into the bathroom.

I turned on the shower and allowed the water to heat up.

She still didn't say anything.

With my hands on her shoulders, I spun her around to face the mirror. She was stunning. Her face was flushed. Her eyes were bright. To any *smart* person, they'd know that she was fresh off a thorough, satisfying fuck fest. Or in our case, in the intermission of a thorough, satisfying fuck fest, because no fucking way were we done tonight.

Tracing my index fingers down her arms, I pressed a kiss to her shoulder. Her hair fell over her shoulders, and the tips kissed her nipples.

I swept the hair away, brushing my fingers along the undersides of her breasts. She trembled against me and ever so slightly pressed her ass against my already rising cock. Her eyes followed my fingers as I moved them around her areolas, making them pucker. I strummed her nipples until they grew hard and pointed directly at the mirror.

My fingers traveled downward, across the flat, toned muscles of her stomach and between her legs.

She took a half step to the side, spreading wider for me.

Our eyes found each other in the mirror. I pushed two fingers between her labia and stroked her clit.

Her eyelids dropped to half mast, and she leaned her head back against my other shoulder.

"I could watch you all night," I said into her ear.

She swallowed, and my eyes zeroed in on her throat. A throat I was aching to come down.

"You say when it's time for sleep," I said, lazily passing my finger back and forth over her clit, feeling it swell. "I can taste you and fuck you all night. You're in control of when we stop." I nipped her shoulder. "I'm in control of your pleasure."

She nodded. "Okay."

"So you want to sleep?"

Alexandra shook her head. "No."

"What *do* you want?"

"To take you in my mouth."

I smiled and kissed the spot on her shoulder I'd just bitten. "Good girl."

She sucked in a breath and the sparkle in her eyes intensified.

I pulled my fingers free of her pussy, took her hand and led her over to the big shower, opening the foggy glass door and pulling her inside with me.

Shoving her against the tile wall, I cupped her face and took her mouth. I couldn't get enough of her mouth. Of her teeth scraping my lips, of her tongue tangling with mine. She tasted so fucking good.

Her hand drifted down between us. She took my cock and began to stroke me.

I groaned into her mouth and deepened the kiss, fucking her mouth with my tongue. I intended to fuck it with my cock a whole hell of a lot deeper. I planned to introduce her tonsils to my crown and get them very acquainted.

She whimpered when I released one side of her face and pinched a nipple. Her hips shot out off the wall, and she began to shamelessly ride my thigh, grinding her clit against my leg.

Just when I knew she was close to coming, I pulled away from her, gathered her wet hair in my fist and forcefully—but gently—pushed her to her knees.

A smile tipped her lips as she sank down in front of me, taking my cock in her hand and immediately guiding it past her lips.

She looked up at me and grinned around my cock.

Holy fucking shit.

My grip on her hair tightened, and I began to move her head back and forth, fucking her face and gradually sliding my dick deeper and deeper into her hot, soft little mouth.

She sucked. Boy, did she know how to fucking suck.

I was in rapture, and it was all I could do to stay focused and not lean my head against the wall, close my eyes and blow my load right then and there.

But I could tell by her enthusiasm and the way she continued to watch me that this was just as much for her as it was for me. She was enjoying this. She was getting turned on sucking my cock.

She liked my cock in her mouth.

I picked up the pace a little and went to pull back, to guide her over my cock and bring the crown to her lips when she resisted and pushed forward more, taking more of me into her mouth. I hit the back of her throat.

Heaven.

And then I went even deeper. She pushed me even deeper. She suppressed her gag reflex, dropped her tongue and took me deeper than any woman ever had, then she started making swallowing motions with her throat, contracting the back of her throat around the head of my cock.

I was going to die.

And it was going to be a beautiful death.

I tugged her hair harder, and with a whimper I knew to be borne of disappointment, she followed me and swirled her tongue around the head when it retreated to her lips. Then she wedged that tongue into the hole at the tip. The entire time, even when I wasn't looking at her, I knew she was looking at me. I knew she was watching my reactions to what she was doing.

I dropped my gaze to hers as I guided her mouth back over my cock and allowed her to take me back as deep as I was before.

Dear sweet baby Jesus. The woman had a throat that never ended.

Heat began to swirl in my belly again, and my balls started to tighten.

She pulled me out to her lips, then released me, only to start stroking me root to tip with her hand while flicking my crown with her tongue.

I watched her. She watched me watching her.

Once more to the back of her throat and I'd be a dead man.

With my fingers thoroughly entangled in her hair, I pulled until her mouth slid back over my shaft and I felt the back of her throat. She began to do that swallowing thing again, hugging my cockhead with her throat muscles while her lips squeezed me at the base.

I couldn't hold on any longer, pushed myself just a half inch deeper until her eyes widened but didn't say no, then I let go.

She didn't balk. She didn't pull away. She didn't even stop contracting her throat. She took every shot I gave her, swallowing down my cum like a pure fucking goddess.

I was in awe of this woman. Of her talent. Of her dedication. Of her perfection.

Only once I was done pulsing did I pull her hair and my dick slipped past her lips. She smiled up at me and blinked through the water spray.

With a deep groan, I hauled her to her feet with my arms under hers, pushed her back up against the wall, then took her mouth again. Because it was mine.

Because Alexandra was mine. You don't let a woman who sucked cock like that go. You marry her, you eat her pussy like you're a starved man on a desert island, and you never fucking let her go.

Two down, one to go.

CHAPTER THIRTY-ONE

Eli

AFTER OUR SHOWER, I ate Alexandra one more time, this time slowly, not wasting a drop, then I curled up around my wife and we fell asleep.

My wife.

How fucking surreal was that?

And yet, I liked the idea of it. I genuinely liked the fact that Alexandra Hartford was my wife. It warmed my heart and made me smile the longer I thought about it. And of course, the longer I thought about her, the harder I got.

When morning came, I got up, pissed, then tugged the drapes closed a little tighter to keep the morning light from sneaking in.

Movement out of the corner of my eye drew me back to the beauty in the bed. She was passed out on her back, naked and fucking gorgeous. The top sheet was draped across her waist, but her breasts were exposed.

My dick twitched as the urge to suck one of those raspberries into my mouth began to take over all other thoughts in my brain.

But then the memory of what was hidden beneath that sheet came barreling back, and I licked my lips.

Wait a sec.

I blinked.

It had been movement out of the corner of my *left* eye.

I blinked again.

I could see.

I blinked and blinked and blinked.

I could see again.

Holy fucking shit balls. I could see again.

Excitement zipped through me, and I wanted to whoop as loud as I could. But I didn't. I didn't want to wake her that way. I did a fist pump in the air, put my hands together in prayer, and said a silent thank-you to the universe, then I decided to celebrate the best way I knew how.

Slowly, I crawled up the bed from the end and slid the sheet off her. She didn't wake. Didn't stir. One leg was bent. She was in a horizontal tree pose, and when the sheet slipped away, exposing her pussy and those glistening pink lips, I just knew I couldn't abstain. I was just too fucking hungry.

I gently moved her legs, spreading them for me, and settled onto my belly.

"Hmmm?" she moaned, stirring above. Her hand fell to the top of my head as I used my fingers to push her labia apart and flick her clit with my tongue.

"The best kind of breakfast is when all you have to do is move the panties to the side," I said. "But here I don't even need to move the panties. It's even better." Then I dove in and had my first breakfast. Because I was a fucking Hobbit, and there would most definitely be a second breakfast, an elevenses, a luncheon, afternoon tea, dinner, and supper. And maybe in among all that, we'd order up room service or a pizza.

If perfect had a taste, Alexandra would be it.

After a delicious first breakfast of Alexandra, followed by a second breakfast of another helping of Alexandra—since we weren't done celebrating me getting my eyesight back in both eyes—she told me to get dressed, postponing my elevenses and luncheon until we returned to the hotel. It was Tuesday, and we had two more days to kill before we were "supposed" to be in San Diego.

She did, however, bend over with her legs spread, plant her elbows on the ground and tell me that this was a great yoga position for sex. For later.

I said *fuck later* and took her right there and then like that.

She was fucking right. It was a great yoga pose for sex.

Then I made her show me more yoga positions that were also great sex positions *for later*. She had a lot to show me.

I had a lot that I wanted to learn.

Alexandra mentioned that she really wanted to go to a dude ranch and ride some horses since she hadn't been riding in ages—I didn't even know she rode.

She also mentioned something about stopping in Utah—and visiting the Canyonlands in Moab. I googled Moab and read that they have some wicked four-by-four ATV tour packages, so we were definitely doing that.

Then it was a straight shot to San Diego, since we no longer needed to stop in Las Vegas to get hitched seeing we'd done that in the best place and way imaginable already.

We'd stopped off on our way out of the city center to the dude ranch and grabbed the marriage license. We planned to drive out later that evening to Ricardo's house and have him sign it. But the paper in our hands didn't make it feel any more real. Last night, under the stars, in front of our new friends, and that kiss, followed by taking my wife to bed was what made it all real.

For me there wasn't anything fake about any of this anymore.

"I didn't know you rode horses," I said as I drove our rental car to the dude ranch about twenty miles outside of Denver called Harris Brothers Ranch.

She nodded. "I started doing it when I was about eight, fell in love immediately. It was what ignited my love of animals. It got expensive, though, and when my parents divorced, I had to give it up. But I'd made such a good impression with the husband and wife who owned the stables that if I went and mucked stalls twice a week, they let me ride one of the horses for an hour afterward. I did that until I went away to college. It was one of my only escapes from the *hell* that was my parents' separation."

"I think I've been on a horse maybe twice in my damn life."

Alexandra's smile had me wanting to pull over on the fucking highway, yank her into my lap and make that smile even bigger. Now that I had her, got a taste, I was becoming this insatiable, Alexandra-crazed beast. She didn't seem to mind though.

"I'm sure they have gentle horses for beginners," she said, sticking her tongue out in a teasing way. "Like the bunny hill for skiers. The bunny horse."

I wrinkled my nose and scowled exaggeratedly. "Har-har."

I took the off-ramp from the highway and followed the tree-lined road for another few miles.

"My sister never mentioned that you liked horses."

"I'm sure Eden kept a lot about me from you, considering how much you hated me."

I sighed. "Yeah, probably. Emphasis on the past tense. Hat-*ed*. I don't hate you now."

"If you did, you have a funny way of showing it. I'm surprised your tongue hasn't cramped or just gone on strike."

I wiggled it and faced her. "Impossible. It enjoys you just as much as the rest of me."

Her grin was demure, and when she bit that bottom lip of hers, I had to push my growl all the way down to my toes.

I wished Eden hadn't kept anything about Alexandra from me. However, the old Eli probably would have looked for a way to weaponize any extra info he had about Alexandra.

The old Eli was such an asshole.

"Up on the left," she said, pointing to the polished wooden sign that hung between two posts over a single-lane gravel road. The sign read: Harris Brothers Ranch.

I turned down the gravel road, which was lined with wood and wire fencing. Four horses clopped through the grass and bent their heads to eat.

"They know we're coming?" I asked, taking in the enormous stable up ahead, along with the big farmhouse and scattering of outbuildings.

Two big black Chevy pickups were parked outside the stable. One was hitched up to a horse trailer.

"They do. I called ahead."

I slowed my roll and parked where it said "Guest Parking."

Alexandra barely let me put the car in park before she was hopping out and inhaling deep.

"Oh, I love that smell," she said, closing her eyes. "Fresh air, hay—"

"Horseshit," I said, closing my car door and coming to stand beside her.

"Manure," she corrected.

"It's horseshit."

"You here to ride?" called a voice from inside the stable.

Two tall shadowed figures walked with confident gaits toward us, each of them wearing Stetsons and cowboy boots.

"Yes," Alexandra said with a smile in her voice. "I'm Alex Hartford. I called a couple of days ago about booking some riding."

"I remember," said the taller of the two men.

They came into view, and when they saw Alex, both sets of nostrils flared and their eyes darkened beneath their hats.

I could see them caress her from top to toe with the gazes. Jealousy and possessiveness began to burn like a white-hot flame inside me.

In two strides I was beside her, looping my arm over her shoulder, which caused both men—I'm assuming the Harris brothers—to flash their eyes my way and reel in their predatory gaze.

Alexandra was not a doe on the heath for them to chase and sink their teeth into. She was my wife. She was mine.

With a grin, I thrust my hand out. "Eli, Alex's husband. Nice to meet you."

Alexandra tipped her eyes to me for half a second before turning back to the two cowboys.

"Nate Harris," the taller one said.

"Asher Harris," said the one with the white scar on his chin.

After pleasantries were exchanged, the brothers led us through the stable.

I could feel Alexandra's excitement and wanted some of that for myself.

"We'll put you on Macklin," Asher said to me. "He's an old boy, but he's reliable and easygoing." He leaned his forehead against the side of Macklin's brown head, then kissed him.

"And we'll put Alex on Hula-Hoop," Nate said. "Sweetest girl you could ever meet." He stroked Hula-Hoop's black cheek. "Aren't you, girl?"

"Oh my God, are those twin foals?" Alexandra asked. She'd wandered down the stable a bit more and was peering into a stall.

"Born last night. Gamble is the filly, and Rumble is the colt," Asher said, stomping his boots over to where Alexandra was. "Long labor. We were out here with their mom, Greenleigh, helping her until three."

I thought back to what I was doing at three in the morning. Oh yeah, Alexandra.

"They're beautiful," she said, her eyes getting all glittery.

"They're going to be champion racers. Greenleigh's blood-line is as long as Route 66, and their sire is a champion out of Wyoming with a bloodline just as long." Asher nodded and patted his hand against the paddock beam. "Let's get your horses saddled up and you guys in some hats."

Alexandra and I followed the Harris brothers to the tack house, and thankfully, we were allowed to wear Stetsons and not helmets.

They had us saddled up and ready to go in no time.

"I think we can handle ourselves," I said to Nate as I guided the easygoing Macklin toward the opening at the fence.

"Sorry, man, no can do. Gotta guide you. But we'll keep a distance if you prefer so you can have your privacy." Nate climbed onto a horse he said was named Umber.

I grumbled.

Asher, at least, was going to stay back at the ranch.

But Alexandra was beaming. The woman could not stop smiling.

I could tell she was in her happy place, which in turn made me happy.

So I sucked it up, squeezed my legs around Macklin's sides so he would pick up speed, and tried to have a good time, even with our cowboy chaperone, who—I am confident enough in my own masculinity and sexuality to say—was a really handsome, and ruggedly so, dude.

I just had to keep reminding myself that Alexandra was my wife, she'd ridden my face all night and morning and would do it again tonight, and there was no reason to be jealous or insecure around Mr. March from the Dudes of the Dude Ranch calendar. I was sure there was such a calendar. There had to be.

I caught up to her, and she glanced over at me, still wearing that jaw-dropping smile. "Macklin is so sweet, isn't he?"

"So far so good," I said.

"And Hula-Hoop is just the most beautiful thing in the whole wide world." She leaned down and patted Hula-Hoop's neck. "Aren't you, baby girl?"

I shook my head and smiled at how she'd flipped into a cooing baby voice when she addressed the horse.

Her head lifted, and she inhaled deep, then exhaled again, looking around the wide-open space of the field. "This is honestly the life, Eli. I would love nothing more than a chunk of land dedicated to rescuing animals—dogs, horses, cats, donkeys—whatever. Those that need a forever home for their last days. Even llamas or alpacas. I'm not picky. Nobody deserves to die not surrounded by love like Jill. She deserved so much more."

My heart hurt at her mention of Jill. "I know, and I agree."

For the first time since we arrived at the ranch, her lips dipped into a frown. "Nobody should die alone."

She wasn't necessarily talking about Jill anymore. Or at least not *just* Jill. She was talking about Eden, too. She'd died alone. She'd taken her own life in her bathroom, and she was completely alone. She'd felt alone, too, since neither myself nor Alexandra had picked up our phones.

The *clip-clop* of Nate's horse behind us grew louder, and soon he was beside Alexandra on his horse, Umber. "There's a beautiful creek about half a mile through the woods. Thought that might be a nice place to stop if y'all packed a lunch."

"We did," Alexandra said, tossing back her smile. "That sounds perfect."

Nate grinned. "All right then."

Macklin and Hula-Hoop were walking close enough together that I could confidently reach out and touch Alexandra. Holding onto the reins and pommel, I leaned over, grabbed her arm and tugged her close. "Kiss me."

She smiled and leaned in, closing her eyes.

I pressed my lips to hers. It was chaste, but I still felt it in my toes.

She pulled away, but I held onto her arm. "I hope your dream of saving animals comes true. Everybody deserves somebody with a heart as big as yours in their life."

Her eyes sparkled with unshed tears back at me. "I'm glad we got married the way we did."

I smiled back at her, released her arm and let Macklin naturally shift away from Hula-Hoop. "Me, too."

But the disappointment in her choice of words hung heavy in my chest. She said she was glad that we got married the way we did, not *that* we got married.

Because this is still a business transaction. You've just gone and muddied it with sex.

I knew that to be true, but I also knew that nothing about how I felt about Alexandra or what was going on between us now felt the least bit transactional or businesslike. It felt real and raw and primal. It felt right.

Did she feel the same?

Or was it all in my head?

Was the tumor not only pressing on my optic nerve, threatening me with eternal blindness, or was it also affecting my ability to see reality?

Because the reality I saw was Alexandra and I developing feelings for each other, mutually. But maybe the *real* reality of it was entirely different.

Maybe, as soon as this wedding was over and the tumor was out of my brain, Alexandra was going to wave goodbye as she wrapped her leg around her head and flipped me the bird with her middle toe.

The thought of that happening made everything inside me hurt.

CHAPTER THIRTY-TWO

Alex

WHAT AN ABSOLUTELY PERFECT day.

I woke up with Eli's tongue between my legs and my body blissfully sore from a night of his overwhelmingly thorough attention, then we spent the afternoon on horseback, riding through the mountains.

Ana messaged me around lunchtime and asked if Eli and I wanted to meet her and Sérgio for dinner at a restaurant downtown, so of course I said yes. Ricardo and Fatima were taking Manuel to the movies, so we all met up before the movie started so Ricardo could sign the marriage license. Ana and Sérgio were more than happy to sign as our witnesses as well.

Dinner with our new friends was better than anything I could have imagined. It was like we'd known Ana and Sérgio for years and not just a few days. We laughed, ate and drank until we were all smiling idiots, stumbling to our respective cabs.

I hugged the crap out of Ana because honestly, I loved the woman. It was like an insta-love friendship that I knew would last a lifetime. I just had this wonderful, beautiful feeling about her, and it had nothing to do with the alcohol we'd consumed.

I promised to go visit her in Portugal, and she promised to visit me in Maine, then we parted like old friends with tears in our eyes as we drunkenly waved goodbye to each other out of the open windows of our cabs.

Back at the hotel, Eli ran me a luxurious bath in our Jacuzzi tub, then climbed in behind me and strummed his finger against my clit until I came. After that, I turned around, straddled him, and came again while he edged himself again and again until he took me on the bed and made me come a third time.

We were on the road and waving goodbye to Denver and all the memories that it held by nine o'clock Wednesday morning.

The plan was to stop in Moab for the night, get a hotel, rent some four-by-four ATVs and tour the Canyonlands before striking off bright and early Thursday morning for San Diego.

There was a cocktail party for Allegra and Ford on Thursday night, and since I'd RSVP'd *yes* to that, Eli and I couldn't miss it. Otherwise, who knew what kind of an invoice Allegra would serve me. Plus, I'd booked four nights at the hotel where the wedding was being held, so I didn't want to waste a night I'd already paid for.

Moab was beautiful. I'd definitely be returning. And Eli knew how to drive an ATV—of course—so that just made the excursion all the more awesome. I tried driving it, too, and after about half an hour I was doing donuts in the sand just like the rest of them.

We fell into bed that night exhausted. It sounds ridiculous to say, but we only had sex once—we were *that* tired.

On the road by six in the morning on Thursday, we made it to San Diego by six that night.

"With two hours to spare," Eli said, coming out of the bathroom proudly naked and drying his hair with a towel. What a difference a couple of days make. This time last week, we could barely stand to be in the same room as each other, let alone parade around naked.

"Whatever shall we do with ourselves?" I asked cheekily, biting my lip and climbing up the bed from where I'd sat on the edge in my plush white bathrobe.

His brow lifted. "I can think of a few things."

The hotel room only had one king-size bed, and up until a couple of days ago, it would have been a problem. But my *husband* was unable to keep his hands off me, so only one bed between us was no longer an issue.

He tossed the towel onto a chair and stalked toward me, climbing up the bed from the bottom like a male lion stalking a gazelle, a starved look in his eyes.

I was beneath him in seconds, wrapping my legs around his back as he sank into me, both of us moaning as he hilted himself.

In bed, and with Eli inside me in one fashion or another, we stayed until we looked at the clock on my phone and realized we were already fifteen minutes late to the cocktail party downstairs.

Whoops!

Eli told me to wear the bandage-style royal blue dress with the shiny black pumps, so I did.

I hated wearing heels, but I deliberately took a pole-dancing class for nearly two years before I discovered Muay Thai and taught myself how to walk in heels. So even though I hated wearing them, I could walk in them without killing myself.

I was finishing up my makeup in the bathroom, standing in front of the mirror, when a hot as fuck Eli wearing one of the button-up dress shirts I'd picked out for him—the maroon-colored one—came up behind me. "I fucking love you in that dress," he said, sweeping my hair off my neck and dropping his lips there.

I grinned at him in the mirror as I applied my lipstick. "It was a good choice." Glancing down at his pants, I bobbed my brows. "You fill out those pants and that shirt nicely."

"They were a good choice," he said, mimicking me.

"How soon can we get away from this party and come back up here so we can have a party of our own?" He made crazy eyes. "I'm going through withdrawals. Haven't tasted your pussy in—" He glanced at his watch. "Nearly forty minutes."

Chuckling, I spun in his arms, draped my arms over his shoulders and nuzzled my nose against his. "Eleven—tops!"

"I'm going to hold you to that. At eleven on the nose, I'm grabbing your hand—I don't care if you're mid-sentence talking to the most important person in the room—and I'm whisking you back up here and taking that dress off with my teeth."

"Promise?"

He growled, and that same hungry look from earlier flashed in his eyes. "Normally, I wouldn't care and wouldn't ask, but I know this whole wedding thing is important to you, so will I fuck up your lipstick if I kiss you?"

That made me smile. "Yes."

His brows pinched, and his lips dipped into a frown.

I pushed my fingers into his hair and encouraged him to move his face in closer. "But I don't care." Then I took his mouth, and we were over half an hour late for the cocktail party.

With a deep breath, I stepped out of the elevator, Eli's big warm hand at the small of my back, a reassuring presence I needed.

I hadn't seen Allegra in years. Of course, I "kept up" with her on social media, but I hadn't been in the same breathing space with her in quite some time.

I was a different person now. An accomplished veterinarian and yoga teacher who did Muay Thai and was saving to buy a chunk of land so I could take in old rescue animals and give them love as they lived out their last days.

And yet, the closer we got to the lounge where Allegra and Ford were holding the private cocktail party, the more I began to feel like the old, insecure, insignificant Alex from veterinary school.

Butterflies, all of them angry, flapped wings made of razor blades in my belly.

Why didn't I just suck up the expenses and tell Allegra I couldn't make it, even after I had RSVP'd yes? This was so stupid.

"You okay?" Eli's mouth was next to my ear, and his fingers curled protectively around my hip.

I swallowed. "I need a drink."

He steered me toward the bar, ordered himself a whiskey and me a glass of rosé. I didn't even let the bartender put the wine glass on the bar before I was reaching for it from his hand and putting the glass to my lips.

"Easy," Eli said smoothly. "Pace yourself. I'm right here. I look hot, you look hotter, and we have an exit time. You got this." He kissed my shoulder. "Just think about what I'm going to do to you when I get you out of that dress."

I glanced at him out of the corner of my eye. "Are you trying to make me blush?"

"You're beautiful when you do."

My cheeks warmed.

"Alexandra?" came a voice that I would recognize until the day I died. It was breathy and feminine and so sexy, I was sure half the men in the room felt their dicks twitch when Allegra spoke.

I moved my eyes from Eli to my frenemy, Allegra, who looked as beautiful as ever, on the arm of her also very beautiful husband-to-be, Ford Grady.

Allegra drew me into her arms, hugging me in that barely-touch-air-kiss, super-fake kind of way. "Hola, darling. *Muaw, muaw.* It's so amazing that you could make it," she said, standing back and stepping into Ford's embrace. "Ford, *mi amado,* this is Alexandra. I've told you about her. She works at that cute little vet hospital in Maine."

I clenched my molars and smiled at Ford. "Nice to meet you, Ford."

Ford was tall, probably two inches taller than Eli, and his hair was the same dark brown as Allegra's. They also had the same spray-tan shade. He was a decent-enough-looking man if you liked that perfectly coiffed, clean-shaven, Botox and fillers, Ken doll look.

I glanced over at my date and his scruff, dark hair, and the ruggedly handsome planes of his face.

No competition.

Ford and I finished shaking hands.

Allegra switched her hawklike stare from me to Eli, her expression turning from judgmental to avid and aroused. She didn't hold back checking him out from top to bottom.

I told the jealous monster in my brain to go sit in the corner and keep quiet. "Allegra, Ford, this is Eli, my—"

"Alex's husband," Eli said, thrusting out his hand. "Pleasure to meet you."

"Husband?" Allegra squeaked, her brown eyes going wide.

I smiled, but I didn't feel that smile in my heart despite how much I loved that I was actually Eli's wife. But in some stupid way, telling Allegra didn't make it feel more real. It actually kind of cheapened it. I'd liked that it'd been our little secret—well, ours and our friends back in Colorado.

Eli nodded, and his grip on my hip tightened. "That's right."

"Since when?" Allegra pressed, her heavily made-up eyes squinting at me. "A month ago you were with Cade, were you not?"

"Alex and Cade parted ways a little while ago. She just didn't update her relationship status right away," Eli said. He knew I struggled to lie. "We've actually known each other since we were five. She was my twin sister's best friend since the first day of kindergarten."

Ford's eyes widened. "Oh wow."

Eli chuckled and sipped his whiskey. "Mind you, Alex and I didn't exactly get along when we were kids, but we bumped into each other a little while ago and—" He squeezed me tighter, then looked at me. I brought my gaze to his and instantly began to relax with how utterly convincing he was being. If I didn't know any better, I'd believe that he was actually madly in love with me. "We've put the past behind us. Right?"

"Yeah," I breathed.

He turned back to Allegra and Ford. "Before I knew what I was doing, I was popping the question. We thought we'd just get married in Vegas on our way here, but something better fell in our laps a couple of days ago, so ..." Eli looked down at me again, still with all that incredibly convincing love in his eyes. "We're married."

I broke our eye contact and turned to Allegra, reaching out and putting my hand on hers. "But we can keep this a total secret. I don't want to steal an ounce of your thunder. This weekend is all about you guys, and I couldn't be happier."

Maybe I wasn't such a terrible liar after all.

Allegra's smile was brittle.

But Ford seemed to be ignorant to her irritation and thrust his hand out toward Eli again. "Congratulations, man. That's awesome." He then leaned in toward me and kissed me on the cheek. "Best wishes, you guys. And there's no thunder to steal. We're all about celebrating all the love this weekend."

He stepped back beside Allegra and looped his arm around her. "Right, pumpkin?"

I nearly spat out my rosé. He just called her pumpkin. Normally it would have been a cute pet name—not one I would have liked, but it was better than poodle or shmoopsie pie—but the fact that Allegra was oranger than normal made the nickname hilarious.

Eli kept his grip on me, and I swallowed my rosé without making a scene.

Allegra flashed me another veneer smile. "You remember Gina, Kymberli, Tavia, and Selena from PenVet, right?" Allegra asked me, her eyes now drifting down my body.

I nodded. "Yes."

"Well, they're just over here. Come." She stepped out of Ford's embrace and tugged me out of Eli's. "You simply *must* come say hi."

Must I?

I looked back at Eli longingly. *Help!*

"Eleven," he mouthed, tapping his watch.

I widened my eyes, smiled, and mouthed back, "Eleven."

"Kymberli, Selena, Gina, you remember Alexandra Hartford, right?" Allegra said, coming up to a group of three women I very much recognized who were all holding wine glasses with white wine. She one-arm hugged and fake-kissed each one of them, all the while not unlooping her thin, fragile arm from mine. "Where's Tavia?"

"She forgot her phone in her hotel room," Gina said.

Allegra towered over me in her heels. On flat feet, she had at least four inches on me. And I knew her heels were at least five inches, while mine were only three.

Kymberli, Selena and Gina's gazes did the exact same thing down my body as Allegra's eyes had. I squirmed and looked away, letting them do their thing. Just get the judgment over with.

Plastic, bleached smiles greeted me, though not one grin made their eyes sparkle or the corners crinkle. I couldn't tell if that meant their smiles were fake or they'd just had a shit-ton of work done.

My guess was both.

Now, I don't judge people who get work done. You do you. But when I saw all these Barbie-like women in front of me, all of them except Allegra with bright blonde hair down to their nipples, French-tipped fake nails, thousands of dollars' worth of jewelry and flawless makeup, I started to shrink.

Not literally, of course. But the longer they stared at me, the smaller and less significant I felt.

Kymberli squinted. "Alexandra ..." Then recognition dawned on her, and her blue eyes went wide. "Oh right, Alexandra. You're the one who got horse jizz in her eye after we went to the stud farm and jerked off stallions." And also the one you shared a house with for a year. We were fucking roommates!

I sighed. "Yes, that's me."

The women all snorted.

"And you changed your hair," Kymberli added. "It has ... red *streaks.*" Which she clearly did not like.

"And this enormous tattoo on her back," Allegra added, forcing me to turn around so the woman could look at my back.

"It's a gigantic tree," Selena said, confused. "Why a tree?"

"It has personal meaning," I replied. They didn't deserve any more information than that.

"It's ... *big,*" Gina said. This was obviously her attempt at some kind of pretend compliment, but she failed miserably.

"Yes, it is," I said plainly as Allegra turned us back around to face her "friends."

"Who are you here with?" Gina asked, looking behind me as if my date was just tagging along like a piece of toilet paper on the bottom of my shoe.

"Um ... my date's over talking to Ford and ..." I spun around only to find Eli laughing and smiling with three other men, Ford not among them. "Eli's the one with the maroon shirt."

Their expressions turned intrigued, and their eyes checked Eli out from top to toe, lingering for a while on the front of his pants.

"He's yummy," Selena crooned. "Model? Actor? Financier with a real penchant for BDSM?"

I turned back around and gaped at her. "Uh ... he's a ..."

What was he? Yes, Eli was a roofer, but that wasn't his *career*, was it? He'd only been doing it for a little over a year. Did he really have a *title?* A career? I mean, if anything, I'd call him an aspiring author and illustrator, destined for amazingness as soon as he took the leap and published his graphic novels. But that was Eli's secret that he'd bravely shared with me. I wasn't about to blab it to these plastic-faced ditzes.

"He's a ...?" Allegra probed, lifting a thick, sculpted brow.

"Eli's a roofer," I finally said, throwing my shoulders back.

I watched as each woman mentally turned up their noses and curled their lips. Of course, either the Botox and fillers wouldn't allow it or they'd just gotten very good at *hiding* their true feelings behind a blank face.

But I'd been around these women too much in the past to not be able to identify their disapproval. I'd felt it for the entire duration of my time in vet school.

I smiled at them all, untangled my arm from Allegra's and stepped to the side. "If you'll excuse me, I need to find the ladies' room." Then I booked it out of that suffocating, pretentious space and ran as fast as I could on my heels to the bathroom.

In the stall, I glanced at my phone. "Shit," I muttered. It was only nine forty-five. Over an hour of this torture to go before Eli and I could retreat to the safety of our room. I plastered my back to the stall door and closed my eyes.

Eleven couldn't come fast enough.

I probably stood there for a good five minutes with my eyes closed, trying to gather my thoughts so I could go back out there and face the world of fake. In under three minutes, four women had managed to subtly tear me down and take me right back to when we were in vet school and I was dealing with the death of my best friend and trying to find myself. It was a dark time, and they preyed on my insecurities back then, just as they were trying to now.

I needed to be stronger. I needed to either not let their judging eyes and poisonous comments affect me, or I needed to stand up for myself.

I was about to open the stall door when the bathroom door opened and several female voices began to echo around the small space. The only one I recognized was Gina's.

"Did you hear what he said?" another woman asked.

"Mhmm," replied a second woman.

"Yeah, but he's a *roofer*," Gina sneered.

I peered through the crack in the stall door to see who the women were besides Gina.

"I don't care if he's a fucking hobo," said the redhead. "I don't know the last time Drake went down on me. I've got six vibrators and a standing weekly 'date' with my son's karate teacher where he sucks my clit until I'm screaming 'hi-ya,' but even he doesn't do what that roofer says he likes to do."

The brunette sighed. "Ralph either."

Gina was quiet.

"Did you see her hair and her tattoo?" the brunette asked, her voice dripping with disapproval. "She looks like a biker chick."

"She was always *odd*," Gina added. "But how she landed a man like that, I don't know."

The other two made "Mhmm" noises.

"I mean ... she's *pretty*, if you like that kind of look with tattoos, weird hair, muscular arms and stuff," the brunette added. "He does, obviously."

"Allegra says she was with another guy like a month ago—had been for several years—and now she's here with the roofer. Did you see the giant rock on her finger? How the fuck does a roofer afford that? Aren't they like a half step up from a gardener?" the blonde said, tossing a nervous giggle in at the end. "I mean, it's not huge but certainly not what I'd expect a roofer to be able to afford."

The brunette scoffed. "My gardener doesn't stick his tongue in my ass, that's for sure."

WHAT?

What the hell did Eli say? What did they overhear?

I pressed my ear to the crack in the door.

I needed to hear it all.

CHAPTER
THIRTY-THREE

Eli

FUCK ME, THESE GUYS were stuck-up fuckers. All of them. Even Ford.

Though I'd go so far as to say that he was the *least* stuck up of the bunch.

I had to work hard to keep my eyes from crossing when they all started talking about cryptocurrency, hedge funds, and buying bigger yachts or sailboats. And don't even get me started on those fuckers who were blatantly, openly talking about their mistresses and which models they'd slept with and how deep their nannies can deep-throat.

My knuckles were white, my fist was so tight. And I was seriously concerned that if I squeezed the crystal lowball that held my whiskey any tighter, I'd shatter the glass and cut my hand.

A guy I'd been introduced to as Ryland laughed, then sneered at something another guy said. "I haven't muff-dived in ages."

A bunch of other guys nodded and chuckled.

"At least not on my wife," another guy said. "When you've seen a pussy during childbirth, the last thing you want to do is stick your mouth there again. No fucking thanks. And I can't tell you the last time I didn't fuck her in the ass. Tight pussy or in the ass is what I say."

More guys nodded and chuckled.

"I told her to get a C-section if she ever wanted me to fuck her cunt or eat her out again," the guy who'd introduced himself as Keith said.

When he told me his name, I had to catch myself. I literally started to say, "Oh, that's the name of my tumor." But I stopped and said, "Oh, that's the name of my tum—*eric* supplier. I buy my turmeric from a guy who grows it himself. Let me know if you want me to hook you up."

Then Keith the human, not the tumor, looked at me like I was speaking another fucking language that wasn't found on planet Earth.

Kirk, another guy, sipped his scotch. "She knows she's got it good, which is why when I say, suck me under the desk at my home office, she hops to it and doesn't ask for me to reciprocate. Because—gross."

Now it was my turn to sneer.

"See," Kirk said. "Eli gets it. Leave the pussy-eating to the young guys without money and a 401K."

I sipped my whiskey and shook my head. "Yeah, I don't eat pussy."

All the guys laughed and nodded.

"I fucking devour it."

Their smiles fell.

My shoulder lifted. "I guess I'm part of the minority, but to me, there's nothing better than diving up to your ears until it looks like you face-planted into a box of honey crullers. And if she gets all squirmy when you stick your tongue in her ass, all the fucking better." I finished my whiskey and turned to the bartender. "I'll have another, please."

The chatter about eating pussy died nearly as fast as it formed—thank fuck—and the men I was unfortunately standing with turned their conversation to something equally arrogant and misogynistic that I couldn't be bothered to pay attention to.

I stood there sipping my drink, counting to sixty over and over in my head, willing the clock to move faster and for it to be eleven o'clock.

I knew I'd glanced at my watch way too fucking much, which was rude as hell, but I did not care.

I was eating peanuts out of a bowl on the bar when Alexandra was suddenly at my side, a shocked but aroused look in her eyes.

I gave her a curious look.

She pressed her lips together.

I lifted a brow.

She lifted a brow, and her mouth curled on one side into a smile I wanted to smother with my lips.

Her eyes moved quickly to the side. To where the door exiting the lounge into the rest of the hotel was. Then she moved them back to me, then back to the door.

I grinned, drained my drink, set it down, reached into my wallet, tossed a fifty on the bar to cover my two whiskeys and her rosé. "Look at the time," I said, grabbing her hand. "Already eleven." Then I whisked her out of there as fast as she would allow in those heels.

We stepped into the elevator, both of us grinning like absolute idiots.

"I heard something in the bathroom," she said as the doors closed in front of us. "Apparently some women overheard your conversation at the bar. Something about a box of honey crullers?"

I scraped my top teeth over my bottom lip. "They did not hear wrong."

Her grin grew. So did my cock.

"Bend over and grab your ankles," I said, losing my smile. I stepped behind her.

Her eyes went wide, and her mouth opened. "Uh."

"Did I stutter? Bend over and grab your ankles, Alexandra."

When I used her full name, her spine snapped straight, her pupils dilated, and her nostrils flared. She hinged at the hips and essentially folded herself in half. I toed her feet apart a little, sank to my knees, and peeled her dress up from the bottom to expose the backs of her thighs, the bottom cheeks of her ass and—nothing else.

"You're not—"

"Wearing any panties," she replied, triumph in her voice.

"Oh, Alexandra ..." I caressed her ass cheeks, "Good girl." Then pushed my face between her legs until my tongue made contact with her clit.

Her legs wobbled, and she sucked in a breath.

I hadn't hit the red *stop* button on the elevator panel, so at any point in time the elevator could stop, that door could chime and people could be standing on the other side.

I did not fucking care.

The idea of getting caught just made what we were doing hotter.

I pushed a finger and then another into Alexandra's wet, hot, tight pussy and pumped while my tongue wiggled over her clit back and forth. She squirmed and mewled.

Her clit began to swell against my tongue.

The elevator stopped moving.

Ding.

I stood up, pulled her dress down, and with my hands on her hips, hauled her against me. Alexandra stood up just as the doors opened and a couple probably our parents' age stepped onto the elevator.

"Going down?" I asked, pinching Alexandra's ass when she snickered at my choice of words.

They nodded. "Yes, to the restaurant," the man said as he hit the big *M* on the panel for *Main*.

As I watched the numbers climb, quietly, I ruffled up the back of Alexandra's dress and slid two fingers back between her legs. My other arm looped around her chest, holding her against me and in place while my fingers fucked her. She buckled against me and trembled. I kept her standing.

I pulled one finger free of her and scraped her clit with it. She shuddered harder. I held her tighter against me.

Bringing my mouth next to her ear, I whispered so only she could hear me, "Before we get to our floor, you're going to come for me. Understood?"

She nodded.

"Answer me, Alexandra." I slid my finger over her clit again.

"Yes," she sighed softly.

My finger wiggled back and forth over her clit again, feeling it swell and her pussy grow slicker as I fucked her with my middle finger.

Thank God the couple in the elevator with us was nattering on, rather loudly, about how obnoxious their son-in-law was because it made what Alexandra and I were up to easier to cover up.

"I just don't understand why he thinks I'd be impressed with the fact that he bought the children each a pony. Do the kids even *like* ponies? Where are they going to keep them? They live in a penthouse on the Upper West Side." The older gentleman shook his head. "I wish she'd married that mechanic. At least he would have gotten the children something practical, like their own cars. You can't ride a pony to school in Manhattan. The kids are already too big to ride them anyway."

"Hush, Conrad," his wife said, shaking her head and patting him on the shoulder affectionately. "But yes, I agree. I much preferred Brian to Preston. Unfortunately, our daughter does not share our taste."

The floors continued to climb while Conrad and Mrs. Conrad kept muttering about their dislike of Preston and the fact that he thought springing for this hotel was a great anniversary gift for the easy-going, no-frills older couple from Kansas.

I was happy for them to keep chatting. It kept their attention off what I was up to with my hand and where it was beneath Alexandra's dress.

I rubbed my finger even more, even faster, and she quivered, her pussy tightened around my finger and then ... she let go.

I couldn't see her, but I could feel her. I could hear her. Her breathing was ragged, and the moan that rumbled in the back of her throat was deep and feral. I covered it by pretending to sneeze.

"Bless you," the older woman said.

"Thank you."

Ding! went the elevator on floor nineteen.

Gently I pulled my finger from Alexandra and pulled down her dress just as the door opened to reveal more people waiting.

I released my arm from across her chest and took her hand, leading her—dazed and wobbly on her feet—out of the elevator and past the people in the hallway.

We walked quietly to our room. I fished the key card out of my pocket and flashed it in front of the door. The light turned green, and I turned the latch, hauling her inside and shutting the door as fast as it would allow.

I had her up against the door and was peeling her dress off before she even had a chance to take a breath. And when she finally did breathe, I stole that breath with a kiss, devouring each and every one of her moans.

She was naked on the bed with my face between her legs in less than five minutes, and there I kept her well past eleven.

Alexandra returned from the bathroom in all her naked glory, a refilled water glass in each hand. She handed me mine, then gracefully slid onto the bed.

"Thank you for getting us out of there when you did," she said, sipping her water. "I was close to pulling the fire alarm."

"It was you who came to me with the 'get me out of here and fuck me' eyes. So I should be thanking you."

"I believe you have—multiple times."

I smiled as I took a sip of my water. "I can't believe we have three more days with these people."

"Yeah ... but tomorrow the day is free. It's just another evening event, and hopefully, more people—more tolerable people will be there. Otherwise, we bail after dinner. I can fake a stomach ache."

"Codeword: Pineapple is what we'll use to get the fuck out of there."

"Deal." She sipped her water again, and a contemplative look flashed behind her eyes.

"What's up?" I could already read this woman like a book.

"I don't want to push, but I'd really like to read the rest of your stories if you'd let me."

Unease wormed through me. She told me she liked the stories, but there was that quiet but persistent negative voice in my head that was telling me she was just being nice but truthfully thought it was total garbage.

She can't lie.

That was only moderately comforting.

"I mean if you don't want me to, I don't have to," she went on. "But I can't get what Eve and Elliott were about to uncover in that cave out of my head. I need to know what happens. I need to know what *happened* before, too. Where did they get their superpowers? Have their superpowers been increasing? Or have they always been this powerful?"

I grinned, then leaned over to my nightstand and unplugged my tablet from the cord. "If you're *that* curious. If you're going to lose sleep over it ..." I flipped the flap on the tablet and brought up book one of the series, then handed it to her.

She bounced gleefully on the bed. "Thank you!"

I slunk down the bed, spread her legs and was about to flick her clit with my tongue when she stopped me, my ears clamped between her knees.

"Hey?" I said, trying to wedge myself free. "What gives? You're busy. I might as well be busy, too."

She glanced at me over the tablet, a sexy, amused smile curling half her mouth. "This book is about children. And one of those children is meant to be your sister. Forgive me if I get a *little* weirded out at the idea of getting aroused and inevitably *off* as I read it. Find me a sexy bodice-ripper with a highland warrior or a Navy SEAL single dad who can't keep his hands off the nanny, and you can go to town, but not when I'm reading this, okay?"

She had a point.

Didn't mean I liked the point.

I shuffled down to the bottom of the bed and glared at her playfully. "Fine. You can read for twenty minutes, then you're coming to find me in the shower, deal?"

She smiled again, instantly causing my cock to thicken. "Deal."

CHAPTER THIRTY-FOUR

Alex

MAKING SURE THAT I didn't wake the gorgeous naked man in the bed beside me, I quietly slid open the balcony door and stepped out into the cool morning shade.

It was only about eight o'clock, but I'd been up since seven, fervently reading the Evans Twins Chronicles and marveling at the incredible graphics and details Eli had added.

He was so talented, it blew my mind.

Tightening the sash around my puffy white robe, I took a seat in the chair and opened the flap on the tablet again. I'd just started book two, and it was already amazing and better than book one—which was also amazing.

I would have liked to make myself a coffee, but I didn't want to wake Eli. The man had been unceasingly devoted to my pleasure last night, so he deserved to sleep in.

Normally, I would have brought my yoga mat out to the deck, since I hadn't actually done any yoga in nearly three days, but I booked myself a class in the yoga studio for eleven this morning, so I figured I could slack off and bury myself in the book instead. It was just so good.

I'd never considered myself to be a creative person. I had my strengths, which were tenacity, math, sciences, yoga, Muay Thai, and time management, but when it came to writing anything besides a necessary paper for a biology class or drawing anything more than a sick man with a bowl cut, I was at a complete disadvantage.

But Eli had not only the creative genius of drawing but also of world-building and writing. I knew he said that Eden was the mastermind behind the stories themselves, but he was no slouch either.

I was flipping pages so fast, desperate to find out what happened next, that when a warm kiss fell to my neck, I nearly jumped clean out of my chair.

"Well, good morning to you, too," he said with a chuckle.

"Sorry, I'm just so into this book."

He came to sit in the chair beside me, wearing nothing but a skeptical look on his face. "Really?"

I bunched my brows. "Yes, *really*. Do you not believe me when I say this is amazing and I can't get enough of it?"

His lips twisted. "You're the only person to ever read it ... so I guess I'm just nervous."

I shook my head. "Eli, you have nothing to be nervous about. This is truly incredible. You *have* to publish it. Either self-publish or submit it to a publisher. But seriously, it could be turned into a movie or a television show. Pitch it to Netflix. The possibilities with this are honestly endless. You've created such a beautiful world." Smiling, I reached for his hand and squeezed it. "And you know I have a hard time not telling the truth, so take some solace in that, okay?"

He nodded and swallowed. "Okay." I brought the tablet up again. "Whereabouts are you?"

"Not quite halfway through book two. I just can't stop reading."

A hungry look took over his brown eyes, and he sank to the floor, shuffling over so he knelt in front of me. "Can you stop for maybe five minutes?"

Starting at the tops of my feet, he drew the backs of his fingers slowly up along my ankles, my calves, the backs of my knees, my inner thighs, and the tops of my thighs. The tickles sent tendrils of need up through my legs, only to converge at the apex of my thighs, causing my pussy to pulse and tighten. My nipples tightened, and I ached for his mouth to suck them, to relieve the sudden throbbing.

I put the flap over the screen and set the tablet down on the small table between our chairs. "Maybe for *five* minutes."

His fingers pushed the bottom of the white robe up my thighs, exposing my bare, now wet, pussy. Thank God for the translucent glass panels that made up the balcony railings and the fact that there were similar glass privacy screens between each unit's deck.

We were in our own little world, hidden from the public to do what our bodies desired. Though I couldn't deny the thrill that shook me at the fact that even though nobody could see us, we were still not in the privacy of our own room, and anybody within earshot would be able to hear us.

Let 'em listen. I was on my honeymoon.

"Inch forward a bit," he said, elbowing my knees farther apart as he settled between my legs, flicking his tongue out to say good morning to my clit.

I sighed and slid down farther in the chair.

"Good girl," he purred, his words sending a decadent buzz through me.

Closing my eyes, I melted deeper into the chair, tossed my arm over my eyes and let Eli do what he did best.

Because the man really was the absolute best at giving head.

I'd been a little more than mortified at first to hear the women in the bathroom discussing what they'd overheard, but then as they said that I was a "lucky woman" and how their husbands could "learn a thing or two" from Eli, my mortification disintegrated, leaving nothing but a warm, wanton feeling in my lower belly and between my legs.

My hips lifted off the chair of their own volition, and I pressed my pussy against his face. He took that as a moment to slide his fingers inside me and seek out that spot he'd gotten to know *very* well in the last few days. I could almost say he knew that spot better than I did. *Almost.*

I didn't have to give him an ounce of direction. He knew what I liked and how to get me to the edge and throw me over better than any man I'd ever been with.

The circles his tongue made over my clit had me seeing stars, and ribbons of pleasure spun and twirled through me, warming my body and awakening all my cells.

Then he did something I wasn't expecting but would be forever requiring from now on. He moved his tongue away from my clit and scraped his stubbly chin over it instead.

I was about to lose my damn mind.

"Oh my God," I breathed out. "Dear God."

Back and forth he dragged his whiskers, the prickling sensation unlike anything I'd ever felt before. It was like he was scratching away a layer and revealing and awakening new nerve endings I hadn't even known existed until this moment. My clit was stunned.

My hips shot off the chair again, and my hands fell to the top of his head, where I gripped his hair and held him in place. "Don't stop."

Don't ever fucking stop.

Exquisite sensations crashed through me, only to create bigger, more beautiful sensations that seemed new and gloriously beguiling. I wanted to explore them further. I wanted to know why, when he scraped his chin up my pussy and then wiggled it across my clit hood, my left leg felt like it was about to go numb. Like I'd just been sitting on it funny and pins and needles were shooting down my leg from my hip to my toes.

I didn't hate it.

I fucking loved it.

But I wanted to know why and how and uncover more secrets that Eli was revealing about my body, about my pleasure.

Did he know what he was doing to me?

Had he read books on sex? Books on female pleasure?

His chin waggled again, and I tightened my grip on his hair. "Just like that," I panted.

His fingers inside me increased their pumping, and he pressed up hard on my G-spot. I felt like I had to pee.

He pressed again and I sighed, then gasped.

He raked his chin over my clit again, pressed up even harder on my G-spot, and I let go.

"That's right, Alexandra," he said, continuing to fuck me with his fingers and rake his chin across my clit. "Good girl."

Why did him calling me a good girl turn me on so much?

But it did. It really did.

Heat flooded my limbs, colliding with the waves of pleasure that burst out from my core while blinding white stars flashed and blinked behind my closed eyes.

He just kept going. Just kept pushing me.

My orgasm seemed to last forever, but alas, all good things must come to an end, and as I scrambled for a solid, deep breath, my body, having stiffened and lifted as I came, dissolved back into the chair. Eli gently slid his fingers from me.

Without a word, he stood up, his cock hard and heavy between his legs, with a drop of precum on the tip, and he went into the hotel room. The sink in the bathroom ran for a moment before he returned to the deck.

He didn't say a word but just reached for me, hauled me out of the chair, positioned me in front of him at the smoked glass and metal deck railing and helped me bend over slightly.

I grinned when he ran his hand over my ass cheek, then he positioned the thick head of his cock between my still throbbing pussy lips.

Easily, he pushed inside, filling me.

We both let out a groan.

I gripped the railing and pushed back into him, but he didn't allow me to be hunched over for long. I was drawn backward so my back rested against his chest. He stepped backward, dropping down into the chair I'd just vacated and setting my legs on either side of his.

His hands untied the sash of my robe, and he slid it over my shoulders, nibbling on my neck and scraping his teeth across the top of my back. We sat there for a moment, connected but not moving as he swept his tongue along my tattoo and sank his teeth into the top of my shoulder.

I sucked in a breath and moved my head to the side so he could do it again.

Knowing what I wanted, he chuckled and acquiesced while slowly beginning to move beneath me. He bucked up into me while one hand navigated down my torso between my legs and the other one made its way up to my throat.

He began to pick up speed. He held my head in place with his fingers. It wasn't rough, but it wasn't gentle either. I loved it. With pressure from his thumb, he made me turn my head, and he took my mouth in an awkward, erotic kiss, pushing his tongue deep against mine and scraping his teeth over my lips.

I bounced up and down on his lap, crying out every time he hit me deep, squeezing my muscles around him.

His fingers worked magic over my clit, and his grip on my throat tightened. I wasn't going to last long. In some ways, I was still coming off my last orgasm and hadn't completely made my way to the bottom of the cliff, yet here I was turning around and making my way back to the top.

His teeth tugged on my bottom lip, and he pinched my clit.

I gasped. I groaned.

"You're so fucking sexy," he said, applying a little more pressure to my throat and taking my mouth again. "I could fuck you for the rest of my life and never tire. I never want to stop."

I knew we were caught up in the moment—he was literally inside of me, and we were seconds from climax—but his words filled my heart and wrapped around it like a protective mantle. I could do this forever, too.

I could make love to Eli, *be* with Eli for the rest of my life, too.

"Please ..." I said, not quite sure I knew what I was asking for but feeling the need to say it anyway.

Was I asking for him to be mine for the rest of our lives?

Was I asking for him to pinch my clit and make me come?

Was I asking for him to call me a good girl again and tighten the hold he had on my throat?

Or was it all of the above?

I was pretty sure it was all of the above.

"Please, Eli ..." I whimpered, begging him for all of it, for everything he could give, for everything that we could be together.

His fingers picked up speed on my clit. I started lifting and dropping harder into his lap, jarred and elated each time he filled me once again. I was close. The storm in my lower belly was brewing wildly.

His grip on my throat tightened until a small amount of breathing discomfort had me feeling light-headed. But I trusted Eli. Implicitly. And I knew he'd never hurt me and that if I asked him to stop, he'd stop immediately.

"Yes," I said against his lips. "God, yes."

He smiled wickedly as he took my mouth once more. I lifted up for a final time, swirled the head of his cock around my opening for a moment, feeling him, teasing him, teasing both of us. Then I slowly dropped back down, inch by luscious inch, accepting him back into my body as I squeezed myself around him.

"Fuck," he grunted as we kissed. He pinched my clit.

And together we came.

Our lips remained locked in a kiss, but neither of us moved. We stilled, breathing in the other's breath through our noses as we panted and allowed the pleasure of our connected bodies to flow out of him and into me and back again. He pulsed inside me; I pulsed around him. My clit throbbed and my belly warmed as heat and pleasure rushed out of my center in glorious waves.

We broke the kiss after several heartbeats but pressed our foreheads together. He removed his hand from my throat and his fingers from between my legs.

Eventually, I faced the ocean and leaned back against his chest. His arms encircled my waist, and he held me in place, his cock still safely inside me as we watched the water erupt into a blanket of diamonds and the shorebirds swoop and dive.

He kissed the side of my head. "I could get used to mornings like this."

"Me, too," I said, lacing my fingers through his.

"Too bad all good things must come to an end." He kissed my neck this time, and a single tear rolled down my cheek.

CHAPTER THIRTY-FIVE

Alex

"OH, FOR FUCK'S SAKE," I murmured as Eli and I entered the yoga studio in the rec and fitness area of the hotel.

"What?" His hand landed on the small of my back.

"The cast of Gossip Girl California is in the class." I waved and smiled at Gina, Kymberli, Selena and Tavia, who were unrolling their mats near the back corner of the room.

"So what?" Eli asked, following me to two of the only side-by-side spots left in the class, which were right at the front with the instructor. "You're a fucking yoga teacher. You can out-bind and out-standing-bow-pose anybody." He unrolled the rental mat next to mine. "Besides, I don't think their kind of plastic is very *bendy*, if you know what I mean?"

I snorted. "It's just not going to be as relaxing knowing they're in the class watching me—literally—the entire time."

"Want me to take off my shirt and pants and do the class in my boxers? I'm sure after what they overheard me saying last night, I've been the nonstop star of their bean-flicking fantasies." He bobbed his brows at me.

He always knew how to make me laugh. I swatted his hand away from the hem of his shirt. "No. And you wish you were the star of their *bean*-flicking fantasies."

"I don't wish for anybody but you to think of me as you flick your bean, but I can almost guarantee you that my confessions about my dietary preferences left more than one woman *hot* and desperate to bean-flick last night."

"Dietary preferences ..." I rolled my eyes and smiled. "You're ridiculous."

"But I got you smiling and thinking about my dietary preferences and how despite my very thorough meal this morning, I'm still fucking hungry." He knelt down beside me and waggled his tongue at me.

I was still smiling. It was impossible not to with Eli. I also wasn't thinking nearly as much about the four women at the back or what they thought of me.

"Just try not to fall out of eagle pose into me, okay?"

He winked. "I'll see what I can do. And if I fall anywhere, it'll be on top of you. Or with my face between your legs."

I rolled my eyes again. "You're incorrigible."

The class was really good, despite the laser beams I felt in the back of my skull from the four women behind me. Yoga was something that no matter where I was or who was around me when I was doing it, I had been doing it long enough that I was able to find my pranayama ujjayi breathing and center myself. The yoga instructor was great, her voice was soothing, and it was refreshing to be led through practice rather than lead it. I forgot how much I enjoyed being able to close my eyes during certain postures rather than scan the room to make sure nobody was going to injure themselves hyperextending a joint.

My body needed the endorphin release. My chakras needed the attention, and my heart needed the grounding. When we all bowed and said "namaste," I wasn't surprised to find my throat tight or tears welling up in my eyes. I kept my hands in prayer on my forehead and bent to the ground just a little bit longer to allow my gratitude to flow into the Earth and collect myself.

When you exhaled that which no longer served you and took that hour for yourself at the mat, the emotions and endorphins could be very powerful things.

It wasn't the first time a yoga class had brought me to tears.

After unfolding myself from the mat, I stood up and approached the instructor. "Thank you so much. That was just what I needed."

She was a lithe, blonde woman probably in her mid-forties. I got a real Reese Witherspoon vibe from her. "You're so welcome. I can tell you practice regularly." Her smile was warm and inviting.

"I teach at a studio in Maine."

"I thought you might be a teacher. Your poses were flawless."

My cheeks got hot. "Thank you."

Her nose wrinkled for a moment, and her eyes studied me. I squirmed under her stare.

"Can I ... can I give you a hug?" She chuckled awkwardly. "I'm not a hippie weirdo, I swear, but just ... your chi is really telling me you need a hug. You probably know better than me, but there was a reason you took my class, greater than because you needed to stretch."

I swallowed and nodded stiffly. I'd encountered empathic and spiritual people like this before during my time practicing yoga, and although I wasn't one of them or big on hugging strangers, my years practicing yoga had taught me not to dismiss when someone felt your energy strongly enough to speak up about it.

She wrapped her slender arms around me, and I wrapped mine around her.

It was only weird for a moment, and then it felt like I'd known this woman for years and was hugging an old friend.

We held on for another twenty seconds or so, and I opened my eyes midway through to find Eli giving me a "what the fuck?" face. I closed my eyes again.

The woman, who I believed was named Basha—or so said the sandwich board outside the studio—pulled away and smiled. "You'll figure it all out, and it'll be better than you ever expected."

I cocked my head to the side. "What will be?"

She shrugged and shook her head. "I don't know. I just ... feel a lot of conflicts in your energy. Confusion, turmoil, and uncertainty. But I also feel excitement and desire. So harness those feelings, and I'm sure they'll guide you in the right direction." She clasped my hands together in hers and squeezed. "Thank you for letting me share in your energy today."

I nodded, blinking in shock. "Thank you for allowing me to be a part of yours."

Smiling, she released my hands, grabbed her yoga mat and headed out the door, leaving just me and Eli.

"What was that about?" he asked, taking my free hand and linking our fingers together, pulling me toward the door.

"I just ... I got a lot out of that class and knew that I needed to thank her personally. Then she felt an energy in me and asked if she could give me a hug."

"And ..."

I shrugged. "And she said she felt a lot of conflicting emotions, told me to focus on the excitement and desire and everything will work out."

Insatiable need flashed in Eli's eyes. "I can help with the *desire* part."

I rolled my eyes. "Do you ever run out of sexual energy?"

"Not where you're concerned."

I shot him a look of disbelief. How was he not running on fumes yet? "I thought we were going back up to our room to change into our bathing suits. A day at the pool with a cabana and drinks sounded like heaven when you mentioned it this morning." I sighed and rested my head on his shoulder. "I can't wait to rub sunscreen all over my handsome husband."

Eli's grin was massive when he gazed down at me, and the look of shock in his eyes was unmistakable. "You called me your husband," he said teasingly.

"Well, you are, aren't you?" I said, lifting my head from his shoulder and wrinkling my nose. Now I was self-conscious for calling him that. Was I caught up in such a sex and orgasm fog that I was misconstruing things? Thinking whatever was happening between us was more than it was? I'd never been so confused, but also deliriously happy in my entire life.

I mean, technically, legally, he *was* my husband. But calling him *my husband* was taking some getting used to. I didn't dislike having to get used to it. Not at all. But I also wasn't going to tell him that.

"I am your husband. And I like it when you call me that." He pressed a kiss to the side of my head and unlinked our fingers, wrapping his arm around me instead. "We will head to the pool in a little bit," he said, leading me away from the elevator. "And you can rub, tug, and whatever else you want to your handsome husband until he's as slippery as an eel.   But not yet. I've booked us massages."

"Oooh."

"We need to be as relaxed as possible if we're going to get through the next three days."

"Agreed," I said, allowing him to lead me across the main lobby toward the sign that said *Serenity Elite Spa.* He held open the door, and I stepped inside. We were greeted with gentle spa music, with maybe some babbling water in the background.

Crystal shot glasses with cucumber and wheatgrass juice were offered to us as we checked in. I loved mine. Eli gagged.

"That tasted like grass," he murmured as we followed the receptionist down the hallway to the massage rooms.

"It is grass," I said with a chuckle. "It's *wheat*grass."

His lips curled like he'd just drunk curdled milk. "And people drink this on the regular? Willingly?"

The receptionist held open the door for us. "Please strip down to your underwear. You're welcome to take your bra off. Your massage therapists will be with you shortly." She closed the door, and unlike even less than a week ago, when Eli and I would have been so careful undressing in front of each other, we just stripped right there, not having a care in the world.

"I want to suck those nipples," he said, climbing onto the massage bed.

"Later." I climbed onto the adjacent bed and put my face in the hole. "This was such a great idea. I can't remember the last time I splurged on a massage."

"We're going by the same rules again tonight, too. Eleven—or sooner—and we're blowing that Popsicle stand."

"Do you see me arguing?"

There was a gentle knock at the door.

"We're ready," Eli called out.

The door opened, and a very handsome, very big, very tall man stepped in. My eyes widened. Eli flipped his head around to see the door, since he had been facing me. I wished I could have seen the expression on his face, particularly when the man stepped aside and a woman possibly not even five feet tall stepped out from behind the man.

"Hi, I'm Helena," she said, stepping up to Eli. "I'll be massaging you today."

Eli's head flipped back around to face me, panic in his eyes.

I stifled a laugh and followed the blond man, who was probably close to seven feet tall, with my eyes as he stepped toward me. "I'm Jake, and I'll be massaging you."

"Uhhh ..." was all that came out of Eli's mouth as he stared unblinkingly at Jake.

I lifted a brow at him.

His gaze narrowed at me, and a cheeky smile slid across his mouth.

"Looking forward to it," he said, glancing up at Helena.

"Me, too," I said to Jake, settling back in with my face in the hole of the table.

The lights were dimmed, and the sheet was pulled down from the tops of my shoulders to just above my ass crack.

"Gorgeous tattoo," Jake said.

"Thank you."

Warm oil was squeezed onto my back, and I closed my eyes, but not for long. I had to see what was going on at Eli's table.

I wasn't jealous about Helena touching him, but I could tell by his reaction when Jake stepped over to my table that he wasn't entirely keen on a man as handsome and big as Jake touching me.

I turned my face toward Eli and opened my eyes. Sure enough, he was facing me, and his eyes were wide open as Helena worked the warm oil into the tops of his shoulders.

I struggled not to smile, but the intensity of his stare was making it hard.

Jake's hands were also magical and working out knots in my shoulders and back I didn't even know I had. At one point I moaned, but that only prompted a chuckle at the flare of Eli's brown eyes and the clenching of his jaw.

"Can you try to relax a bit, sir?" Helena asked. "Your muscles are very tense."

"Sorry," Eli grunted.

I rolled my lips inward, trying not to laugh.

When Jake moved down to my thighs, I thought for sure Eli was going to leap off the table and put an end to everything, but he remained calm-*ish* and let the man do his job.

I, meanwhile, was in pure heaven as Jake slid his big, strong thumbs up the backs of my hamstrings and pulled his middle and forefingers back down the sides of my legs. And don't even get me started on the foot massage. I was close to an orgasm there, one hundred percent.

"Please try to relax, Mr. Evans," Helena said again when Jake had moved around my body and the front of his pants was right next to the top of my head as he worked on my neck, head, and shoulders.

"Sorry," Eli murmured again.

"Anything else you'd like me to focus on before our time is up?" Jake asked, those big fingers of his working out a knot in my left upper back.

"You've hit all the right spots," I said, only half awake. "No suggestions."

Jake chuckled, finished up, and then he and Helena left.

I hadn't realized it, but I'd closed my eyes again.

The door *snicked* closed, and then the noise of Eli climbing off his table flitted around the room. There was a *click* of the door being locked, and then I was being yanked by the ankles down the length of the bed.

I squealed.

Eli flipped me over, spread my legs and pushed my underwear to the side. He was inside me before I had more than half a second to register what was going on.

My legs were draped over the edge of the table, my back horizontal.

Lifting up onto my elbows, I watched him, with a feral, possessive look in his eyes as he held onto my knees and pumped into me.

"A little jealous?" I asked, teasingly.

He growled. "Not doing that again."

"I wasn't jealous that a beautiful woman was touching you," I said, the pleasure in my center and lower belly beginning to build. He released one hand from behind my knee and pushed my panties further aside to get at my clit.

"You're hotter than her. No need for you to be jealous." He grunted. "Watching another man touch you …" His head shook, and he bared his teeth. "Fucking unbearable."

I bit my lip and smiled, loving the primal and hungry gleam in his eyes.

Like I was his and his alone and he would kill any man who ever laid a hand on me. I wasn't one for murder, but the possessiveness in his eyes was something I could get used to.

"You're mine," he said, pumping harder but not speeding up. The slow pull of his length across my channel had me squirming on the massage bed and my pussy quivering. Then when he pushed back in, I squeezed and welcomed him home.

His fingers on my clit were bringing me to that sweet, sharp edge fast.

Eli gritted his teeth. "Say you're mine."

"I'm yours," I breathed.

"My wife."

"Your wife."

"Fucking right you are."

He pinched my clit, drove into me harder, and away I went off up into the stratosphere, flying high on my climax and loving the way Eli made me feel, how he felt about me and the way that look in his eyes turned me to mush.

He closed his eyes, tilted his head back, and stilled, coming inside me, filling me and claiming me. Because I was his. Utterly and entirely. Fully and completely. I was his.

CHAPTER THIRTY-SIX

Alex

WE MADE SURE TO handsomely tip Jake and Helena, since not only did we leave the massage room smelling like sex, but we most definitely overstayed our welcome in the room, considering the mild look of impatience on their faces when we met them at reception and paid for our massages. But when they saw the tip on the receipt, they were nothing but smiles.

Eli and I spent the rest of the day by the pool, soaking up the sun, enjoying cocktails and indulging in fish tacos from the taco food truck down the block from the hotel. He'd downloaded an app and discovered that a highly rated food truck was parked just one street over, so leaving me to protect our lounge chairs from sneaky pool-goers, Eli ran out and grabbed us a late lunch.

Exhausted from a day of doing nothing and loving it, we headed back to our room around five o'clock. Dinner was at seven.

Sex, a long bubble bath together, then more sex, followed by a rushed dress and makeup, and we were exiting the elevator at six fifty-five.

"I fucking love this dress on you," Eli said, looping his arm around the top of my shoulders and letting his gaze lazily traipse its way down my body. "I have good taste."

"Not going to argue with you there," I said. Because I couldn't. The dress I was wearing tonight fit me perfectly.

I put my hair up in a high ponytail and kept my makeup minimal—which was basically the way I did my makeup every day (when I even wore it at all) because I had no idea how to go *glam*, particularly for the evening.

But the dress I was wearing, a black sparkling thing with full sleeves and absolutely no back, was amazing and made me feel more beautiful than any contouring or smoky eye ever could. It was quite short, so I had to make sure not to bend over or crouch. Pretty much, if I dropped something, it either stayed there forever or I had to ask Eli to pick it up for me.

My heels were a cherry-red pump, to match the bright chunks in my hair, and I'd found an old lipstick in the bottom of my purse to match. I forgot to bring any jewelry on this trip—not that I owned much—so the simple gold studs in my ears would have to do.

"It shows off your sexy tattoo," he said, leaning in and pressing his lips to the side of my head. "Yesterday's dress was hot, but the fact that your entire front is covered but your back is completely bare ... that you're not wearing a bra." He growled. "Tell me you're not wearing panties again."

We entered the dining room. "I had to," I said with a sigh. "Dress is too short to risk it."

He pretended to pout but then smiled. "Ah, well, I'll just have to remove them with my teeth later."

We approached the bar. He ordered us both drinks while I scanned the dining room for anybody I might know and be interested in talking to. It looked like seating was assigned.

"I'm just going to go find where we're sitting," I said, untangling myself from Eli's arm and slaloming my way through the round six-person tables, people and chairs.

I found my name at a table. *Alexandra Hartford.*

But Eli wasn't sitting with me.

What the fuck?

I kept looking around for his name only to find him sitting with Kymberli, Gina, Tavia, Selena, Ford and Allegra.

What in the fucking nightmare was this?

"Here you go," Eli said, finding me, handing me my wine and pecking me on the cheek before taking a sip of his whiskey.

He was so attentive, so affectionate. So ... wonderful. So ... believable. I knew he was attracted to me. We'd started sleeping together, after all, and he confessed to liking me when we were kids—despite how much he also hated me. But his affection, his attentiveness caught me off guard. It didn't at all feel like he was playing or pretending. Were they real? Or was I too caught up in post-multiple-orgasm bliss to see past his impeccable acting skills?

His hand drifted down, and he cupped my butt. "Where are we sitting?"

The anxiety spinning a wicked and twisted web inside of me started to surround my heart and lungs, restricting my breathing and making my pulse begin to pound.

"You're *here*, with the Gossip Girls of California and the happy couple. Meanwhile, I'm alllll the way over there." I glanced at the table where my name tag had been. It was the table with the old, single aunts and uncles. There was only one seat not filled now, and it was mine.

Why was my hand shaking?

Why did Allegra do this?

"Fuck that noise," Eli said calmly, grabbing his name tag off the table. He left me standing there watching him as he draped his coat over two chairs at an empty table, picked up the name tags belonging to those seats and swapped out my name on my table for one of those names. Then he was back and set down "Keith" where Eli's name had been at the table with Allegra and Ford.

He reached for my hand. "My understanding is Keith and his wife don't like each other anyway. I'm sure they'll be glad not to be seated with each other. Now come on. Let's grab our seats."

I grinned at him and followed.

"I don't know why she did that," I said, sipping my wine and watching the door, with black tendrils of dread threatening to wind their way around my heart the moment Allegra realized what we'd done. Because she would notice. She noticed everything.

Eli shrugged and plainly said, "Because she's an Oompa-Loompa bitch."

I nodded. "She is."

He brought his head in close to mine. "I'm here for you because, for some reason, you feel you need to be here. I don't know what went down in college for you, but I know that I made your high school life—"

"And elementary and junior high—"

"Don't remind me." He pressed his lips together. "I know I made your life hell for a long time. And I will do whatever I can to make it up to you. But tell me, Alexandra, is there anything nice about Allegra? Anything redeeming? Is she even a frenemy, or is she just an enemy?"

I didn't want to answer him.

It would be easy to say that she was my enemy because for all intents and purposes, she was. And yet, the compulsion I felt to come to her wedding when I received the invitation was overwhelming. I felt bullied into coming by a piece of cardstock. I was reduced to that insecure, twentysomething-year-old whose best friend had just died and who didn't have any other meaningful social connections in the world.

"After Eden died, Allegra and her group were the only friends I had," I said quietly. "I've never made friends very easily, and I think after Eden, I was afraid to make any more meaningful connections. So being on the outside of a group like Allegra's was the safest place for me." I tipped my eyes up to his.

He pressed his forehead to mine.

"I know it wasn't healthy. I know she's not a nice person. And as much as I shouldn't care about what they think of me now, I do. It's sick, but I do. I haven't made any friends in Maine, not really. And I've lived there since I finished vet school."

He nodded. "Okay. I get it."

Commotion at the entrance to the dining room caused us to lift our heads. Allegra, Ford, their wedding party and families were walking through. Allegra's eye found mine. She took one look at where we were sitting and the fact that we were sitting together, and rage filled her face.

I was about to crumple under her glare when Eli pressed his mouth to my ear and took my free hand under the table. "Don't you dare."

I inhaled deep.

"Sit up straight," he ordered. That commanding tone clung just on the edge of his voice. "Look her in the eye and smile that gorgeous smile, Alexandra. Don't crumble. Don't shrink. You are such a fucking badass. You are the last person in here who should be cowering under that bitch's glare."

Swallowing, I did as he said, following Allegra and her posse to their table with my eyes and keeping a super big, super fake smile on my face.

Murmurs behind us at their table made my ears perk up and the hair on my arms began   to tingle.

"They did it on purpose. It was a joint effort," Eli said. "They're talking about how we foiled them right now and deciding whether it's worth causing a fuss over. If they come to our table, you do not say a word, understand?"

I nodded.

"Good girl."

I sipped my wine, hating that my hand trembled as I brought it to my lips.

A throat cleared behind us.

I set my wineglass down on the table and lifted my head, turning away from Eli. He squeezed my hand.

"Allegra, you look beautiful," Eli said. "Tavia, Kymberli, Selena, Gina, radiant, ladies. Radiant."

"Thank you," they all said, their voices breathy and croony.

"I think there's been a mix-up," Kymberli said. "Eli, you're supposed to be at the table with us."

Eli sipped his whiskey and fixed them all with a very bored look. "Yeah, I saw that. But I figured it had to be a mistake, since why would *I*, a plus one who all you guys have never met before, be with the bride and groom and the bridesmaids? And why would Alex be at a table with a bunch of single aunts and uncles?" He glanced at the table I was supposed to be at. "So I just fixed things. Besides, based on the horrible shit Keith was saying about his wife last night, I figured they wouldn't want to sit with each other. And he's the best man, isn't he? Shouldn't he be there?"

The women's faces all went red.

"We just wanted to get to know you better," Tavia said, her eyes darting to Allegra for approval as she twisted her fingers in front of her.

Eli shrugged. "Appreciate it, but I wouldn't feel right having laughs with you guys while my wife was all the way across the room. We'll be sitting here tonight."

I risked another glance at their faces as I sipped my wine.

It was all I could do not to smile, let alone laugh.

They were all opening their mouths and closing them, but no words were coming out.

"No harm, no foul," Eli said. "Return to your tables, ladies. I'm sure we can catch up and you can get to know me better a little later." He left zero room for argument and basically told them to *git*, only in a much more commanding, alpha, hot-as-fuck way.

I could see all their spines straighten, but at the same time, they melted.

Yeah, Eli had that effect on people. Women in particular, anyway.

He lifted his brow at them. "Anything else?"

They shook their heads.

"All right, good girls. Bye."

Four sets of pupils dilated, and not that I was thinking about their underwear, but I would bet a lot of money that from those two little words, *good girls,* that all four women were wet as fuck. I know I was.

They turned around and walked back to their table, and only once they'd sat down did Eli remove his hand from mine, cup the back of my head and pull my mouth to his for a kiss.

I was breathless and wanting more when he pulled away, his eyelids hooded and filled with lust. "You are ten times the woman, person and wife those harpies are. You don't need them. You don't need their validation, approval or friendship. They are *not* your friends. Got it?"

I nodded.

"But if this is what you need to do, I will support you. I will have your back. I will always have your back."

I nodded again.

"Drink your wine."

I lifted the glass and took a sip, flushed from how turned on I was right now.

"Good girl."

Well, shit, now I had to worry about a damn wet spot on my dress.

If I ignored the feeling of laser beams shooting into the side of my head all night, it wasn't a terrible evening.

The food was good, and now that I was sitting with Eli and not at a table with old, single aunts and uncles, but with people my own age and in relationships, I felt like I could bring my shoulders away from my ears and relax.

I'd done an hour of yoga, had a beautiful massage from Jake, and spent the day by the pool with my sexy husband. You'd think I'd be super relaxed, but that wasn't the case. At least not until I had a couple of drinks in me and Eli's arm draped around me most of the night like a protective suit of armor.

Eli was deep in conversation with the man beside him as we ate our dinner, so I casually chatted with the woman to my left. Turned out she was in this morning's yoga class and did yoga multiple times a week as well back home in Arizona.

I was nibbling on my halibut when I overheard Eli saying something to the man he was chatting with that made me tune the rest of the world out and tune into him. "Huge traveler," Eli said. "I've got the bug, and the bite is very itchy. I haven't been anywhere in ages, but I tell you, man, as soon as I'm in the clear from the surgeon, I am booking a flight and getting the fuck out of here."

The other guy chuckled.

My perfectly cooked fish no longer tasted perfect. I set down my fork, swallowed the bite in my mouth, and washed it down with wine.

So he was planning to leave again once the doctor cleared him for travel. He wasn't sticking around Maine, wasn't going to continue his roofing job. He would file for divorce, things between us would end, and he would go on his way.

How could I have been so stupid as to think that what we had was anything more than just a momentary transaction? He was scratching a different itch with me, but it was nothing more. I was his ... *for now.* But not forever.

And I had been an idiot to think anything otherwise.

A hollow began to form in my chest, as if someone scooped it out, except I was still upright, still breathing, still existing, and my heart was still beating, so I guess I was fine, technically.

I went back to my conversation with the woman beside me, tuning out Eli and the other guy completely, but I struggled to focus on what Rebecca was saying, to hear her over the roaring sound in my ears and the crushing and crumbling feeling in my heart.

There were speeches from the bride and groom's families, followed by a roast kind of toast from Keith for Ford, then before I knew it, we were standing up and heading to the elevator.

Eli took my hand and smiled, giving my fingers a squeeze. "I can't wait to get you out of that dress."

"I, um ... I don't think I'm ready to go back to the room just yet," I said, stopping us in our tracks and forcing a few people to walk around us.

We moved off to the side by the wall, Eli's brows pinching together. "Everything okay? You want to go for a walk? It's not even eleven."

I nodded. "I do want to go for a walk, but I think I actually want to go alone, if you don't mind?"

His smile dropped heavily into a frown. "Have I done something?"

Knowing I was a terrible liar, I quickly shook my head. I needed to get out of there. "I just need to think about what happened earlier and what Basha the yoga instructor said to me. I think I'll just go sit on the beach for a bit." I gave his fingers a gentle squeeze. "But I'll see you back in the room. I won't be long."

The reluctance to let me go was clear on his face.

I smiled reassuringly, but it hurt to lift the corners of my mouth, given how weighted my heart felt at the moment. "We've been together nonstop for over a week. Absence makes the heart grow fonder, right? Go work on Eve and Elliott. I'll be okay." I let go of his hand and turned to go, but before I was even half a step away, he stopped me, draped his suit jacket over my shoulders and kissed my cheek. "You know that if you say *no* to sex, I respect that, right? I'm not a pressuring asshole."

"I know," I said, glancing back at him. "Thank you for your jacket." I slid my arms into it, then headed toward the door that led out of the hotel and down toward the beach.

I just needed to think.

Everything that had transpired today at dinner was making my head hurt.

How unnecessarily mean Allegra and her friends had been to me, that they seemed to be favoring Eli and trying to split us up, and of course, what he'd said to the guy he was talking to about leaving the moment his doctor gave him the green light to travel.

I was an idiot to think that this marriage was anything but part of a deal between two people. And yet, the things he said to me, the way he kissed me, the way he worshiped my body and protected me had me feeling like it was all so much more real than it was.

But then I remembered that he'd also said he would play a convincing boyfriend, that nobody at this wedding would think we weren't together and madly in love. Apparently, that included me.

Was this something I could get upset about though? I'd agreed to the marriage. I'd agreed to the sex. Hell, I might have been the one to initiate it. And I certainly wasn't keeping my legs closed now.

It'd just been so long since I'd felt this kind of a connection with anybody that my brain was mistaking civility and a truce, a deal and an arrangement for love, devotion and desire.

I couldn't be mad at Eli. He was playing his part perfectly.

Perhaps *too* perfectly, because he'd duped even me.

I found an empty lounge chair in the sand and sat down. It was dark out, and there were a few stars overhead. Solar tiki torches lined the area of the beach that was meant for hotel guests, and the not-quite-full moon reflected off the calm water.

There was no need to run back up to the room and talk to Eli about any of this. I needed to just suck it up and recognize it all for what it was. A fun, sexy road trip with my former enemy. He needed my insurance plan, and I needed a hot, convincing date for Allegra's wedding. He was simply holding up his end of the deal.

As I sat there, I began to wrap a protective shield around my heart. I wasn't going to be cold with Eli. He'd done nothing wrong, but I also wasn't going to let myself fall any further in love with him than I already was.

Because I was in love with him.

That much I knew.

So I had to tell my heart to stop falling, to buck up and start falling out of love with him before it was too late.

I sat there staring at the water and torches for probably another twenty minutes, making sure the rivets on my shield were extra tight and would hold up to his convincing devotion.

Walking back to the hotel, I practiced some deep breathing, drawing air in through my nose for a count of four, holding it and then exhaling for a count of four. It helped ease the tension that surrounded my heart and to fill the hollow in my chest.

I was walking past the pool when a rustle of bushes and a giggle made me stop in my tracks.

The pool area was well lit, and there were several cabanas around, but only one had its privacy panels facing the pool drawn.

"Ford ..." came a girly giggle.

My eyes widened.

I'd already taken my heels off, so with bare feet, I padded around the pool to the cabana.

Grunts, groans and moans filtered out from the cabana.

Were Allegra and Ford having one last pre-wedding romp?

I went to turn away but was stopped by the manly uttered word of "Brittney."

What?

Who?

Huh?

My eyes were peering through the thin crack between canvas panels before I'd sucked in my next breath.

And there was Ford standing behind a blonde woman who I think was one of his vet techs, pumping wildly into her ass as she bit her lip and moaned.

Oh my.

I watched for way longer than I should have, but it was kind of like a car wreck. Then I was transported back to when I was sixteen and what I'd walked in on then.

I pulled back abruptly and did what you're never supposed to do. I ran on the pool deck back toward the hotel.

Then I ran to the elevator, and as soon as it hit my floor, I ran to our hotel room.

I didn't have the key card, so I started knocking furiously on the door.

Eli opened it, his eyes wild and wide. "What happened?"

CHAPTER THIRTY-SEVEN

Eli

"You're not saying a word," I said sternly after Alexandra returned to our room looking like she'd just seen the ghost of who the fuck knows. "It's none of our business. She's not your friend."

Alexandra gaped at me. "I have to."

My head shook, and I paced through the room, pulling at my hair. I'd been an absolute fucking mess since she told me she needed time to herself, pacing the room, then standing out on the balcony watching her down on the beach below. Yes, we'd spent twenty-four hours a day together for over a week, but I hadn't grown tired of her and certainly didn't need time to myself. What the fuck happened, what the fuck changed between when I put Allegra and her friends in their place and the end of dinner? She'd completely changed, and not for the better.

Why didn't she want to talk about how she was feeling with me? Why keep it bottled up inside? Hadn't I proved to her that I could be trusted? Hadn't I shown her that I genuinely cared about her and wasn't just in this for the kick-ass insurance policy anymore?

"Listen to me," I said, facing her again and taking her by the shoulders. "This is not your cross to bear. This is not your responsibility. For all we know, Allegra knows about the affair and is fine with it. A bunch of the other wives seem to know about their husbands' mistresses."

She shrugged me off and stepped away. "Doesn't make it right. And I doubt they're *fine* with it. They probably just signed insane prenups and know they're fucked if they file for divorce." She planted her hands on her hips. "Even if Allegra is a bitch, she doesn't deserve to marry a cheater. She doesn't deserve to start her life with someone with such a secret being kept from her."

"And if they call the whole thing off and her life is ruined, how are you going to feel about that?"

Her eyes widened. "Better now than a year from now when she catches him with that woman or someone else. Better now than if they have kids and an entire family is blown apart."

"Or you say nothing. He stops cheating, and they have a family and live happily ever after."

If thunder had a look, Alexandra was the definition of it. A storm brewed behind those blue eyes, and lightning flashed. Her scowl was menacing as she shook her head. "I knew it."

"Knew what?"

Her head shook again. "Don't play dumb with me. Admit it, Eli. Admit that you still blame me. That you believe had I kept my mouth shut, that your parents and my parents would still be together."

I shrugged and lifted my hands. If she wanted to hash this out now, then so be it. "We'll never know, will we?"

"You honestly think that had I not gone to my dad and told him what I saw, my mom and your dad would have just *miraculously* stopped sneaking behind everyone's backs, gone back to their spouses and pretended nothing ever happened? That your dad and my dad would remain business partners and best friends? Our moms would stay best friends and we'd all continue to have summer barbecues with each other as if not a damn thing had gone down in secret?"

I shrugged again. "Maybe."

"And you think that after what *I* saw that I'd be able to look any of our parents in the eye? Let alone speak to my mother and not feel like I was betraying my dad?"

What the fuck did she see?

I'd never asked her, never asked Eden if she knew.

I just assumed she'd caught them kissing, but what if it was more?

Did I want to know?

Her lip curled up, and her eyes turned fierce, her smile smug. "Your dad was up to his fucking wisdom teeth in my mom's ass. Had her bent over the kitchen counter and was trying to see what she had for fucking lunch. That's what I walked in on. That's what's burned into my retinas for the rest of my life. What I see when I close my eyes every night. Why I can't even think about my mom, let alone look at her or speak to her."

"Jesus fuck," I muttered, shoving all my fingers into my hair and pacing the length of the hotel room.

"Yeah," Alexandra went on, her tone harsh. "She did that to your mom, her best friend, and my dad—her *husband.* Your dad did that to my dad, his *best friend,* and your mom—his *wife.* Your dad went home and kissed your mom with the same mouth. Smiled at you and Eden with the same mouth that had just earlier that day been molars-deep in my mom's ass. And how many times before had he done it? They'd been sneaking around for months." Her smile was wicked and satisfied, but the pain behind her eyes was something that tugged so hard at my heartstrings, I thought I might collapse to the ground. "And now that image is in your brain, too."

My mouth was as open as it could go.

"So yeah, forgive me for not holding that in and hoping that things just 'went back to normal' because I sure as fuck couldn't have looked at any of our parents after that without wanting to puke. I love my dad. He was a good husband and a good friend and business partner, and he didn't deserve what your dad and my mom did to him."

"My mom didn't deserve it either," I said quietly.

She shook her head. "I know she didn't. And in a perfect world, maybe your mom and my dad should have just said fuck it and got together, but they didn't." Glancing away, her throat moved on a swallow. "Not that I gave a shit after seeing what I saw, but my mom actually had the audacity to say that I betrayed *her*. She thought that I preferred her to my dad and should have kept her secret or come to her so she could tell my dad. She called me a shit daughter."

Fucking hell. I didn't know that.

"Your dad came after me, too. Said I ruined two families in one go. So I have you, my mom, and your dad blaming me for what happened. Telling me I poked my nose in business that wasn't mine and because I did that, I broke up two families."

Well, now I wanted to put a hole through the wall—or my dad's face.

"My mom started drinking shortly after." I had no idea what else to say.

"I know she did. My dad went through a bit of that, too."

"It destroyed Eden."

Her eyes went from ready to maul to watery and sad quickly. "I know it did. She was my best friend. And I blame myself for that."

"Did you tell her what you saw?"

Alexandra nodded. "She begged me to tell her. Wouldn't let it go. I tried to tell her she didn't want to know, that she was better off not knowing. But she wouldn't let up. So I told her." Her gaze fell to the floor. "Second biggest mistake I've ever made."

The first was going to Thailand and leaving Eden alone. She didn't have to say it for me to know that was what she meant.

"How's your dad now?" I asked, wanting to get off the topic of Eden before I lost my composure as well. I also hated fighting with Alexandra. It didn't feel right. It didn't feel natural. Not anymore.

A month ago it would have felt as habitual as riding a bike, seeing as we'd done nothing but fight for our entire lives. But now, that was the last thing I wanted to do with her. I wanted to love her like she deserved. Protect her. Worship her and start a life with her.

"Better," she whispered, the ire in her tone slipping away. "He hired a personal trainer a couple of years after the divorce and got super ripped. He's big into fitness now. Goes to the gym every day. He's known as the Silver Zaddy at his local gym, which makes me want to barf, but it's good for his self-esteem. He's assured me he doesn't date anyone within a twenty-year age range of me. That he prefers women closer to his own age." She shrugged and glanced upward. "I don't know if that's the truth, but he's happy, so that's what matters. And your mom?"

"Better, too. She drank hard for at least three years following the divorce. Things got scary for a while there. But she's seeing a really great guy now. She's been sober for seven years, she does Pilates, and she and Arnold go on lots of cruises and down to Florida several times a year. He treats her well, and she's happy. Which, as you said, is what matters the most."

"I'm glad she's doing well. Eden mentioned that her drinking got a bit dicey. That she had to call 911 at least twice when she couldn't rouse your mom after she blacked out."

I nodded. "Yeah. It was not fun."

We fell into silence, but it wasn't awkward. There was a sense of companionship there. And the tension that I'd been feeling was gone, too. Alexandra's shoulders weren't nearly as close to her ears, and her features weren't bunched in frustration. I could only imagine that to tell me what she saw had to be cathartic. As much as she knew it would inevitably scar me for life, holding that in, particularly when someone else blamed you for something like what I blamed her for, had to take its toll on you.

And truth be told, I was ashamed to admit that until now, I did still blame her. I blamed her because I didn't understand.

But I understood now why she did what she did, and I didn't blame her one bit.

That's not something you can keep to yourself. That kind of secret would destroy even the strongest of people—and Alexandra was one of the strongest people I'd ever met.

I cleared my throat, and she lifted her gaze to mine. "I'm sorry I blamed you. I wouldn't have done the same thing in your shoes if I saw that. You did the right thing, telling your dad. Even if the domino effect was catastrophic, your dad and my mom had a right to know."

"Thank you," she whispered.

"You're still not telling Allegra though. You shouldn't have to be that person twice." She didn't deserve to be the bearer of bad news a second time. I understood now why she told her dad. And chances are, had I been in her shoes, I probably would have told my mom. But Allegra wasn't of any relation to Alexandra. She wasn't even a good friend. She wasn't even a friend.

Her throat moved on a swallow, and she stepped around me to the open deck door, stepping out into the cool evening breeze. "Whatever, Eli. You obviously know best." Then she stepped to the side of the deck and out of my view.

I wanted to go to her but knew that I wouldn't be welcome. She'd just divulged a lot and needed to process.

Fuck, I needed to process. And yeah, she was right. The image, the idea of my dad doing to her mom what Alexandra just described was something I'd never be able to scrub from my brain. I was surprised Alexandra didn't have a psychiatrist on speed dial. Maybe she did.

I sat on the edge of the bed for a while, willing her to come back inside, but she didn't. I also knew that I couldn't "demand" she come back in, because as much as she "obeyed" me when I used her full name and that specific tone of voice, I couldn't abuse that control she gave to me. I was on thin ice with Alexandra. I just didn't know why.

I went over everything we'd just discussed, dissecting it and searching for hidden meanings and a reason as to why she'd suddenly flipped a switch. She didn't know about Ford's affair at dinner, did she?

The longer I thought about things, the more I realized that she was right. Allegra deserved to know. She had a right to decide whether she was going through with the wedding. She deserved to go into it with open eyes.

But Alexandra didn't deserve the inevitable wrath that playing messenger would invite.

Taking one of the key cards with me, I left the hotel room and headed down to the lobby.

Apparently, Allegra and Ford were spending the night apart—so he could bang his vet tech—so I told the guy at the front desk that I was with the Ruiz-Grady wedding and had to deliver something to the bride. They told me her room, but as I was walking back to the elevator, I saw a flash of long brown hair, orange skin, and a white bathrobe ducking out to the covered patio.

I'd recognize that Oompa-Loompa spray-tan anywhere.

Following Allegra to the patio, I made sure to stick to the shadows in case she was meeting up with the pool boy or perhaps a drug dealer. Maybe the secret behind her "glowing" skin was illegal Oompa-Loompa fetal cells that she had injected into her skin biweekly and she was getting another dose before the big day. Who the fuck knew?

But she didn't meet anybody. She just took a seat on the foot of an empty lounge chair, pulled a pack of cigarettes out of her robe pocket, and lit up a menthol.

I turned up my nose at the smell.

Now was not the time to preach about lung cancer, crow's-feet and rotten gums.

I gently cleared my throat, which caused Allegra to startle and frantically search for an ashtray.

"Your secret is safe with me," I said, coming out of the shadows but not failing to miss the irony in the words I chose to use.

"Oh, Eli!" She smiled wide. "You smoke?"

I shook my head. "No."

She took a pull off the cigarette, and I resisted the urge to make a face of disgust. "I don't normally either. But I'm so stressed out about this wedding."

I sat down on the foot of the adjacent lounge chair to hers. "Weddings can be stressful. Especially big ones."

She took another drag off her cigarette, blowing the smoke out the side of her mouth and away from me. "I'm sorry that I split up you and Alexandra tonight. That was petty of me."

I nodded. "Yeah, it was."

The gaze she flicked my way held about two percent amusement. She didn't hate that I'd agreed with her or that I'd stood up to her and defended Alexandra.

"Ford would never stick up for me the way you did for Alexandra."

"No?"

She shook her head.

"The man doesn't do much in the way of anything. Besides golf, sail and try to land us bigger celebrity clients by buying more and more billboards."

Was this my opening?

"Can I ask you a question?"

Nodding, she flicked the ash off the end of her cigarette. "Nothing else to do right now."

I took a deep breath. "Are you and Ford in an open relationship?"

Her head whipped around from where she'd been glancing back into the hotel lobby. "Are you asking for *you?* For you and Alexandra?"

I held up my hands and shook them, along with my head, so fucking hard that if I knew I didn't have a strong neck, that sucker would have snapped clean off. "No. No. Sorry. You misunderstand."

Her gaze narrowed. "What are you getting at?"

"Are you and Ford in a closed, exclusive relationship? No ... *side* pieces? Like a lot of his friends ... and *your* friends have?"

She shook her head. "No. Nothing like that. We're exclusive. Why?" Panic filled her brown eyes, and her hand trembled as she brought it to her mouth and sucked hard enough on the cigarette to cause lines to form around her puckered lips.

"He was seen with a woman ... *Brittney?* In one of the cabanas by the pool only an hour ago, and they were ..."

"What?" she whispered. "What?" That next one came out on more of a hiss.

"Having sex. Ummm ... in the ass." Why I felt the need to add that last part is beyond me, but I said it, so I would have to suffer the consequences.

Allegra's eyes filled with tears as she put out the cigarette on the slate rock ground, only to grab another one from the box in her pocket. Her hands shook so bad when she tried to light it that I took pity on her, grabbed the lighter and lit it for her.

"Thank you," she said on a rattled breath. She was almost too calm. It was as if she had a suspicion and I'd just confirmed her theory.

"I thought you should know."

She nodded. "Yeah." The woman was starting to scare me with just *how* calm she was. If it were me, I'd be losing my fucking mind. Unless she was a seether and the anger was slowly building inside her like a sleeping volcano, then when we least expected it, she'd erupt and burn every villager in a ten-mile radius with her lava rage.

"You want to talk about it?" I asked hesitantly. "About your options? About where to go from here?"

She was quiet for a moment, then her head shook, her jaw tight. She finished that second cigarette and stood up.

I stood up, too. "Are you going to be okay?"

"Yep."

We were too close for my comfort, standing directly in front of each other between the two lounge chairs. They weren't parallel, but rather the ends of the loungers tapered until the footrests of each touched.

I couldn't figure out a clean exit without insulting her or getting even closer. She was blocking the exit at the wider part. The only other option would have been to climb over the chair itself.

"I'm really sorry," I said. "You don't deserve to find out on the night before your wedding. Or from someone you barely know."

"There's nobody I'd rather hear the news from than you," she said. "Ford's not even half the man you are. I want a man like you." A haunting look passed behind her eyes before she reached out, grabbed me by the front of the shirt and kissed me.

What the fuck?

Her grip on my shirt was scary-tight. Then again, she had long-ass fake, white painted fingernails. I'd noticed them as she held the cigarette between two fingers. It was like eagle talons puncturing my polo. I lurched my head back and broke the kiss, only to stumble back and trip over the lounge chair, landing hard on my back on the other side.

"Fuck," I growled. "What the fuck, Allegra?" I stood up, brushing the dirt from my pants and rubbing my sore lower back.

There was no remorse in her eyes, only defiance ... and pain. The woman was definitely hurting.

"You can't tell me Alexandra makes you happy. You can do so much better."

"Extremely happy," I said, glaring at her. "And no, I can't. It's Alexandra who could do better. I definitely married up." I turned to go. "Go figure out your own fucking marriage and stop trying to ruin other people's." Then I left her standing there on the patio with her pack of cigarettes, in her robe, and with the news I came to tell her. What she chose to do with it was up to her.

I took the stairs up to our floor two at a time. In the moment it felt like the right idea. The I-need-to-get-to-my-woman-as-fast-as-possible kind of adrenaline pushed me to take the stairs two at a time, but around the twelfth floor, I realized it was a stupid plan and was winded by the time I arrived at our door.

I opened the door, expecting to find Alexandra either in bed or still on the deck. She wasn't in either place.

She wasn't in the goddamn room.

Neither was her purse or the keys for the rental car.

I pulled my phone out of my back pocket and called her, but it went directly to her voice mail.

"Alexandra, where are you? Call me back immediately."

I tried texting her. *Where are you? I went and told Allegra. You were right, but you shouldn't have been saddled with the job of telling her. Call me please. Let me know you're okay.*

I waited five minutes, pacing the room before I called her again.

No answer.

What the actual fuck?

Where was she?

Where did she go?

Her suitcase was still in the room, but upon further inspection, I realized that her toiletries bag and the bag that held her dress for the wedding tomorrow were not in the room.

Did she go to another hotel?

Still catching my breath from my impromptu StairMaster, I ran out of the hotel room and took the elevator this time back to the lobby.

I brought up a beautiful picture of her on my phone. "Did you see this woman walk out of here in the last twenty minutes?" I asked the woman at the front desk.

She nodded. "Yes. Is there a problem?"

"Did she head to the underground parking?"

Her head shook. "I'm sorry, sir. We had a big arrival of some Japanese tourists, so I was preoccupied. Did you want to leave a message for her here for when she comes back?"

If she comes back.

Just because she left her suitcase didn't mean she wasn't running.

I shook my head. "No thanks." Then I took off out to the front of the hotel where the big fountain with Spanish influence and mosaic tiles bubbled and shone in brightly colored lights.

I didn't know why I was outside. We'd parked in the garage.

I had no idea what to do. No idea what I'd done.

Was Alexandra gone?

Would I ever see her again?

Would I ever get the chance to tell her that I loved her?

CHAPTER THIRTY-EIGHT

Alex

I DROVE FOR HOURS. I wasn't sure where the hell I was going, but I just kept driving. Eventually, I reached a sign that said "sky-diving" and realized I was damn close to the Tijuana border, so I turned around and headed back toward San Diego. But I couldn't go back to the hotel. Not after what I saw out on the patio.

Eli was kissing Allegra.

How could he?

He didn't tell me he was leaving the hotel room when I was out on the balcony, so when I came back inside and found him gone, I didn't know what to think.

Did he go tell Allegra about Ford and Brittney?

Did he go confront Ford?

Did he go for a walk on the beach to clear his head?

At least when I needed some space, I had the decency to tell him that I was going, but he couldn't offer me the same courtesy.

I went down to the front desk to ask if they'd seen him, only to not even make it to the front desk.

He was standing there, on the beautiful garden patio, kissing Allegra, who was in nothing more than her robe.

My jaw nearly hit my sandals.

He's playing the part, but deep down, he's still the same Eli. You can't teach an old dog new tricks when he's been rabid since he was a pup. He lives to hurt you. He lives to break your heart and cause you pain.

And he succeeded, just like he did when we were kids.

Only this time, it felt a million times worse, because I'd fallen for his ploy, for his act. He'd played the role of the devoted and convincing husband so well that I believed it, too.

When I saw him kissing Allegra, my heart slammed hard against my rib cage, then fell straight to the floor, the protective shield I'd carefully placed around it suddenly becoming porcelain and shattering into hundreds of jagged pieces I scrambled to collect. But there were too many shards, and every time I reached for one, I cut my hand and bled a little more.

I only needed a moment to see what was going on before I ran back up to the room, grabbed what I could in haste, and fled to the rental car.

I debated getting another hotel but eventually decided that I wouldn't and would just wait until I saw Eli at the wedding tomorrow and tell him to get his own damn room, since I paid for the one we were in.

I hadn't made up my mind about what to do, but one thing I knew for sure: I couldn't spend the night with him in that room. Not after I saw him kissing Allegra. Not when I knew he was just pretending to care for me, to be my loving husband, but deep down he was planning to hop on the first flight he could and get as far away from me as possible once he got his surgery covered and was tumor-free.

I wasn't somebody who went back on her word, so I would honor our agreement and allow him to use my insurance, but

I didn't have to torture myself or my heart with his company anymore.

Tomorrow, after I went and got my makeup and hair professionally done, I would meet him in the lobby and tell him that he needed to find another room to stay in. That we needed to go back to how things were before we started sleeping together, before we started acting like more than just enemies who no longer hated each other.

That was a safer relationship.

Safer for my heart, at least.

I parked along the beach, not too far from the hotel, and tried to close my eyes for a while, but I never slept. I couldn't.

I couldn't shut off my brain and tell it to stop picturing Eli kissing Allegra. And then, of course, the image of Ford fucking Brittney popped into my head, which only prompted those long burned-in images of Eli's dad and my mom.

I hadn't planned to tell him what I saw our parents doing, but when he told me not to tell Allegra and then admitted that he still blamed me—without knowing the whole truth—that truth just came out. And I wasn't conservative in my details.

I wanted him to feel my pain, my disgust and my horror. I wanted him to understand what I walked around knowing and seeing behind my closed eyelids every day since we were sixteen.

But now, I worried that he was angry with me for telling him and took that anger out by kissing Allegra.

I also felt guilty for telling him. Just like I'd felt guilty for telling Eden.

I understood why Eden wanted me to tell her. She wanted to help me get through it. But I should have known better. Eden had always been a sensitive soul. And when I finally told her, she'd taken it worse than anybody else.

I told her on more than one occasion that her level of empathy, just how sensitive she was, was not only her greatest strength but her greatest weakness as well. She felt her mother's sadness and depression and all of her anger—and Eli's—and it destroyed her. She couldn't organize it. Couldn't let it go. Couldn't keep it from consuming her. It didn't help that when we graduated high school, I attended Brown, Eli went to MIT, and Eden stayed in Greenfield, Connecticut, and attended acupuncture school. She was too close to home. Too close to her mom and her dad, and she let their anger and hurt seep into her life and ultimately ruin it.

Because unlike Eli and I, who had cut off our cheating parents completely, Eden couldn't just walk away from her dad. She tried to maintain a relationship with him, but that just ended up hurting her mother more. Her parents put her in the middle of their war, and she ended up being the biggest casualty.

Tears flooded my eyes as I thought about my best friend.

I thought she was doing better when I left for Thailand. She loved the new healing clinic she'd started working at. She was an accomplished acupuncture therapist and had just started with a holistic healing company that had naturopaths, chiropractors, physiotherapists, counselors and dieticians. She was in her element with people just like her. She'd recently broken up with her boyfriend, had gone back on her depression medication, and was seeing her counselor. She said she was excited to start dating again and looking for Mr. Right.

She assured me that she was okay and feeling good about life.

I told her I didn't have to go. That my trip could wait. But she practically made me go. She told me she'd stop speaking to me if I canceled my dream to finally go and visit the Golden Triangle.

She probably said the same thing to Eli, which was why he went to Africa on a safari.

I had a crappy phone with a Thai sim card when I was over there. I called her as often as I could, but for her to call me was a bit more difficult.

Eli and Eden's mom had fallen off the wagon after being sober for a couple of years—probably because my mom and their dad had gone and gotten married in Hawaii. Eden had to take care of her mom alone, and it was just too much.

I wiped away another tear and closed my eyes as I stared out at the black sky and water. Even though it had happened sixteen years ago, it might as well have happened yesterday for how vivid all the memories were.

It was my sophomore year. I'd turned sixteen two months earlier and had just started driving. I had a chemistry test last period, but I forgot my study flash cards at home, so during second period, which was my free period, I drove home—since I had my own car—to get them.

I didn't expect anybody to be home. There were no vehicles in the driveway, and my mom's car wasn't in the garage. But I'd never been an overly *noisy* person when I came into rooms or buildings, so I just parked in the driveway, used my key like I always did, opened the front door and ran to my room to grab my flash cards. I was at the bottom of the stairs, flash cards in hand, when the sounds of heavy moaning and sighing drew me to the kitchen.

Because my mom's car wasn't in the driveway, I stayed extra quiet. What if someone had broken into the house? I mean, those were NOT the typical sounds I assumed a burglar would make, but then again, I'd never met one. Perhaps the burglars were a boyfriend and girlfriend and robbing people turned them on so much, they had sex in their crime scene. I was sixteen, imaginative and naïve as hell. I had no idea what to think.

Cautiously, I approached the kitchen, the sounds of someone experiencing extreme pleasure growing louder. And also more familiar. I recognized that woman's voice. Though I couldn't say I'd ever heard my mother in the throes of ecstasy before—thank God—but I knew what she sounded like when she sighed.

I was seriously surprised that I didn't drop my flash cards. I stood there for probably a good twenty seconds, stunned by the image of my mom with her funky patterned leggings hanging on only one ankle, her bare ass in the air as she was bent over the kitchen counter. Eli's dad, Mr. Evans, Roger, had his face shoved between her cheeks and was moving his head.

I didn't breathe. I didn't make a sound.

What happened after that, I couldn't specifically recall, but the next thing I knew, I was at my dad's office—the office that he shared with Roger, since they were business partners and had opened up an accounting firm together seven years earlier.

Stunned, as if I'd just stumbled away from a car wreck and was the only survivor, I walked into my dad's office.

"Alex, honey?" He was up and out of his chair and around his desk, taking me by the shoulders. "What's wrong? You look like you've seen a ghost."

I blinked up at him.

He was such a handsome man. So kind and patient. He'd never made me feel like a "girl." He asked me to help him in the garage, split firewood, and taught me how to do some simple plumbing and electrical stuff. But he also never made me feel like I was the son he never had. I was just "his Alex," "his kid," and he was going to invite me to do stuff with him, teach me things and love me for me. I was sure he liked that I enjoyed all those activities more than some stereotypical girlie things and that he could relate to me more, but I knew that if I had been a tutu-wearing, tea-party-holding, hate-to-get-dirty kind of kid, he would have made the best of it and found something for us to bond over anyway.

"Honey, you're scaring me. What's wrong?"

"I ..."

"You can tell me anything. You know that. Anything."

I nodded. I knew that. He'd never made me feel afraid to confide in him, like if I did, I'd get in trouble.

"I ... I went home to get my chemistry flash cards ..."

He nodded. "Okay ..."

"And I saw Mom."

"Is she all right?"

Define all right.

I nodded again. "Her car wasn't there so I thought the house was empty. But ... M—Mr. Evans was there and so was mom."

His thick black brows scrunched. "Roger was there?" Then he glanced through the glass wall into Mr. Evans's office, where his desk sat empty. "He told me he had a meeting with Murphy Contracting."

I swallowed.

"What were they doing, Alex?" His tone turned dark and serious.

My heart hammered against my rib cage, and my stomach threatened to return that bowl of oatmeal I had for breakfast. My bottom lip trembled. "They ..."

"Alex ..."

"Um ..."

"What. Were. They. Doing?"

I glanced into Mr. Evans's office again, where a picture of his family—of Eden's family—hung on the wall. Eden, Eli, Roger and Louisa were all sitting in the grass in a field somewhere with their German shepherd Misty sitting between them. Everyone was smiling. Everyone was happy.

My dad had a similar photo of our family on the bookcase behind him. It was on one of the rare occasions my sister Sidney came home from England. We were on a sand dune at the beach smiling. Like a big, happy family.

Two families, multiple friendships and a business partnership would be forever changed the moment I told my dad what I saw. Did I want to do that? Did I want to destroy Eden's family? My family? Two marriages, a thriving business and all these friendships?

"Alex?" My dad's voice snapped me out of my trance, and I lifted my eyes back up to him from where I'd been staring at our family photo. "The truth is always better than a lie. Lies grow like a virus. The truth is the antidote. What were they doing? I won't be mad at you. You have my word."

I nodded again. "Um ... they were *together.*"

My father's face became a storm cloud. "Together how?"

"Dad ..." I squirmed where I stood.

"Together *how*, Alex. I need to know."

I squeezed my eyes shut. "Mr. Evans's face was in Mom's butt, and she was naked, bent over the kitchen counter," I blurted out.

The bile in my throat lifted. I opened my eyes, grabbed his trash can from beside his desk, and puked.

The front door for their office opened and chimed.

I heard my dad walk past me, and just as I lifted my head, a string of puke connecting my mouth to the plastic lining of the garbage can, I watched my dad haul off and punch his best friend in the face—the face that had just been smashed clean against my mother's ass.

After that, life turned horrible.

Their friendship ended immediately. Their business partnership ended. My dad filed for divorce and had assault charges to deal with, since Roger had actually gone and pressed charges for the two punches that my dad threw at him.

Roger and my mom bought a place together. I stayed with my dad, and Eden and Eli stayed with their mom.

My dad started drinking. So did Eden and Eli's mom.

Luckily, my dad was able to be a functional alcoholic and still work during the day, only to get lost in a bottle at night. He also wasn't an angry or aggressive drunk but rather a sad one. He also made sure to give me his keys the moment he got home from the liquor store so he wouldn't be tempted to drive to get another bottle. For all intents and purposes, he was a very responsible, easy-to-live-with alcoholic.

I knew that was not the case with Eden and Eli's mom, however.

The summer following the explosion of our families was when I went to go stay with my dad's sister in The Hamptons. We all agreed that it would be a nice change of scenery and a break from the chaos the last few months had been. That was where I met Dereck Sharpe and when I had sex for the first time.

We'd both been "virgins," and even though it hurt a little, he was gentle, patient, and kind. I think we had sex a total of like twenty times that summer. We tried everything, figured why not? His parents had a pool house, which was where he stayed, so we had total privacy. And my aunt wasn't the controlling or super conservative type. She knew what Dereck and I were up to, so she sat me down, asked me if I was on the pill—which I was—and if we were using condoms—which we were. Then she told me to make sure I didn't give my heart away to some teenage boy during a summer fling, that I could have fun—because after the year I'd had, I deserved some fun—but that I had a bright future ahead of me and didn't need to get caught up with a broken heart over some "Hamptons boy."

I loved my Aunt Leah.

So I did just that. I had fun, I learned what I liked when it came to sex, I learned how to give a decent blowjob—a skill which I've only perfected over the years—and that you need A LOT of lube when it comes to anal sex. Then Dereck and I hugged goodbye and went our separate ways. I had no idea where he was now or what he was doing, but whoever he was with, that woman was definitely having some amazing orgasms because Dereck was nothing if not a perfectionist when it came to giving head.

Though Eli was certainly no slouch either.

That thought of Eli brought me back to the present.

My heart was still heavy, and my head hurt. I missed my best friend.

"What do you think I should do, Eden?" I said out loud. "You know him better than I do. But you also saw what he was capable of when we were kids. He's the reason I'm so fucked in the head when it comes to people. When it comes to trust. Well, him and my mom. My insecurities about *everything* stem from how horrible Eli treated me. And yet, after all of that, I really thought he'd changed. And I forgave him for what he did." I glanced up at the ceiling of the car. "Has he changed at all? Or has this all just been a giant prank?"

I never should have let down my guard. Shown him my soft underbelly, and in the end, gave him my heart. Because as much as it pained me to acknowledge it, the fact of the matter was, I'd fallen in love with Eli. So if this was all just a big ruse, the agony of that revelation would be that much more unbearable because of the heart shattering that would come with it.

I waited for Eden to reach out, but I didn't hear or feel anything.

"What about you, Jilly Bean? You there? You got any words of wisdom for me?" A patch of warmth bloomed on my upper thigh, and a spot on the back of my hand tingled. It was like Jill had just rested her chin on my lap and licked my hand.

I closed my eyes and tried to feel her presence.

"I know you loved him, Jill. But you only knew him as he is now, not what he used to be. You don't know what he's capable of. How much hate filled his heart before. Are people able to change that much? Do we really change at all? Or do we just get better at pretending, become better actors as we grow up?"

I waited for another sign or message from Jill or Eden but didn't get anything. The heat on my thigh disappeared, along with the tingle on my hand. Jill had run off to go chase a rabbit. Or maybe she was snuggled up under a tree with Eden. A glowing sensation filled my heart at that thought. I hoped they found each other in the afterlife.

I assumed he told Allegra what I saw, then they shared a moment and kissed.

Did that mean that the wedding was off?

I hadn't heard anything otherwise.

Wait?

Where was my phone?

I grabbed my purse off the passenger seat and opened it, shoving my hand inside to look for my phone, but it wasn't in there. Then I dumped my purse onto the passenger seat, but still, it wasn't in there.

I threw open the driver's side door, unbuckled my belt, and went on the hunt for my phone under the seat and between the seat and the center console.

Still no phone. Did I leave in such haste that I forgot my phone?

Shit.

I must have. It was probably back in the hotel room on my nightstand or the dresser.

Crap.

Maybe the wedding was off. I needed to get back to the hotel and find out, but I needed to steer clear of Eli.

Climbing back into the car, I put the key in the ignition and drove back to the hotel, parking in the back of the parking lot and between two big trucks. Hopefully, Eli wouldn't be able to see the car with the way I parked it.

I kept to the shadows as I headed for the lobby. It was still quite early in the morning, so hopefully, he was sleeping and not sitting in the lobby waiting for me.

I could only hope.

I opened the door to the lobby.

The place was quiet.

The woman at the front desk smiled at me, then her brows scrunched. "A man is looking for you."

I figured. Nodding, I said, "I thought he might be."

"Did you want to leave a message for him?"

"No, thank you. I'm just wondering if you know anything about the Ruiz-Grady wedding and if there are any updates?"

She shook her head. "Not that I'm aware of."

"Okay, thanks."

The elevator dinged, and I froze, turning my head to watch the doors slide open.

An elderly couple shuffled off, but that was it.

I let out a sigh of relief and headed back out to the car. My hair and makeup appointments were at a salon two blocks away. I didn't want to get ready at the hotel salon in the event the bridal party was using it for their own hair and makeup. That would have been an absolute nightmare.

I debated running back up to the hotel room to get my phone but ultimately decided against it, since Eli was probably there and would most definitely not let me leave.

I hated and loved the control he had over me. I reacted to his demands in a way I'd never reacted with any other man before. My body was compelled to listen before my brain even had a chance to go, "Excuse me?"

And yet, I relished that side of him. It turned me on.

I wasn't a doormat, and Eli wasn't "controlling," but he did make me want to give up control to him. I had a hard time explaining it any other way. I trusted him—or at least I did. And *had* trusted him not to abuse that control. Until he did.

And when he used my full name or called me a good girl, forget about it. I was unable to stop myself from swooning.

No, I couldn't see him. Not until the wedding. I needed to remain strong. I needed to rebuild that shield around my heart but this time make it ten times as thick.

My appointment wasn't until ten, so I headed out, grabbed some breakfast—despite my lack of appetite—and just waited. I had no phone to preoccupy me. Nothing to take my mind off my raging thoughts and broken heart. So I just watched the sky get brighter and the sun climb up through the fluffy white clouds.

I was exhausted when I finally walked into the salon. The makeup artist was going to need to break out her extra heavy-duty concealer to cover up the purple bags under my eyes.

The wedding was at one o'clock, with a cocktail party to follow while the bride and groom and wedding party went by helicopter to go and get photos taken. Then dinner was scheduled for five.

I was out of the salon by noon, then used the bathroom in the hotel off the lobby to get dressed.

The champagne-gold slip dress that pooled at my feet with a small train had a side zip, so fortunately it wasn't an impossible task getting myself dressed alone.

This wasn't what I envisioned when Eli and I finally got together as more than just non-enemies, but alas, this was my reality. I had to make the best of it.

The makeup artist had worked her magic and hid the purple bags under my eyes like a pro, while the Brazilian blowout and thick voluminous waves that the hairdresser put into my hair had me taking a second and a third look at myself in the bathroom mirror.

I never could have pulled this look off myself.

I was still without my phone, but there was a Walgreens beside the hairdresser, so I swung in there before my appointment and bought a twenty-dollar watch just so I could keep track of the time.

By the time I was changed into my dress and my black strappy heels and everything I didn't need was stored back in the car, it was twenty minutes to one.

Taking a deep breath, I tried desperately to calm my nerves and walked with as much confidence as I could muster through the lobby toward the back atrium where the wedding was being held.

Most of the guests had already taken their seats.

Two seats were saved by a blue suit jacket draped across. I knew who that was.

Even though I shouldn't have, I glanced around the busy glass- and wood-framed space filled with fragrant flowers and people.

He was impossible to miss.

A gasp snagged like a fishhook in the back of my throat at the sight of him.

He was in the blue suit with the vest, those perfectly tailored pants and a white long-sleeved shirt. His back was to me, and he had one hand on the window frame as he casually leaned over, displaying the muscular breadth of his back and that really great ass.

I took a moment to appreciate just how beautiful he was.

I wasn't the only woman doing so, either.

And as if he felt me watching him, slowly, he turned around.

His gaze found mine, and relief consumed his face, followed quickly by anger edged with confusion and hurt.

It was the look of hurt that got me and made my insides twist violently.

I turned and made my way through an aisle of people to a single empty chair on the opposite side of the aisle from where he'd set his jacket down.

I was being an idiot, I knew. Childish, even.

But we couldn't talk now, and I hadn't finished repairing my shattered shield. I needed more time.

His eyes seared me as he walked to his seat and sat down. Even when I couldn't see him, I knew he was watching me. I felt the heat of his stare, heard the questions he was asking with every second that passed.

There was a wedding program being passed around, and I busied myself by pretending to read it.

Eventually, Ford made his way to the front of the aisle, with Keith at his side, both of them smiling and laughing. I searched Ford's face for even a glimmer of reluctance or guilt, but I saw none. I did, however, see him glance quickly over to Brittney, who sat with a man, their fingers linked together.

The plot thickened. Brittney was in a relationship.

The man she was holding hands with brought their intertwined hands up and kissed the back of hers. Her engagement ring damn near blinded me.

Another twist.

Brittney was not only in a relationship, but she was engaged. And sleeping with her boss, who was about to get married.

Did people not have ANY scruples anymore?

No. Because Eli kissed Allegra, when he was for all intents and purposes legally married to me. Even if it was just a business arrangement with sexual perks, he was supposed to be showing everyone that we were madly in love. Most of all Allegra.

The minister at the front nodded, and the music started to play over the speakers.

One by one, Kymberli, Tavia, Gina and Selena all walked down the aisle, smiling like perfectly painted, coiffed and freshly waxed Barbie dolls in floor-length blush-colored maxi dresses.

Once those dolls were all neatly lined up at the front, as if they were in their boxes with twist-ties around their limbs keeping them upright, the music changed and we all stood up.

I couldn't stop myself from looking up, and as I expected, I found Eli staring at me.

"Where did you go?" he mouthed. "What did I do?"

I pressed my lips together and shook my head, staring at the ground. A tear slid down my cheek.

Allegra looked beautiful as her father escorted her down the aisle toward Ford.

Ford was smiling. Allegra was smiling.

Everyone was smiling.

Everyone but me and Eli.

We all turned to face the front, then sat when the minister told us we could.

There was a lot of pomp and circumstance, a lot of talking, but I didn't hear any of it. It was all just a dull, annoying hum in my ears as I tried to figure out how I was going to face Eli when the ceremony was over. What I was going to say to him.

"Does anyone have any reason why these two people should not be joined in holy matrimony?" the minister asked.

I didn't even think that this was the perfect moment for Brittney, Ford or someone else to stand up and call the union of Allegra and Ford a sham until Allegra herself loudly declared, "I do."

CHAPTER THIRTY-NINE

Eli

Where the fuck had she been all night?

Did she get another hotel room somewhere?

I figured out why she wasn't answering her phone when I found it between the bed and her nightstand after I returned to the hotel room to wait for her.

I didn't think she'd be able to go this long without her phone, but this wasn't the first time I'd underestimated Alexandra.

She was stronger and fiercer than any other woman I knew, and if she didn't want to be around me, she'd walk away from her phone and her suitcase full of clothes if she wanted to.

Of course, she looked hot as fucking hell. I knew the moment I saw that dress on her in the store that it was made for her body, and with her hair and makeup, she looked like a fucking model.

I wanted to run to her, pull her aside and ask what the hell was going on, but she made sure that we didn't sit together and that there were many people between us to make getting to her nearly impossible.

Once the ceremony was over, I wouldn't let her escape, though. She owed me answers—at the very least.

The guests in the crowd gasped when Allegra snatched the microphone from the minister and loudly said, "I do," when he asked if anyone objected to the marriage.

Oh, here we go.

Where was the popcorn when you needed it?

"Allegra?" Ford asked, his hands open, his eyes confused and panicky.

She shook her head and sneered. "Don't *Allegra* me. Where were you last night, Ford?"

His brows pinched, then he turned to Keith. "I was with Keith. We had drinks and cigars down on the beach. Right, Keith?"

Keith nodded. "Can confirm."

"Bullshit," Allegra spat out. "You were fucking Brittney in one of the pool cabanas. In the fucking ass."

Ford's eyes went saucer-size, and he spun around to face Brittney.

Her fiancé had pushed to his feet and was staring down at her in complete shock. "What the fuck, Britt?"

Brittney had the decency to bury her face in her hands.

"Who the fuck told you that?" Ford asked, turning back to Allegra.

Allegra glanced into the crowd in search of me, but thank fuck she didn't point and say my name.

"Does it matter?" she asked.

"It does when you're being a two-faced fucking hypocrite, *Allison.*"

Allison?

Murmurs of confusion echoed around the atrium, meanwhile Allegra or *Allison* looked like she'd just been slapped in the face with a piece of raw chicken.

Smug, like he suddenly had the upper hand, Ford turned to the crowd and nodded. "Yeah, you heard right. She's not *Al-*

legra Ruiz. She's Allison Reins. And her parents aren't *Carlos and Paloma.* They're Carl and Paula."

"You son of a bitch," Allegra said, shooting darts from her eyes at her fiancé.

"Yeah, yeah," he said, brushing her off. He had an audience now and was going to use it to his full advantage. "Miss *Reins* here was once told that she looked like a Latin beauty because of her dark hair, dark eyes and naturally tanned skin."

Naturally tanned skin?

I wasn't aware that her particular shade of orange was a natural pigment for anybody but an Oompa-Loompa.

Ford continued. "So when she started college, she changed her name—legally—to Allegra Ruiz and started pretending that her family was from Mexico. She likes the attention she gets from being thought of as exotic. She even bullied her parents into following along with the scheme and told any family members who spoke out against her or called her Allison that they'd have hell to pay."

Allison ... Allegra or whoever was positively seething on the altar now. People were looking at her like she had three heads—including her bridesmaids.

This was news to nearly everyone, apparently, and had I not been focused on Alexandra and how she was reacting to all of this, I would have probably laughed.

Allegra's face was beet-red, and the way her eyes bugged out gave me serious serial-killer vibes. Particularly after the way she calmly took the news I gave her last night.

"You will fucking pay for this," Allegra whispered, though because she had the microphone, everyone heard her.

Ford scoffed. "Yeah? More than you already are? Come on, Allison, be honest. The only Latin you've ever had in you was Raul the tennis pro when we had a threesome with him at our resort in Belize last year." He chuckled and glanced out into the crowd, finding me and smiling like a smug, smarmy bastard. "Besides, I heard you and Alex's husband were getting it on last night on the lobby patio, so fuck you and your righteousness."

I stood up from my chair, sending it teetering and falling into the knees of the guy behind me.

"Uh, no." I held up a finger. "I went to find Allegra ... Allison or whatever the fuck her name is, and tell her that I saw you with your vet tech, because dude, nobody should go into a marriage not knowing that they're marrying an asshole. She kissed me. I turned her down."

I turned to the crowd.

"I have spent the last two nights hearing about all the affairs, the mistresses, the tennis pros, the karate instructors, the models, the deep-throating nannies, and how ridiculously unhappy a lot of your relationships are." I faced Ford again. "And you have the audacity to point fingers. I would *never* step out on the woman I love." I turned to Alexandra and pointed to her. "And I am madly fucking in love with this woman. I'm completely content with the idea of her being the only woman I sleep with ever again. With hers being the only pussy I eat ever again."

A few older people in the crowd made gasps and uncomfortable noises in their throats.

I did not care. All I cared about right now was letting Alexandra know that she was the only woman I wanted. The only woman I wanted to kiss, fuck and do anything with.

And then it hit me. Had she seen Allegra kiss me? Was that why she took off? That and whatever happened at the rehearsal dinner last night had to be it.

I kept my attention on her but spoke loud enough for the crowd to hear me. "Even after she gives me babies, I will gladly continue to eat that pussy."

"Oh my goodness," said a grandmother somewhere.

"Because I fucking love you," I said straight into Alexandra's unblinking eyes.

She swallowed, and her bottom lip wobbled.

Awkwardly, I shuffled past the people beside me to the aisle and walked to the row where she was, holding my hand out for her. "Let's get the fuck out of here before the poison of these people rubs off on us anymore."

She stood up, stepped past the guests beside her and placed her hand in mine, then we ran-walked out of the atrium, across the concrete pavilion and through the wisteria-trellised pergola Allegra or Allison or whatever had just walked through with her father.

We rode the elevator up to our room in silence, but I could barely breathe from the thick tension between us. I was vibrating.

I was pissed right the fuck off at Allison and Ford.

At Alexandra.

At myself.

She'd taken off with the rental car and left her phone in the hotel.

I was pissed off she didn't just talk to me. Didn't tell me what was bothering her, what I'd done or said to upset her. Because the last thing I ever wanted to do was hurt her ... again.

I was still holding her hand, and when the elevator door opened onto our floor, I yanked her down the hallway, fishing the key card out of my pocket with my free hand.

I had the room door open in under a second and was pulling her inside.

Once inside, I dropped my jacket to the ground, gripped her by the throat with one hand and the hip with the other and shoved her against the wall, taking her mouth.

Because it was mine.

It was all I could think of to do. All I wanted to do. Well, besides giving the woman who I loved more than anything a piece of my mind. I also wouldn't mind hauling her perfect ass over my knee and teaching her not to run like she did last night.

She kissed me back, whimpering when I bit her lip and pushed my tongue deeper into her mouth.

I broke the kiss, turned, and stomped into the bedroom. "Don't you ever fucking run like that again."

She followed me deeper into our room. The blinds were pulled closed since we were in a west-facing room and the sun was blasting this side of the hotel. Neither of us had bothered to turn on the light. She looked hot in the muted, hazy light in that incredible gold dress. But I couldn't think about how badly I wanted to tear that dress off her.

"Did you mean—"

"What I said out there? Yes. I meant every fucking word." I pulled at my hair, spun on my heel, and paced the room. "Yes, Alex. I'm in love with you. Have been for possibly ever, I don't know. But you leaving last night ..."

"I saw you kissing Allegra ... Allison."

"And instead of coming to me, instead of *talking* to me, you fucking ran."

"Yes ... but ... I ... it wasn't just that."

I let go of my hair and stopped where I was, closer to the bathroom. "Yeah, I kind of figured. But again, instead of talking to me, you just shut down and shut me out."

Her chest lifted and fell heavily with strained breath. "I overheard you talking to that guy you were chatting with at the table last night about how you couldn't wait to get back to traveling and seeing the world. That once your medical procedure was done, you were booking a flight the next day since your travel bug bite is getting really itchy."

I shrugged. "Yeah? That's not a lie. We're going to go to Portugal, right?"

Her mouth dropped open. "But I ... I thought that you meant traveling by yourself. That once you got the surgery, you were going to just leave." She swallowed and looked down at the floor. "Leave me."

Fuck.

I swooped in and grabbed her hips. "Alexandra, look at me."

She lifted her head. Her blue eyes were full of tears. "I thought you were playing me again. Pranking me like you did when we were kids. That this was all just you being the convincing husband like you said you were going to be and me stupidly believing it was all real."

Fuck me. I'd really done a number on her self-esteem and ability to trust. I deserved her ire. I deserved her reservations and the hurt that was in her eyes as she looked at me. I deserved that absolutely agonizing feeling in my gut right now, like someone just took a hot poker and human shish-kebabed me. I deserved it all.

And all she deserved was the safety and comfort of knowing how much she was truly loved.

I swallowed, pushing down the pain in my stomach and ignoring the way that burn began to bleed up into my chest and surround my heart.

"Not a second of this has been acting. I'm not playing you. My love for you is not a prank. Please ... I swear on Eden's grave that I am being truthful here. I am madly, insanely, psychotically in love with you. I *want* to be your husband, to be married to you. To *stay* married to you when this is all over. When I go traveling, I'm taking you with me. I'm not in this for the insurance anymore. I'm in this because I fucking love you from here to goddamn eternity."

A tear slid down her cheek. Her bottom lip wobbled as she whispered, "I love you, too."

"I'm sorry that you saw me and Allegra, but I swear to you, Allegra kissed me, and I pushed her away as soon as it happened. I didn't kiss her back. There was no tongue, no reciprocal feelings. And she tasted like a fucking ashtray since she'd been smoking. But that should not have been your message to deliver. I was trying to protect you from more of her wrath. Show you that I agreed with you when you said the truth is better than a lie and she deserved to know the truth.

Because I agree with you. Now and when we were sixteen. You did the right thing, telling your dad."

She nodded.

"I don't blame you for anything anymore. Not Eden's death. Not our parents' divorces. Nothing. You were just as innocent and hurt in all of it as me, and I was an asshole and an idiot and a horrible person to take it out on you. You didn't deserve it, and if you'll let me, I plan to spend the rest of my life making it up to you for the hell I put you through." My throat ached, it was so tight, and a hot tear slid down my cheek. "Tell me you believe me, please."

Her head bobbed again. "I believe you."

"And do you believe me when I say that I'm not pretending to be the hopelessly in love, devoted, obsessed husband? That I'm not trying to convince anybody of anything because what I feel for you is entirely real?"

She nodded again. "I do now."

Pulling her against me, I took her mouth again as our salty tears slid down between our lips. She grappled at my shirt, her hands unable to stay still on my back and shoulders. She shoved her fingers into my hair and tugged, pulling me down to her and grinding her pussy against my leg.

"I love you so much," I said, tearing my mouth away from hers and scraping my teeth along her jaw. "So fucking much."

"Me, too," she whispered, tilting her head to the side so I could get better access to her neck.

I needed to be inside her. As close as two people could possibly be.

My body wasn't functioning properly. My brain was an absolute mess without her. I needed that connection, that grounding, that sense of total peace that took over my soul when I was inside Alexandra. When I claimed her as mine and she claimed me as hers.

Because I was hers. Infinitely and irretrievably.

Her dress had a high slit, so it was easy for me to hoist her up onto my hips. I carried her over to the dresser and plunked her ass down, then went to work on freeing my cock.

I was inside her in seconds.

Thank fuck.

I was home.

Calm began to settle inside me. My brain was no longer a maelstrom of panic and overwhelming love. Synapses began to fire normally again, thoughts took proper shape, and the edges grew less blurry.

I bucked up into Alexandra hard, and she locked her legs around my ass, taking every thrust and demanding more and that I give it to her harder.

I would give this woman anything and everything she ever asked for.

If I could, I would deny her nothing.

She deserved the world. And I planned to do my best, until my dying breath, to give it to her.

Her nails dug into my shoulders. I welcomed the bite of pain.

I'd known for a while that what we had was love, but the understanding and completeness I felt knowing that she loved me back, that she wanted me, flashed through me as I moved inside her, as I felt her body ripple around me and worshiped it with my own.

It was love. Undeniably.

It was dirty. It was rough.

It was physical and tangible.

But holy fuck, was it ever love.

The way I craved her constantly was love.

The way I felt her so purely in my soul was love.

The way my name breathed past her lips as she shuddered when I scraped my thumb across her clit and she said my name as the first orgasm rocked through her, was love.

It was hard.

It was deep.

It was ruthless, raw and primal.

It was needy and messy, and it came with so much fucking baggage we could barely stand under the weight of it all, but it was ours, and it was love.

She trembled around me, and I pushed up into her once more. She stilled, her mouth opened on a silent cry, and together, we came.

The pleasure ripped through me, and I took her mouth again. I wanted us joined in every way possible. I wanted to feel what she felt and for her to feel what I feel. I wanted to taste her breath, feel every pulse and quiver of her orgasm around my cock as I came inside her for the first time since we confessed our love.

When she relaxed, I relaxed.

But we didn't stop kissing.

I never wanted to stop kissing her.

When our breathing returned to normal and I began to grow soft, we broke the kiss, and I gently slid out of her.

I went to the bathroom, ran a washcloth under warm water and returned to clean her up. As I cleaned her up, I looked up at her and smiled.

She smiled right back.

Then we both started to laugh.

Fuck, I loved this woman.

She hopped down from the dresser, and her eyes glimmered. "So we're staying married then, even after the surgery?"

"I'm sure as fuck not going to be the one to file for divorce."

She grinned. "Me either."

"So then I guess we're staying married."

She bit her lip on a smile. "Guess so."

I glanced at my watch, then sprang into action.

There was a basket of towels on top of the toilet, so I dumped the towels on the bed, then did the same with the basket that was next to the television that had a bunch of wedding guest favors in it. "Come on. We don't have much time."

She'd used the washroom and was just coming out, drying her hands on a towel. "Much time for what?" With both baskets in one hand, I reached for Alexandra's hand and tugged her toward the door.

"Before the restaurant catering is told *not* to put out the food for the cocktail hour. 'Cause let's be real—that wedding was not going to end with a happily married couple."

She grimaced. "Yeah, probably not. I bet two relationships ended today. Poor Brittney's fiancé looked devastated."

"He dodged a bullet. But come on, let's go load up on grub these assholes paid for, then drive down to the beach and celebrate that we *actually* love each other and will never need deep-throating nannies or clit-sucking karate instructors on standby."

"I'm down for that," she said, a giggle in her voice as we stepped back onto the elevator. "I'm down for anything, as long as it's with you."

I squeezed her fingers and glanced down at the woman I was obsessed with. "And I'm down for anything as long as it's with you."

Then we went down to the cocktail lounge, loaded our baskets with food, and took them to the beach, where my wife and I spent the rest of the evening together, madly in love and planning our beautiful future.

Alex

SIX MONTHS LATER ...

"Alex, is that you?" His voice was slow and groggy as he came out from being under the anesthetic.

"It's me." I took his hand and put it to my cheek. How much of the Eli I knew and loved was still in there? And how much did he need to relearn?

The doctors warned us that although the tumor was solid and it had generally clean lines, Eli might need time to return back to how he was before. I prepared myself for the worst.

He blinked. "You're going to have to help me walk."

I nodded and swallowed. "Yes, of course."

"And eat."

"Okay."

"And wipe my ass."

I opened my mouth, but then closed it.

"And jerk me off. I forget how to do that, too."

I pursed my lips and narrowed my eyes.

His mouth split into a big smile.

I glanced up at the doctor. "Any chance you can cut out the wise-ass part of his brain? Get back in there and take off a few slivers of gray matter?"

The doctor chuckled, leaned over and shone a light into Eli's eyes, checking on things. Another doctor at the foot of the bed checked his reflexes by running her pen up the center of his feet. His toes wiggled.

Thank God. I exhaled in relief.

"Don't look at me like that, Alex."

"Like what?" I croaked through a tight throat as I blinked back the tears that burned the backs of my eyes.

"Like you're offering me your heart. Because if you do, I will take it and I will never give it back."

"I gave you my heart quite some time ago."

"Ah, but seeing the relief on your face after I could have died on the table just confirms how much you love me."

"You mean, if I didn't look at you like this, you'd think I was hoping you'd die on the table?"

He shrugged. "I *do* occasionally leave the toilet seat up. It's not *that* far of a stretch."

I swatted his shoulder, then looked back up at the doctors. "Seriously. I'll pay out of pocket if you just go in with a scalpel and take off a few more slivers of gray matter, just the part that's making him a joking jackass. Do you have a dog that needs to be neutered? We can do some kind of swap thing. Service for service. I take off a little between Fido's legs," I pointed at Eli's head, "you take off a little between Smart Ass's ears."

The doctors smiled and chuckled.

"If this is who he normally is, that's a good sign," said the resident at the foot of the bed.

"Oh, I'm normally much more unbearable," he said, flashing them all a cheesy grin.

"Get some rest, Mr. Evans. You did very well in the surgery, and there is nothing to suggest anything but a full recovery," said the attending surgeon.

Eli and I thanked them both, then they left.

He scooted over in the bed and insisted I join him. My head fell to his shoulder, and he slowly looped his arm around me, stroking my hair.

"I was so worried," I murmured.

"I know."

"I'm glad you survived. And that for the most part, you're normal."

"I'll never be normal, baby. That's part of my charm."

I snorted. "You've never had charm."

"Charmed the pants right off you."

"Only took you twenty something years."

"I'm all about the slow burn. I like to really woo a woman, take my time." He pressed his lips to the top of my head and sighed. I could tell he was getting tired.

"Well, don't take your time recovering. Rita says she has a couple more properties she wants us to look at, and two haven't even gone on the market yet. Says they're perfect for what we want."

He squeezed me tight. "I trust you to find the right fit for us. You know what you want when it comes to land, and I want you, so as long as the price is right, I say go with your gut."

I wanted his input. We were in this together. We should choose our forever land and home together. "And if my gut is wrong?"

"Then I lord it over you for the rest of our lives."

I huffed a laugh.

He kissed my head again. "The right property will come along. Don't you worry. You, me and all the dogs we're going to rescue. We're all going to live happily ever after, just wait and see."

"Horses, too?"

"We'll talk about that later. Right now, I think I need to sleep. Dream of taking you, naked in a field—our field—as the sun burns my ass cheeks and you scream so loud you disturb a flock of Great Tits."

I snorted and rolled my eyes before closing them. "You had to choose *that* bird?"

"Great Tits go where there are great tits. I'm pretty sure there is a whole flock in the tree outside my room here, because they know *you're* here."

I yawned. "Yeah?"

"Mhmm."

I was pretty tired, too. No, I hadn't just had brain surgery, but I hadn't been able to sleep the last couple of days. First, I was up all night worrying about Eli's upcoming surgery, then I couldn't sleep or rest or relax during his surgery. It'd been at least three days since I'd had more than about thirty minutes of shut-eye.

A week ago, Eli woke up unable to see anything. He'd completely lost his vision in both eyes. His surgeon, however, was on vacation, so we had to wait until Dr. O'Shea returned in order to perform the surgery.

As much as I loved my husband, that had been the longest and one of the most difficult weeks of both of our lives. I ended up taking the week off work so I could help him, since he had no idea how to function around our apartment without his sight. A couple of times, as I cut up an apple, I had actually stared long and hard at the paring knife and thought, *I'm a doctor. I perform surgeries. It's just a simple tumor removal, right?* Then I'd put the knife in the dishwasher, pour more wine, and take the apple over to my husband, where we'd curl up on the couch together and listen to a podcast.

"Sleep, Alexandra." He ran his hand over my head. "Then, when we wake up, I'll fuck you properly."

"After I feed you and wipe your ass?" I said with a chuckle, followed by another yawn.

"Yeah."

"Okay. I look forward to the five hours post-brain-surgery fucking you're going to give me. I expect edging, stamina, multiple positions, and a lot of you eating me out."

"You got it. But sleep first."

"Okay," I said sleepily.

"Good girl."

A tremor of desire whipped through me at his praise. But I was too tired to let it take root anywhere. Within seconds, I fell asleep in the arms of my husband, my favorite place to be, dreaming of our life together and the many beautiful years to come.

EPILOGUE

Alex

"All right, Ana, we'll see you in a couple of hours," I said into the Bluetooth as I turned right off the road down our long, dirt driveway.

A chorus of woofs and barks greeted me before I saw my wolf pack at the fence. Like they did every night, they chased my Jeep as I drove. Though the older ones in the pack couldn't really keep up as much as some, they gave it their best effort.

"I hear the pack," Ana said with a chuckle.

"They're all just as excited to see you as we are. I do wish you'd let us pick you up from the airport, though."

"You know Sérgio. He wants to be able to drive himself around, which was why we got the rental car."

"And you know my husband is exactly the same."

We both laughed.

"All right, my love. We will see you shortly."

I spied my favorite person—correction, *two* favorite people—in the world in the field and smiled. "See you soon." Ana and I disconnected the call, and I rolled down my window, which only invited the insanity of all the barking dogs to become even louder.

Eli waved at me, then glanced down at the baby on his chest, kissing the top of baby Ana's head.

My heart swelled.

Bandit and Stardust, two of our rescue horses, were in the corral. They weren't big fans of sharing their field with the wolf pack, so Eli put them in the corral when he let the dogs run. The other two horses, Yemmi and Inez, had just run to the far end of the field, as far away from the crazy dogs as possible. Gertie and Phineas were in the barn, most likely.

As it almost always was, Bandit's chin rested on Stardust's back as they stood watching the antics in the field.

Bandit was a retired Shire, a carriage horse, and Stardust was a Clydesdale, who despite the expected "gentle giant" temperament that came with her breed was too skittish and uneasy with new people and traffic to pull carriages. They'd been here since we first moved in, having a barn of their very own, a land to roam, while we still lived in the RV my dad found us for dirt-cheap on Craigslist.

But the RV—which Eli had gutted and redone—was now for guests, ranch hands or vet students who came to work at the rescue ranch.

Yes, Jill's Rescue Ranch had officially opened its "doors" a little over two years ago. We started with two horses and one dog and had since amassed four horses, one donkey, a miniature horse, nine barn cats, and eight dogs.

And of course, we couldn't forget about the guinea pig that Eli fell in love with and begged me to rescue—Peanut Butter.

We also had chickens that constantly chased the dogs, a flock of ducks that adopted us, and two geese to keep the eagles from nabbing the chickens.

I loved our little hobby farm, and on weekends we opened up to the public as a petting farm.

With his gut in knots, Eli, at my insistence, published his graphic novels, and it came as absolutely no surprise that they had become a massive success. Almost overnight.

If I wanted to, I could retire and just do the pet rescuing as a hobby—we were doing that well.

But I loved my job. I loved working with animals, so I continued to work at the animal hospital in Linley Park three days a week and teach yoga at the studio two days a week.

Something had to give, though, when we had Ana, so I stopped going to H&J, and Eli and I built our own little sparring ring in the loft of the barn. Once in a while, we popped back in to say hi to Hector and Jao, but with a baby at home, it made getting there on the regular nearly impossible.

But I wouldn't trade my life for anything in the world.

I parked the Jeep in front of our beautiful white-with-green-trim farmhouse and turned off the ignition.

The dogs attacked my feet as I stepped out of the Jeep, zipping up my coat against the chill. I greeted each one of them while ordering Harvey, the newest addition to the pack, to get down. He still thought jumping up was okay. He'd learn quickly that at Jill's Rescue Ranch, jumping up on people was not kosher.

The change of season stole its way into the air in mid-September, turning hot summer days into cold fall nights almost without warning. A shiver vibrated through me as I spied my handsome husband and our heavily dressed six-month-old, so I ate up the distance between us just so I could be near them quicker.

"There's mama," Eli said in the voice he reserved for Ana. "Home just in time."

"Is she hungry?" I asked.

He nodded. "Been bopping her face against my chest for the last fifteen minutes. I gave her a bottle right before I brought the dogs out, but you know our ravenous little beast."

He loosened the straps on the carrier and hoisted Ana out. She was in a bunting bag and wearing a knit cap, but her cheeks were rosy and cool when I kissed them.

As soon as she saw me, she started grunting.

"Ana and Sérgio are on their way. I was just talking to her as I pulled in."

"Are you excited to meet your Aunt Ana and Uncle Sérgio?" Eli asked as I turned Ana onto her side, whipped out a boob, and started nursing her. It hadn't always been this easy, but eventually, my baby and I found our rhythm, and now we could nurse just about anywhere.

Eli leaned in and kissed me. "How was work?"

I bit my lip. "I might have another dog to add to the pack. I don't know yet. Sharon called and said there is an old codger at the shelter who just got brought in, the same situation as Jill. Owner was elderly and died; owner's adult children don't want the dog."

He rubbed my back as we turned to head into the house. "Breed?" Not that it really mattered.

I shrugged. "A border terrier, like Jill."

His eyes widened.

"And his name is Jack."

"Oh my God."

I nodded. "We kind of have to, right?"

Eli opened the door to the heated utility room where we kept all the dog kennels. The dogs were only allowed into the house with us three at a time. Otherwise, it was absolute chaos.

The dogs—besides Harvey—knew the drill and went to their designated kennels.

Eli fed them one by one, double-checking the chart and making sure those who needed medication got what they needed.

I continued to nurse Ana.

Once he was done, we left the dogs to eat and wind down, and retired to the main house.

Ana popped off, so I tucked my boob away and propped her up on my shoulder.

"I'll call Sharon in the morning and let her know that we'll take Jack if nobody else does," I said as I removed Ana from her bunting bag and put her in the swing in the living room.

"Screw anybody else getting him. That boy is meant to be ours. Jill sent him to us." Eli handed me a glass of wine. It'd become a bit of a routine with us. When I was home for the night, after he, Ana, and the dogs greeted me outside, he welcomed me home with a glass of wine.

I didn't know when it started, but I wasn't interested in ever having it end.

I sipped my wine. "Okay, I'll let Sharon know that we'll take him. That he's ours."

He nodded. "Good." Then, taking my wine glass, he set it down on the counter and drew me into his arms, taking my mouth with his in a proper kiss.

I draped my arms over his shoulders and melted into him.

My husband, my partner, the father of my daughter, and the most wonderful man I'd ever met.

No, our relationship didn't start off on the best foot. And yes, I did fantasize about stabbing him in the back of the hand with a fork on more than one occasion as we grew up. But Eli wasn't that person anymore.

I wasn't that person anymore.

People could change, and I believed that we both had. For the better.

He made me want to be a better version of myself. He was my backbone when I was too weary to hold myself up. He was my shield when my arms were too full to protect myself. He was my soft place to land when my day was nothing but hard.

He was the other half of my whole heart, and I was so glad that he suggested I marry him, because otherwise, I wouldn't know how amazing life could be.

He pulled out of the kiss, and I snuggled into his arms, my cheek against his chest as I inhaled his deliciousness.

"My mom called earlier today," he said with a sigh.

"Yeah, and how is she?"

"Misses Ana."

"She was *just* here."

"Wants to come back next weekend."

I chuckled. "The following weekend is fine, but we need a break between guests. My dad is coming that weekend, but we have the space, and they get along."

"Your dad bringing Janet?"

I grumbled. "Probably." My father had started dating a woman seventeen years older than me. Apparently, they were madly in love, and even though he promised me he wouldn't date anyone younger than twenty years my senior, in his words, "when it's love, it's love." And who was I to deny him such happiness when I myself had fallen in love with a man I'd at one point loathed? "She makes him happy," I said with a sigh. "I just wish she was a little older."

Eli's deep, rumbling chuckle next to my ear was soothing and made me instantly melt and relax deeper into his arms.

We stood there in the kitchen like that for a little while. Wrapped up in each other. I closed my eyes and inhaled his deliciousness, allowing his warmth and the calming rhythmic beat of his heart beneath my ear to lull me into an almost catatonic state.

Who knew life could be this good?

Certainly not me.

But I was grateful that I had the opportunity to experience such a beautiful life. To experience this kind of love.

No, our origin story was not a fairy tale, but it was our story, and it was magical in its own way.

I thought back to Allegra and Ford and how perfect every-thing looked on the outside until you peeled back a couple of layers. In truth, their veil of perfection had been disastrously thin and made of crepe paper.

I heard that their practice had closed and Allegra's friends abandoned her. She was forced to move back in with her parents. She also went back to being called Allison. Ford, from what I understood, took up Brittney the vet tech, and the two of them opened up a practice in Florida somewhere, though he wasn't nearly as successful as he had been in L.A.

When I returned home from San Diego, I made sure to delete everyone in that circle from my social media, and I blocked most of them, too. I was over that part of my life. Over them and the influence they had on how I behaved and the value I put on my success.

Allegra and Ford's practice might have been more glam-orous than mine, but their lives were in shambles.

I had so much to be proud of. And now, finally, I was.

I sighed and hugged my husband tighter.

Eli kissed the top of my head. "I signed the contract with the German publisher today."

I lifted my head. "That's amazing."

"But they want to fast-track things since there is a big comic convention there in the spring they want to pay to fly me over for."

My eyes widened. "Germany?"

He nodded. "In the spring. I said I'd have to talk to my wife first."

"And tell her how amazing our trip to Germany is going to be?"

Eli chuckled. "They offered to pay for you, too."

"Holy shit."

"There's a convention like two weeks later in Italy that the Italian publisher wants me to attend, too."

"Germany *and* Italy?"

He nodded again. "You up for it?"

"I'm sure Sharon would have no problems staying here to help with the animals again. She keeps asking if she can just move into the RV."

"We should just build her a tiny house on the back of the property."

"I'm sure she'd move in before it was ready." I chuckled.

We swayed in the kitchen, looking into each other's eyes.

We really had it all. Everything we'd ever dreamed of.

Ana squawked in the swing, making the noise we knew well was a sound of discontent, heavily laden with a threat that said, "If you do not get me out of this thing in ten seconds, I will lose my fucking mind."

Eli let go of my waist and retrieved our grunting baby, bringing her back to me in the kitchen as I stole another sip of my wine.

He reclaimed my waist with his hands, this time sandwiching Ana between us. She was happy as could be now, glancing back and forth between her father and me, grabbing our faces.

"This is the good life," Eli said, tightening his grip on me and kissing Ana on the cheek.

"No regrets," I said, catching his eye over the top of Ana's head.

He smiled, his brown eyes glimmering and the flecks of gold and copper around his irises sparkling. "My only regret is not telling you I loved you sooner. But otherwise, not a one."

Then I leaned in and kissed him. "As it should be."

For a Bonus Scene of Eli and Alex

Go here --> *https://whitleycox.com/bonus-material/*

If you enjoyed this book
If you've enjoyed this book, please consider leaving a review.
It really does make a difference.
Thank you again.
Xoxo
Whitley Cox

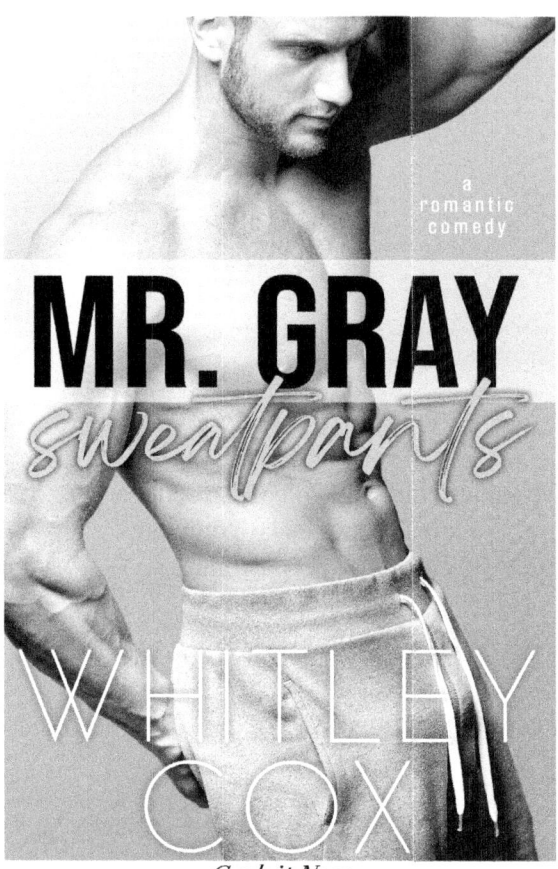

a romantic comedy

MR. GRAY
sweatpants

WHITLEY COX

Grab it Now

SNEAK PEEK

CHAPTER ONE
MR. GRAY SWEATPANTS

"I THINK I CAN see the line of his dick this time! Simon! He's back, come quick!" Jared's voice echoed through the two-story Seattle suburb home.

Casey heard Simon's footsteps on the reclaimed wood floor as he made his way through the house to wherever Jared was yelling from.

"Well, hello there Mr. Gray Sweatpants," Jared cooed.

Casey's brows pinched while she stared at herself in the bathroom mirror and brushed her teeth.

What on Earth were they talking about?

More like, who were they talking about?

She spat, rinsed and wiped her mouth, then descended the staircase to find her surrogate brothers—who were actually married to each other (long story)—standing by the front living room window wearing very swoony faces.

"What are you looking at?" she asked, nearly tripping over Trevor, their cat as she joined them in the living room.

"Well, if you didn't work so damn much and were home once in a while, you'd know that we have a new neighbor," Jared said, tossing his floppy-on-top-shaved-on-the-sides blond hair. "And he is delicious."

Simon rolled his blue eyes. "You can look, but you can't—"

"Touch, yes I know." Jared turned and planted a kiss on Simon's cheek. "You're the only one I want to touch." Then he turned to Casey and mouthed, "Not really."

Casey snorted as she tilted her head to look where they were looking and holy flying crap, Batman!

"See?" Jared said, elbowing her. "Mr. Gray Sweatpants, meet Casey, our workaholic sister."

"If only," Casey muttered, unable to take her eyes off the man who was wandering around the front yard of the house across the cul-de-sac and wearing nothing but scrumptious-looking gray sweatpants that left little to the imagination—and nothing else. No socks, no slippers, no shirt. Yes, it was summer, so there was no begrudging the man his attire, but still. Was he trying to give Casey's brothers—and anybody else who had eyeballs—a heart attack?

"You should go over and introduce yourself," Jared said. "Say, *hello, my name is Casey, I work too much, have no time for friends, and haven't gotten laid in*—" He lifted his brows toward her. "How long has it been?"

Nine months, but she wasn't about to divulge that.

Jared shrugged when she didn't respond and just kept talking, his green eyes glittering. "*And I haven't gotten laid in forever. Won't you be my neighbor with benefits?*"

Simon snorted and elbowed Jared. "Leave her alone."

"But she's so much fun to tease."

The two of them wandered away from the window and into the kitchen, but Casey's feet were full of concrete and her eyes appeared to have undergone some kind of paralysis where they were unable to move from the man's torso. He looked like he'd been carved out of damn marble.

Mr. Gray Sweatpants was carrying a handmade ceramic mug and as he sat down on the porch swing next to the front door and propped his big feet on the railing, he took a sip from the mug as he scrolled through his phone with his other hand.

Casey's insides clenched at just how disgustingly jealous she suddenly was of that mug and the fact that Mr. Gray Sweatpants had his mouth on that mug and not a part of Casey's body.

Sigh.

It really had been a long time since she'd been with a man. And it wasn't just about the sex. She loved kissing. She loved cuddling. She loved laughing at ridiculously stupid shit with someone until her sides hurt, then they spontaneously kissed her.

"You want some oatmeal, Case?" Simon called from the kitchen.

Taking one last glance at the god in the gray sweats, she sighed again then took off to the kitchen, but not before nearly tripping over Trevor again.

"Dear God, Trev, watch it!"

He meowed and glanced up at her with his yellow-brown eyes. That's when she noticed something attached to his collar. It was a small plastic tube of sorts.

Bending down, she held on to a squirming Trevor and removed the tube. Inside was a rolled-up piece of paper.

She patted Trevor's head, then headed to the kitchen, unfurling it as she went.

It read:

Hello,
It would appear your cat is two-timing you.
He/She/They come over here several times a day
and meow at my door for food.
I've only given them a treat or two, as they seem

well fed and taken care of. But I just wanted you
to know that your cat is cheating on you. If I
was being cheated on, I would want to know.
Sincerely,
Your cat's hot side-piece AKA The Mistress

Casey snorted and re-read it a couple of times before passing it to Simon and Jared who were giving her curious looks.

"Why that two-timing little bastard," Simon said with a grin.

"I like how progressive the note is. Very cool," Jared added.

"I'm going to reply," Casey said, tearing a piece of paper off the notepad on the roll-top desk she'd refurbished for the guys.

She quickly scrawled a note.

Hello Mistress,
Why that wily little bastard. I wondered where
he was taking off to. Telling me he had to stay
late at work when all the while he's been out
trolling for strange. I will have a word with him.
I appreciate you coming forward and the fact
that you haven't been overfeeding his cheating
ass.
Much obliged,
Trevor's pissed-off owner AKA The Cuckold

She rolled her note up, then went on the hunt for her two-timing feline. As was to be expected, since he'd probably been off gallivanting all night, he was curled up in a ray of sun streaming through the living room window. She scratched behind his ears a couple of times as she refastened the tube to his collar. "Stepping out on me, Trev? *Tsk tsk.* I hope whoever it is, they're worth it." She kissed his head, then went to find breakfast, but not before taking one more long look out the window at Mr. Gray Sweatpants.

Hello Cuckold,
It's good that you're being such a good sport about it all.
I've been stepped out on before and can say first hand, it's not much fun.
I hope Trevor is fixed, otherwise who knows what kind of kitten-support payments the two-timing bastard could get saddled with.
Weird question, but do you have any burger recipes? I'm tired of the same old same old. I'm sure I could Google something new, but I thought I'd ask.
Sincerely,
The Mistress

Dear Mistress,
Trevor lost his balls many moons ago, so he's leaving broken hearts in his wake, but no illegitimate kittens—thank the universe for that.

Funny you should mention burgers—my brother is a big-time foodie and just got a bunch of venison from an avid hunter friend. Eating Bambi or any of his kin isn't my jam, so they made me a turkey burger, but the rest of the ingredients were all the same. Google "Peanut Butter Jelly Burger" and I swear to Trevor's incinerated balls you will not be disappointed. Now it's your turn to hit me with a recipe tip.
Best,
The Cuckold

Dear Cuckold,
Pardon my proper French, but holy fucking shit balls! A PB & J burger was amazing. I had to go "authentic" and went to the butcher and grabbed some venison. Just picture me kissing my three fingers and pulling them away like a Michelin Star chef. My tastebuds haven't been on such a wild ride in a while. So, thank you. And I'm going to just say that the deer I ate was probably a massive dick who liked to raid people's gardens and eat all their hydrangeas. So he had what was coming to him and tasted delicious.
A recipe tip, hmmm. Walnuts or pecans make a tasty and affordable substitute for pine nuts in pesto.
Fuck, now I want something slathered in pesto. I'm thinking pasta.

*Glad ol' Trev won't be forking over his
hard-earned cash to a plethora of baby mamas.
Thanks again for the PB & J burger tip!
Thankfully yours,
The Dirty Mistress*

*Dear Dirty Mistress,
You can also add a handful of spinach to pesto
to stretch your basil and add some much-needed
iron. Thanks for the tip and I'm glad the burger
recommendation worked. Believe it or not, but
Trevor is jobless. He has been for some time.
The lazy bastard. Does nothing but eat our food,
get fur all over our furniture and try to kill
defenseless butterflies and hummingbirds. If the
asshole wasn't already walking around with no
globes between his legs, I'd have half a mind to
take him in to get them lopped off just for being
suck a jerk.
Are you a green thumb? I only ask since you
mentioned hydrangeas specifically. I'm a landscaper so anything plant-related makes my
neurons fire extra hot.
Sweating my ass off in this heatwave,
The Cuckold*

Dearest Cuckold,
I wouldn't say my thumb is green per se, but more like a light teal. I know a few plants, but I have no idea how to care for them or where they're more likely to thrive: all-day sun/shade/acidic soil/peat moss, etc. Just ask my dead cactus, Craig.
That's cool that you're a landscaper. I'm in construction. Just moved back to Seattle.
Did you know that by caramelizing onions and then pureeing them you can add more flavor depth to dishes like soups, gravies, stews, and stuff? I made a pot pie the other day and my gravy was weak sauce (literally) so I added the onion puree and it worked wonders.
Favorite movie, song, band, television show, and go!
Preparing to die from dehydration in this heat dome,
The Dirty, sweaty Mistress

Dear Dirty, sweaty Mistress,
Favorite movie: The Princess Bride. Song: Work Bitch by Britney Spears. Favorite band: Foo Fighters. Favorite TV Show: Anything on HGTV (obviously), but I really like that one where they transform backyard dumps into garden oases.
Your turn!

I found a Chef John recipe for pickle brine chicken the other day. I have to say, it tasted damn delicious. Now I know what to do with my leftover pickle juice. Plus, everything tastes good when it's been cooked over a fire. I'd consider eating Bambi if he were properly marinated and had those sexy AF grill marks.

Over and out, my anonymous mystery friend!
The Cuckold who saw melted blacktop downtown today. WTF is with this heat?

For the Cuckold taking it all in stride,
I saw melted blacktop, too when I went to the hardware store. Fucking nuts. This isn't right. If I wanted this heat I'd move to Qatar or something.

Did Trevor get a bath? He looks fluffier.

Favorite movie: Memento. Favorite Song: It's My Life (Bon Jovi). Favorite band: Foo Fighters (crazy coincidence). Favorite TV Show: Letterkenny (it's based in Canada and it is fucking hilarious. HIGHLY RECOMMEND). I have one pickle left in my pickle jar, so now I know what I'm doing with that juice. Thanks! Agreed that grill marks are sexy AF and everything tastes better when its been kissed by flames.

Don't melt away, anonymous mystery friend!
The Dirty, Sweaty, Foo Fighter loving Mistress

Hey Misty!
Trevor DID get a bath. Do you want to know
why? Because that little fuckhead decided to
jump at a hummingbird coming to the feeder
and proceeded to knock the feeder down and get
covered in sugar water. Then that asshole went
and rolled in the goddamn fish fertilizer I just
laid in the garden. I swear he's lucky his balls
have already been burned.
Favorite Foo Fighters song?
Feel free to tell Trevor he's an asshole and can
fuck right off. He doesn't deserve treats.
I think I'm more a dog person now.
Can you divorce your cat?
~The cat bather with a million scratches AKA
Cuck (though honestly, if it wasn't for how much
fun these notes are I'd say you could keep the
damn cat).

Damn, Cuck, I'm really sorry about the scratch-
es. My screen door learned the hard way that
Trevor has sharp claws. I stuck both middle
fingers up in the air at him today, then told him
to go fuck himself, which he then took as per-
mission to go and use my screen as a scratching
post. I'm 100% a dog person over a cat person
and Trevor has just confirmed it. Thanks for the

offer to adopt your dick of a cat but I'm going to pass. I'd have long stopped feeding him if it wasn't for these notes. They're a highlight for me, too. And I'm okay keeping it anonymous if you are. I think it just adds to the fun.
I don't think you married your cat, so you can't divorce him.
Unless you did ...? And in that case ...
I'd say no judgment, but we both know that wouldn't be true.
Cheers,
Misty the mosquito-bitten Mistress (because of the broken screen door and all)

Oh shit!
PS. Favorite Foo Fighters Song: Everlong

Leo wiped the drywall dust from his hands onto his carpenter pants.

That was it for the day.

The place would be here tomorrow, and the next day, and the next day.

Normally, he loved his construction job, but when you lived where you worked, it was hard to quit at five o'clock and call it a day when the wall that needed spackling was staring at you as you ate dinner or watched television.

Which was why it was now eight o'clock on a Wednesday night in the middle of June, his stomach was trying to devour him from the inside out, and he knew his fridge would be as empty now as it was this morning.

A meow at the back door brought him out of his exhaustion fog.

That motherfucking cat again.

Wiping his hands for a second time, he went and opened the sliding door. "Good evening, you fuzzy-faced bastard. Back to rip my window screens now?"

The black cat with white paws and a white tip on its tail sauntered in like it owned the place, rubbing his tail against the front of Leo's dusty pants and meowing again.

"Yeah, yeah, hold on."

He went to the counter and grabbed the bag of treats he'd purchased and shook it a couple of times. The cat paused, sat down at stared at him. That's when Leo went in for the little plastic tube he'd fastened to the cat's collar two weeks ago. He could not express how happy he was that Trevor's owner not only found the note but wrote back. And now Leo and his anonymous mystery friend AKA The Cuckold were engaged in a friendly, anonymous, carrier-cat pen-pal correspondence.

Since the majority of his friends from high school were too busy, had families or had moved away he didn't have a ton of friends in Seattle, after moving back. He found a bizarre sense of comfort in his interactions with the cat's owner. Probably a neighbor somewhere. He dropped a treat on the floor and Trevor gobbled it up while Leo unfurled the rolled-up strip of yellow lined paper.

He snorted at his nickname. He had no idea if the person he was corresponding with was male or female, and he'd given no indication as to his sex or gender either. It all just added to the mystery.

Hello Mistress,
That little motherfucker! FUCK! I am so sorry.
You need to let me pay for it. Please! I would
love to include cash in my next note, but I fear
Trevor would just dick off with the money and

spend it on strange pussy and blow. Let me know if you have a PO Box or something I can send money to. Or we could do it Shawshank Redemption style where I leave you cash in a tin box under a slate rock at the base of an old tree. I did what you suggested and pureed up some caramelized onions, they added a lot of flavor depth to my soup. Before you say it's too hot for soup, I disagree and will do so until the day I die. It's always soup season.
Take care.
-The Cuckold

So far, Leo and this mystery person had talked about all kinds of things. Their favorite movies, music, and recipes. He'd gotten to know them quite well in a short amount of time. But still had no idea of their gender or their age.

He couldn't assume that the person was male even though they called themselves a *Cuckold*. He was allowing himself to be called *Mistress*. Truthfully, it all just added to the mystery and fun of it.

He grinned at their mention of it always being soup season. He had to agree. It was never too hot for soup.

Normally, Leo loved to cook. It was one of his few creative outlets. That and his guitar. But since he was determined to finish renovating his late grandmother's house in order to put it on the market, he hadn't had much time for anything—let alone a creative outlet.

He wanted to get this place on the market before the end of the year so that he and his sisters could get their inheritance and he could put his portion into starting his own construction company. He was tired of working for someone else—which was why at the moment he was jobless and only working for himself.

He wrote back to the Cuckold, declining the offer of payment for the screen, attached it to Trevor's collar, fed the cat one more time, then booted him outside.

After a quick shower to remove the remainder of the drywall dust from his hair and skin, he tossed on a pair of denim shorts and a loose white T-shirt.

It was hot as fuck outside and if he could, he'd have wandered around topless—like he did all day in the house as he renovated. But he planned to eat inside an establishment and they tended to frown on their patrons arriving half-naked. This wasn't Venice Beach.

He jumped in his white GMC pickup and backed out of his driveway narrowly missing Trevor as he darted across the street, a shadow among all the shadows.

"Fucking cat," he muttered, his attention now focused on the house three doors up and on the other side of the cul-de-sac.

A hottie lived there.

A hottie with a dirty blonde bob, an ass that wouldn't quit, and very toned arms.

Since he moved in almost two months ago, he'd been watching her—not in a creepy way—but she was hot and when she was home, he took notice. He was pretty sure she hadn't noticed him. She was gone by eight-thirty in the morning, often sooner, arrived home just after five, then was gone again by quarter to six. He was in bed when she arrived home again.

She seemed to have Sundays off though. But she was rarely home even on Sundays.

She also lived with two guys.

Were they a thrupple?

Their ages weren't too far apart. The guys looked like they were in their late twenties—like Leo—while she looked early to mid-twenties.

He hadn't met any of them—hadn't met any of the neighbors—though he was sure they all knew his grandmother, and also probably knew that she had died six months ago.

Was it just not that friendly of a neighborhood?

He came to the stop sign at the end of the street, cast one final glance at the house where the hottie lived, then headed out into traffic.

His gut told him to eat, but his dick told him to get back in the game.

He'd been on the bench, licking his wounds long enough.

It was time he did some calf stretches and played the field again. Not every woman was going to throw the ball at his heart and send him to the ground in agony, right?

Not every woman.

PREORDER
MR. GRAY SWEATPANTS
HERE --> *https://mybook.to/mrgraysweatpants*

Don't forget to Subscribe to my Newsletter!

Be the first to hear about pre-orders, new releases, giveaways, 99cent deals, and freebies!

—————————————————————————————————————

Click here to Subscribe

http://eepurl.com/ckh5yT

ACKNOWLEDGMENTS

There are so many people to thank who help along the way. Publishing a book is definitely not a solo mission, that's for sure. First and foremost, my friend and editor Chris Kridler, you are a blessing, a gem and an all-around terrific person. Thank you for your honesty and hard work.

Thank you, to my critique groups gals, Danielle, Felicia and Jillian. I love our meetups where we give honest feedback. You are my bitch-sisters and I wouldn't give you up for anything. Kathleen Lawless, for just being you and wonderful and always there for me. Thank you to Clarissa Kwan and Author Brooke Burton for their beta-reads on this. I really appreciate your feedback, it made the story 100,000x better. Author Jeanne St. James, my friend, what would I do without you? BBB Publishing for their proofreading. Megan J. Parker-Squiers from EmCat Designs, your covers are awesome. Thank you. My reader group, Whitley Cox's Fabulously Filthy Reviewers, you are all awesome and I feel so blessed to have found such wonderful fans. Thank you to Sharon Abrams and Ana Rita Clemente for helping me with the plot, characters and careers of our hero and heroine and for being the perfect walk-on characters to bring this story to life. And another thank you to Sharon for her proofreading on the ARC. I very much appreciate your attention to detail.

Thank you to the ladies and gent of Vancouver Island Romance Authors, your support and insight have been incredibly helpful, and I'm so honored to be a part of a group of such talented writers. Author Cora Seton, I love our walks, talks and heart-to-hearts, they mean so much to me. Author Ember Leigh, my newest author bestie, I love our bitch fests—they keep me sane. All the other writers out there who take part in NaNoWriMo in November and manage to bang out 50,000 words in 30 days. This was my NaNo project and although it's a lot more than 50,000 words, all my NaNo peeps, you are undeniably amazing. I literally felt hungover on December 1st after writing this behemoth. I don't recommend 124,000 words in 30 days. Just don't do it.

Thank you to my parents, in-laws, and brother, thank you for your unwavering support. The Small Human and the Tiny Human, you are the beats and beasts of my heart, the reason I breathe and the reason I drink. I love you both to infinity and beyond. And lastly, of course, the husband. You are my forever, my other half, the one who keeps me grounded and the only person I have honestly never grown sick of even when we did that six-month backpacking trip and spent every single day together. I never tired of you. Never needed a break. You are my person. I love you.

FIND WHITLEY HERE

Website: WhitleyCox.com
Email: readers4wcox@gmail.com
Twitter: @WhitleyCoxBooks
Instagram: @CoxWhitley
TikTok: @AuthorWhitleyCox
Facebook : https://www.facebook.com/CoxWhitley/
Blog: https://whitleycox.com/fabulously-filthy-blog-page/

Exclusive Facebook Reader Group:
https://www.facebook.com/groups/234716323653592/
Booksprout: https://booksprout.co/author/994/whitley-cox
Bookbub: https://www.bookbub.com/authors/whitley-cox
Goodreads:
https://www.goodreads.com/author/show/16344419.Whitley_Cox
Subscribe to my newsletter here:
http://eepurl.com/ckh5yT

ABOUT THE AUTHOR

A Canadian West Coast baby born and raised, Whitley is married to her high school sweetheart, and together they have two beautiful daughters and a fluffy dog. She spends her days making food that gets thrown on the floor, vacuuming Cheerios out from under the couch and making sure that the dog food doesn't end up in the air conditioner. But when nap time comes, and it's not quite wine o'clock, Whitley sits down, avoids the pile of laundry on the couch, and writes.

A lover of all things decadent; wine, cheese, chocolate and spicy erotic romance, Whitley brings the humorous side of sex, the ridiculous side of relationships and the suspense of everyday life into her stories. With mommy wars, body issues, threesomes, bondage and role playing, these books have everything we need to satisfy the curious kink in all of us.

OTHER BOOKS BY WHITLEY COX

Quick & Reckless
Book 3, A Quick Billionaires Novel
https://books2read.com/QReckless-QBS
Silver and Warren

Quick & Dangerous
Book 4, A Quick Billionaires Novel
https://books2read.com/QDangerous-QBS
Skyler and Roberto

Quick & Snowy
The Quick Billionaires, Book 5
https://books2read.com/QSnowy-QBS
Brier and Barnes

Hot Dad
https://books2read.com/Hot-Dad
Harper and Sam

Lust Abroad
https://books2read.com/Lust-Abroad
Piper and Derrick

Snowed In & Set Up
https://books2read.com/SISU
Amber, Will, Juniper, Hunter, Rowen, Austin

Love to Hate You
https://books2read.com/Love2HateYou
Alex and Eli

Hired by the Single Dad
https://books2read.com/HBTSD-SDS
The Single Dads of Seattle, Book 1
Tori and Mark

Dancing with the Single Dad
https://books2read.com/DWTSD-SDS
The Single Dads of Seattle, Book 2
Violet and Adam

Saved by the Single Dad
https://books2read.com/SBTSD-SDS
The Single Dads of Seattle, Book 3
Paige and Mitch

Living with the Single Dad
https://books2read.com/LWTSD-SDS
The Single Dads of Seattle, Book 4
Isobel and Aaron

Christmas with the Single Dad
https://books2read.com/CWTSD-SDS
The Single Dads of Seattle, Book 5
Aurora and Zak

New Years with the Single Dad
https://books2read.com/NYWTSD-SDS
The Single Dads of Seattle, Book 6
Zara and Emmett

Valentine's with the Single Dad
https://books2read.com/VWTSD-SDS
The Single Dads of Seattle, Book 7
Lowenna and Mason

Neighbors with the Single Dad
https://books2read.com/NWTSD-SDS
The Single Dads of Seattle, Book 8
Eva and Scott

Flirting with the Single Dad
https://books2read.com/FWTSD-SDS
The Single Dads of Seattle, Book 9
Tessa and Atlas

Falling for the Single Dad
https://books2read.com/FFTSD-SDS
The Single Dads of Seattle, Book 10
Liam and Richelle

Hot for Teacher
https://books2read.com/HFT-SMS
The Single Moms of Seattle, Book1
Celeste and Max

Hot for a Cop
https://books2read.com/HFAC-SMS
The Single Moms of Seattle, Book 2
Lauren and Isaac

Hot for the Handyman
https://books2read.com/HTHM-SMS
The Single Moms of Seattle, Book 3
Bianca and Jack

Doctor Smug
https://books2read.com/DoctorSmug
Daisy and Riley

Hard Hart
https://books2read.com/HH-HB
The Harty Boys, Book 1
Krista and Brock

Lost Hart
The Harty Boys, Book 2
https://books2read.com/LH-HB
Stacey and Chase

Torn Hart
The Harty Boys, Book 3
https://books2read.com/THART-HB
Lydia and Rex

Dark Hart
The Harty Boys, Book 4
https://books2read.com/DH-HB
Pasha and Heath

Coming Soon

The Asshole Heir
Winter Harbor Heroes, Book 2
https://books2read.com/the-asshole-heir
Amaya and Carson
August 16, 2022

Mr. Gray Sweatpants
A Single Moms of Seattle spin-off book
https://books2read.com/MrGraySweatpants
Casey and Leo
September 10, 2022

Not Over You
https://books2read.com/not-over-you
Rayma and Jordan
October 1, 2022

Raw, Fierce and Awakened: Part 1
The Dark and Damaged Hearts Series, Book 9
Jessica and Lewis

Raw, Fierce and Awakened: Part 2
The Dark and Damaged Hearts Series, Book 10
Jessica and Lewis

Yes, absolutely the sexy ranchers at the dude ranch are getting their own stories.
I'm expanding my world once more and pairing Asher and Nate Harris with a couple of the Young sisters.

Preorder
Snowed in with the Rancher
Asher and Triss's story
Coming March 4, 2023

https://books2read.com/snowed-in-rancher

Preorder Now

Preorder
Second Chance with the Rancher
Nate and Mieka's story
Coming May 13, 2023

https://books2read.com/second-chance-rancher

Preorder Now

Treat yourself to awesome orgasms!
This one only ships to the US.

https://tracysdog.com/?sca_ref=1355619.ybw0YXuvPL

Treat yourself to awesome orgasms! This one
ships to Canada!

https://thornandfeather.ca/?ref=734ThbSs

Printed in Great Britain
by Amazon

45124080R00263